Chi's Sweet Home

チーズ　スイートホーム

5

Konami Kanata

contents
homemade 75~92+🐾

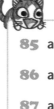

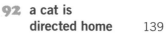

homemade 75: a cat greets

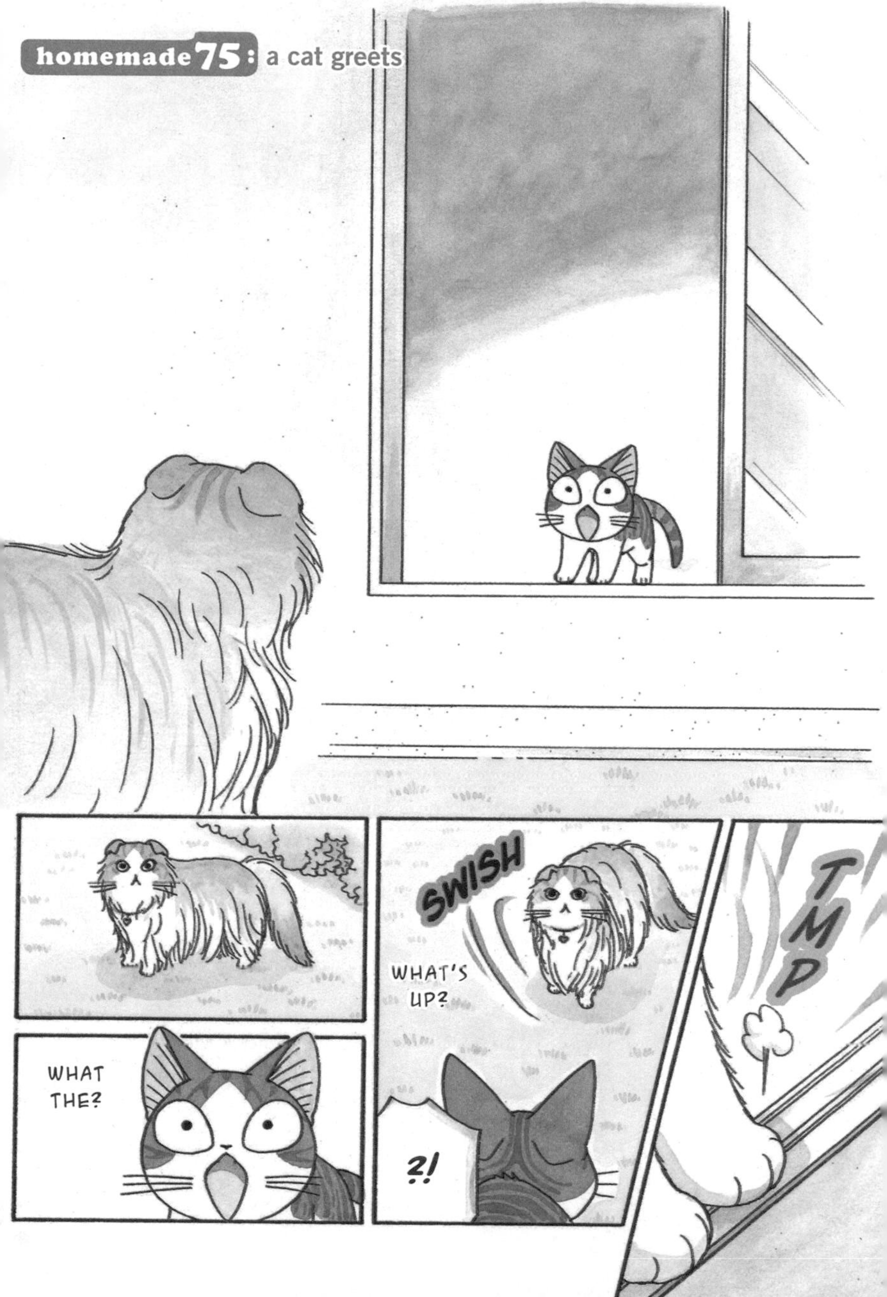

WHAT THE?
SWISH
WHAT'S UP?
?!
TMP

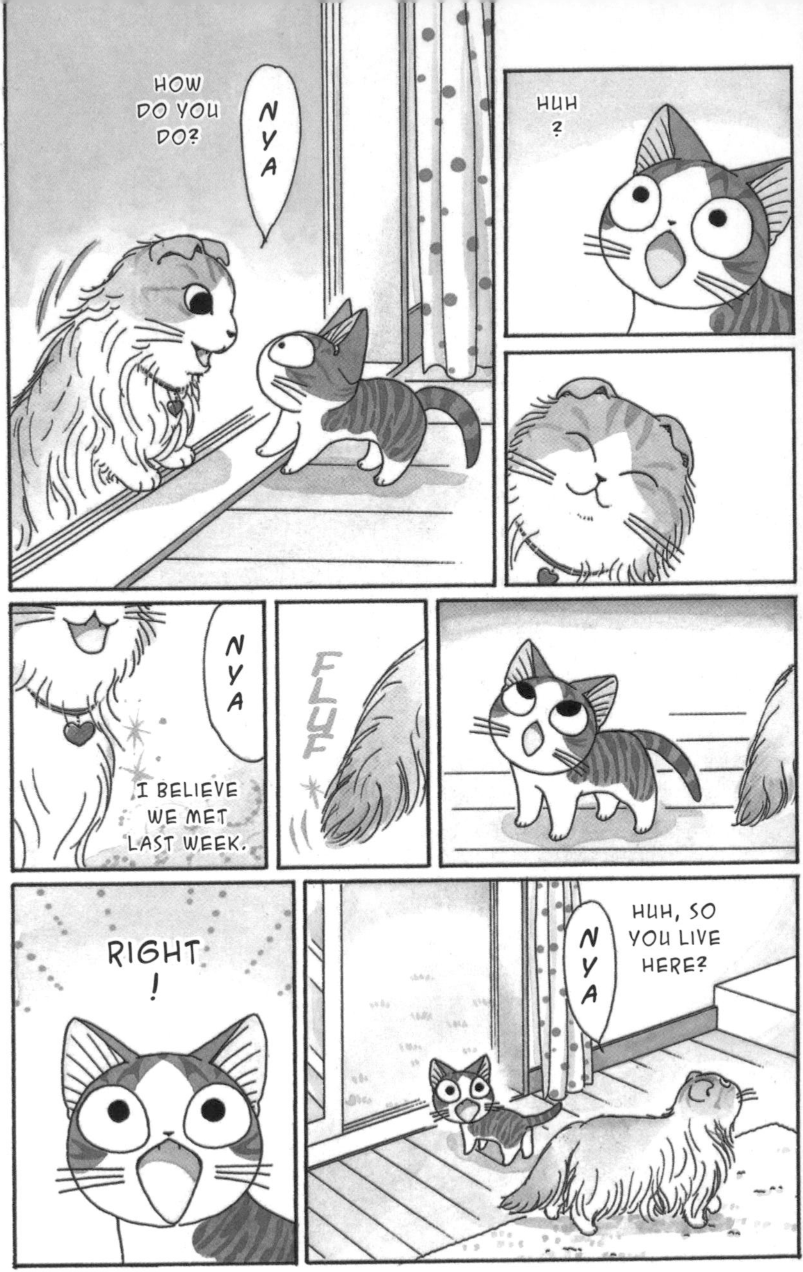
HOW DO YOU DO?
NYA
HUH ?
NYA
I BELIEVE WE MET LAST WEEK.
FLUF
RIGHT !
NYA
HUH, SO YOU LIVE HERE?

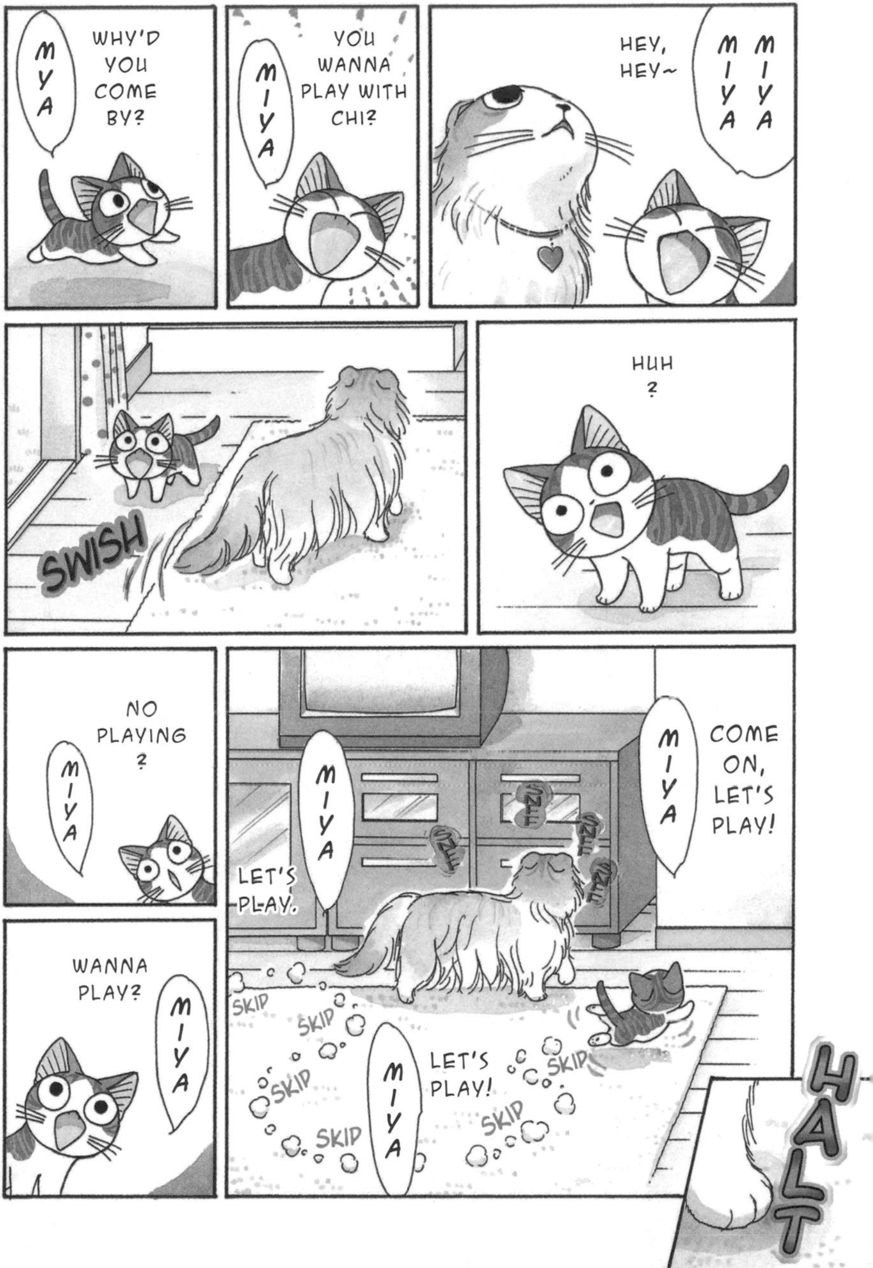

MYA
WHY'D YOU COME BY?
MIYA
YOU WANNA PLAY WITH CHI?
HEY, HEY~
MIYA MIYA
SWISH
HUH?
NO PLAYING?
MIYA
WANNA PLAY?
MIYA
MIYA
COME ON, LET'S PLAY!
MIYA
LET'S PLAY.
SNF
SNF
SNF
SNF
SKIP
SKIP
SKIP
SKIP
SKIP
SKIP
MIYA
LET'S PLAY!
HALT

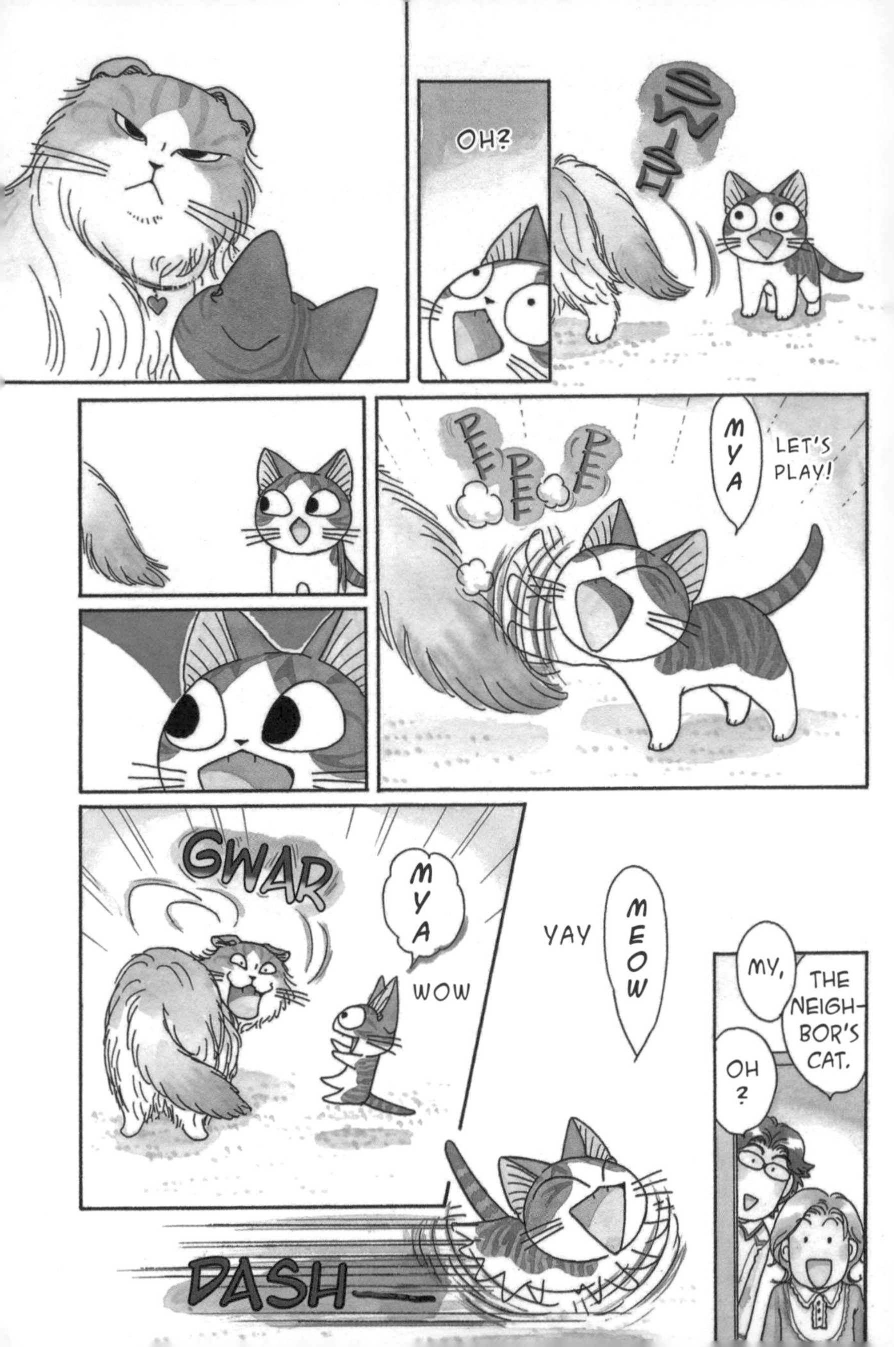
OH?
SWISH
PFF
PFF
PFF
MYA
LET'S PLAY!
GWAR
MYA
WOW
YAY
MEOW
DASH—
MY, THE NEIGHBOR'S CAT.
OH?

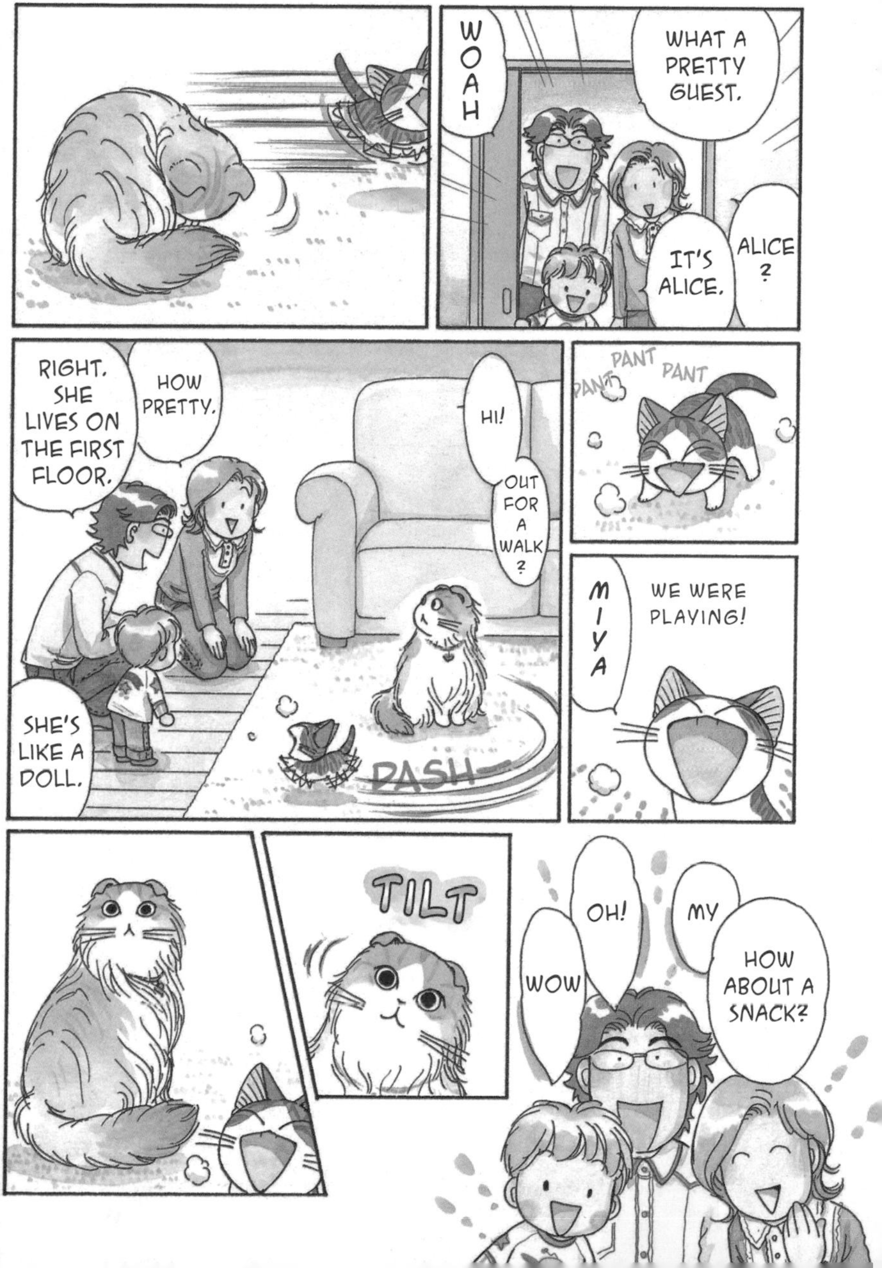
WOAH
WHAT A PRETTY GUEST.
IT'S ALICE.
ALICE?
RIGHT. SHE LIVES ON THE FIRST FLOOR.
HOW PRETTY.
SHE'S LIKE A DOLL.
HI!
OUT FOR A WALK?
DASH
PANT
PANT
PANT
MIYA
WE WERE PLAYING!
TILT
WOW
OH!
MY
HOW ABOUT A SNACK?

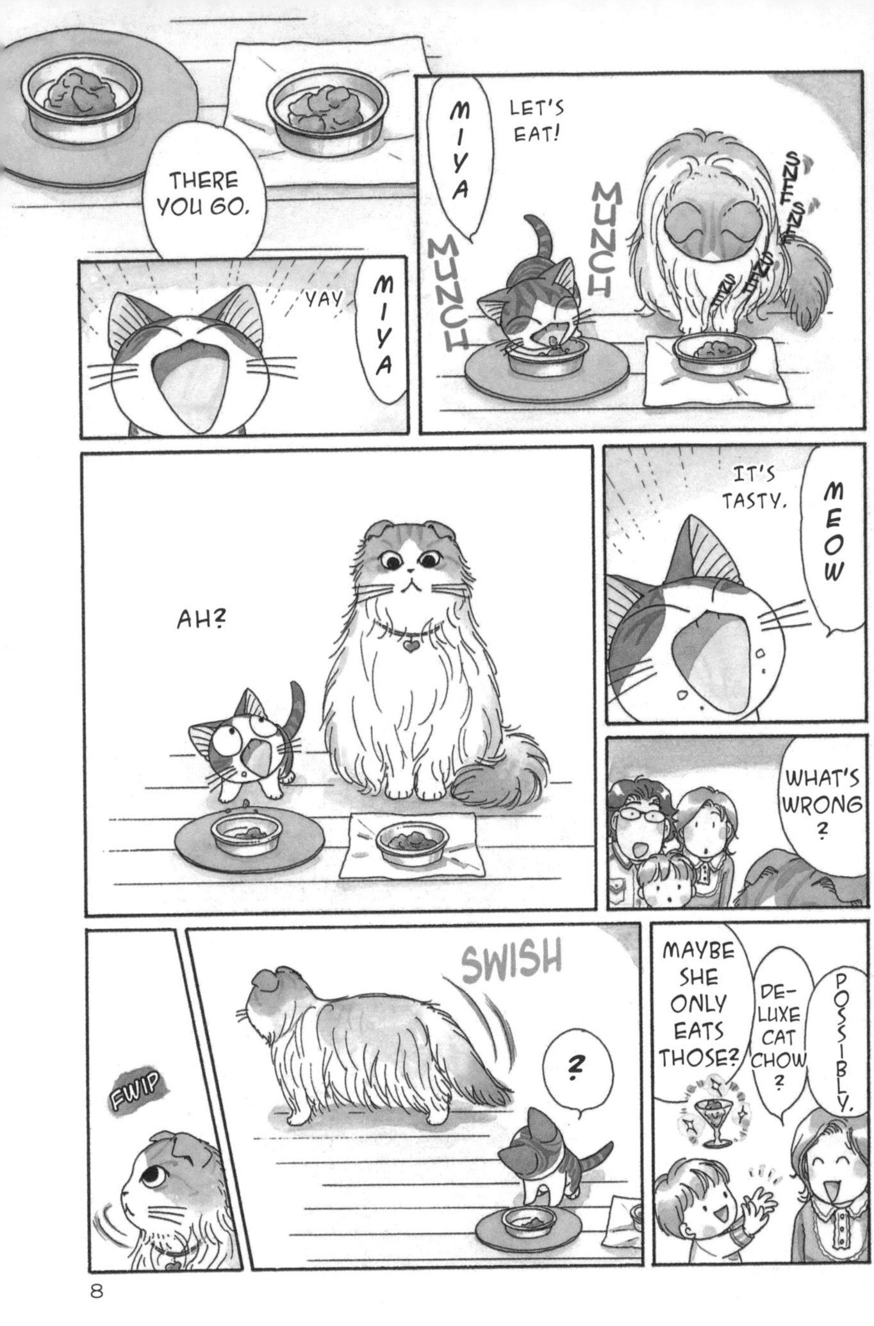
THERE YOU GO.
YAY
MIYA
MIYA
LET'S EAT!
MUNCH
MUNCH
SNIFF SNIFF
AH?
IT'S TASTY.
MEOW
WHAT'S WRONG?
FWIP
SWISH
?
MAYBE SHE ONLY EATS THOSE?
DE-LUXE CAT CHOW?
POSSIBLY.

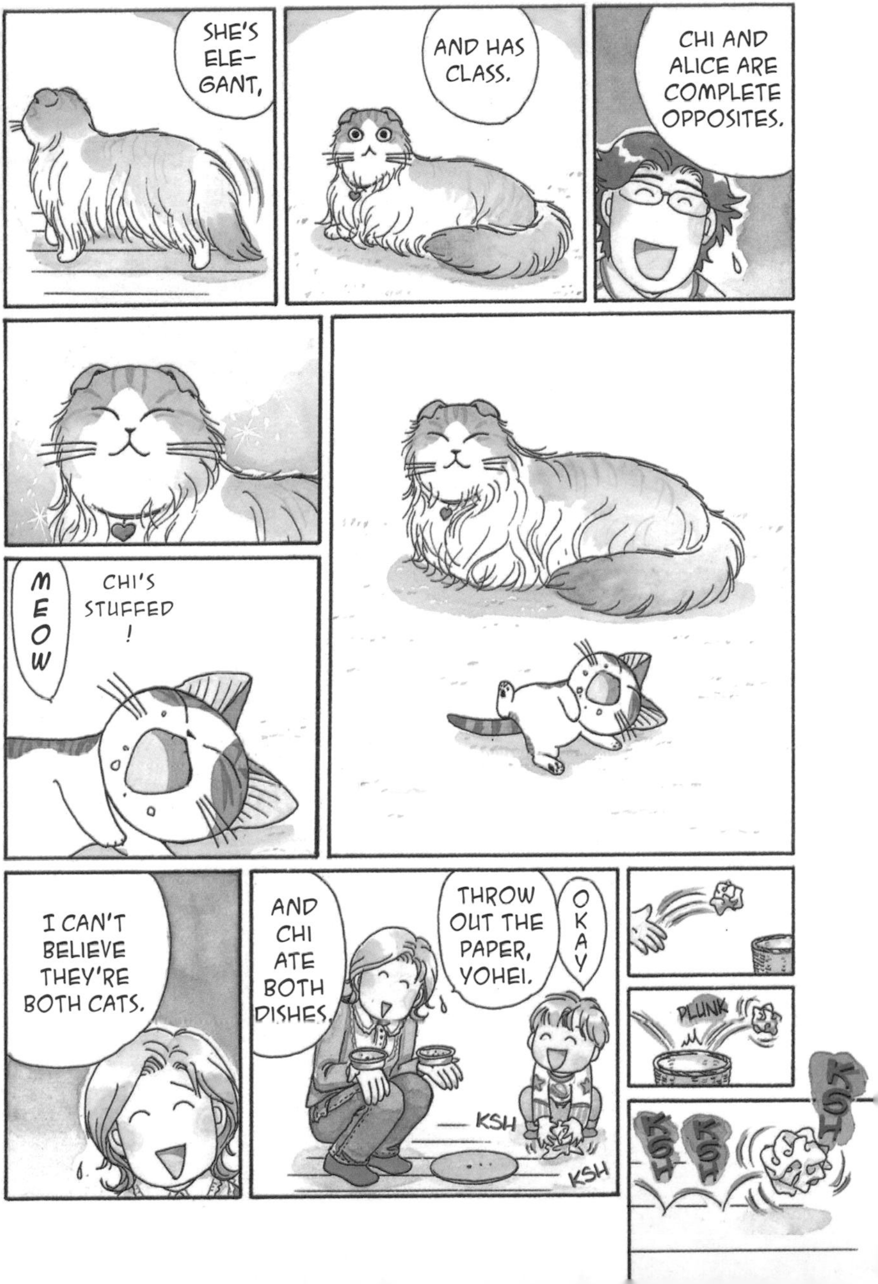
SHE'S ELE-GANT,
AND HAS CLASS.
CHI AND ALICE ARE COMPLETE OPPOSITES.
MEOW
CHI'S STUFFED!
I CAN'T BELIEVE THEY'RE BOTH CATS.
AND CHI ATE BOTH DISHES.
THROW OUT THE PAPER, YOHEI.
OKAY
KSH
KSH
PLUNK
KSH
KSH
KSH

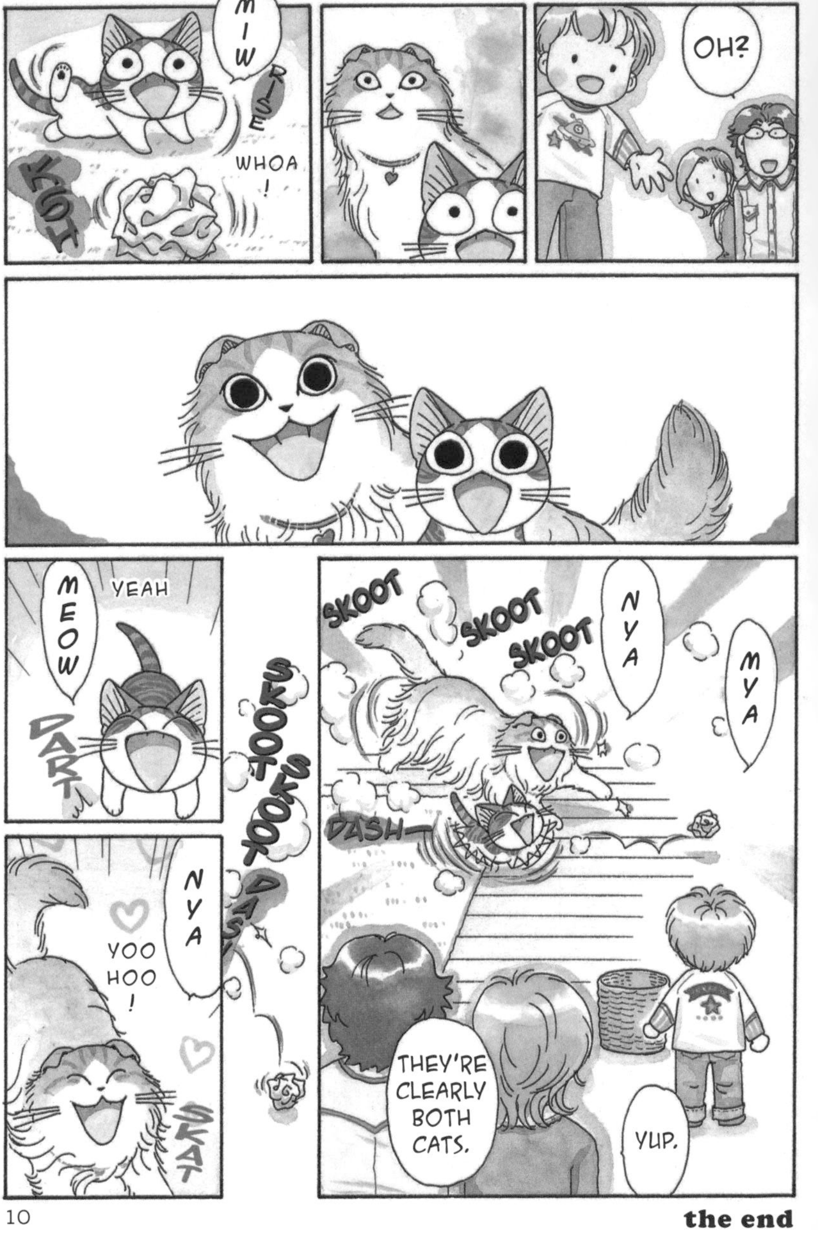
MIW
RISE
WHOA!
KSH
OH?
MEOW
YEAH
DART
NYA
YOO HOO!
SKAT
SKOOT SKOOT
DASH
SKOOT
SKOOT
SKOOT
NYA
MYA
DASH
THEY'RE CLEARLY BOTH CATS.
YUP.

the end

homemade 76: a cat sleeps

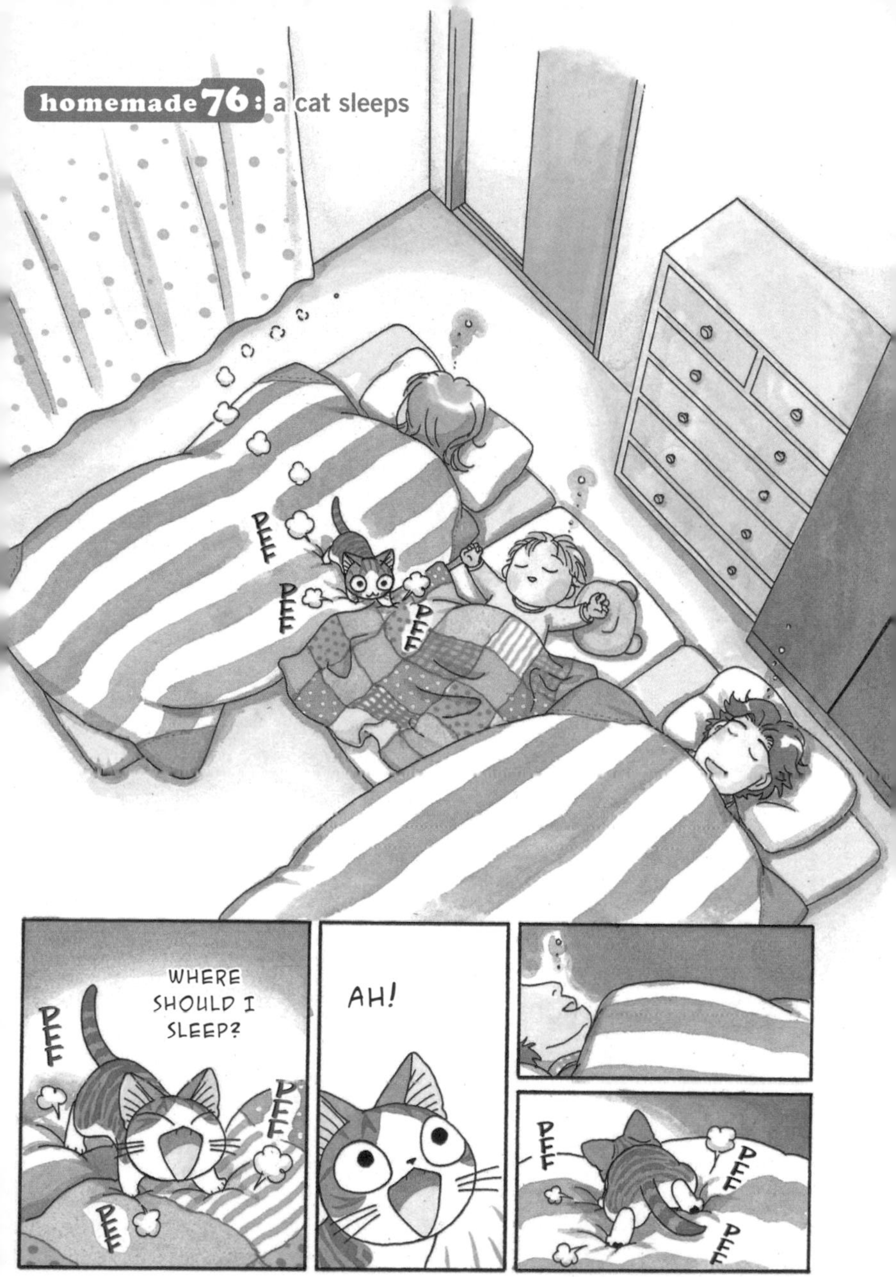
PFF
PFF
PFF
PFF
WHERE SHOULD I SLEEP?
PFF
PFF
AH!
PFF
PFF
PFF

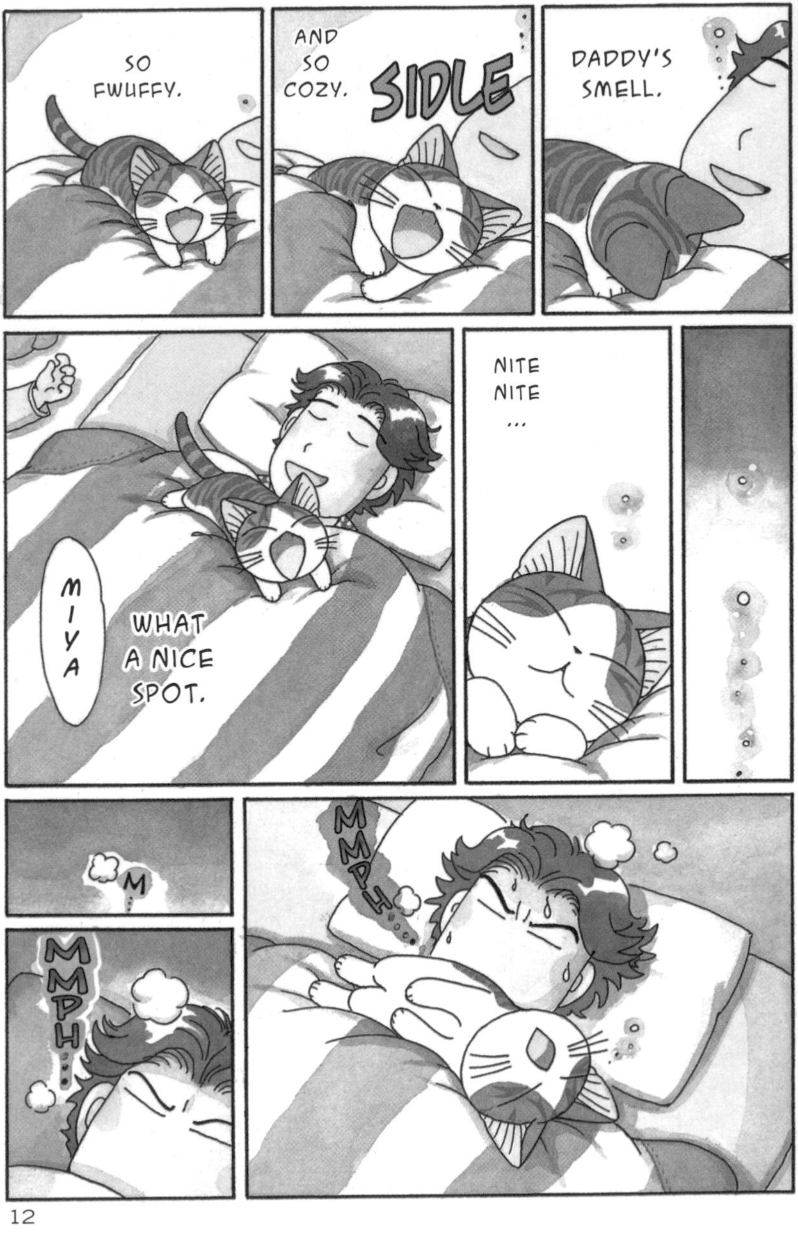
SO FWUFFY.
AND SO COZY.
SIDLE
DADDY'S SMELL.
MIYA
WHAT A NICE SPOT.
NITE NITE ...
M...
MMPH...
MMPH...

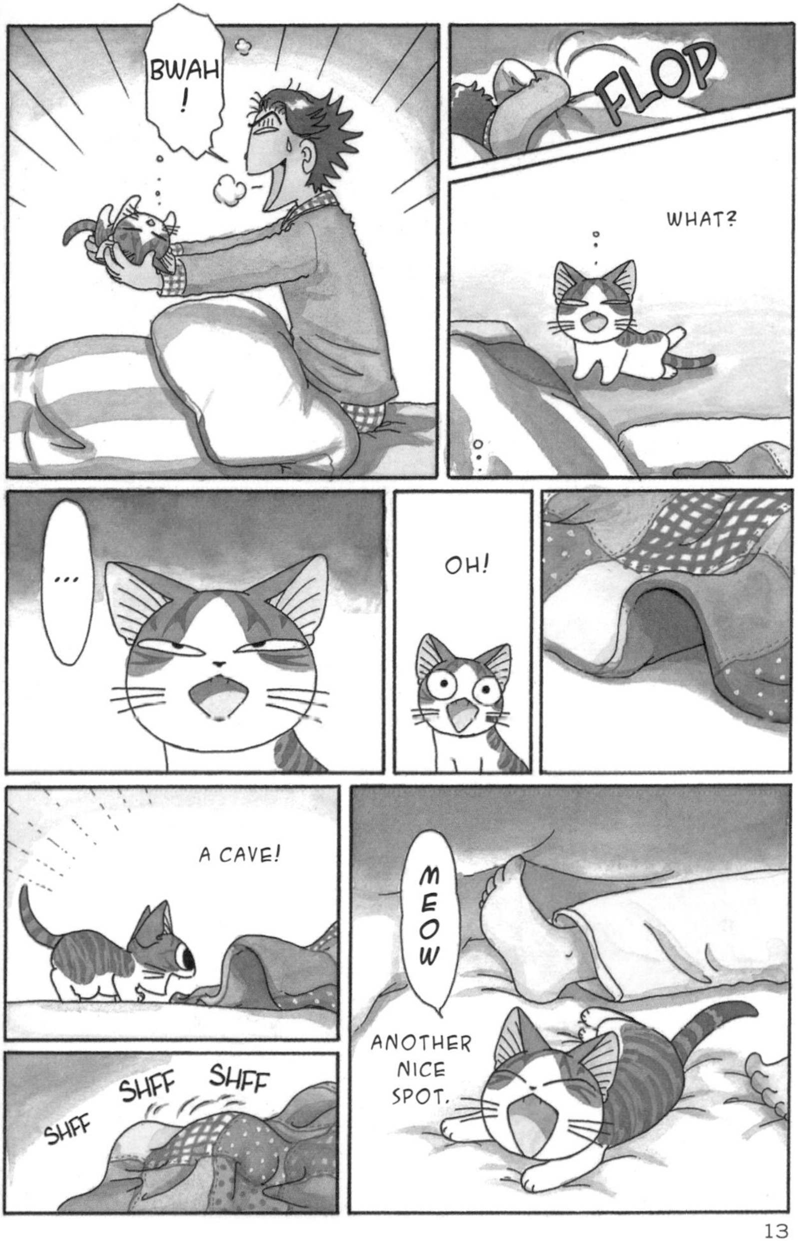
BWAH!
FLOP
WHAT?
...
OH!
A CAVE!
SHFF
SHFF
SHFF
MEOW
ANOTHER NICE SPOT.

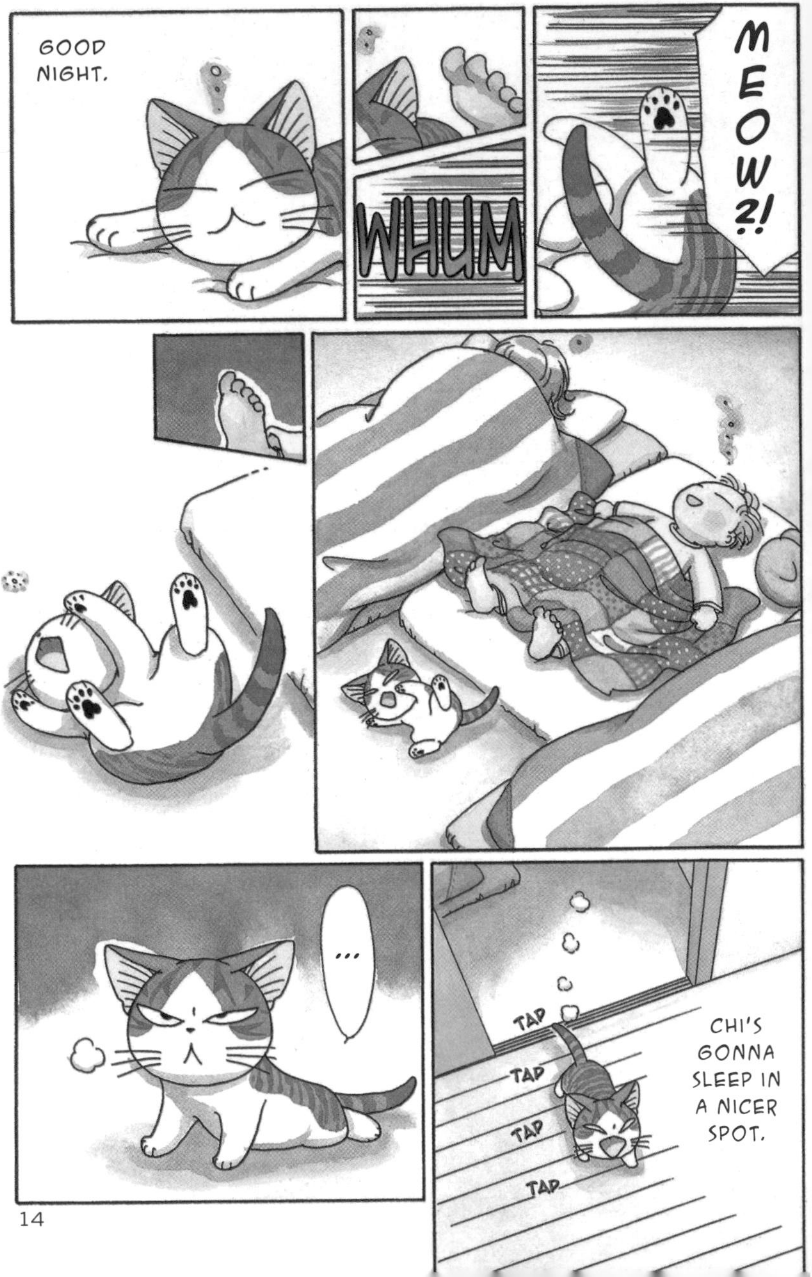
GOOD NIGHT.
WHUM
MEOW?!
...
TAP
TAP
TAP
TAP
CHI'S GONNA SLEEP IN A NICER SPOT.

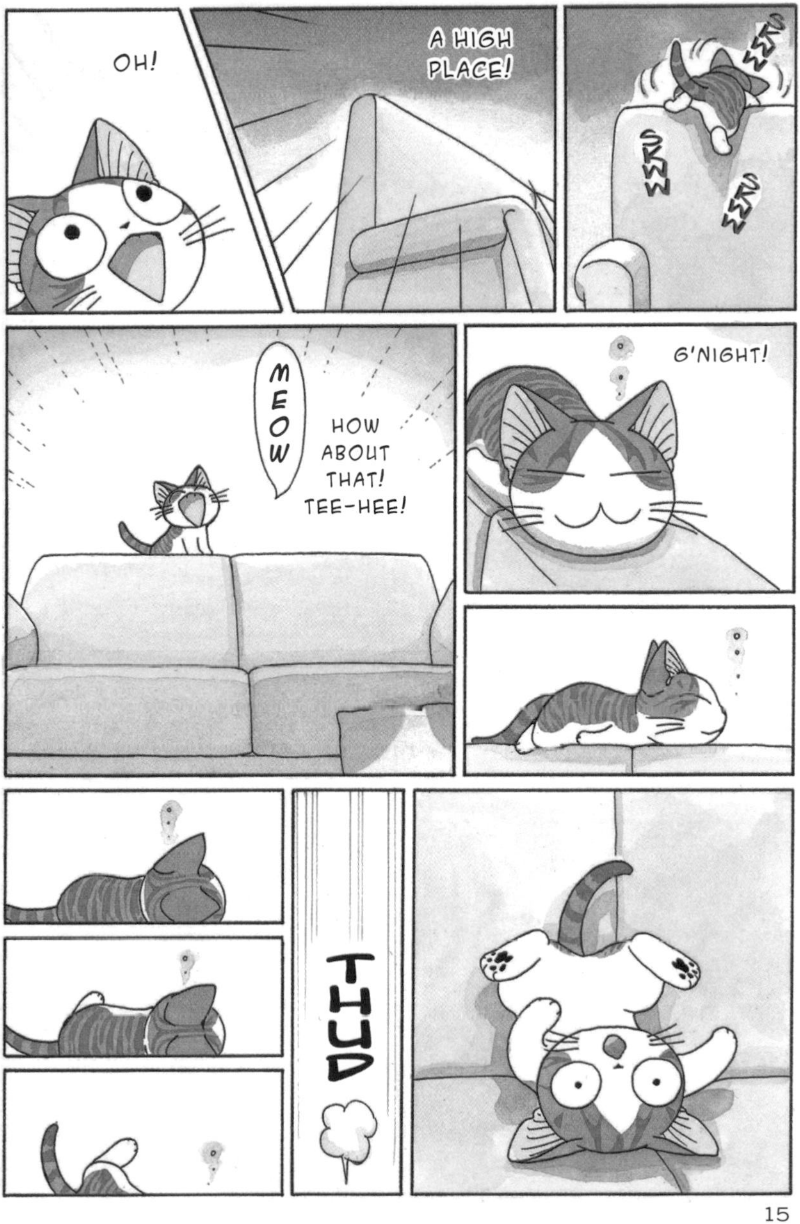
OH!
A HIGH PLACE!
SKRTS
SKRW
SKRW
MEOW
HOW ABOUT THAT! TEE-HEE!
G'NIGHT!
THUD

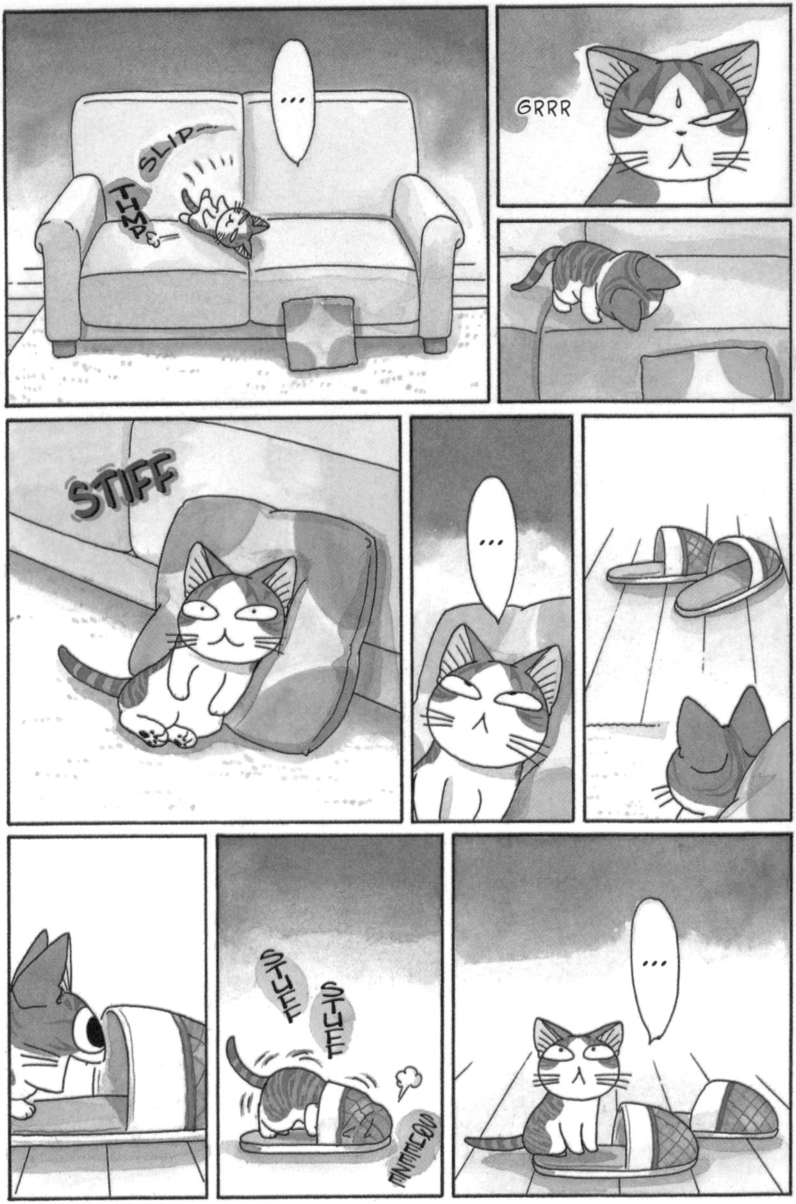
SLIP—
THMP
...
GRRR
STIFF
...
STUFF
STUFF
...

ISN'T THERE A NICE SPOT?

YAWN

MYA

OH!

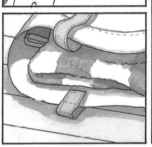

FOUND ONE!

IT'S A FWUFFY CAVE!

MYA

A NICE SPOT!

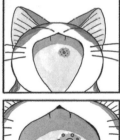

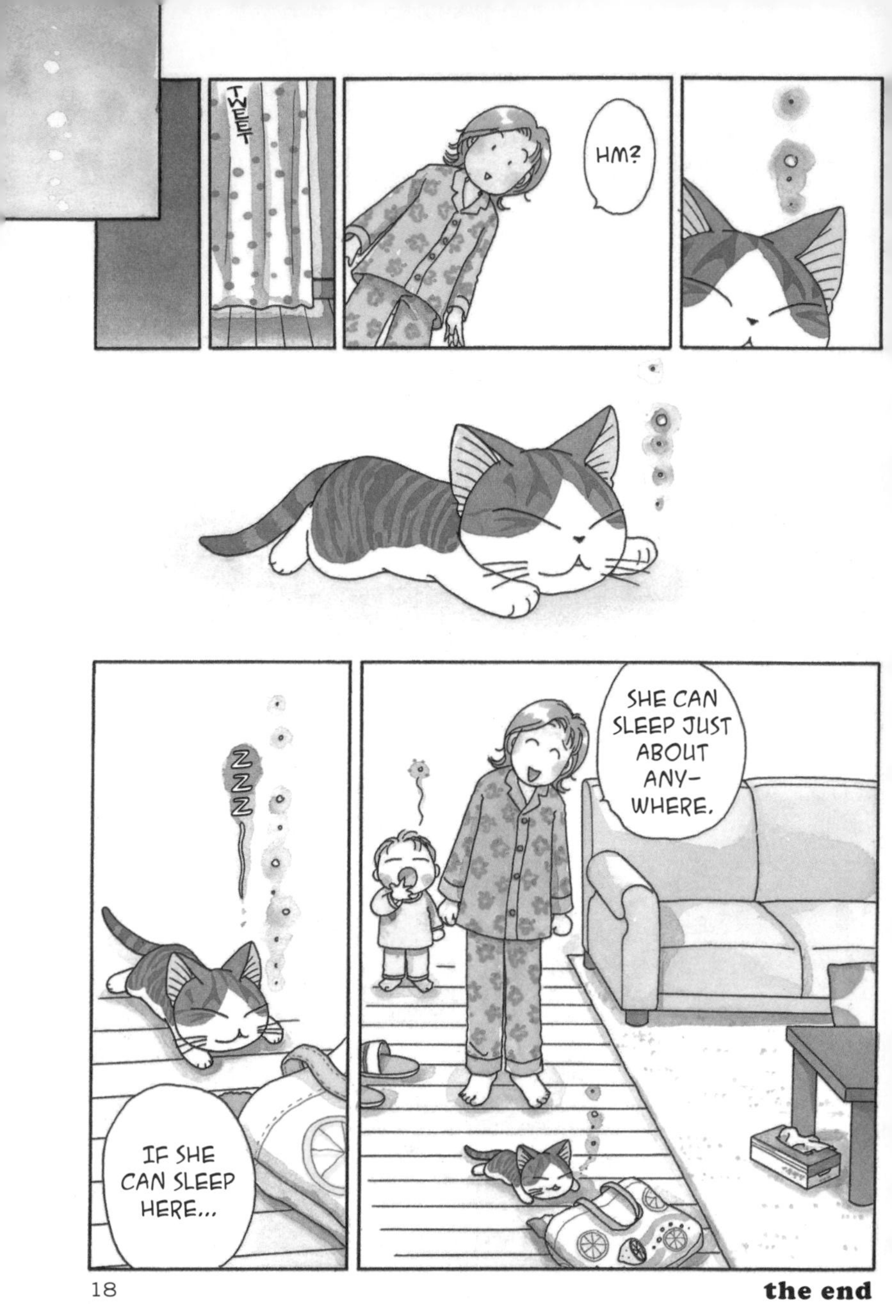
TWEET
HM?
ZZZ
IF SHE CAN SLEEP HERE...
SHE CAN SLEEP JUST ABOUT ANY-WHERE.

the end

homemade 77: a cat investigates

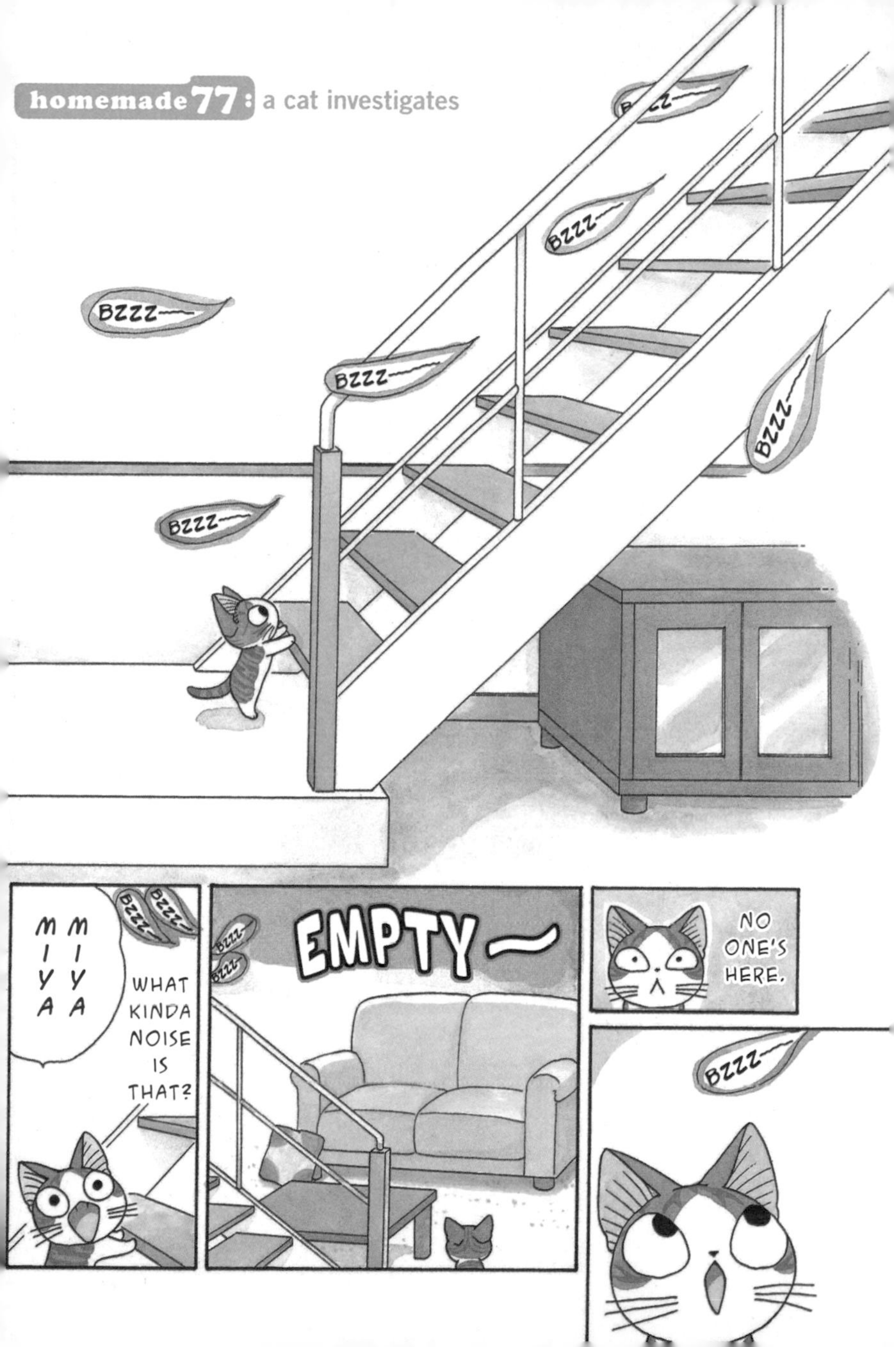
BZZZ—
BZZZ—
BZZZ—
BZZZ—
BZZZ—
BZZZ
BZZZ
MIYA MIYA
WHAT KINDA NOISE IS THAT?
BZZZ
BZZZ
EMPTY~
NO ONE'S HERE.
BZZZ—

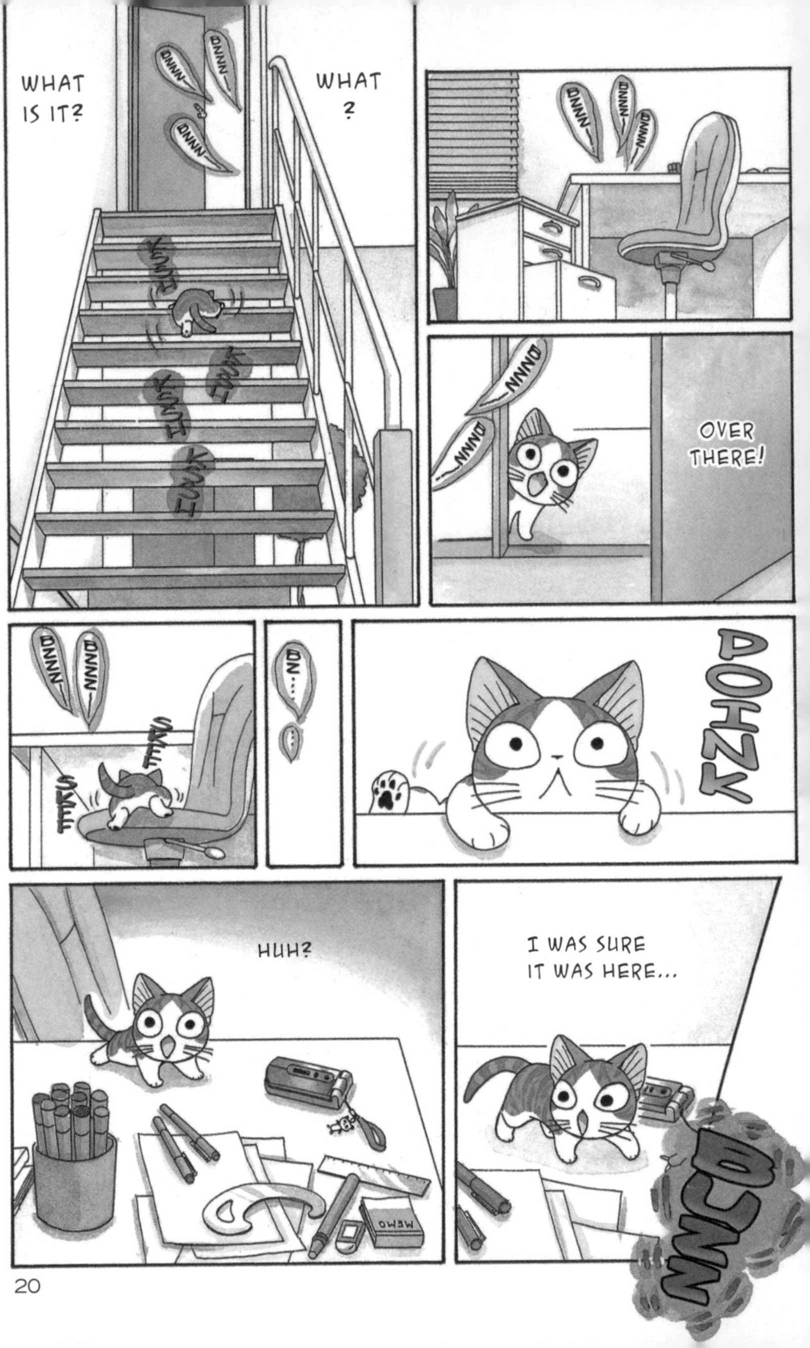
WHAT IS IT?
DNNN—
DNNN—
DNNN—
WHAT ?
DNNN—
DNNN—
DNNN—
DNNN—
DNNN—
OVER THERE!
DNNN—
DNNN—
BZ...
...
POHNK
HUH?
I WAS SURE IT WAS HERE...
DNNN

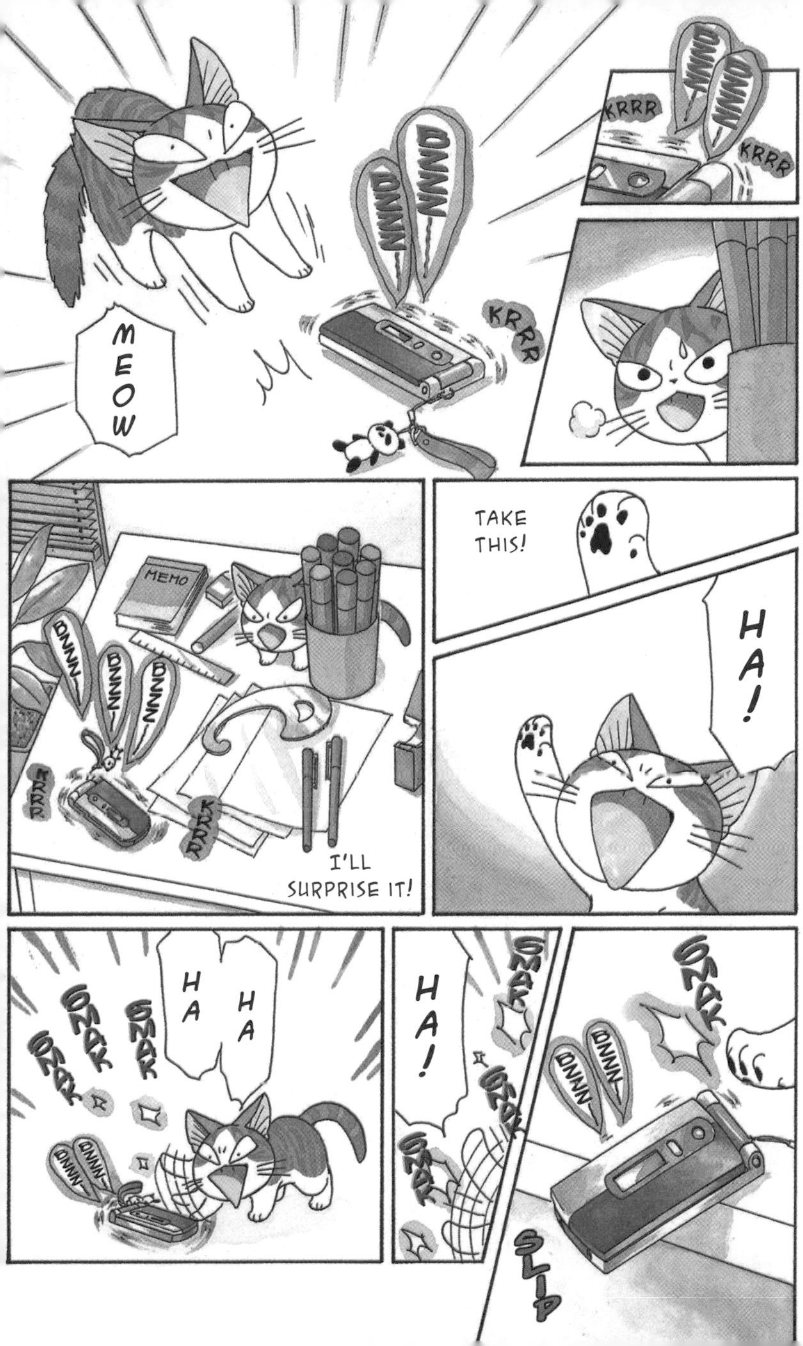
MEOW
DNNN
DNNN
KRRR
KRRR
DNNN
DNNN
KRRR
DNNN
DNNN
DNNN
KRRR
KRRR
I'LL SURPRISE IT!
TAKE THIS!
HA!
HA HA
SMAK
SMAK
SMAK
HA!
SMAK
SMAK
SMAK
SMAK
DNNN
DNNN
SLIP

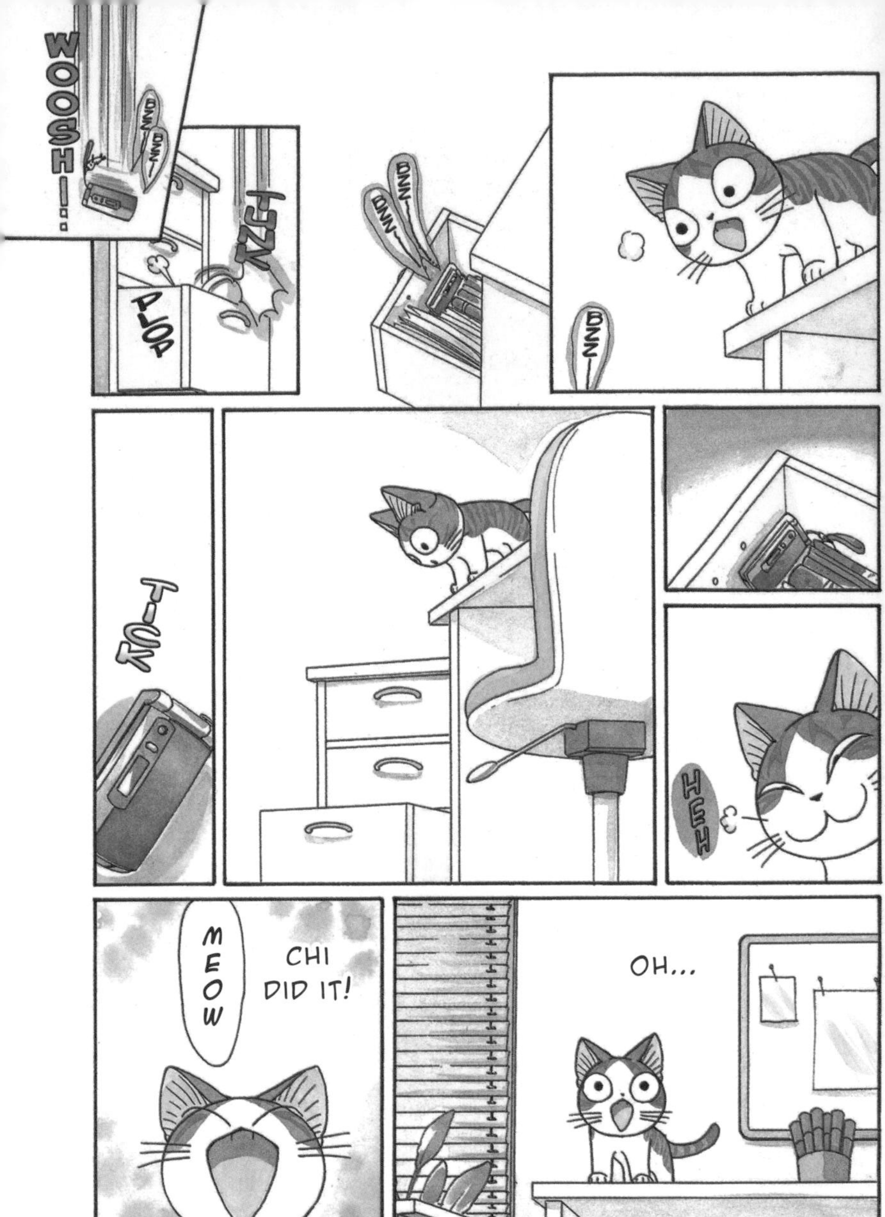
WOOSH!!
BZZ
BZZ
TUNK
PLOP
BZZ
BZZ
BZZ
TICK
HEH
MEOW
CHI DID IT!
OH...

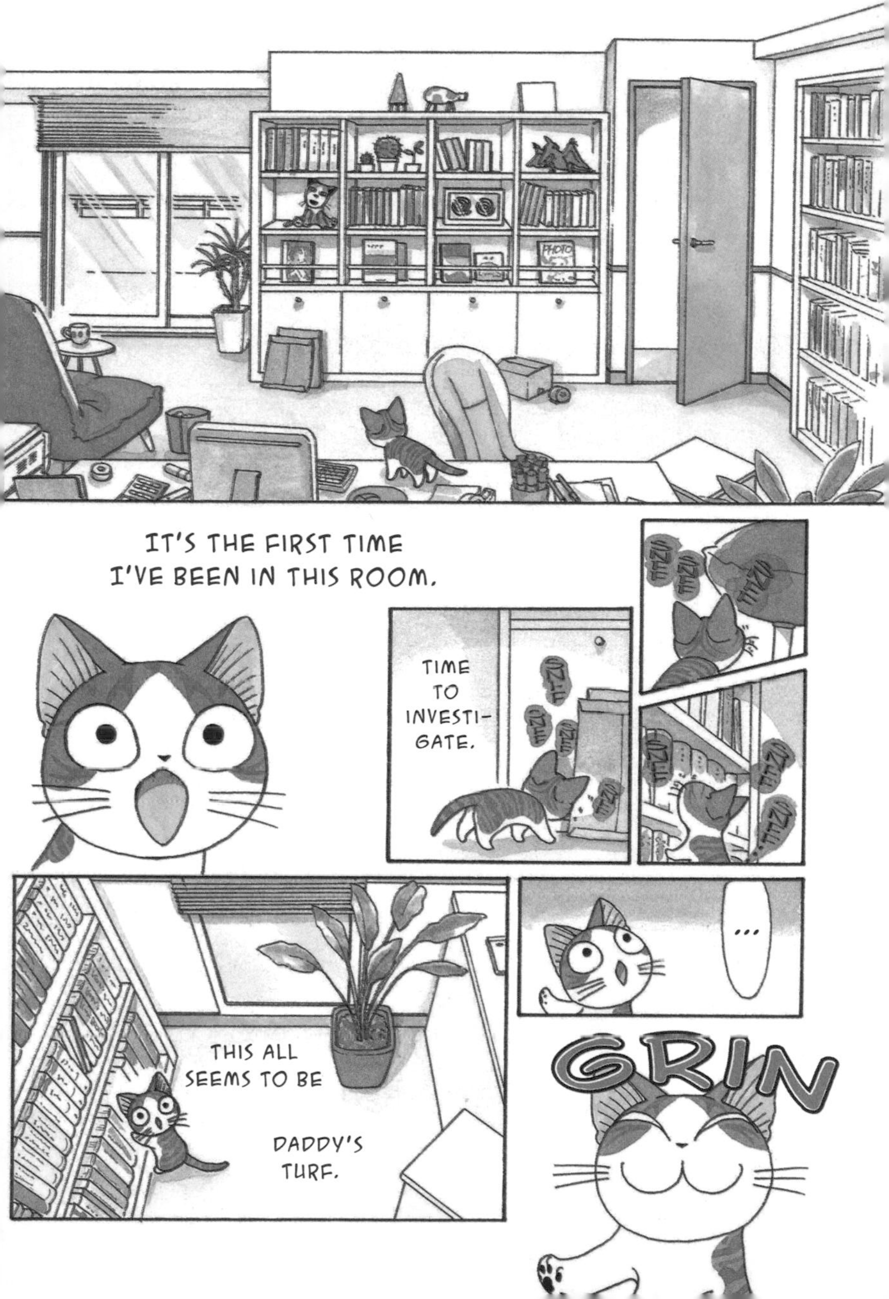
IT'S THE FIRST TIME
I'VE BEEN IN THIS ROOM.
TIME TO INVESTI-GATE.
THIS ALL SEEMS TO BE
DADDY'S TURF.
...
GRIN

MYA

IT'S CHI'S, TOO!

RUB RUB RUB RUB

THIS TOO.

SKFF SKFF SKFF

CHI'S STUFF!

HERE! AND OVER HERE TOO!

ROLL ROLL ROLL...

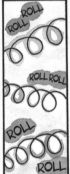

ROLL ROLL

ROLL ROLL

ROLL

ROLL

IT'S ALL CHI'S STUFF!

HA

MIYA

HUH?

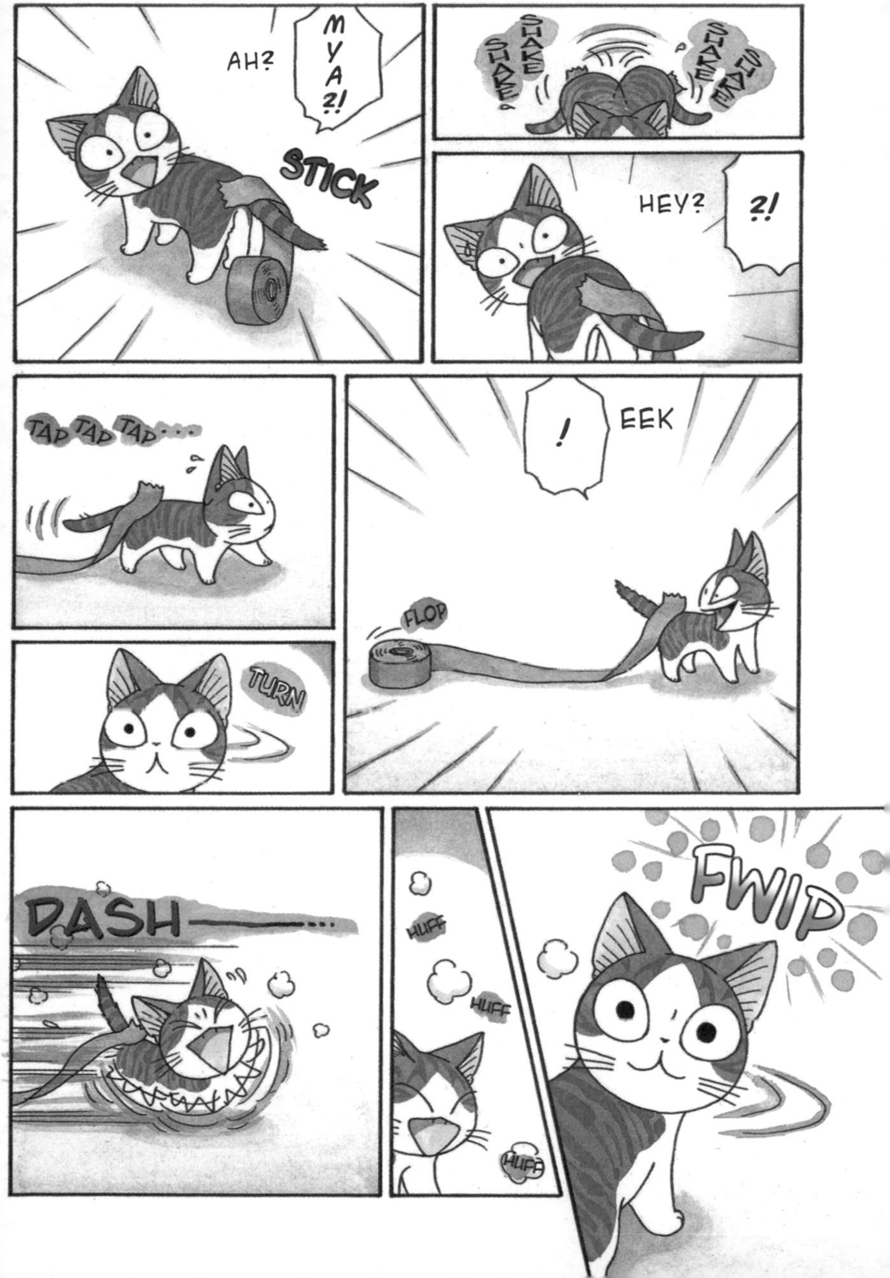
AH?
MYA?!
STICK
SHAKE SHAKE
SHAKE SHAKE
HEY?
?!
TAP TAP TAP...
TURN
!
EEK
FLOP
DASH
HUFF
HUFF
HUFF
FWIP

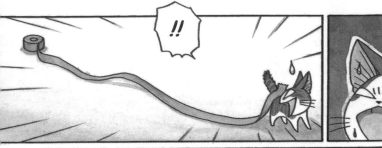

HEWLP ME!!

MEOW

SOME-ONE HELP!

MEOW MEOW

...

NO ONE'S HOME.

OH...

the end

homemade 78: a cat feigns ignorance

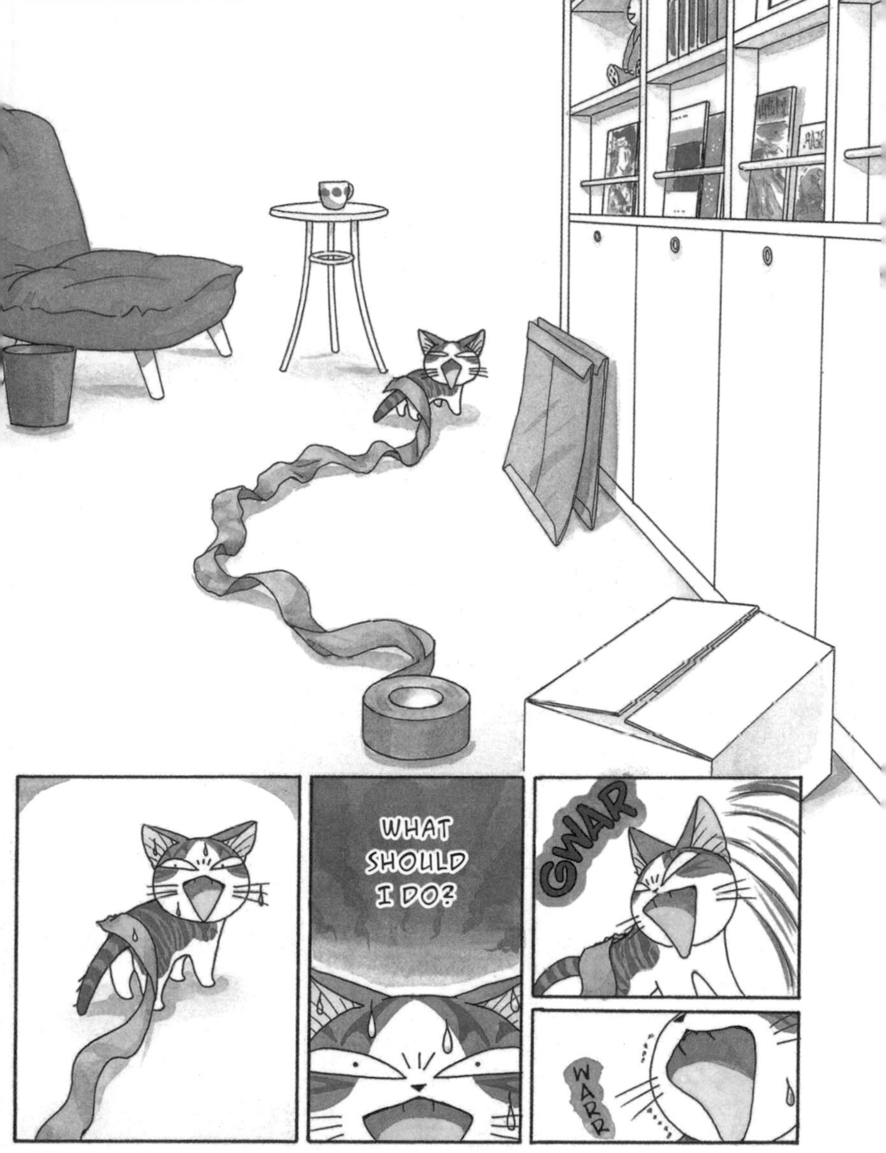
WHAT SHOULD I DO?
GWAR
WARR

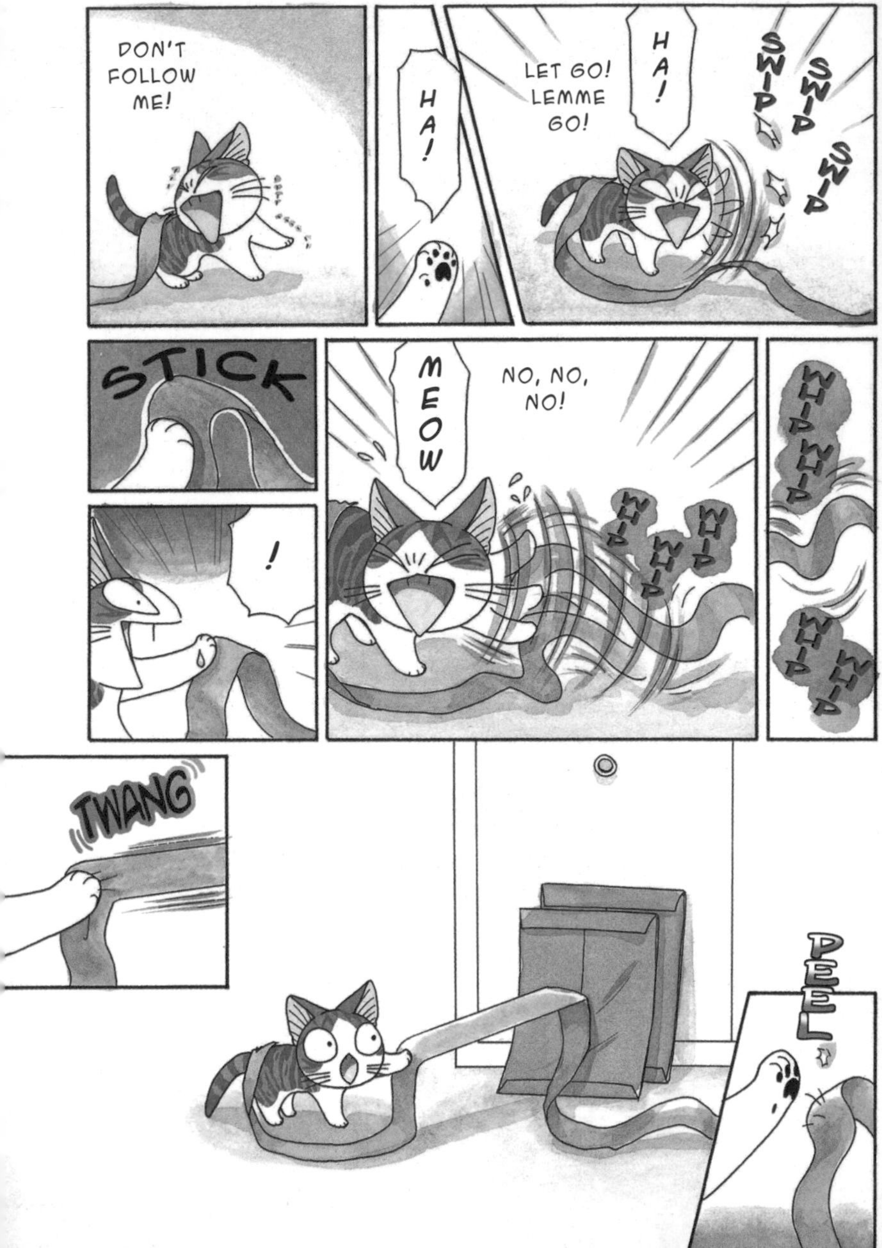

DON'T FOLLOW ME!
HA!
LET GO! LEMME GO!
HA!
SWIP
SWIP
SWIP
STICK
!
MEOW
NO, NO, NO!
WHIP
WHIP
WHIP
WHIP WHIP
WHIP
WHIP
TWANG
PEEL

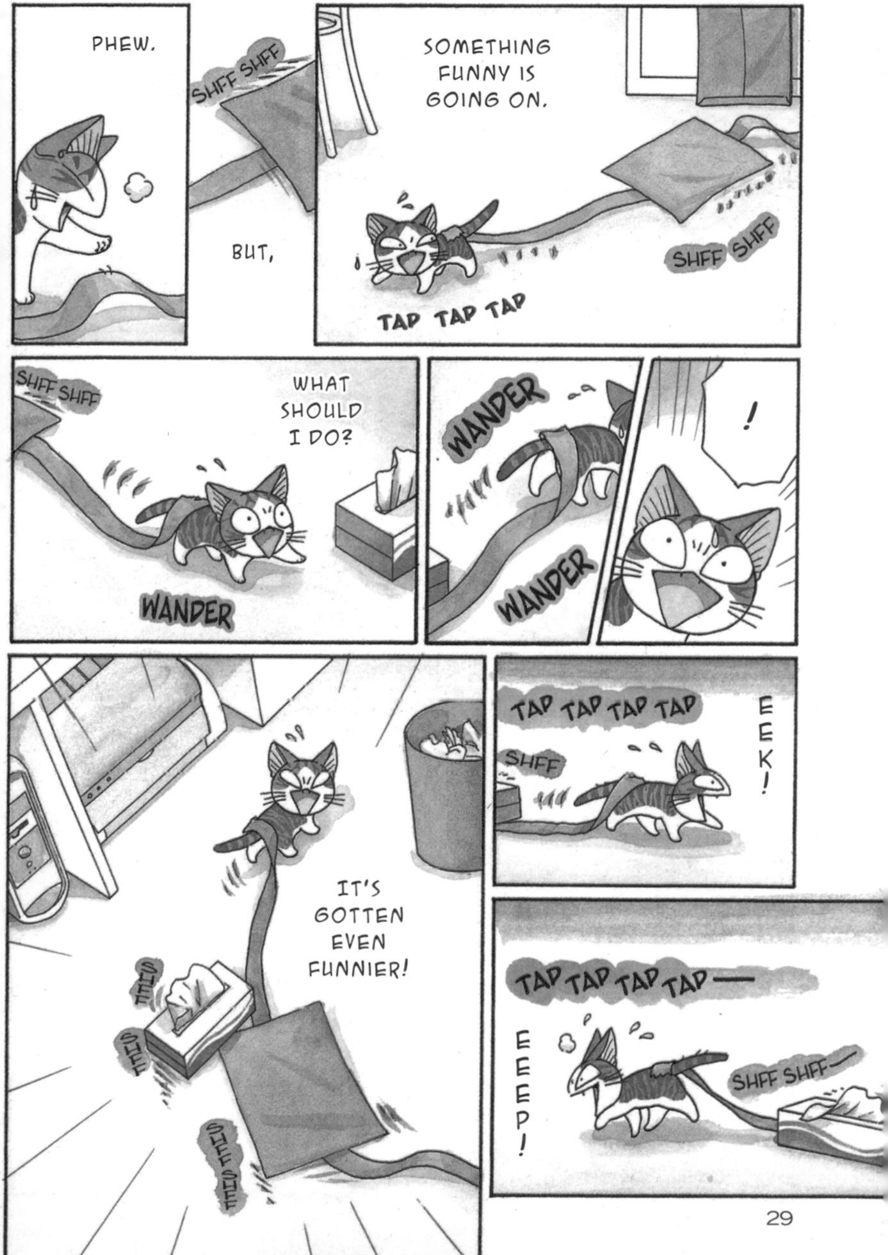
PHEW.
SHFF SHFF
BUT,
SOMETHING FUNNY IS GOING ON.
SHFF SHFF
TAP TAP TAP
SHFF SHFF
WHAT SHOULD I DO?
WANDER
WANDER
WANDER
!
IT'S GOTTEN EVEN FUNNIER!
SHFF
SHFF
SHFF SHFF
TAP TAP TAP TAP
SHFF
EEEK!
TAP TAP TAP TAP—
EEEEP!
SHFF SHFF—

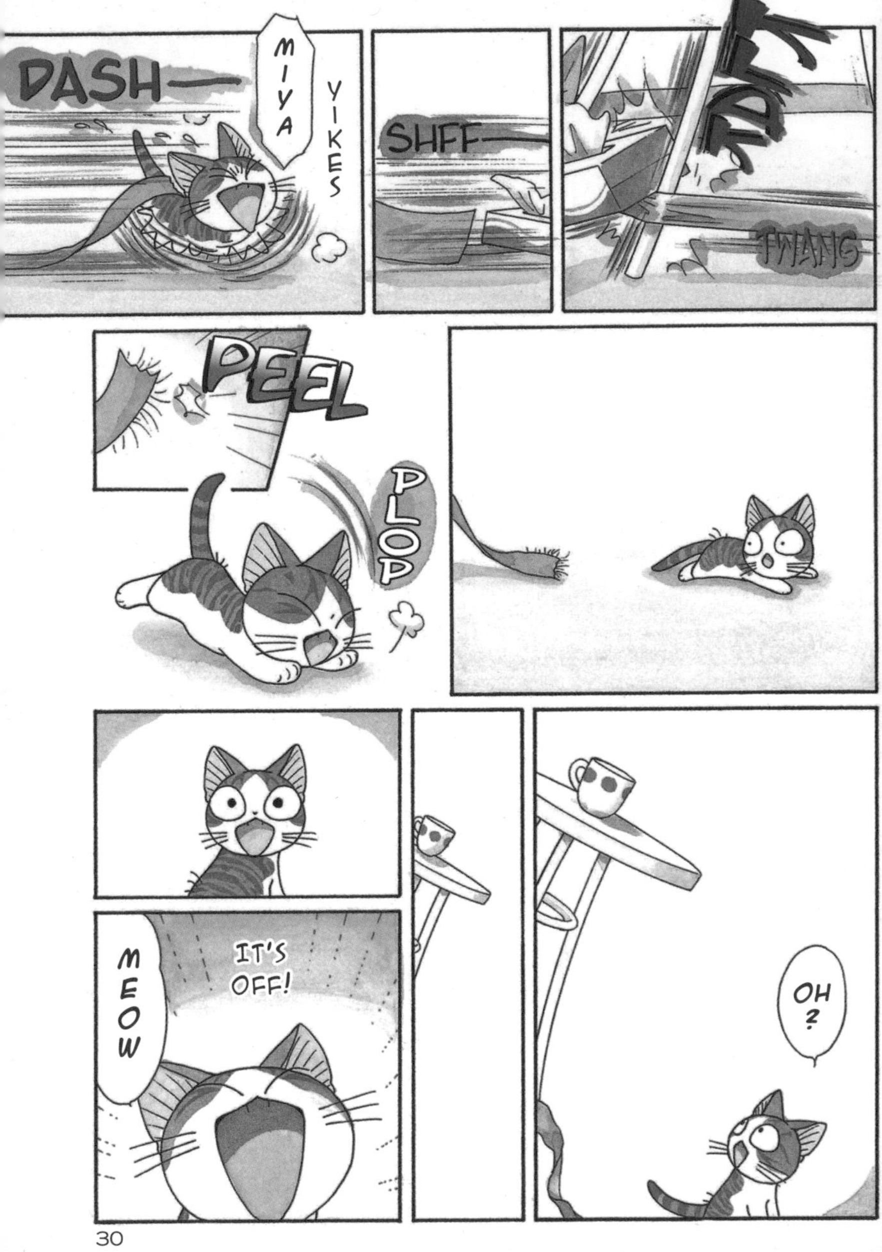
DASH
MIYA
YIKES
SHFF
TWANG
PEEL
PLOP
IT'S OFF!
MEOW
OH?

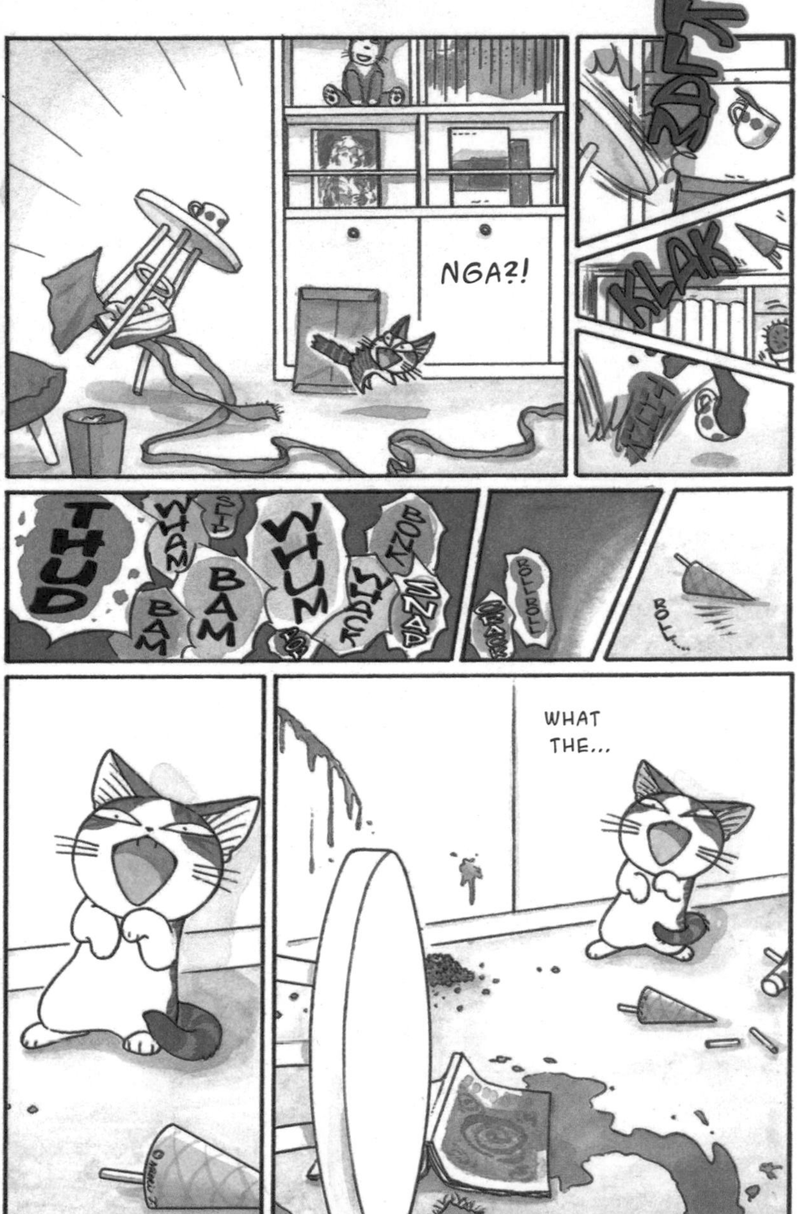

NGA?!
KLAM
KLAK
THUD
WHAM
SLID
BAM
BAM
WHUM
BONK
SNAP
ROLL ROLL
ROLL...
WHAT THE...

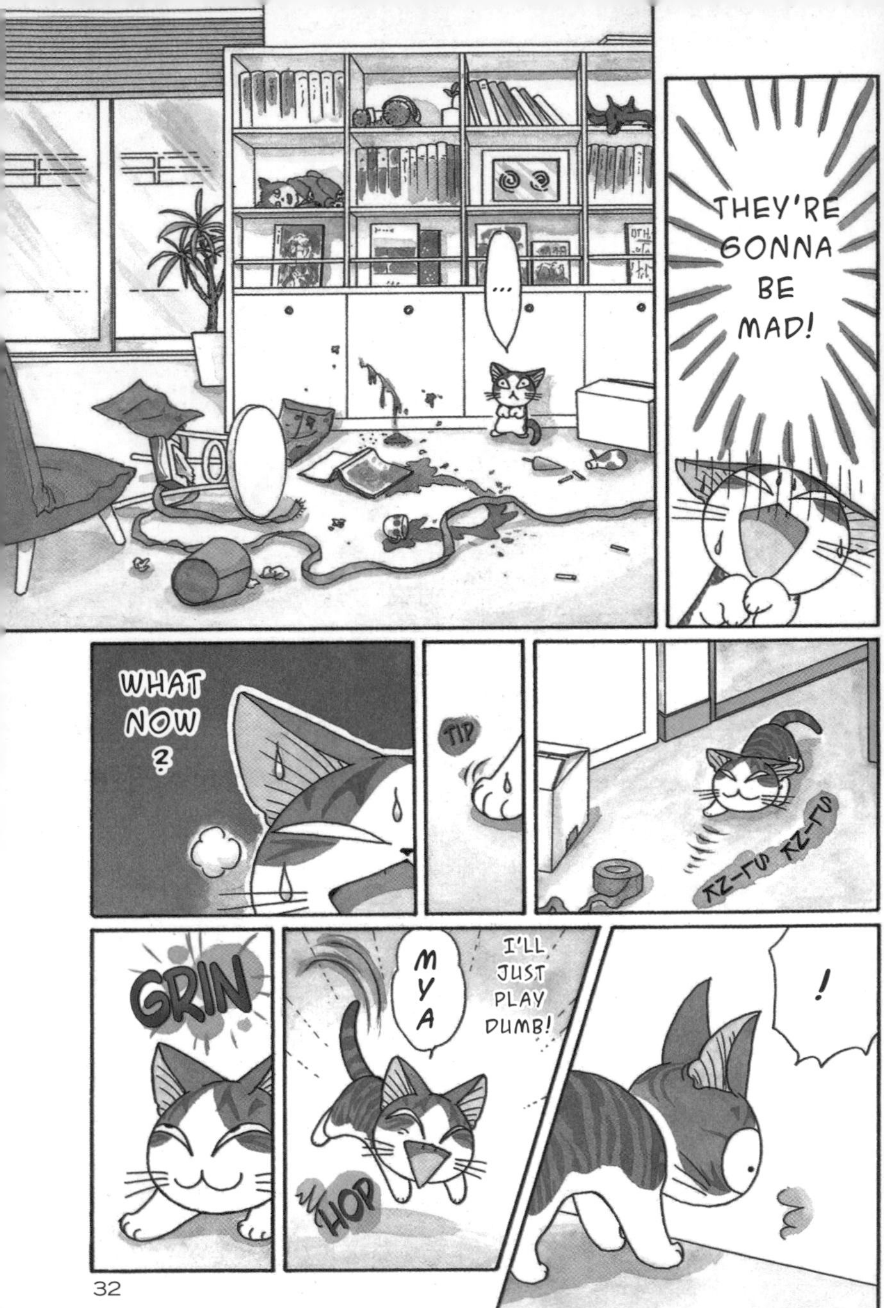
...
THEY'RE GONNA BE MAD!
WHAT NOW?
TIP
GRIN
MYA
HOP
I'LL JUST PLAY DUMB!
!

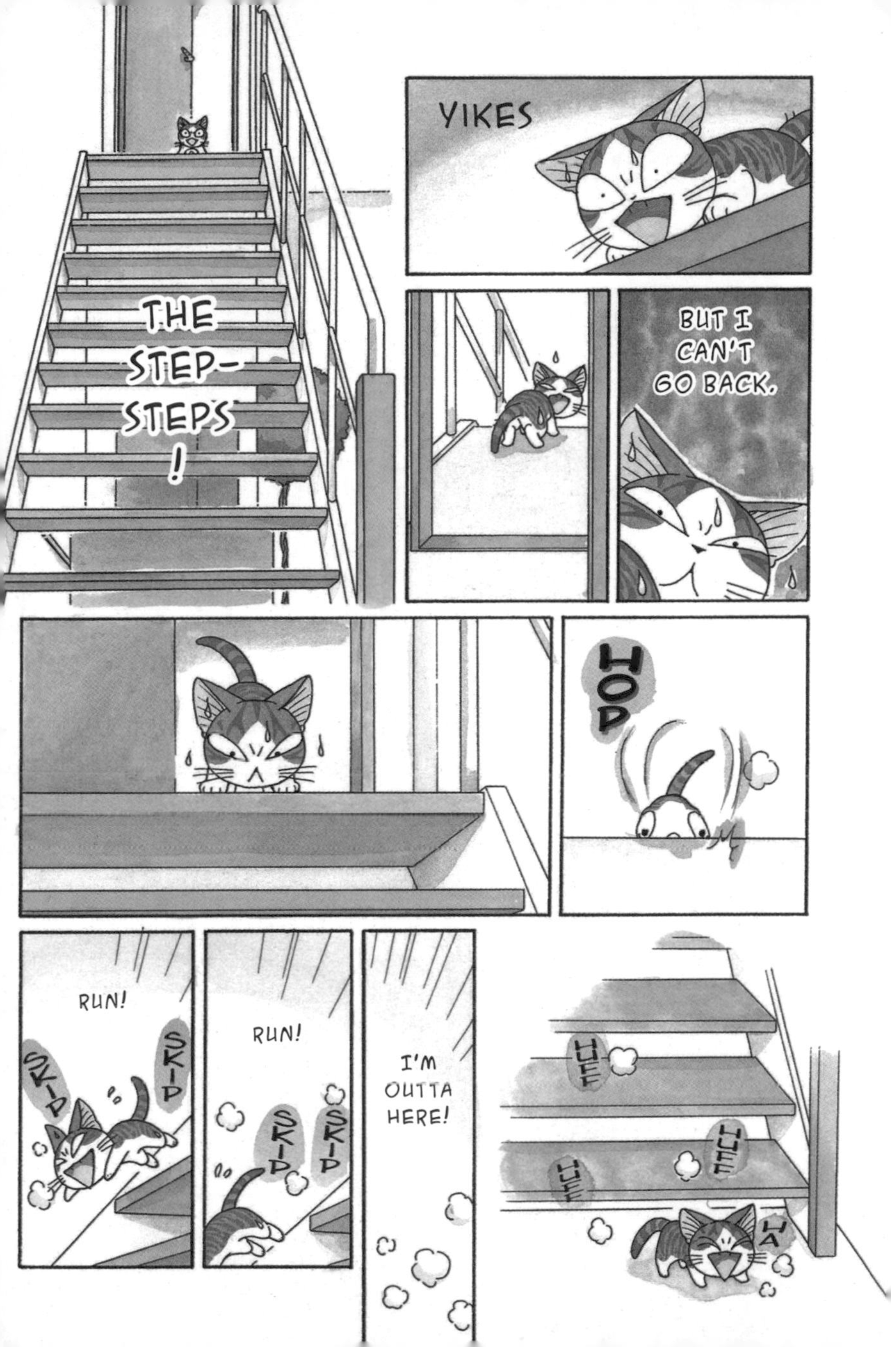
THE STEP-STEPS!
YIKES
BUT I CAN'T GO BACK.
HOP
RUN!
SKIP
SKIP
RUN!
SKIP
SKIP
I'M OUTTA HERE!
HUFF
HUFF
HUFF
HA

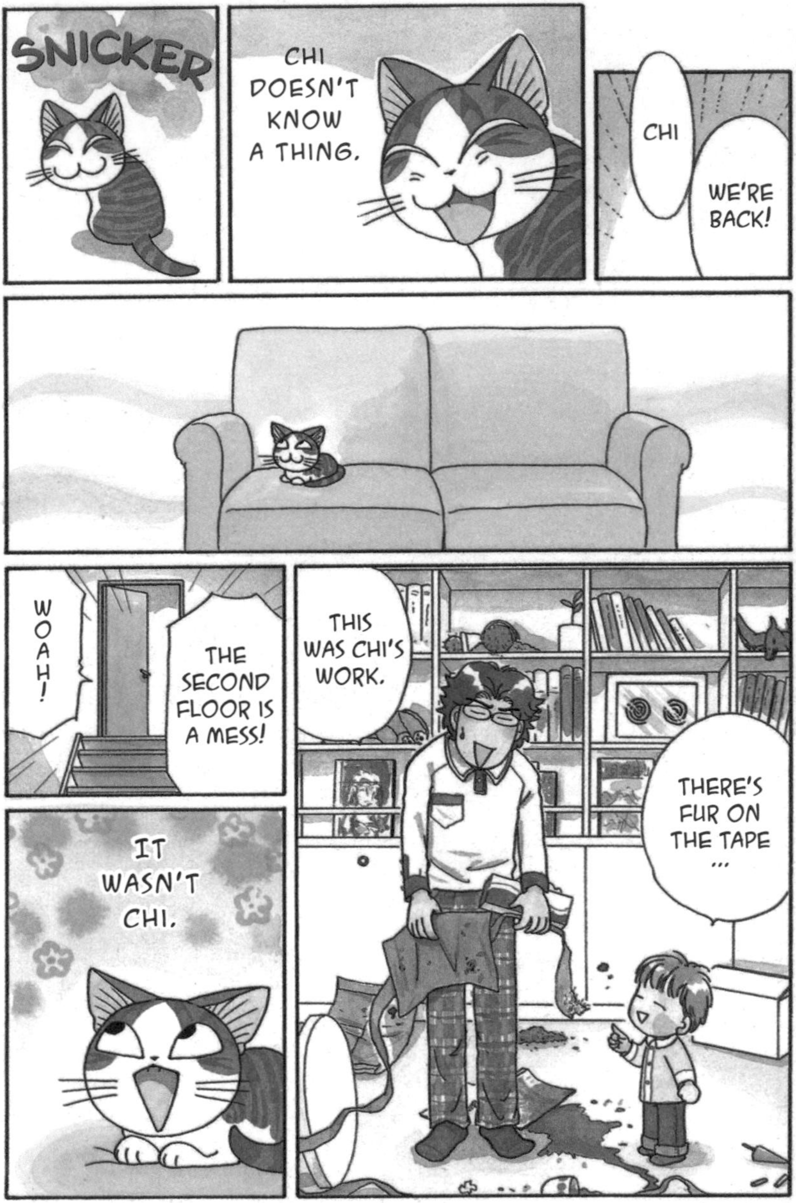
SNICKER
CHI DOESN'T KNOW A THING.
CHI
WE'RE BACK!
WOAH!
THE SECOND FLOOR IS A MESS!
IT WASN'T CHI.
THIS WAS CHI'S WORK.
THERE'S FUR ON THE TAPE ...

the end

homemade 79: a cat contrives

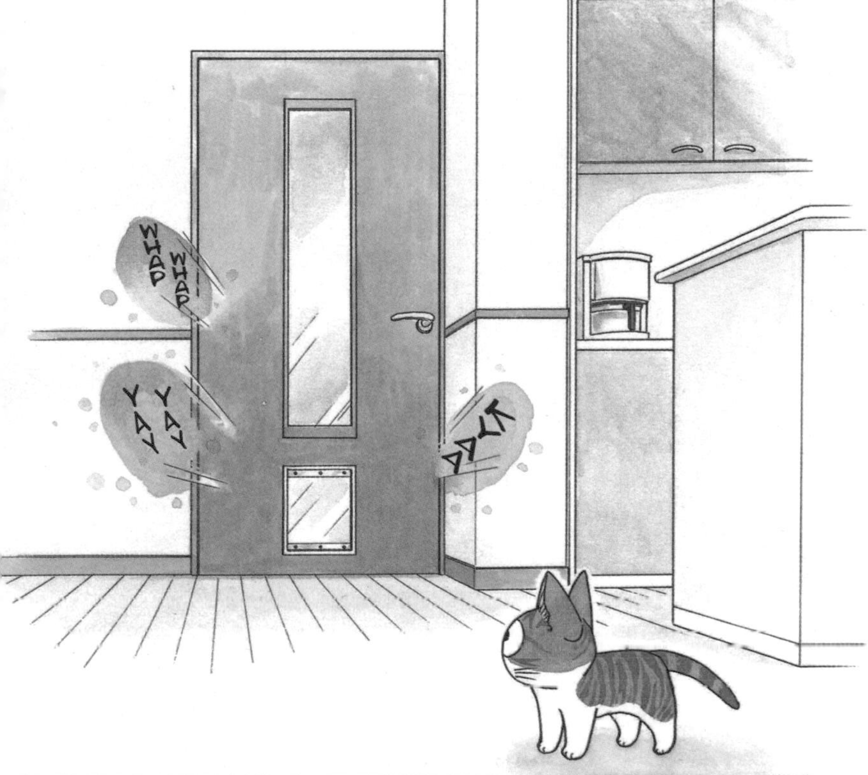
WHAP WHAP
YAY YAY
YAY

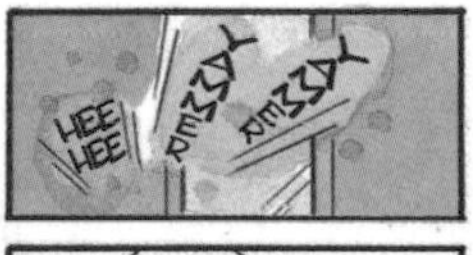
HEE HEE

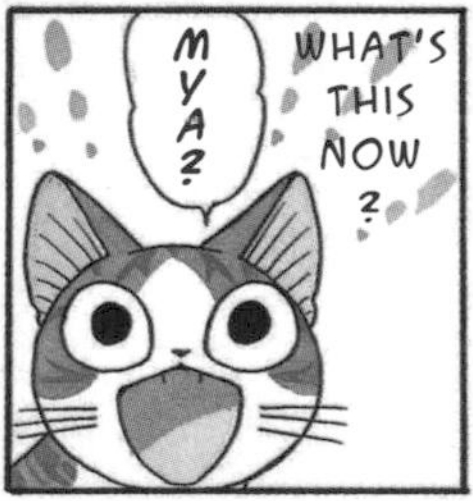
MYA?
WHAT'S THIS NOW?

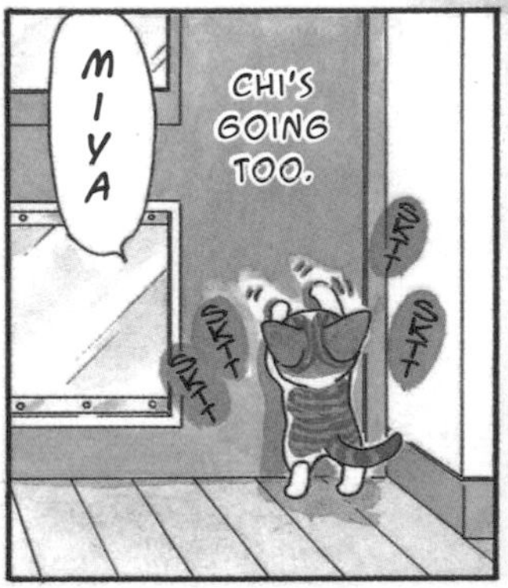
MIYA
CHI'S GOING TOO.
SKTT
SKTT
SKTT
SKTT

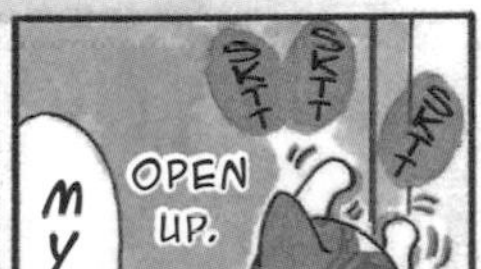
SKTT SKTT SKTT
MYA
OPEN UP.

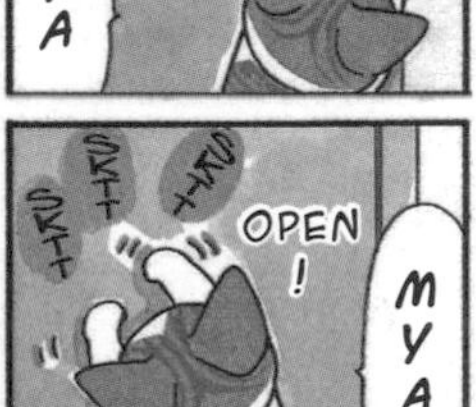
SKTT SKTT SKTT
OPEN!
MYA

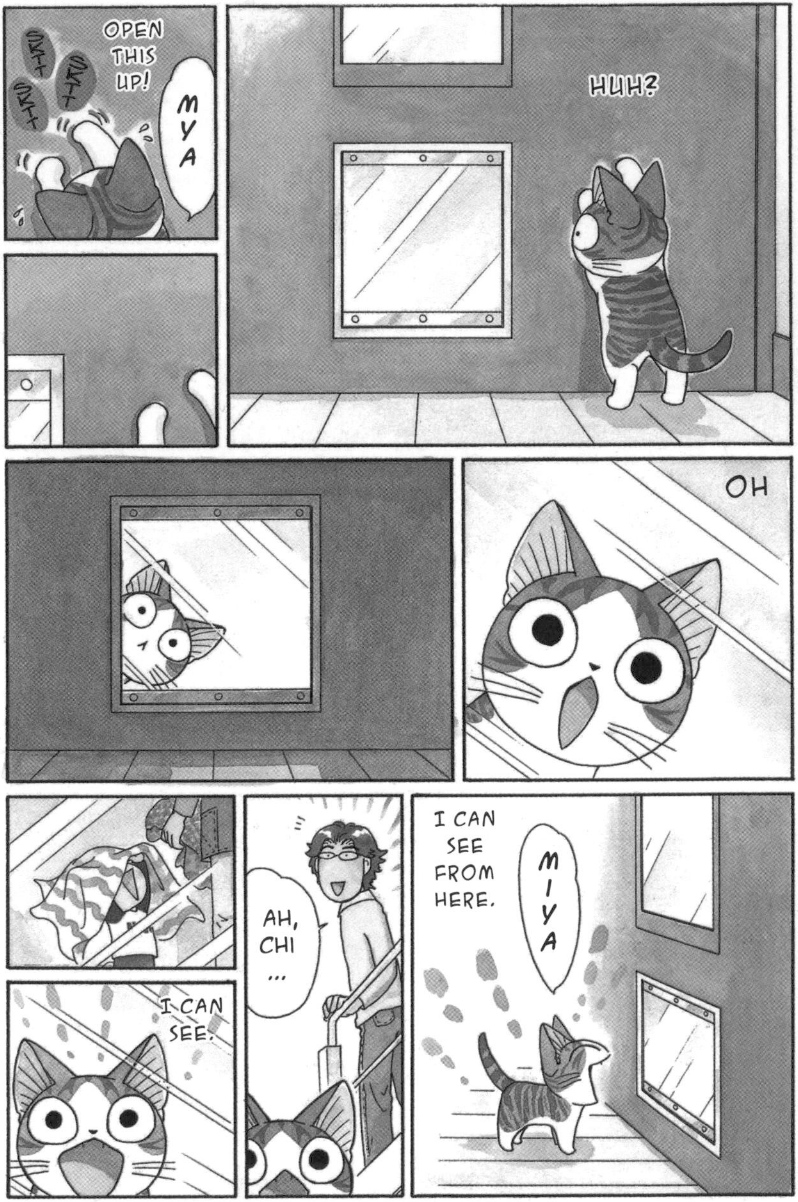
SKTT
SKTT
SKTT
OPEN THIS UP!
MYA
HUH?
OH
I CAN SEE.
AH, CHI ...
I CAN SEE FROM HERE.
MIYA

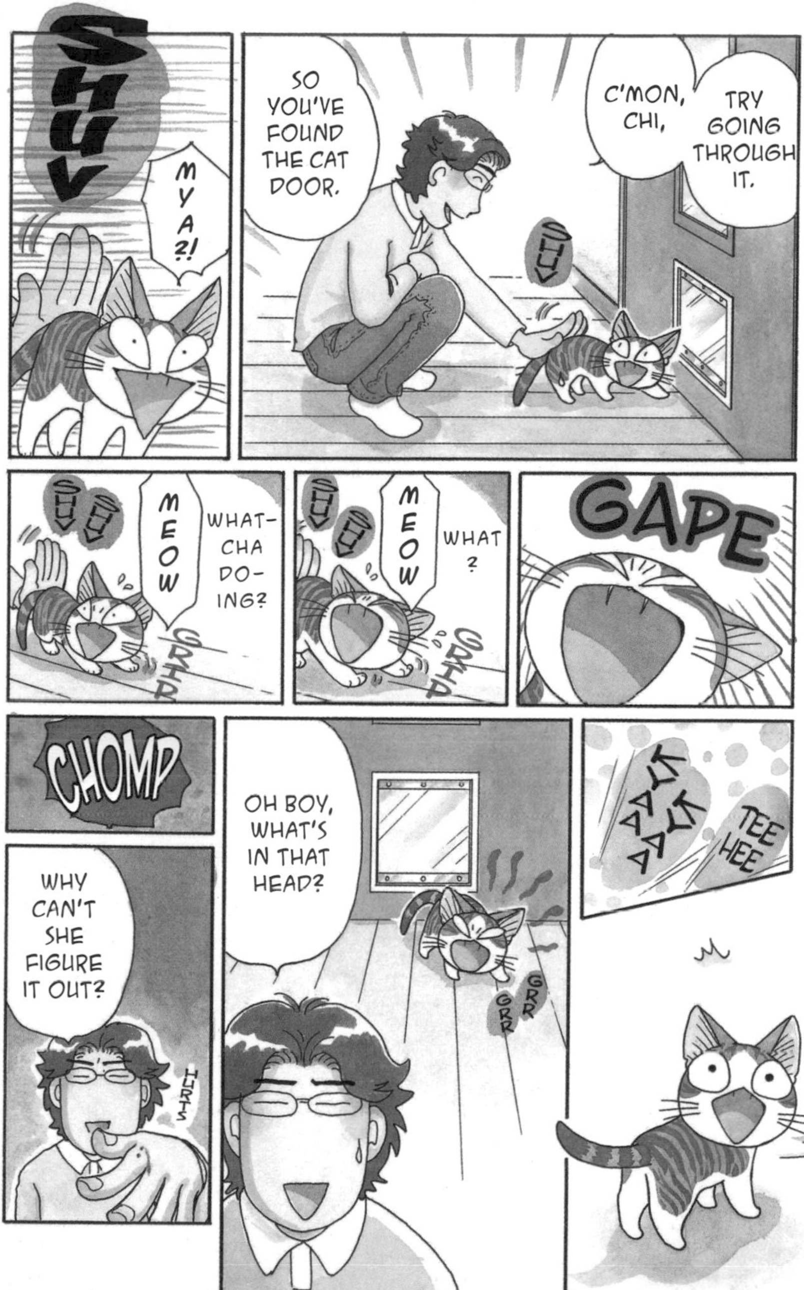
SHUV
MYA?!
SO YOU'VE FOUND THE CAT DOOR.
SHUV
C'MON, CHI,
TRY GOING THROUGH IT.
SHUV
SHUV
MEOW
WHAT-CHA DO-ING?
GRIP
SHUV
SHUV
MEOW
WHAT?
GRIP
GAPE
CHOMP
WHY CAN'T SHE FIGURE IT OUT?
HURTS
OH BOY, WHAT'S IN THAT HEAD?
GRR
GRR
TEE HEE

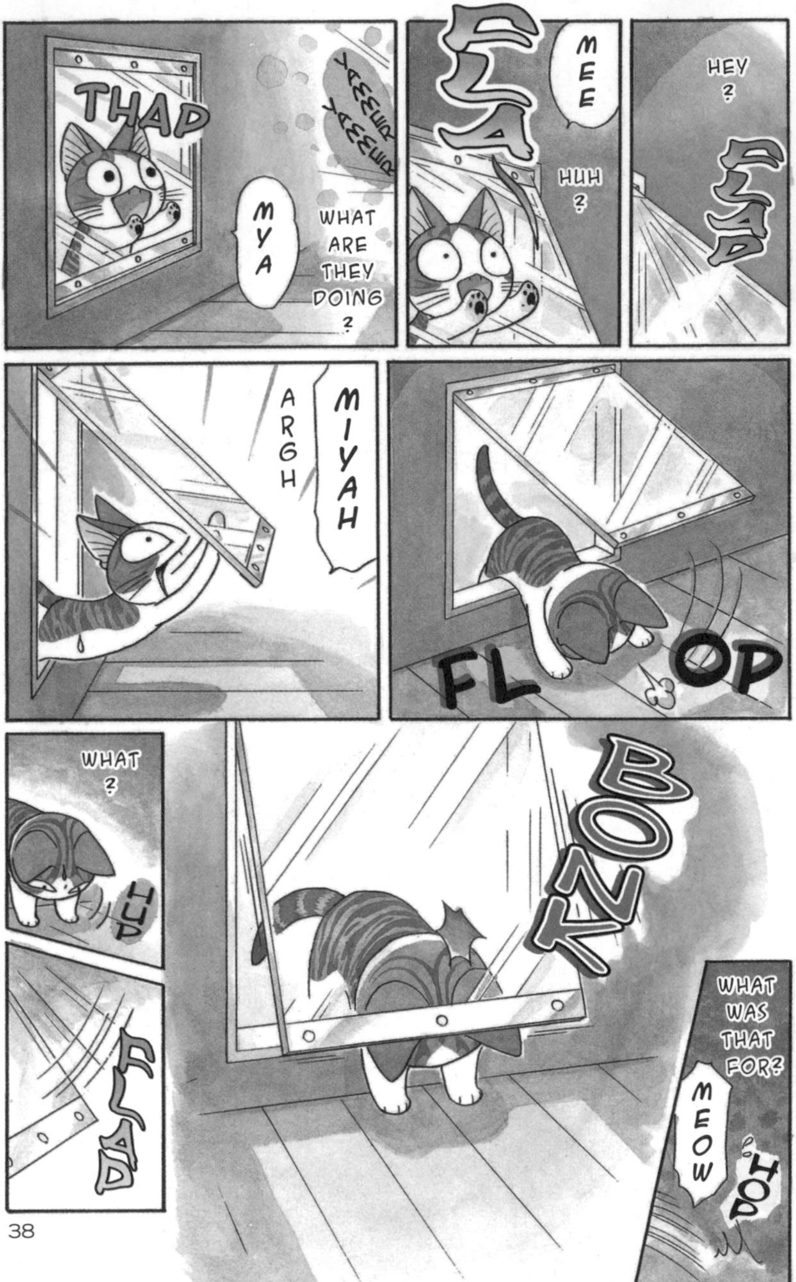

THAP
MYA
WHAT ARE THEY DOING?
FLA
MEE
HUH?
HEY?
FLAP
ARGH
MIYAH
FLOP
WHAT?
HUP
FLAP
BONK
WHAT WAS THAT FOR?
MEOW
HOP

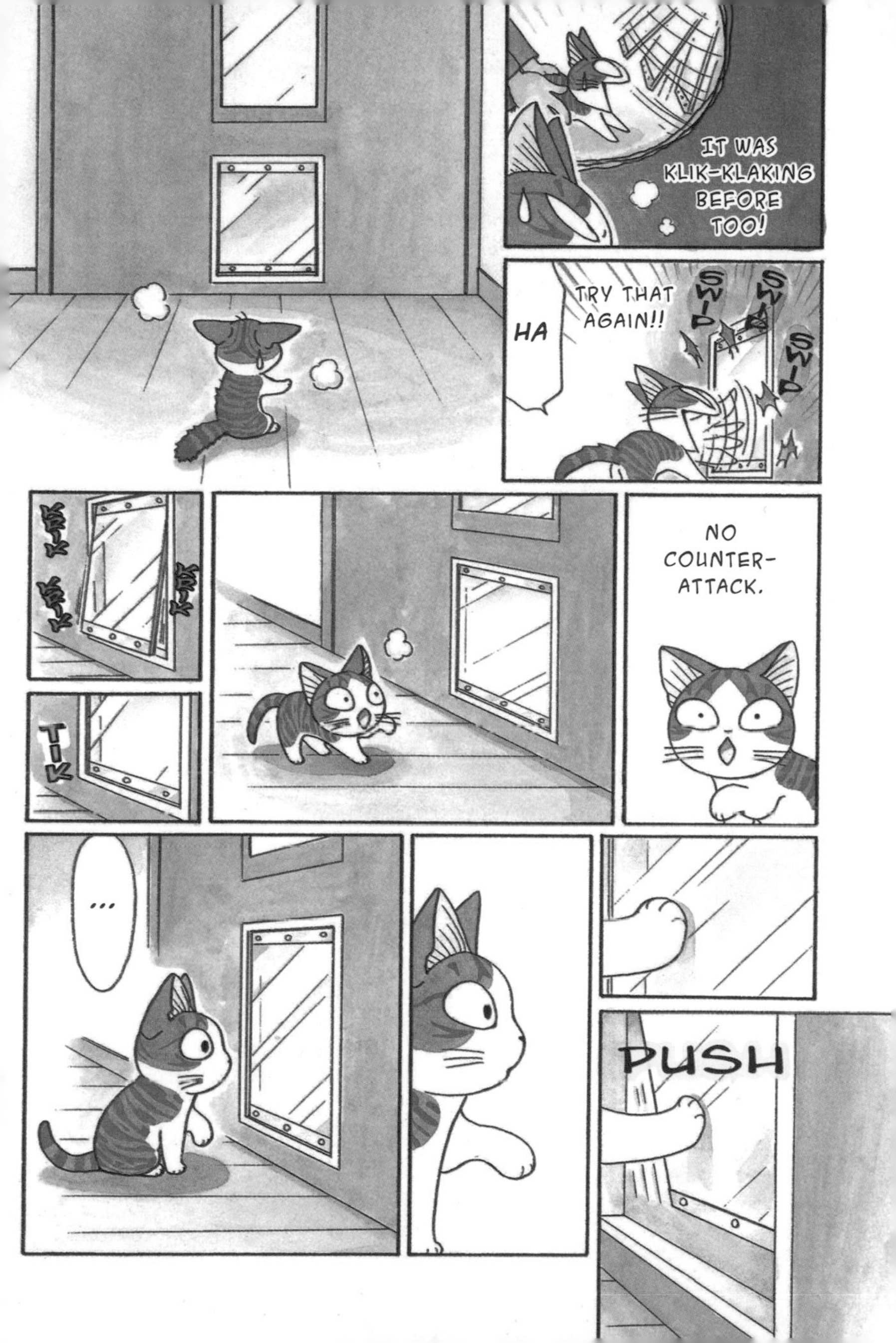
IT WAS KLIK-KLAKING BEFORE TOO!
HA
TRY THAT AGAIN!!
SWID
SWID
SWID
KRIK
KRIK
KRIK
TIK
NO COUNTER-ATTACK.
...
PUSH

OPEN

CLOSE

OPEN

CLOSE

WHAT IS THIS?

I'VE GOTTA THINK ABOUT THIS.

THINK

THINK

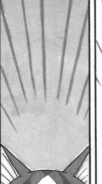

?!

OH!

40

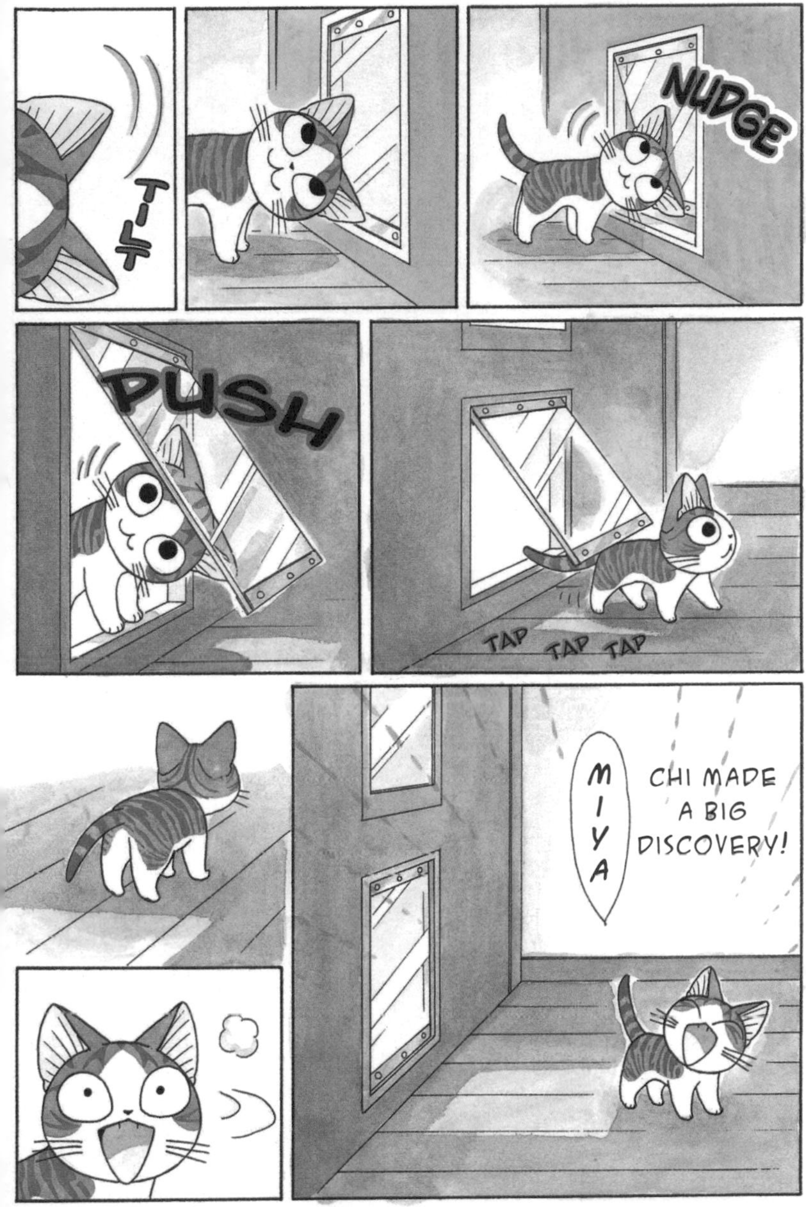
TILT
NUDGE
PUSH
TAP TAP TAP
MIYA
CHI MADE A BIG DISCOVERY!

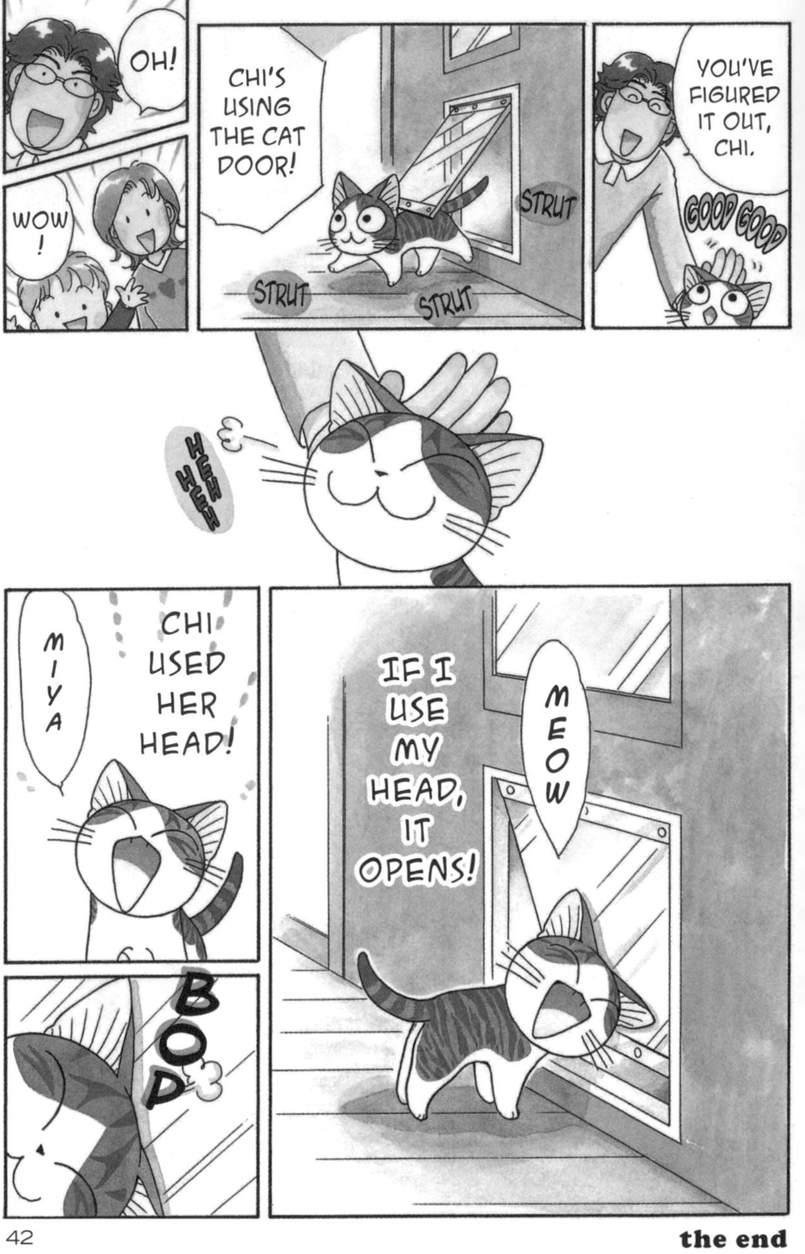
OH!
WOW!
CHI'S USING THE CAT DOOR!
STRUT
STRUT
STRUT
YOU'VE FIGURED IT OUT, CHI.
GOOD GOOD
HEH HEH
CHI USED HER HEAD!
MIYA
BOP
IF I USE MY HEAD, IT OPENS!
MEOW

the end

homemade 80: a cat is brushed

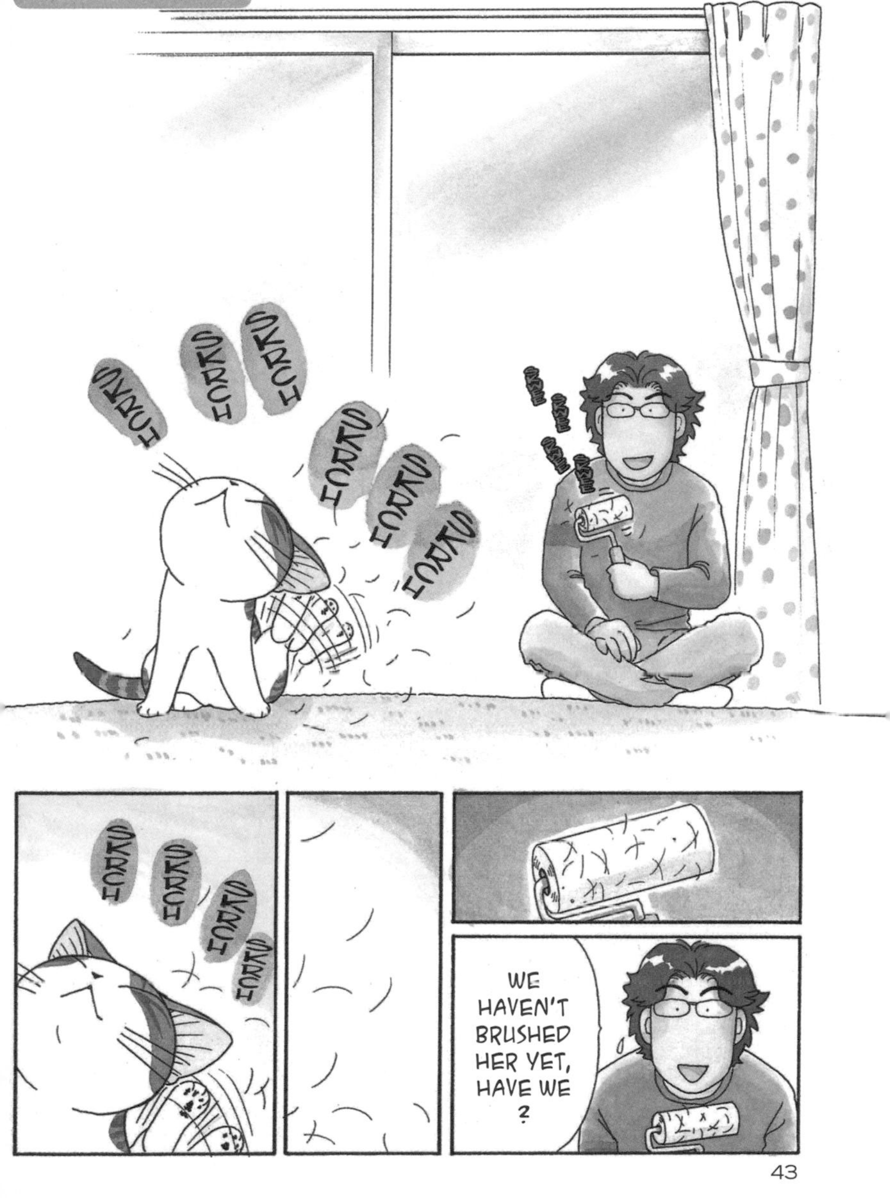
SKRCH
SKRCH
SKRCH
SKRCH
SKRCH
SKRCH
SKRCH
SKRCH
SKRCH
SKRCH
WE HAVEN'T BRUSHED HER YET, HAVE WE ?

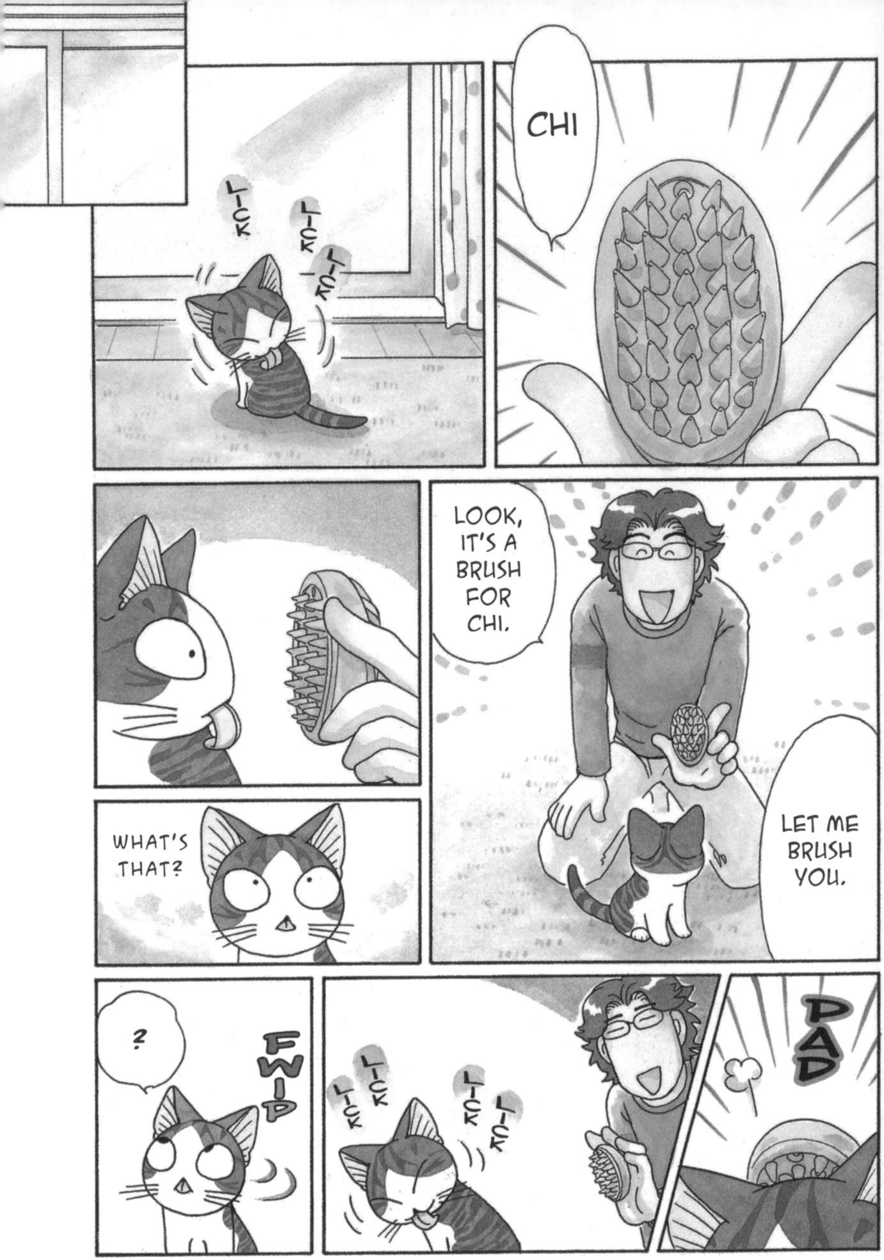
LICK
LICK
LICK
CHI
WHAT'S THAT?
LOOK, IT'S A BRUSH FOR CHI.
LET ME BRUSH YOU.
?
FWIP
LICK
LICK
LICK
LICK
PAD

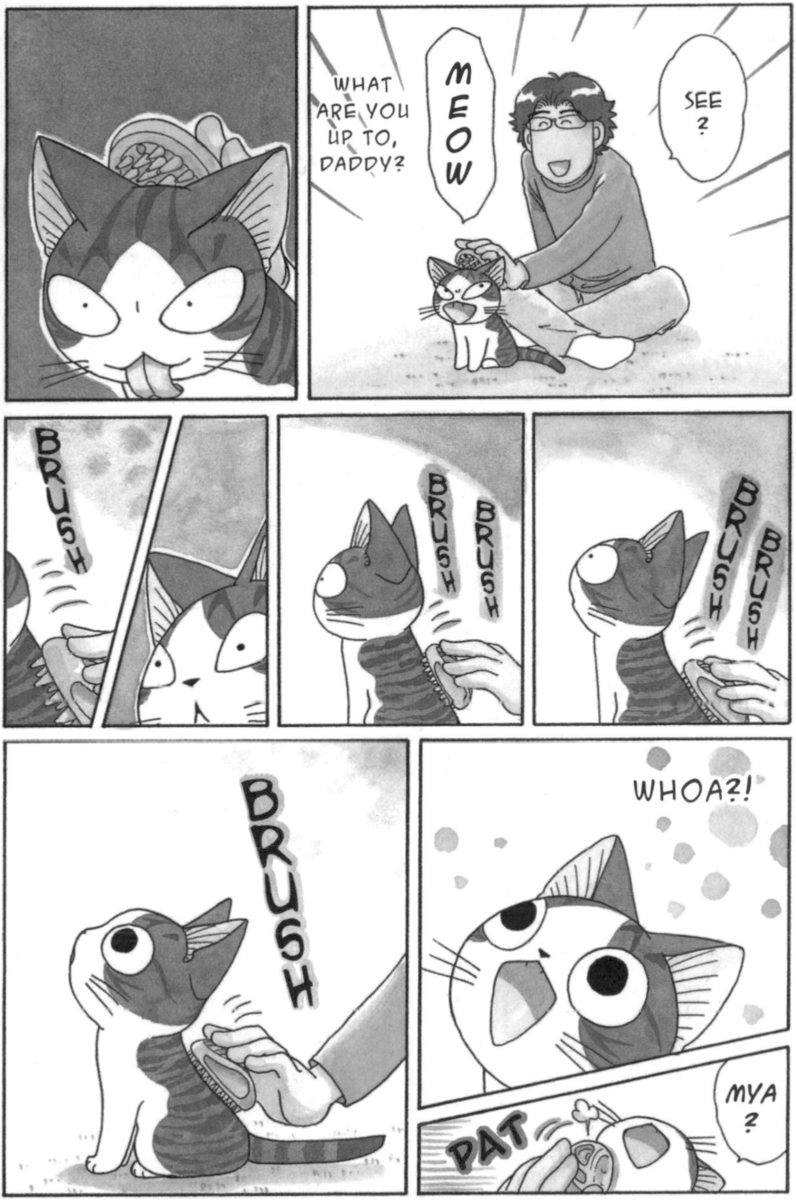
WHAT ARE YOU UP TO, DADDY?
MEOW
SEE?
BRUSH
BRUSH
BRUSH
BRUSH
BRUSH
BRUSH
WHOA?!
PAT
MYA?

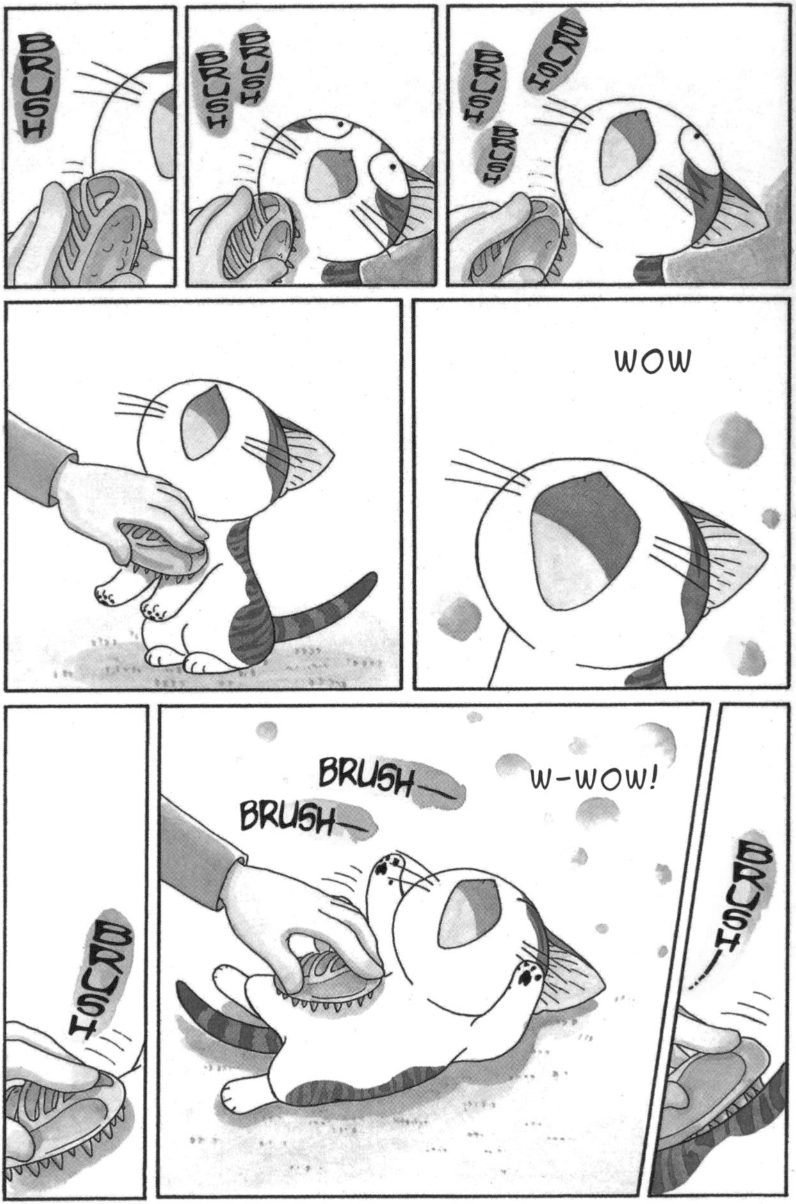
BRUSH
BRUSH
BRUSH
BRUSH
BRUSH
BRUSH
WOW
BRUSH—
W-WOW!
BRUSH—
BRUSH—
BRUSH

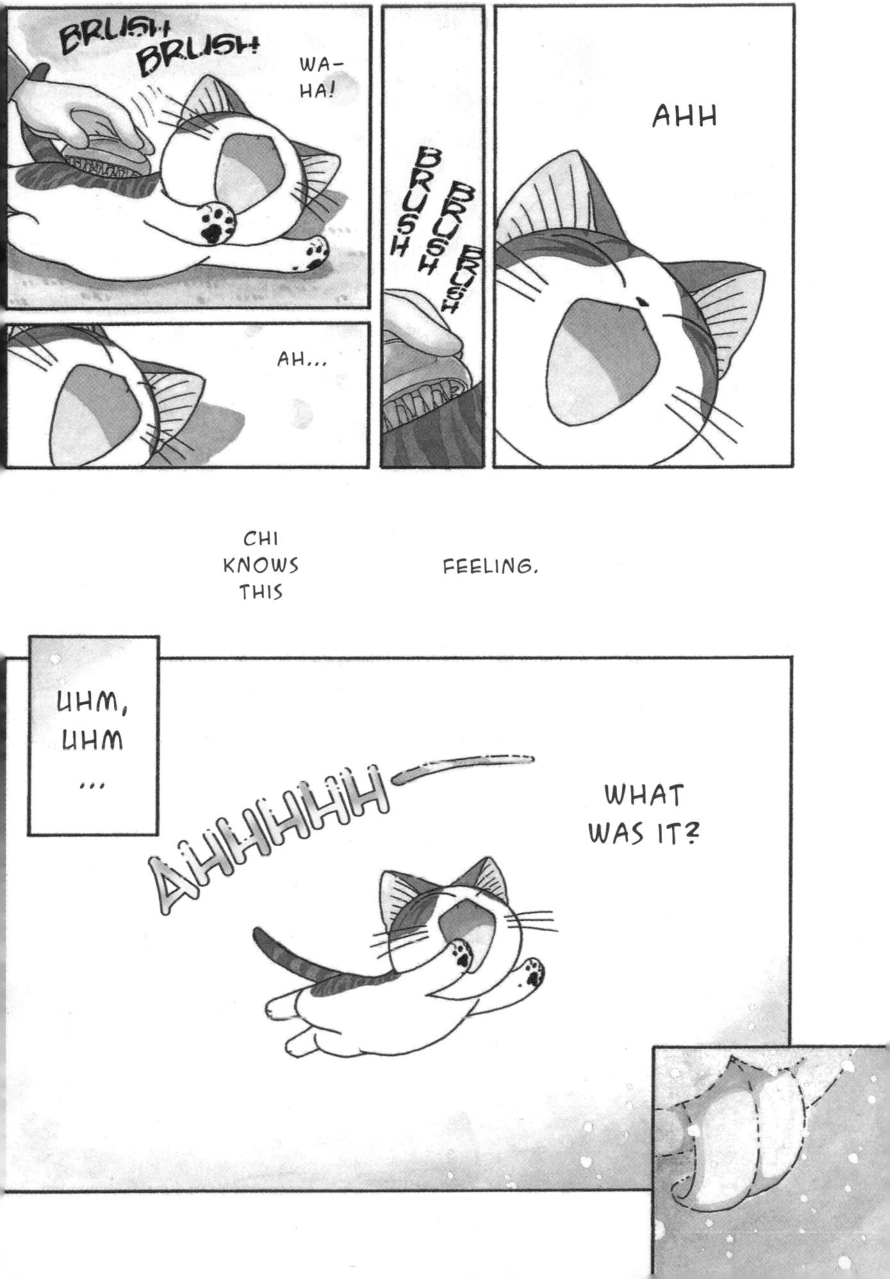
BRUSH BRUSH
WA-HA!
AH...
BRUSH BRUSH BRUSH
AHH
CHI KNOWS THIS
FEELING.
UHM, UHM ...
AHHHHHH—
WHAT WAS IT?

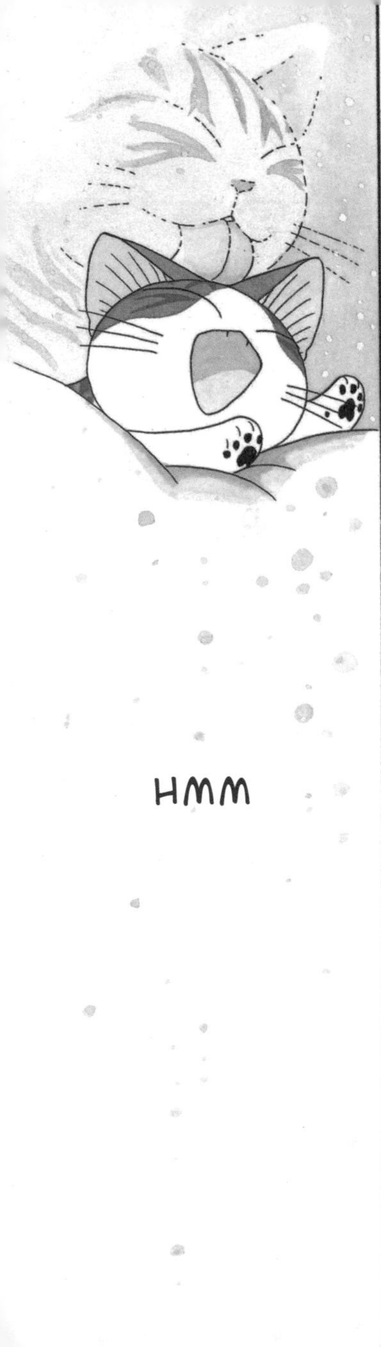
HMM

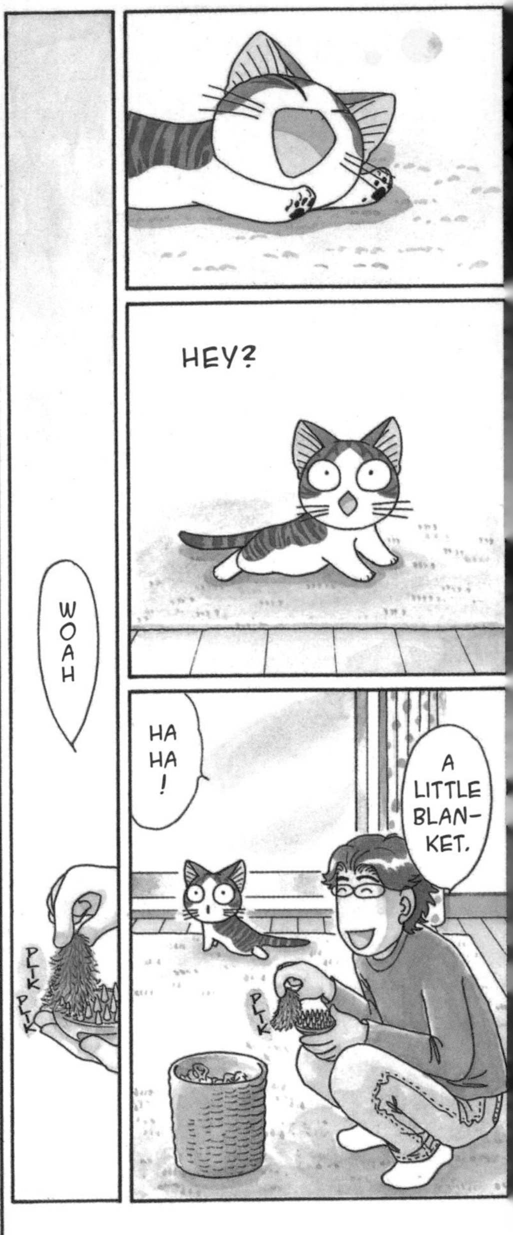
WOAH
PLIK PLIK
HEY?
HA HA!
A LITTLE BLAN-KET.
PLIK

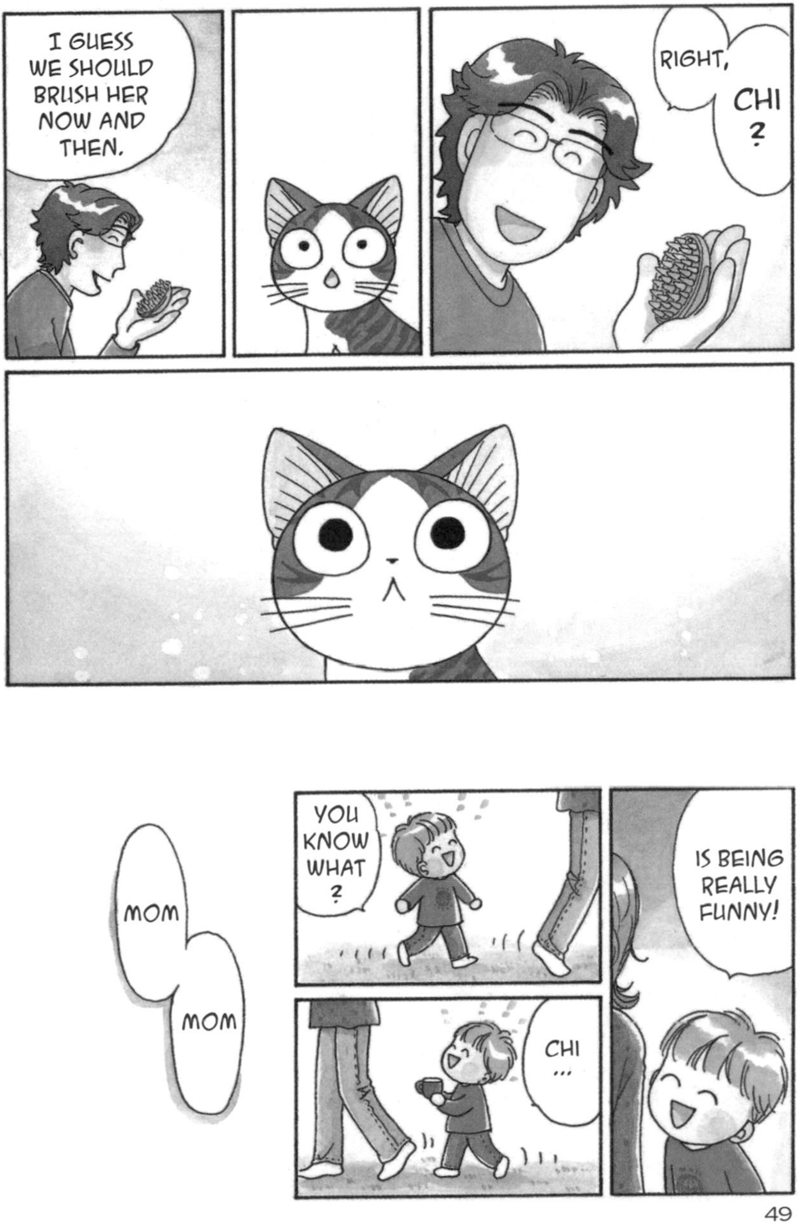
I GUESS WE SHOULD BRUSH HER NOW AND THEN.
RIGHT, CHI?
MOM
MOM
YOU KNOW WHAT?
CHI...
IS BEING REALLY FUNNY!

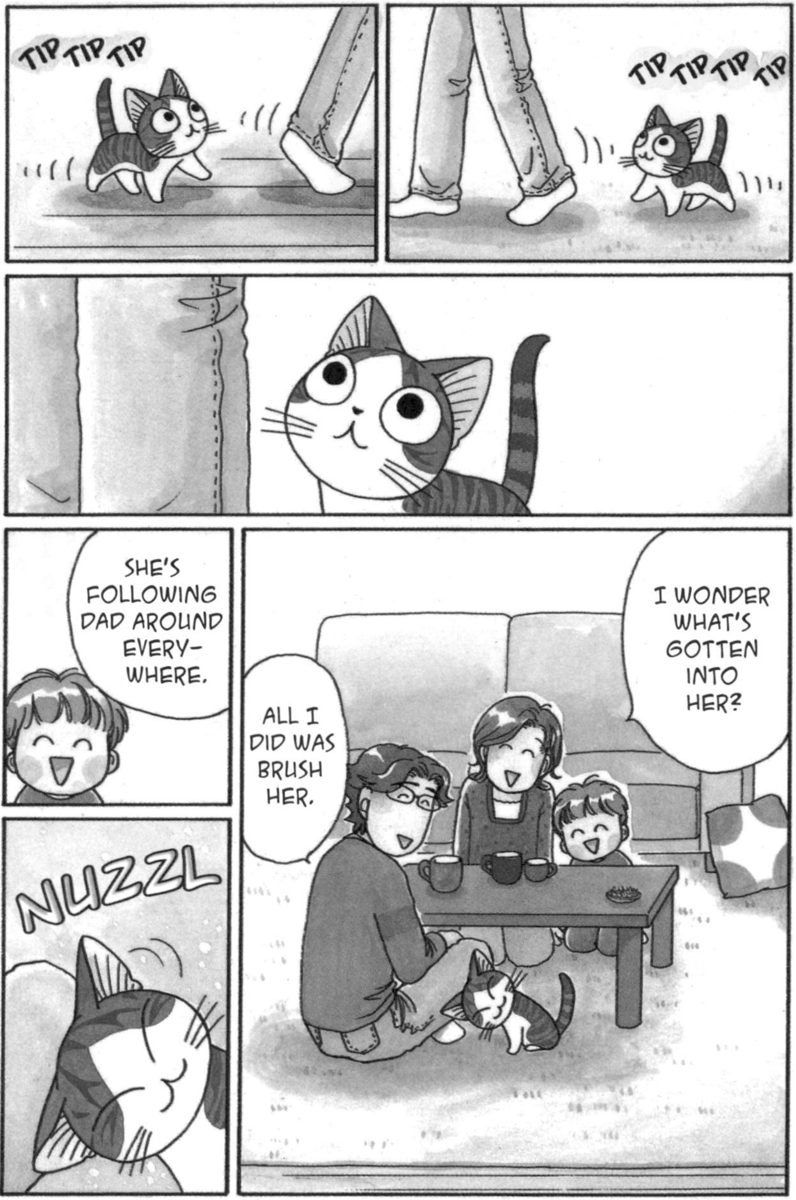
TIP TIP TIP
TIP TIP TIP TIP
SHE'S FOLLOWING DAD AROUND EVERY-WHERE.
NUZZL
I WONDER WHAT'S GOTTEN INTO HER?
ALL I DID WAS BRUSH HER.

the end

homemade 81: a cat goes out

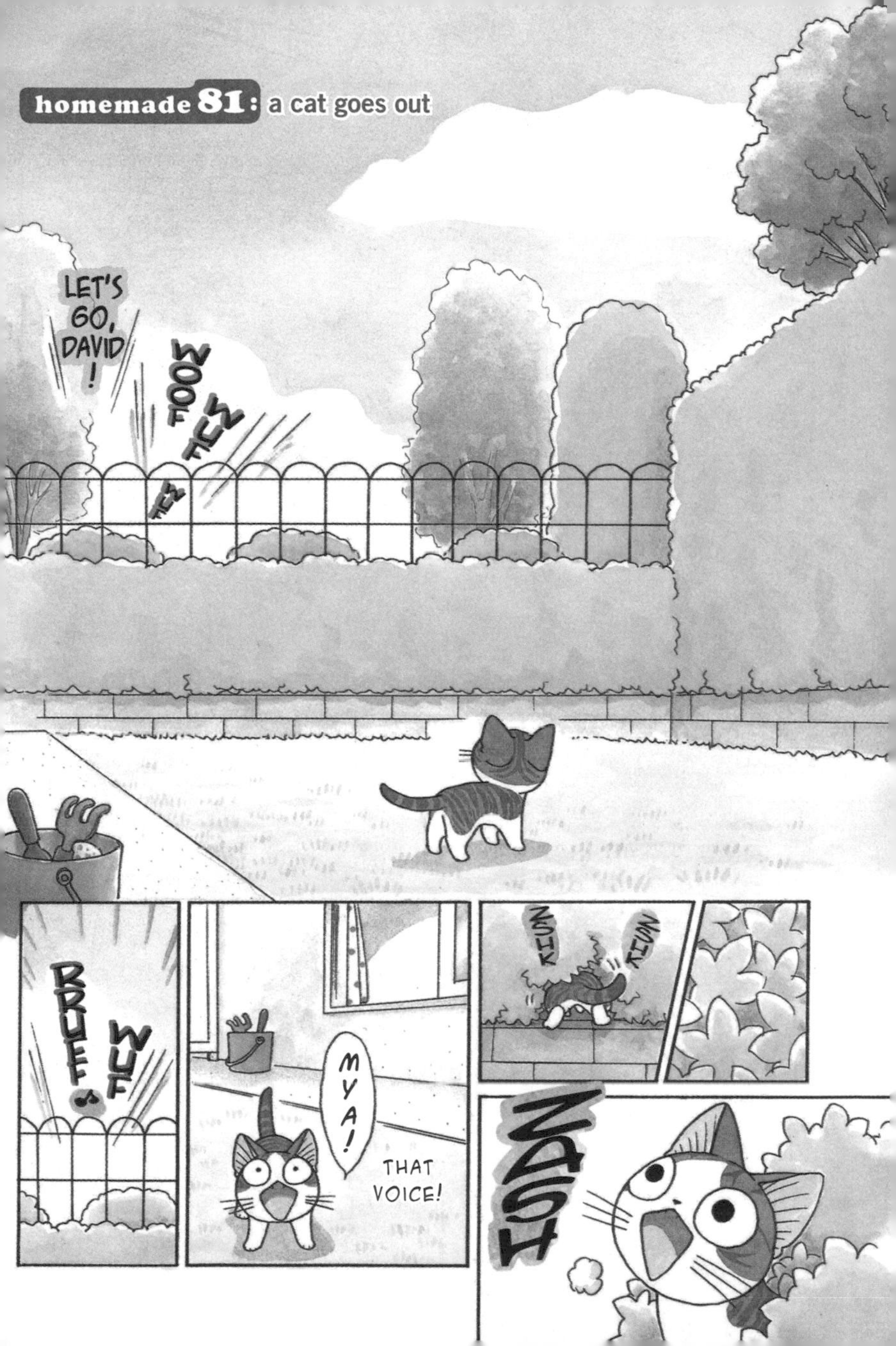
LET'S GO, DAVID!
WOOF
WUF
RRUF
WUF ♪
MYA!
THAT VOICE!
KIUN
KIUN
ZASH

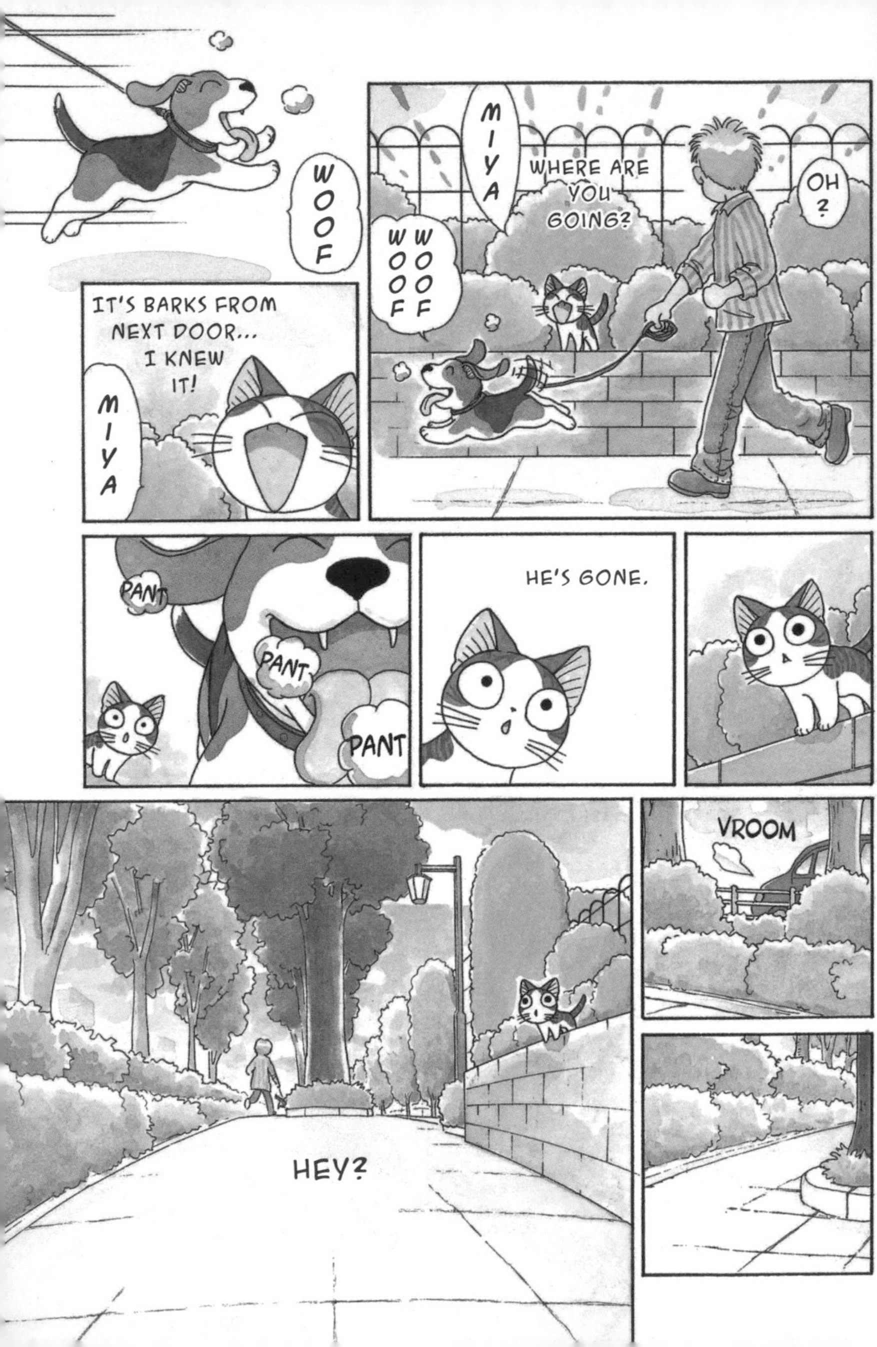
WOOF
IT'S BARKS FROM NEXT DOOR... I KNEW IT!
MIYA
MIYA
WOOF WOOF
WHERE ARE YOU GOING?
OH?
PANT
PANT
PANT
HE'S GONE.
HEY?
VROOM

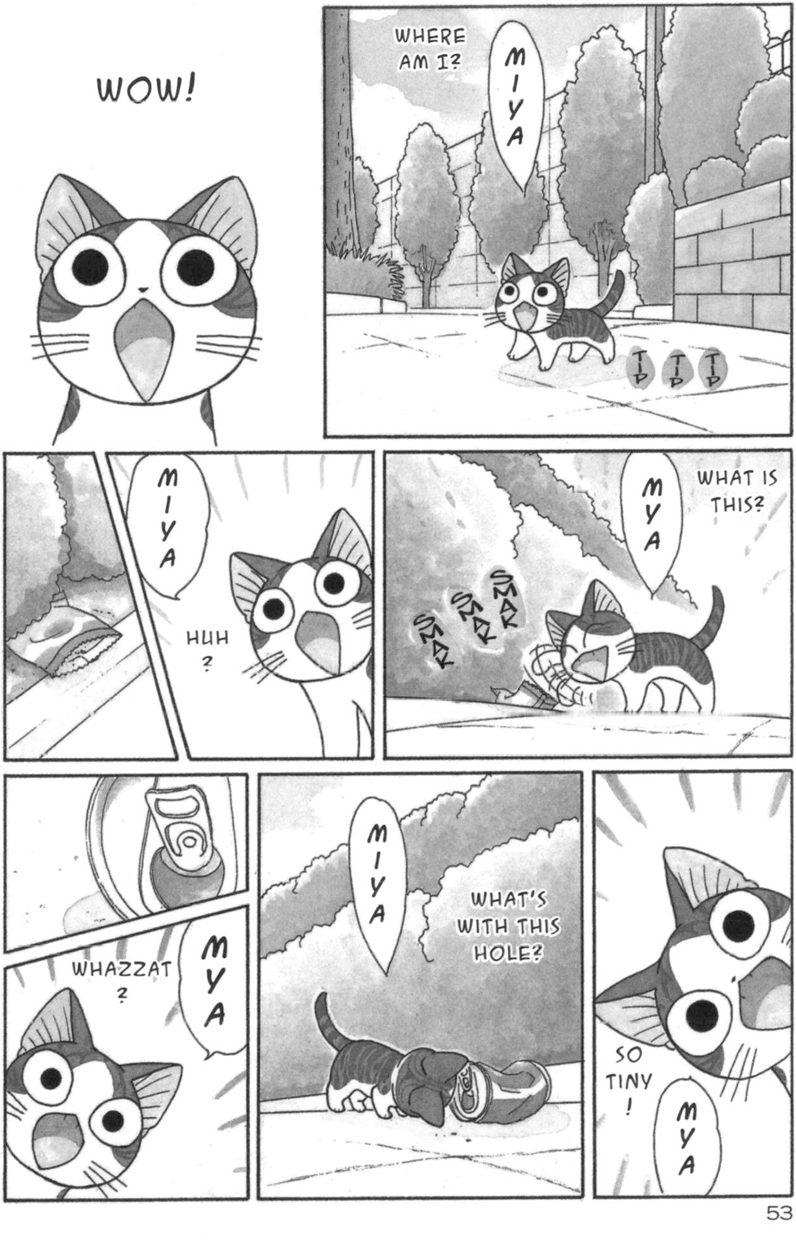
WOW!
WHERE AM I?
MIYA
TIP
TIP
TIP
MIYA
HUH?
MYA
WHAT IS THIS?
SMAK
SMAK
SMAK
WHAZZAT?
MYA
MIYA
WHAT'S WITH THIS HOLE?
SO TINY!
MYA

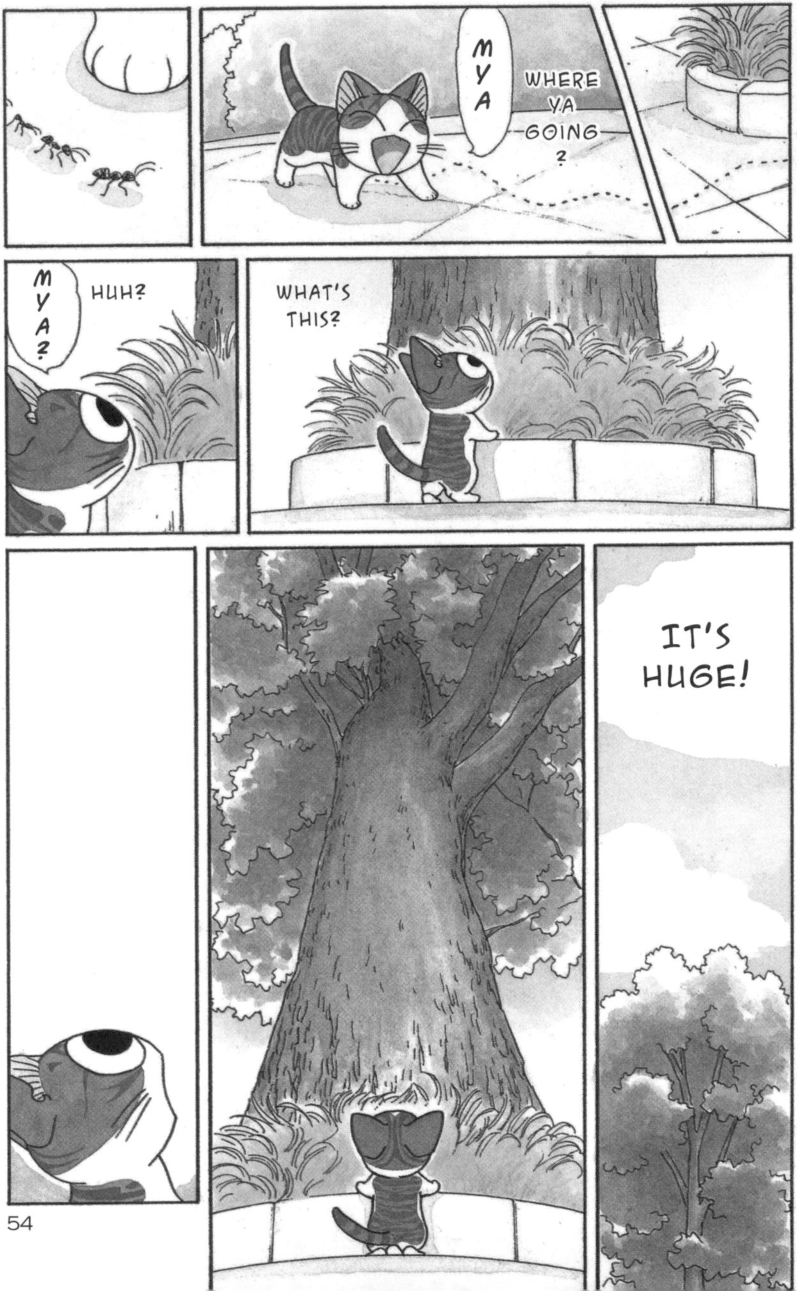
MYA
WHERE YA GOING?
MYA?
HUH?
WHAT'S THIS?
IT'S HUGE!

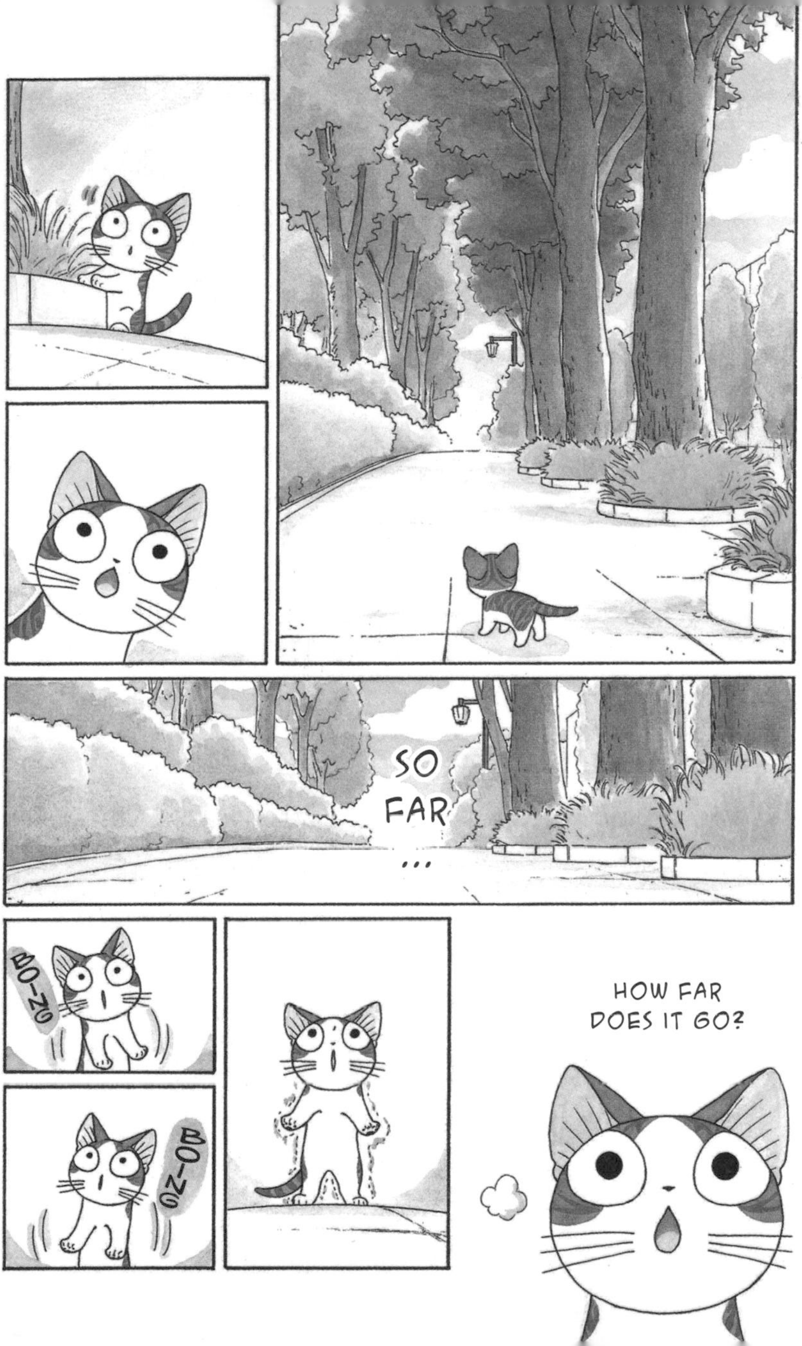
SO FAR ...
BO-ING
BO-ING
HOW FAR DOES IT GO?

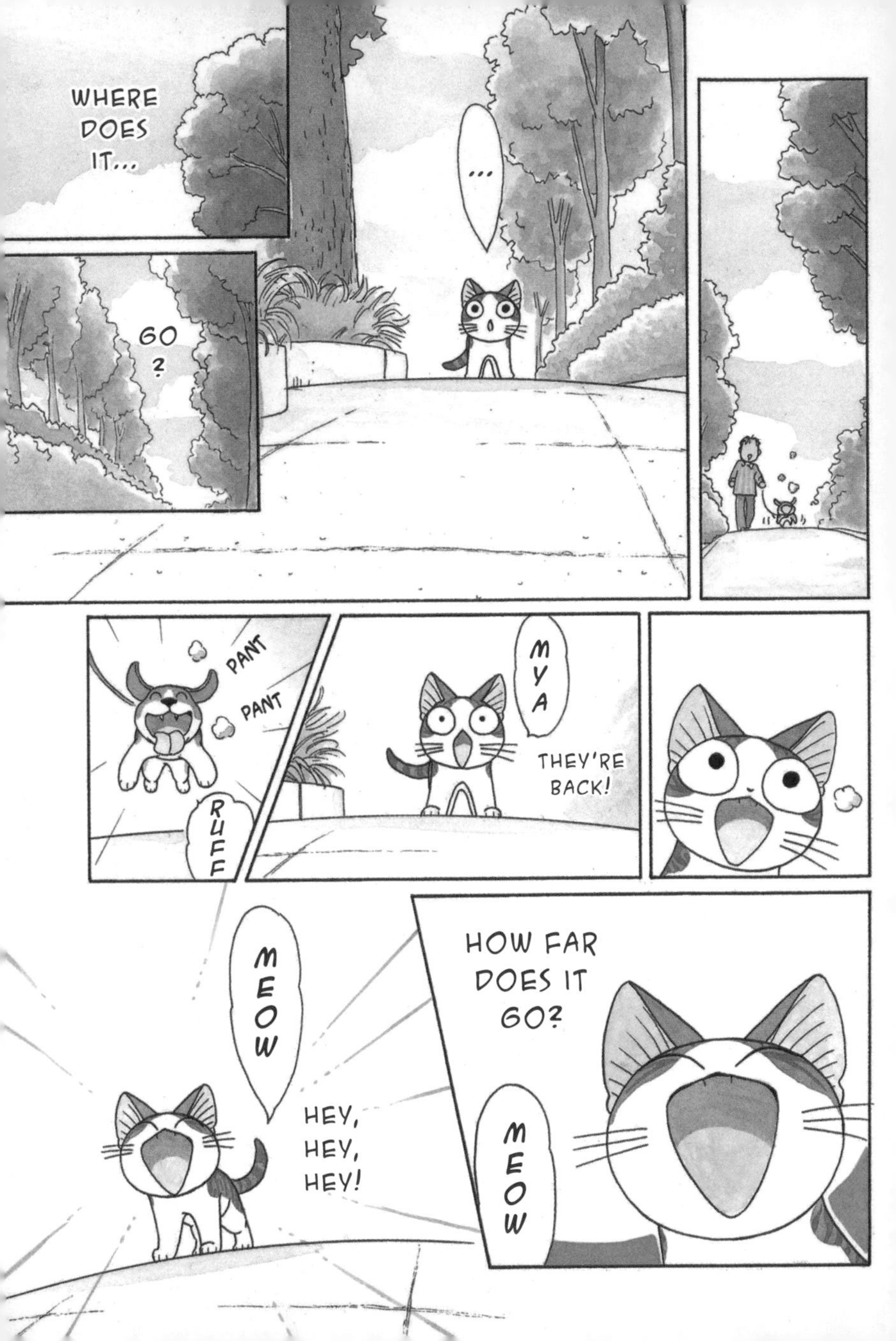
WHERE DOES IT...
GO?
...
PANT
PANT
RUFF
MYA
THEY'RE BACK!
MEOW
HEY, HEY, HEY!
HOW FAR DOES IT GO?
MEOW

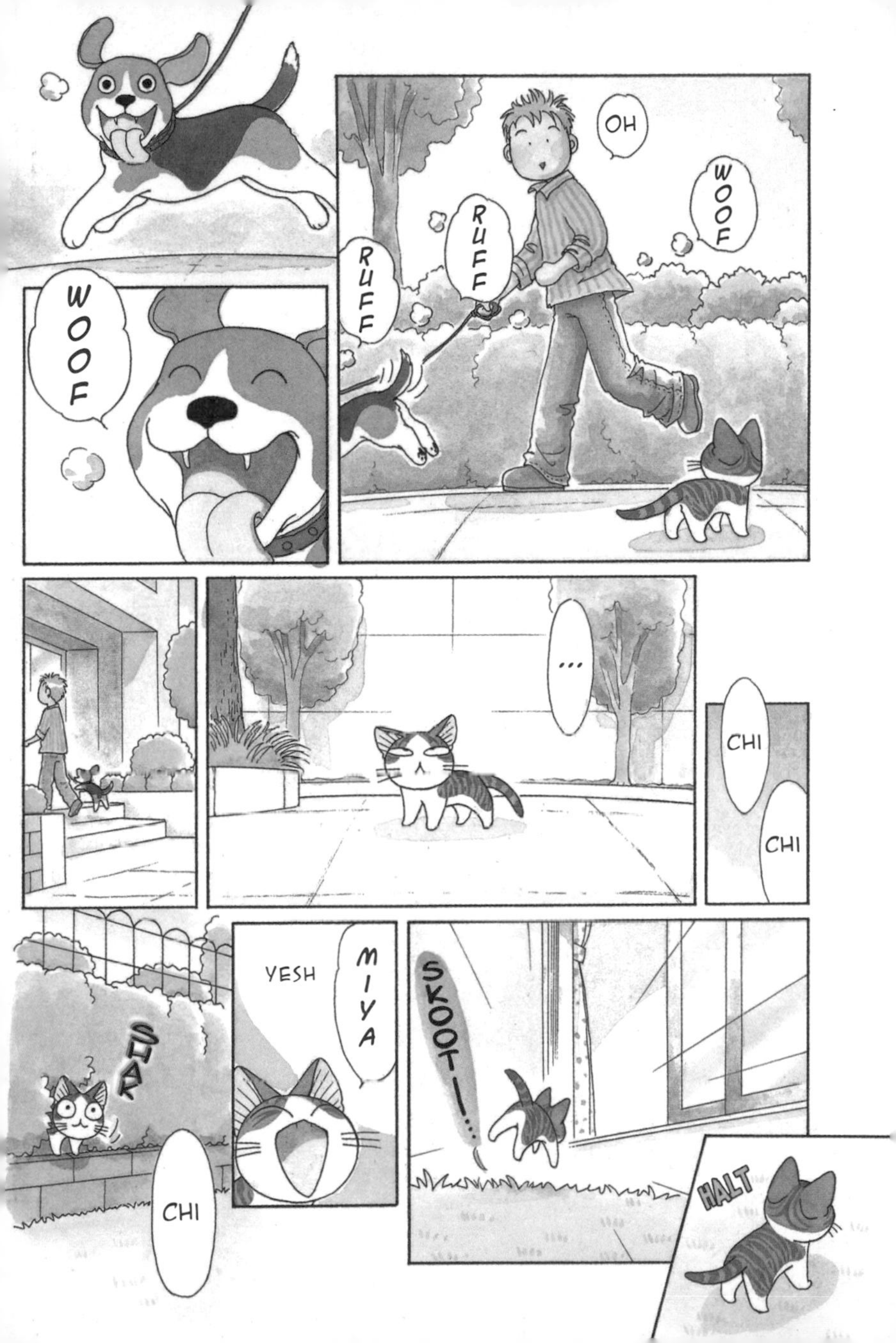
WOOF
OH
RUFF
RUFF
WOOF
...
CHI
CHI
SHAK
CHI
YESH
MIYA
SKOOT!...
HALT

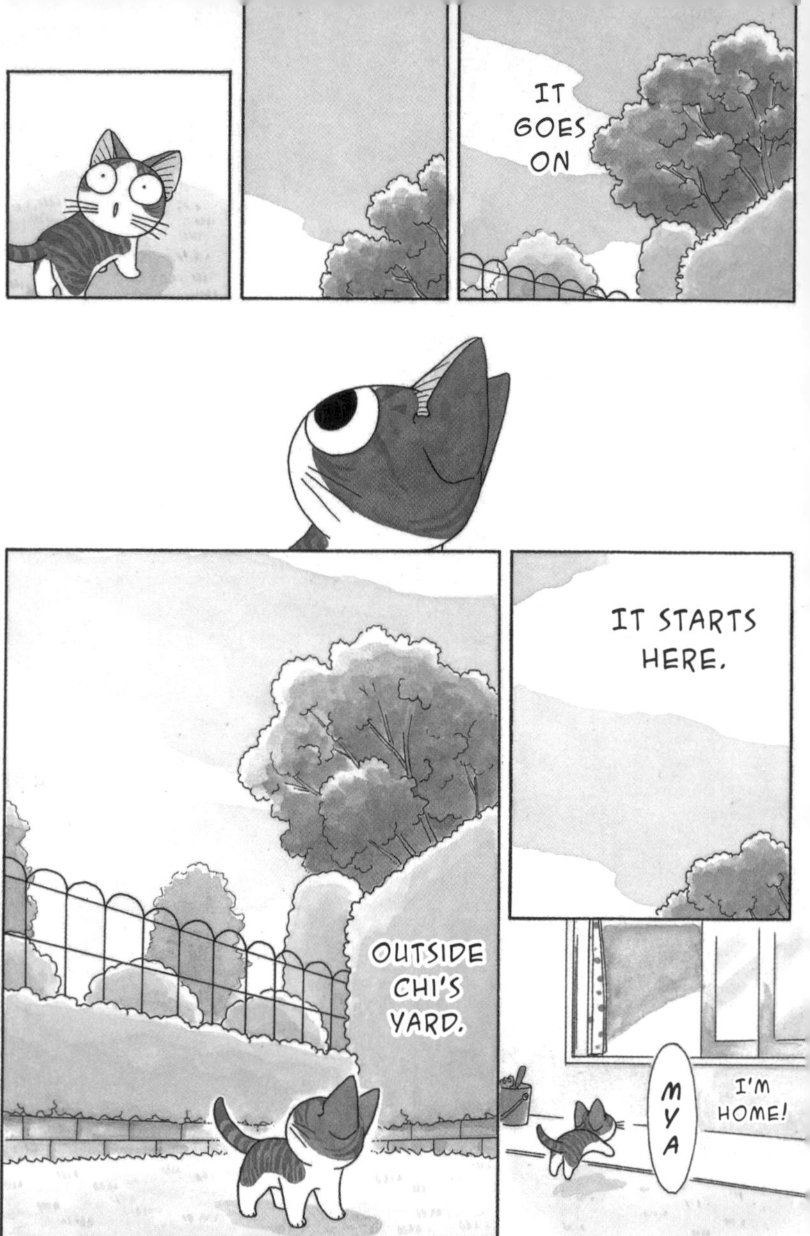
IT GOES ON
OUTSIDE CHI'S YARD.
IT STARTS HERE.
MYA
I'M HOME!

the end

homemade 82: a cat is thrilled

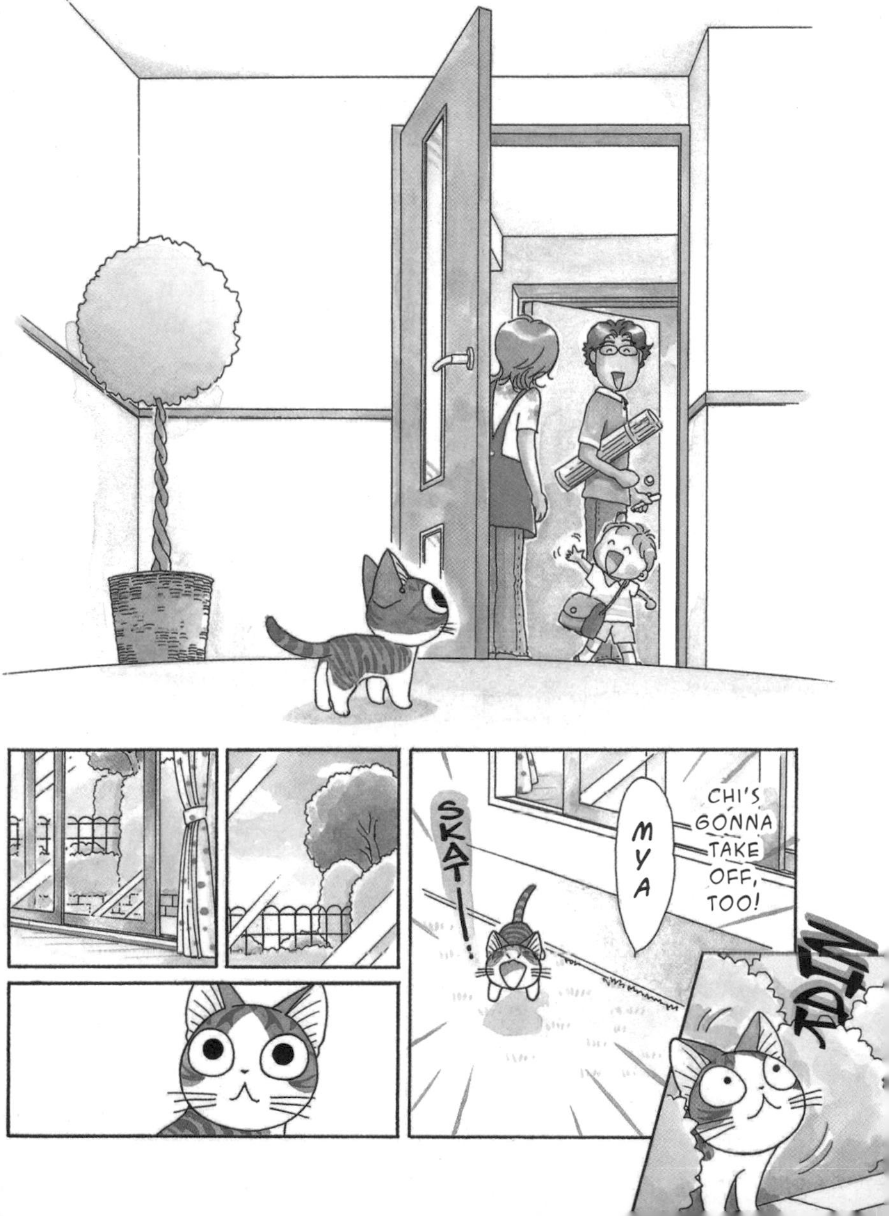

SKAT!
MYA
CHI'S GONNA TAKE OFF, TOO!

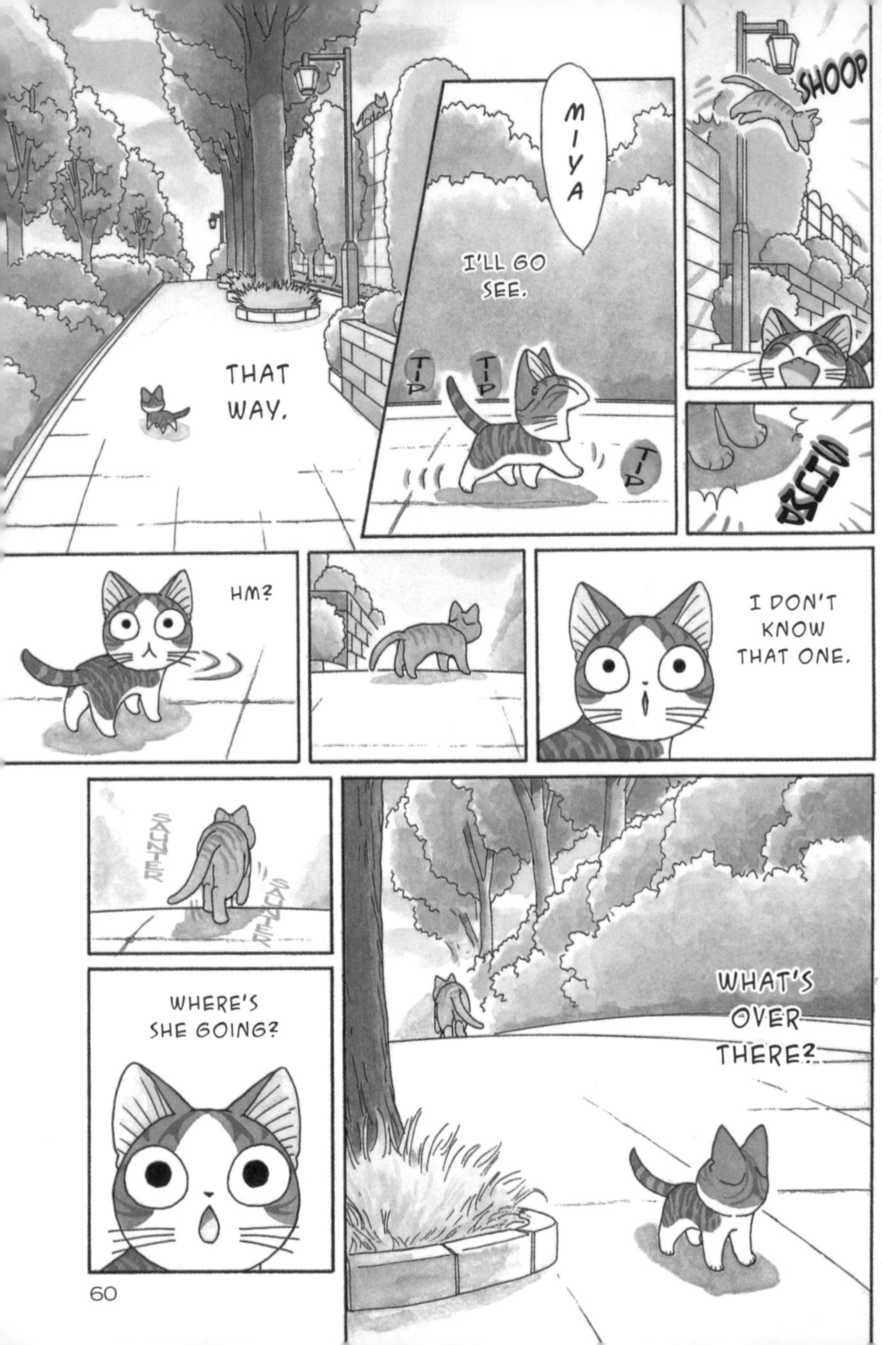
THAT WAY.
MIYA
I'LL GO SEE.
TIP
TIP
TIP
SHOOP
HM?
I DON'T KNOW THAT ONE.
SAUNTER
SAUNTER
WHERE'S SHE GOING?
WHAT'S OVER THERE?

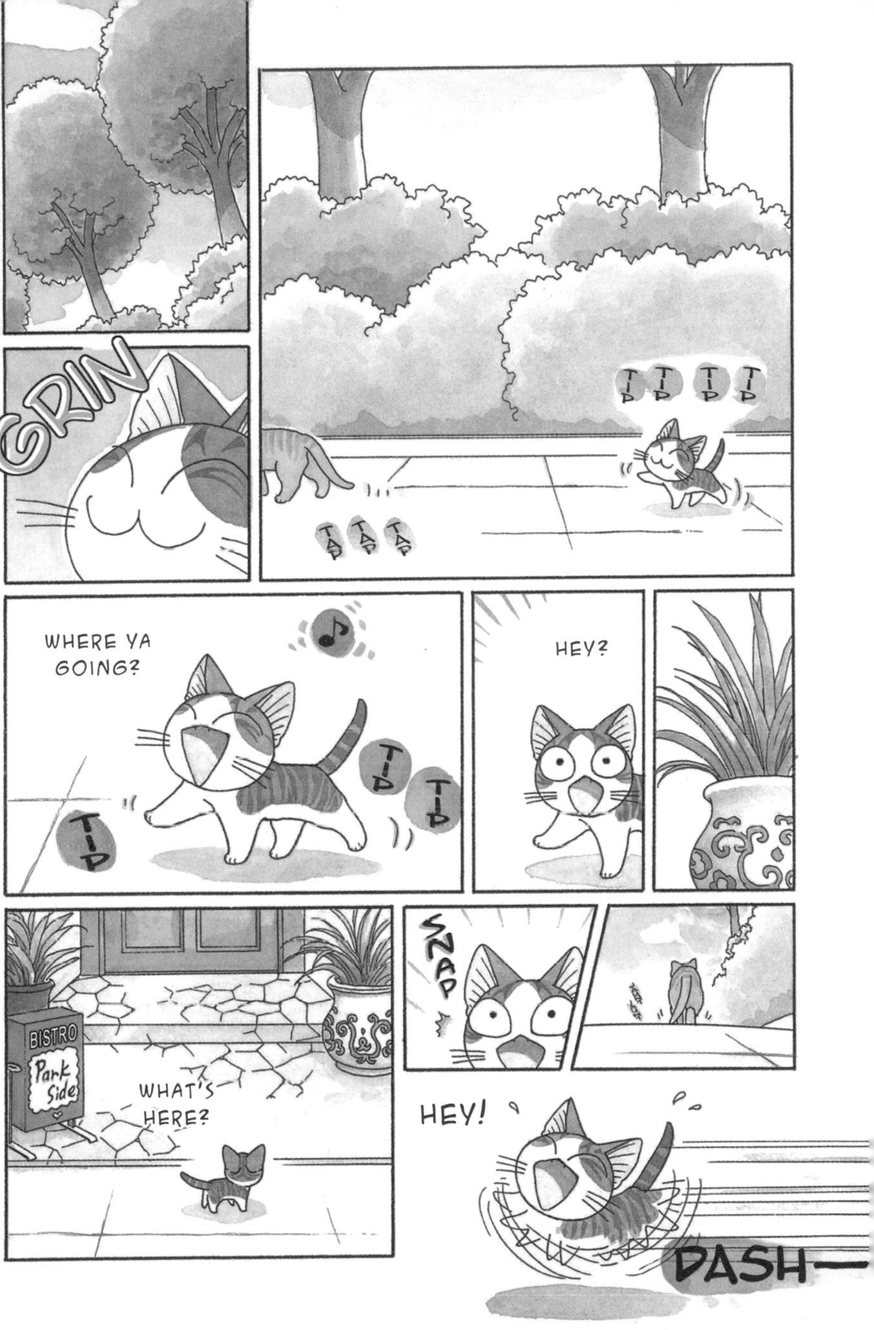
GRIN
TAP TAP TAP
TIP TIP TIP TIP
WHERE YA GOING?
TIP
TIP
TIP
HEY?
WHAT'S HERE?
SNAP
HEY!
DASH—

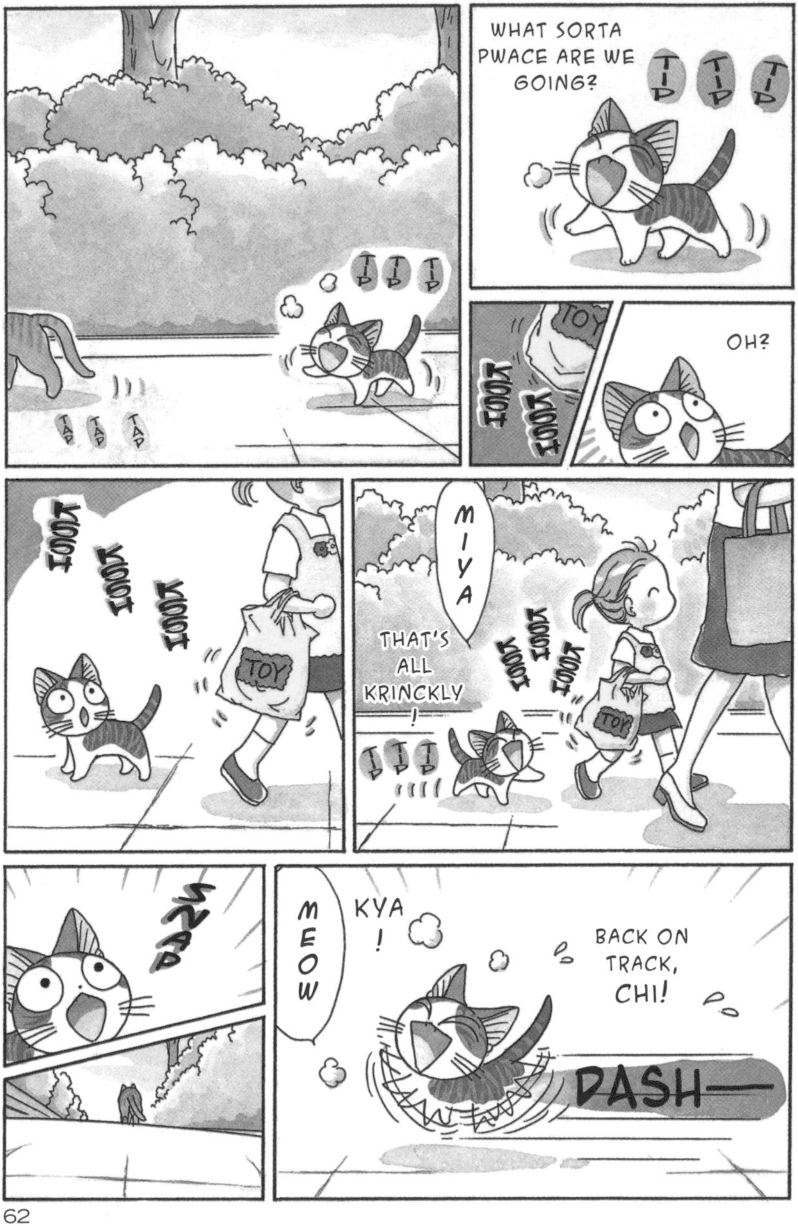
TIP TIP TIP
TAP TAP TAP
WHAT SORTA PWACE ARE WE GOING?
TIP TIP TIP
KOSH KOSH
TOY
OH?
KOSH KOSH KOSH
TOY
MIYA
THAT'S ALL KRINCKLY!
KOSH KOSH KOSH
TOY
TIP TIP TIP
SNAP
MEOW
KYA!
BACK ON TRACK, CHI!
DASH—

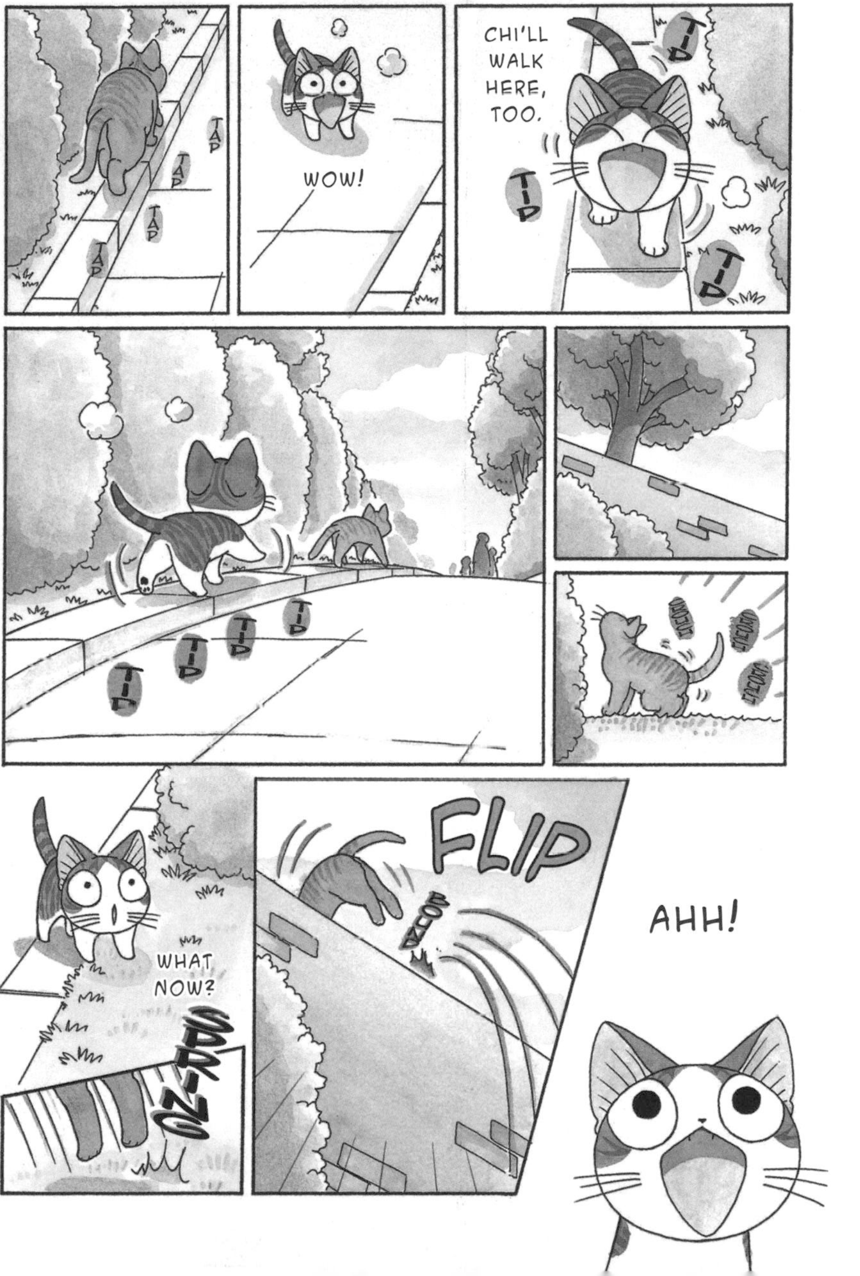
TAP
TAP
TAP
TAP
WOW!
CHI'LL WALK HERE, TOO.
TID
TID
TID
TID
TID
TID
TID
WHAT NOW?
SPRI-NG
FLIP
BOUND
AHH!

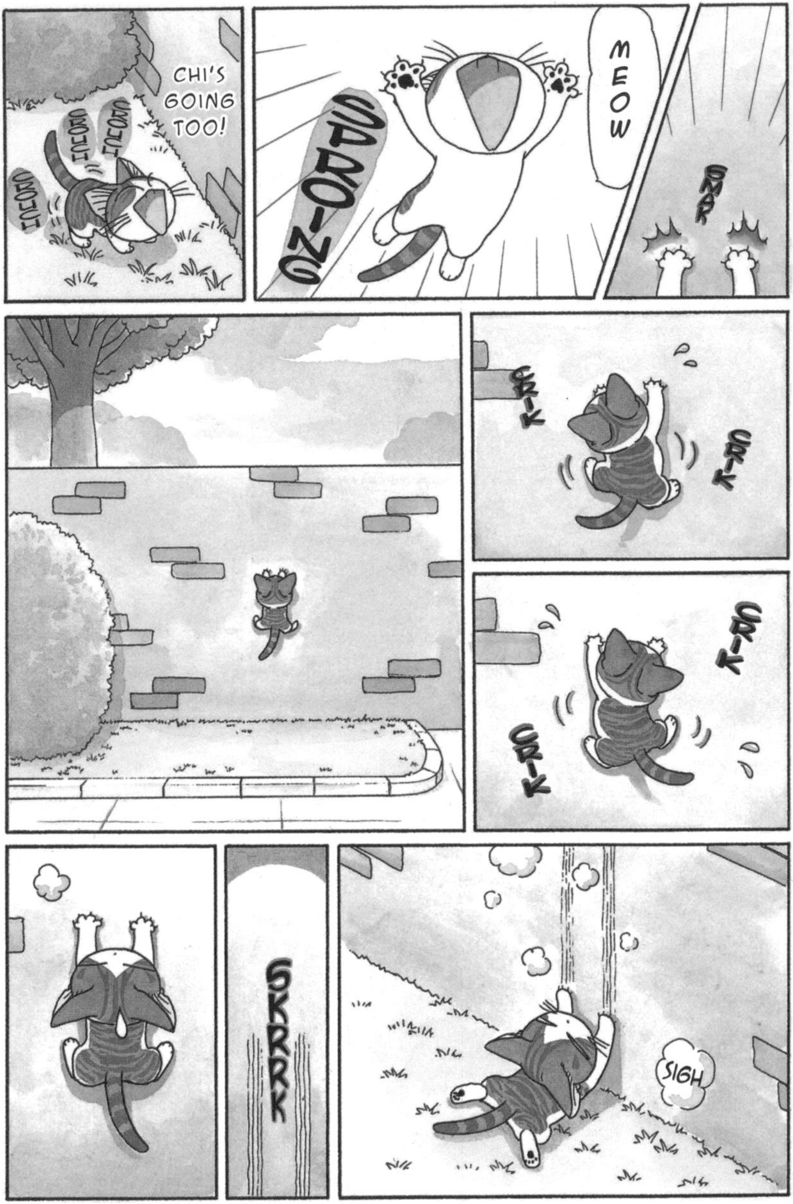
CHI'S GOING TOO!
UROJUI
UROJUI
UROJUI
SPROING
MEOW
SMAK
CRIK
CRIK
CRIK
CRIK
SKRRRK
SIGH

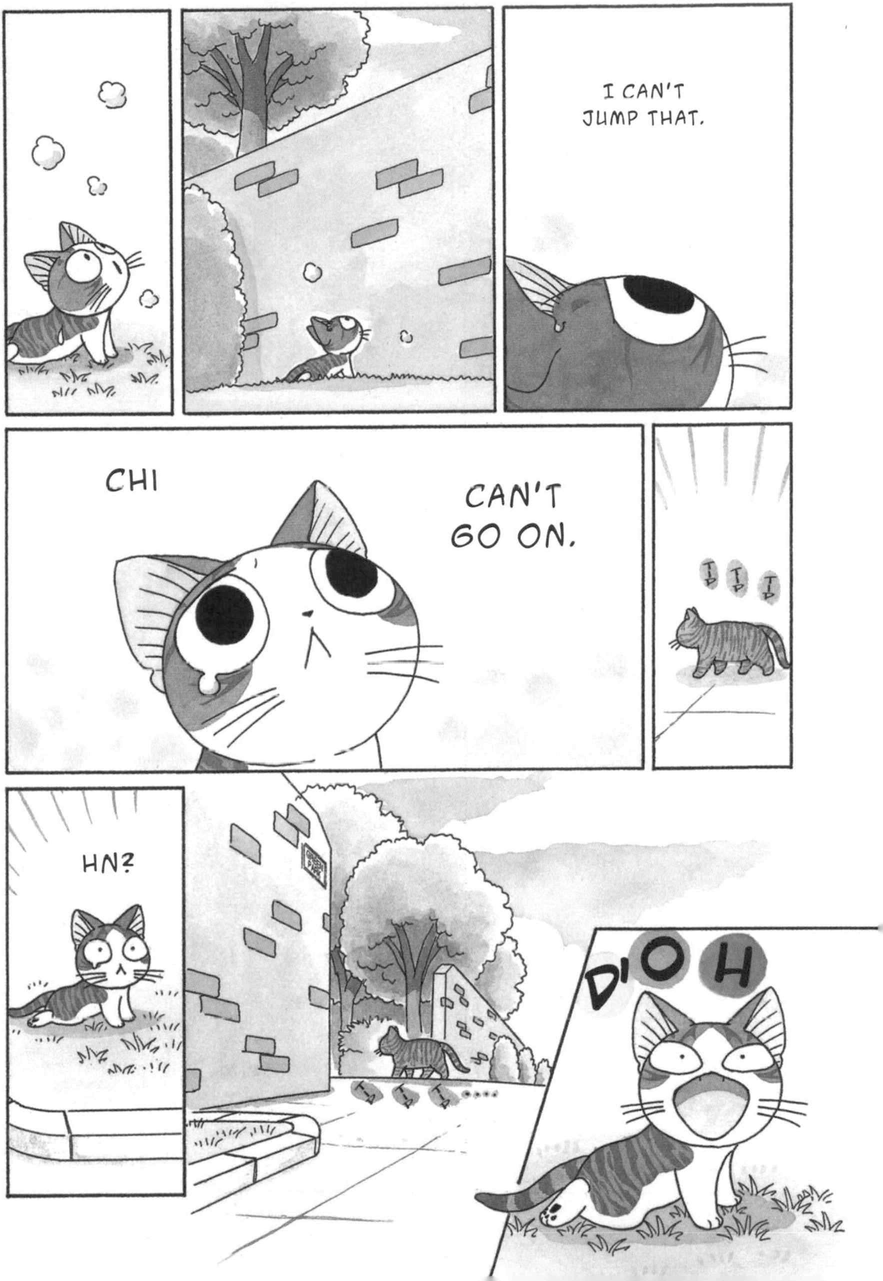
I CAN'T JUMP THAT.
CHI
CAN'T GO ON.
TIP TIP TIP
HN?
TIP TIP TIP
OH

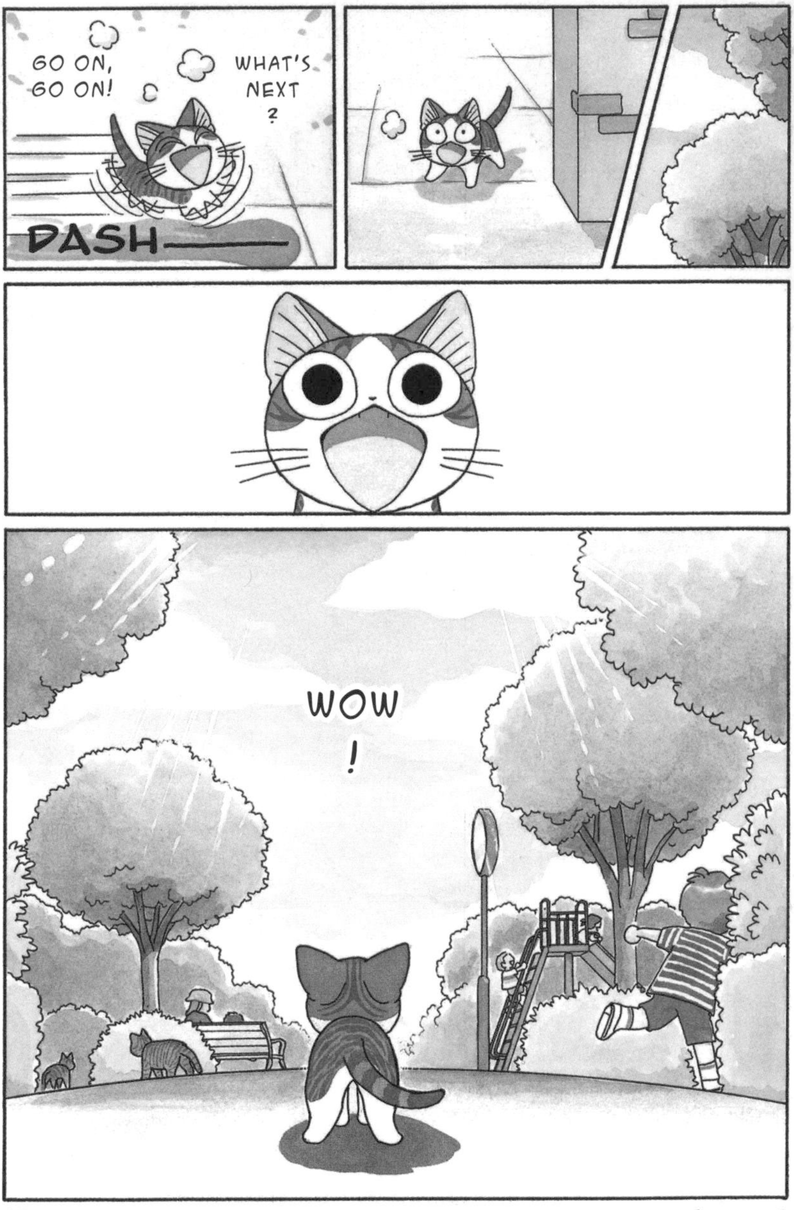
GO ON, GO ON!
WHAT'S NEXT ?
DASH
WOW !

the end

homemade 83: a cat explores

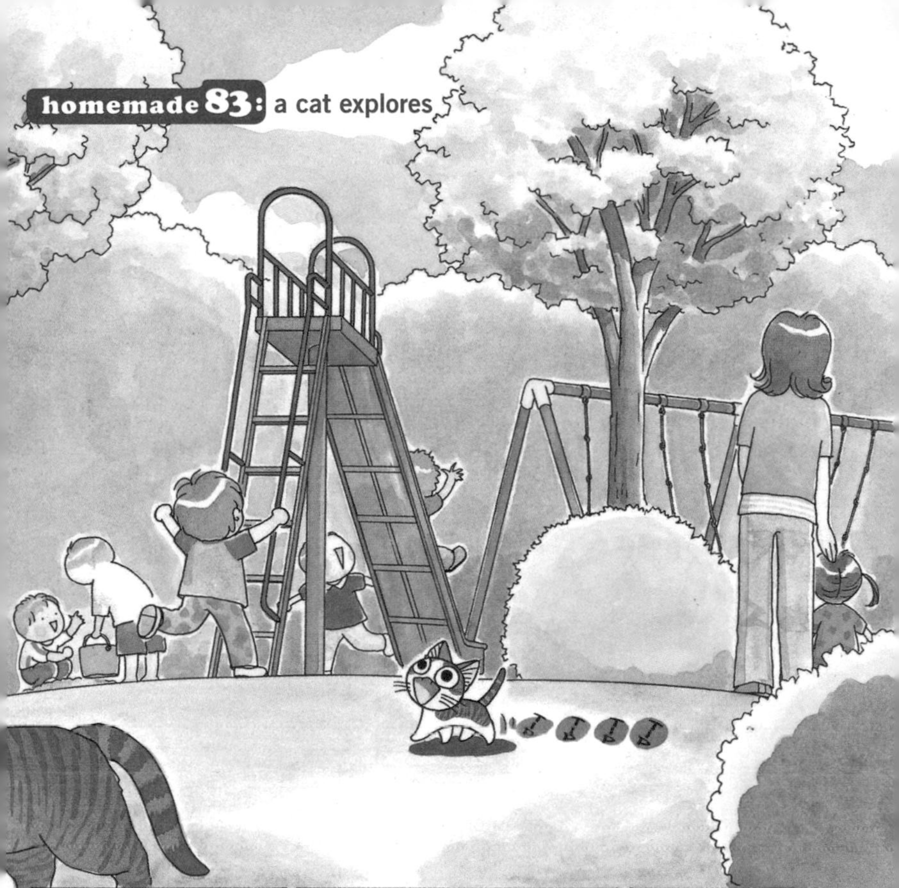

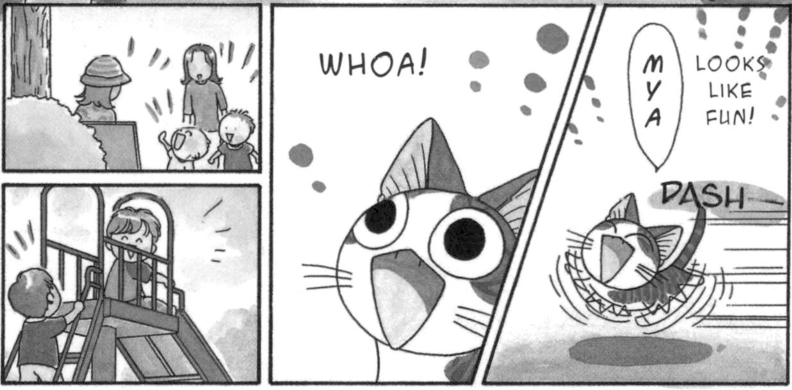
WHOA!
MYA
LOOKS LIKE FUN!
DASH

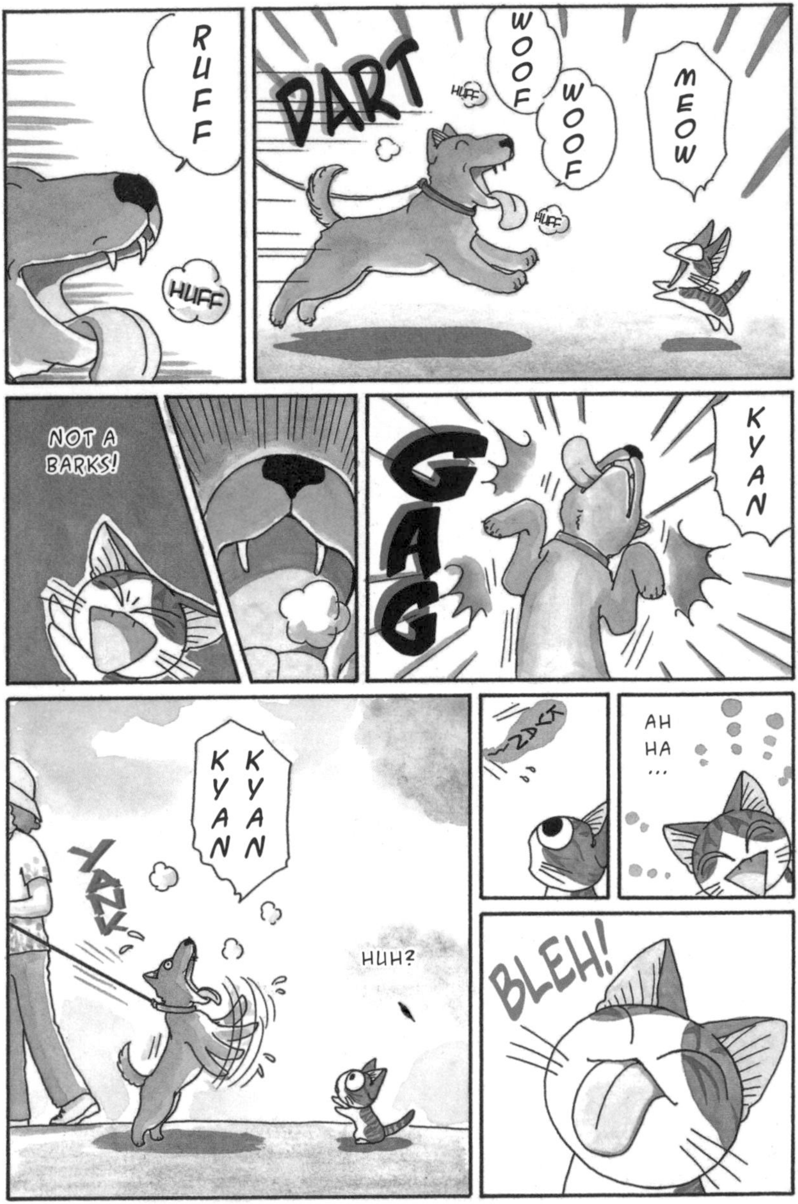
RUFF
HUFF
DART
HUFF
WOOF
WOOF
HUFF
MEOW
NOT A BARKS!
GAG
KYAN
KYAN KYAN
YANK
HUH?
AH HA ...
BLEH!

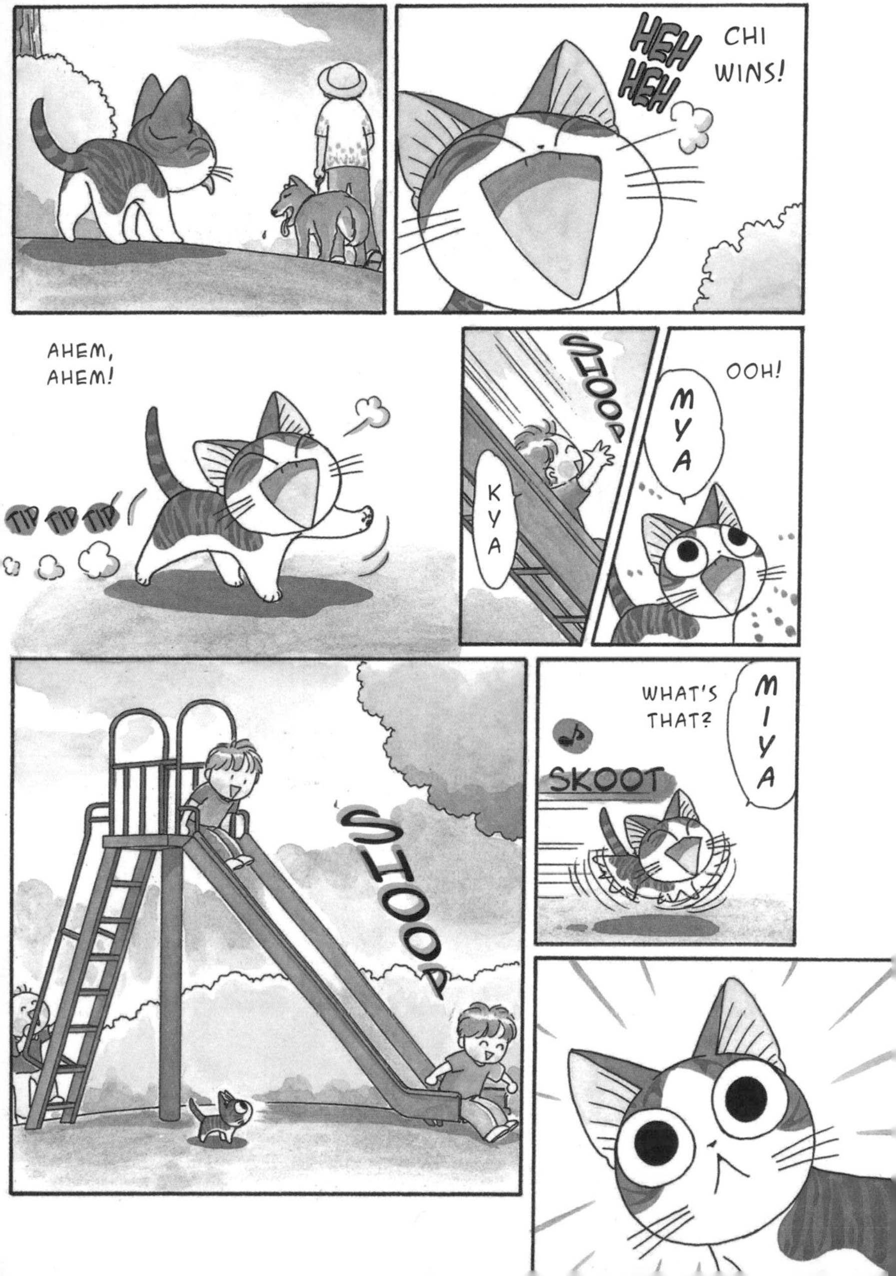
HEH HEH
CHI WINS!
AHEM, AHEM!
TIP TIP TIP
SHOOP
KYA
OOH!
MYA
SHOOP
WHAT'S THAT?
MIYA
SKOOT

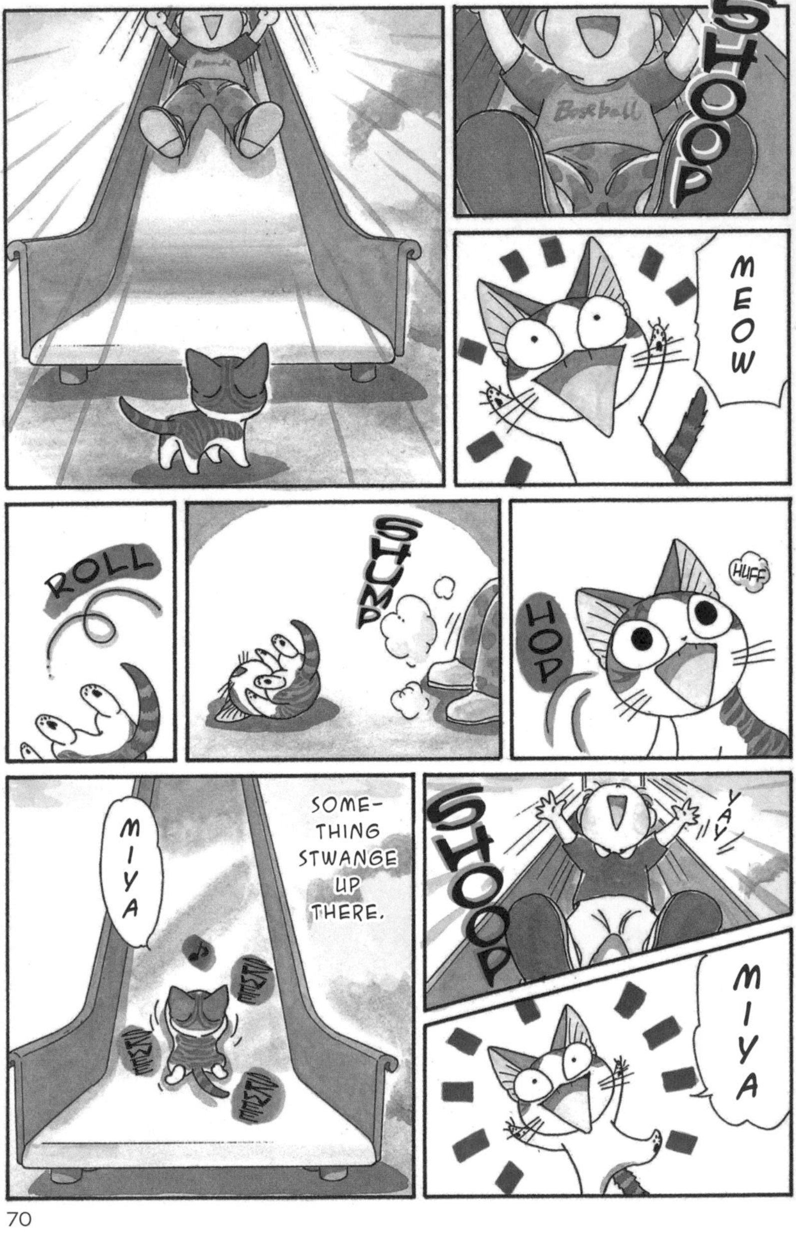
Baseball
SHOOP
MEOW
ROLL
SHUMP
HOP
HUFF
MIYA
SOME-THING STWANGE UP THERE.
SHOOP
YAY
MIYA

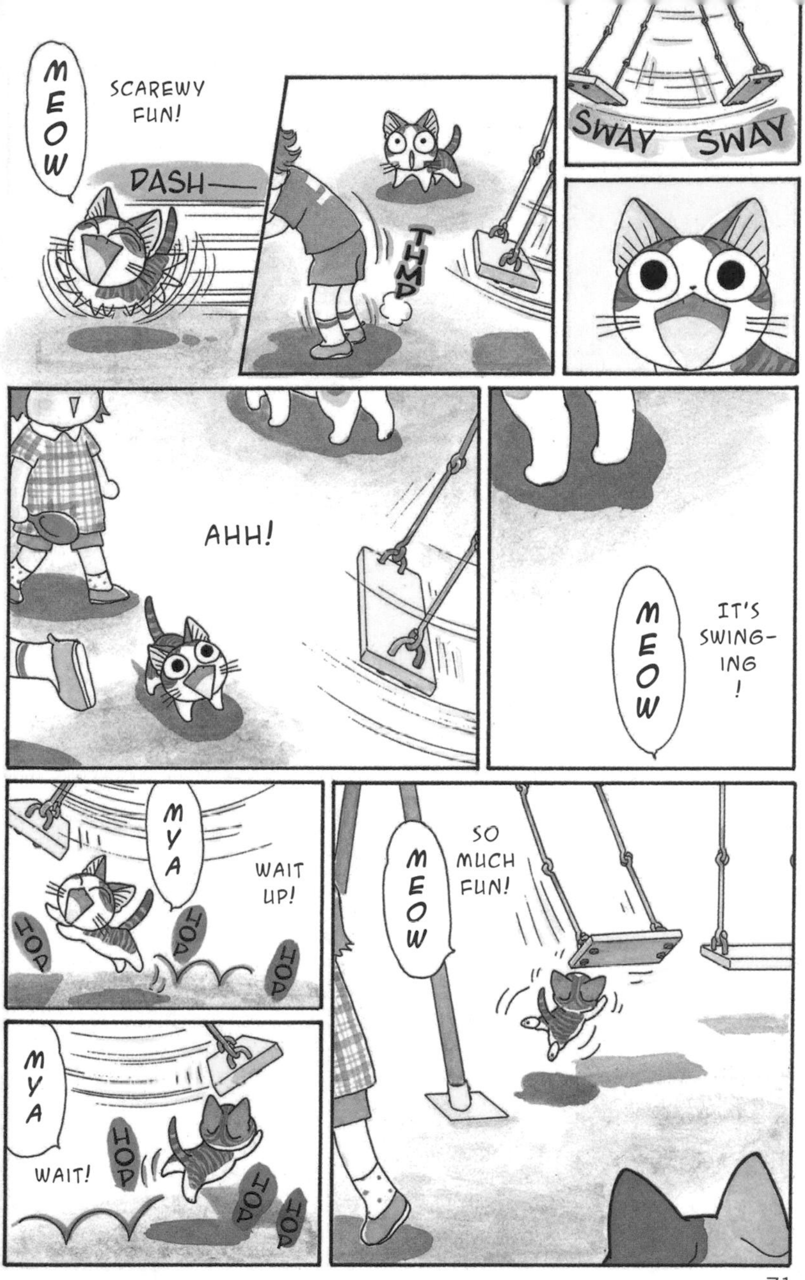
MEOW
SCAREWY FUN!
DASH—
THMP
SWAY SWAY
AHH!
MEOW
IT'S SWING-ING!
MYA
WAIT UP!
HOP HOP HOP
MYA
WAIT!
HOP HOP HOP
MEOW
SO MUCH FUN!

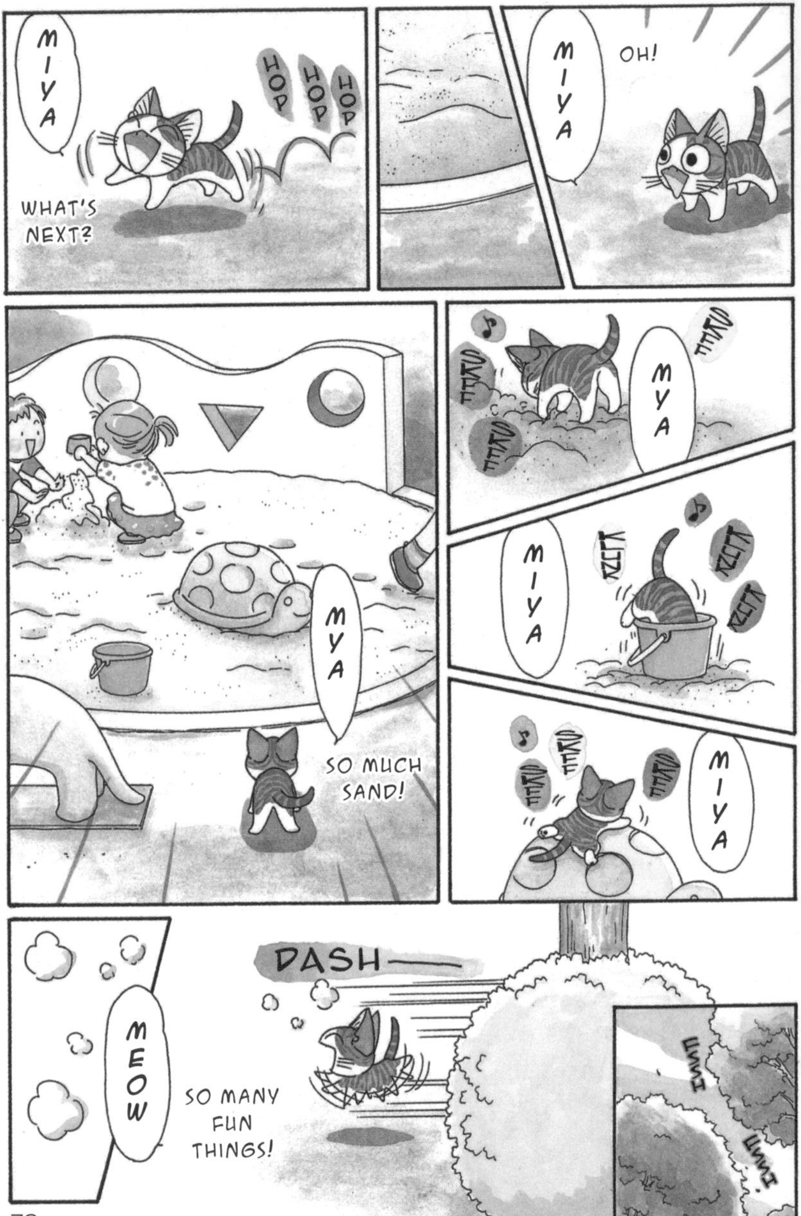
MIYA
HOP HOP HOP
WHAT'S NEXT?
MIYA
OH!
MYA
SO MUCH SAND!
SKREE
SKREE
MYA
SKREE
MIYA
SKREE
SKREE
SKREE
MIYA
MEOW
DASH
SO MANY FUN THINGS!

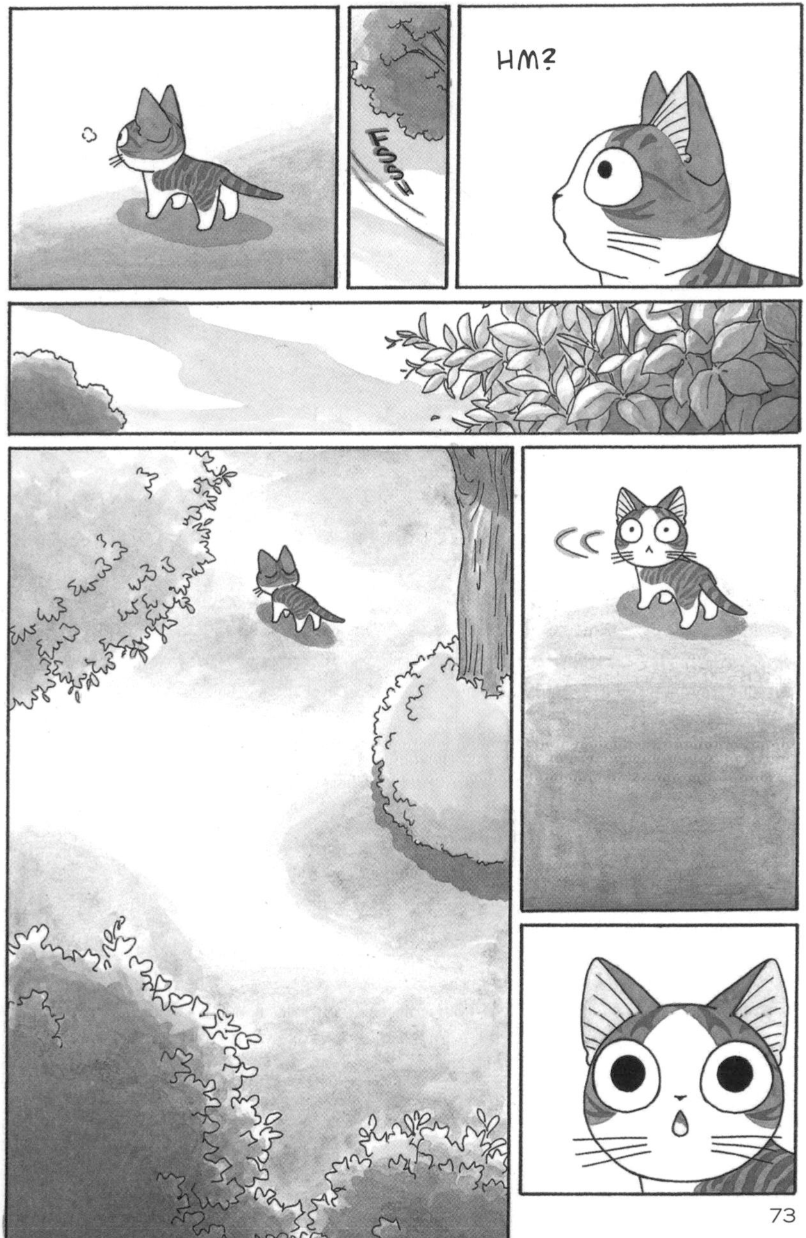
HM?

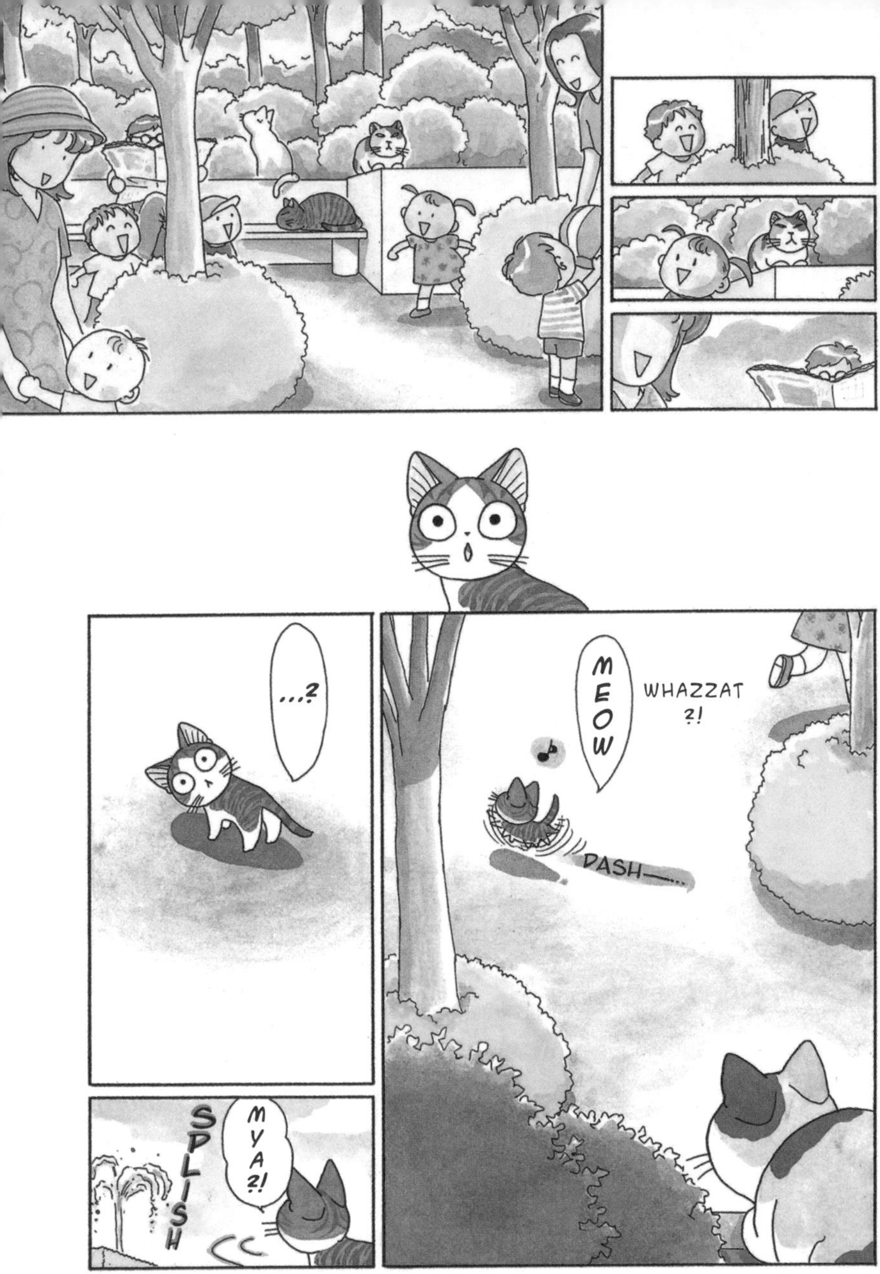
...?
MEOW
WHAZZAT ?!
DASH—...
MYA ?!
SPLISH
the end

homemade 84: a cat returns

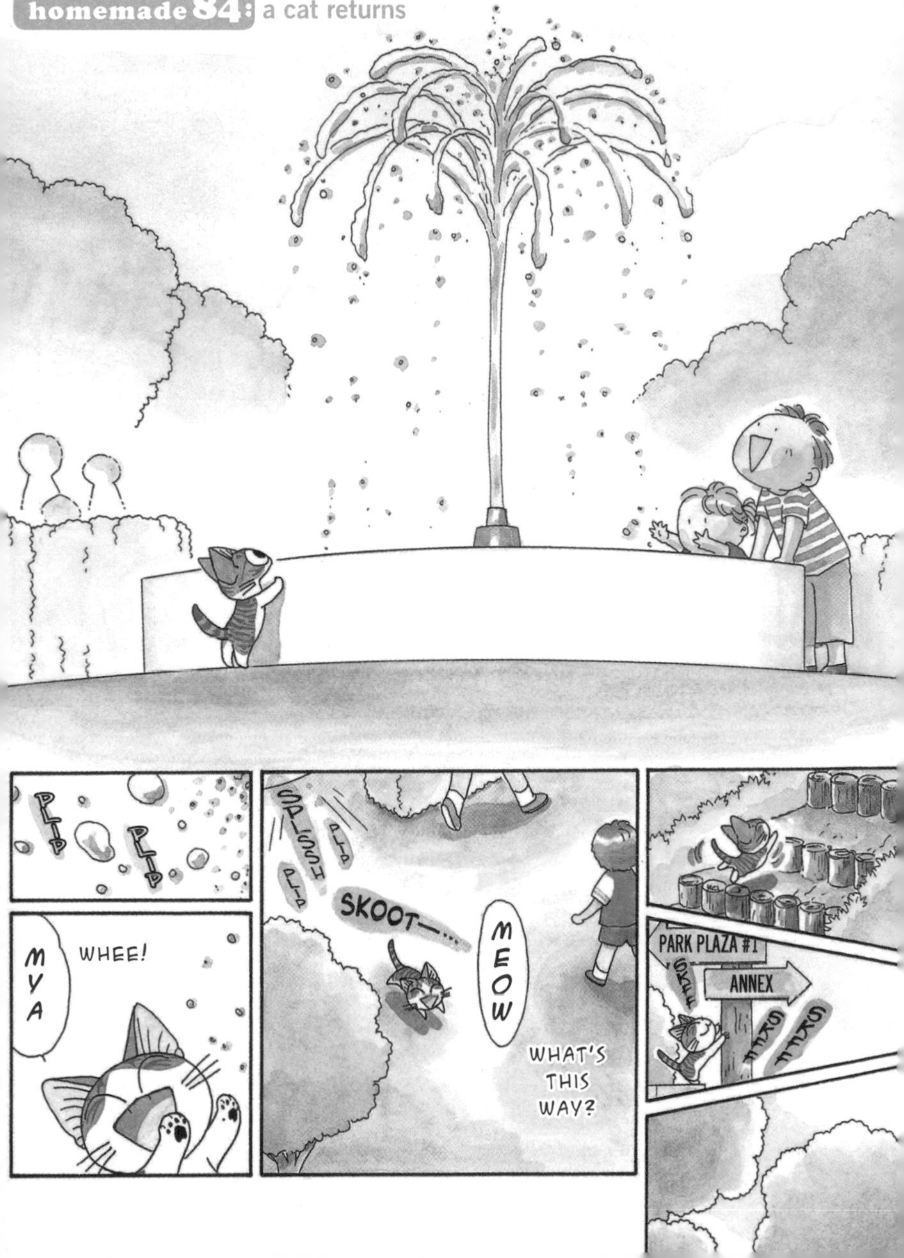
PLIP
PLIP
MYA
WHEE!
SPLISSH
PLIP
PLIP
SKOOT—...
MEOW
WHAT'S THIS WAY?
PARK PLAZA #1
ANNEX

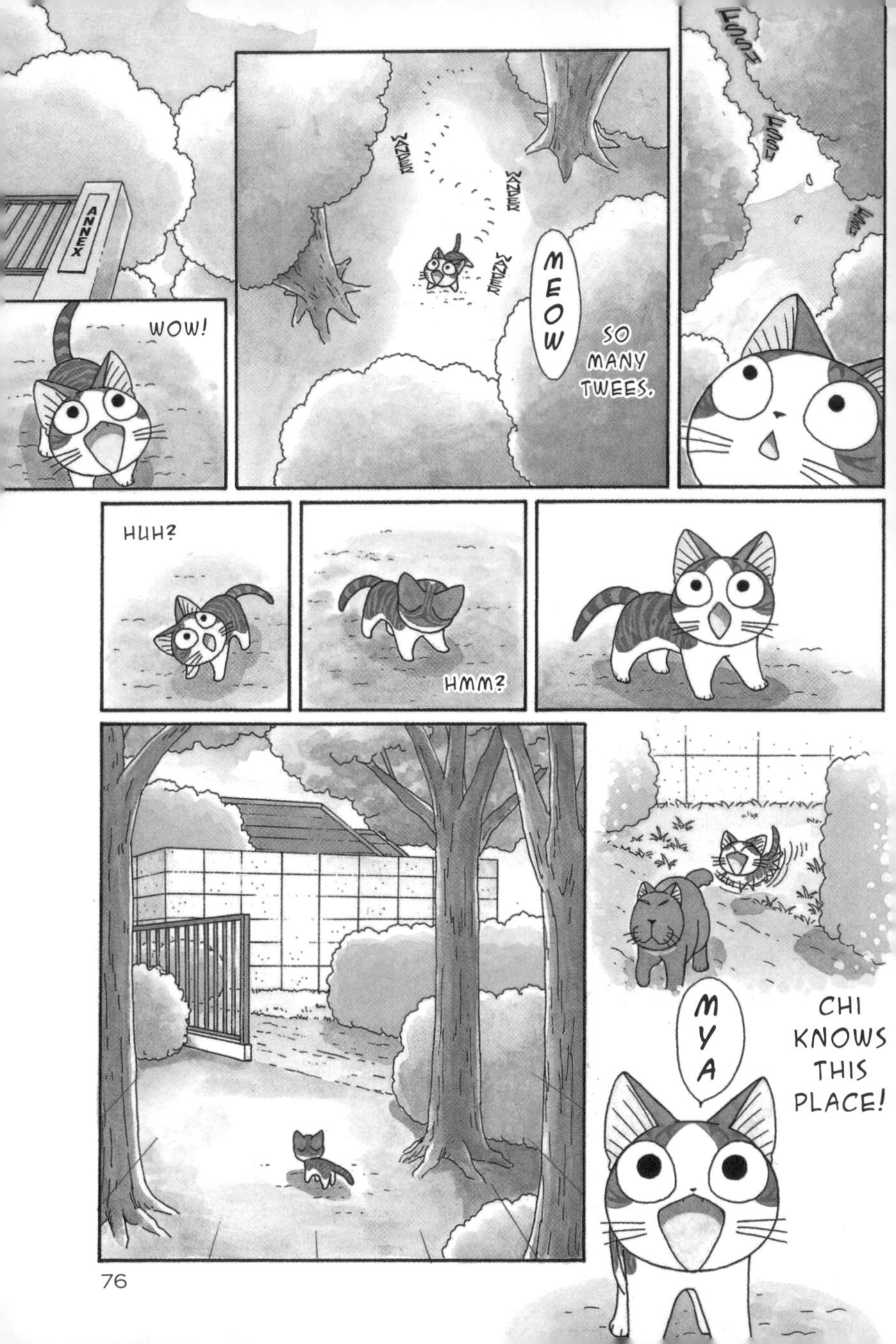
ANNEX
WOW!
WANDER
WANDER
WANDER
MEOW
SO MANY TWEES.
FOOSH
FOOSH
FOOSH
HUH?
HMM?
MYA
CHI KNOWS THIS PLACE!

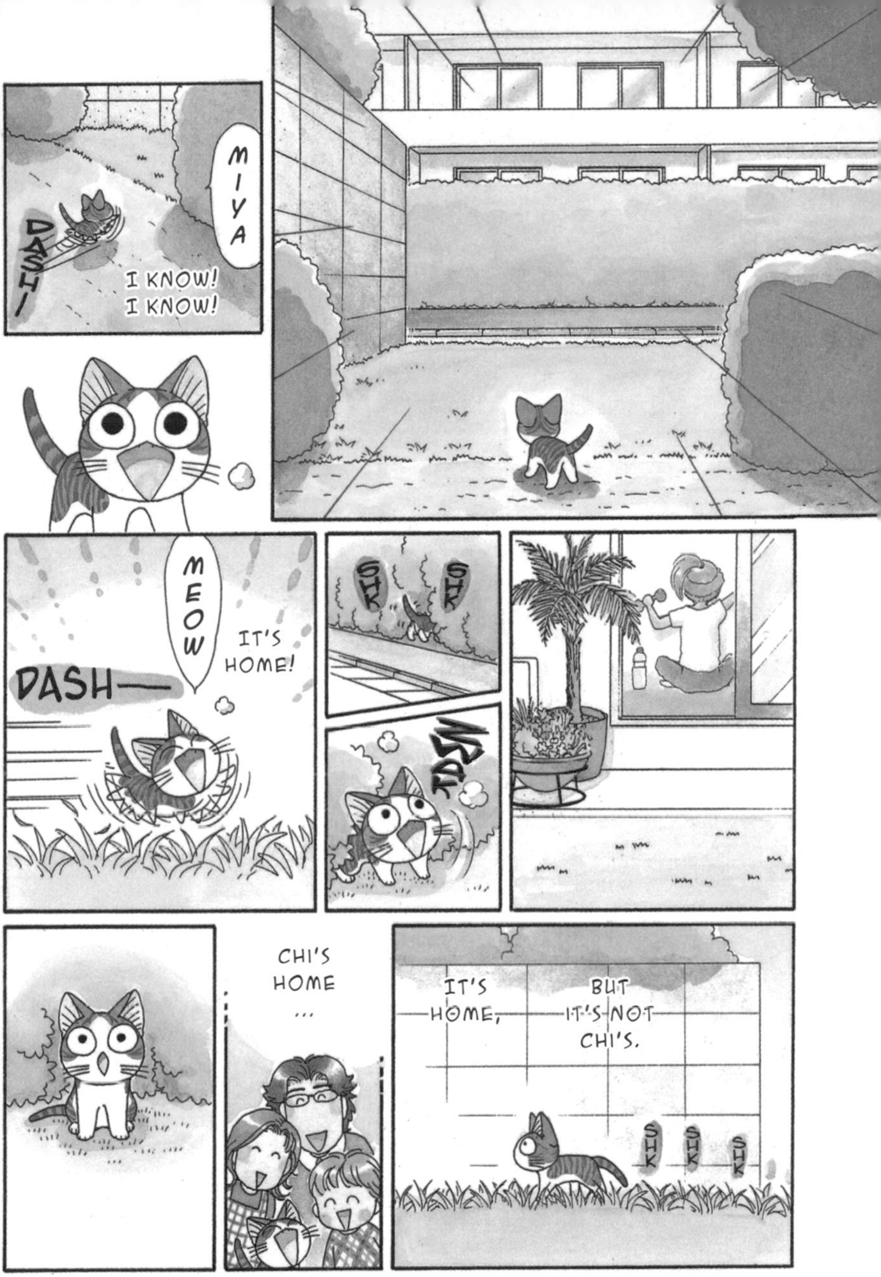

MIYA
DASHI
I KNOW! I KNOW!
MEOW
IT'S HOME!
DASH—
SHK SHK
TDSW
CHI'S HOME ...
IT'S HOME,
BUT IT'S NOT CHI'S.
SHK SHK SHK

WHERE HAVE I SEEN HER BEFORE...

NYA

NYA

SAY, YOU...

HMM?

NIYA

WHERE ARE YOU FROM, LITTLE ONE?

I'M NOT LITTLE ONE!

MYAH

I'M CHI.

I'M CHI...

MEOW

OF CHI'S HOME!

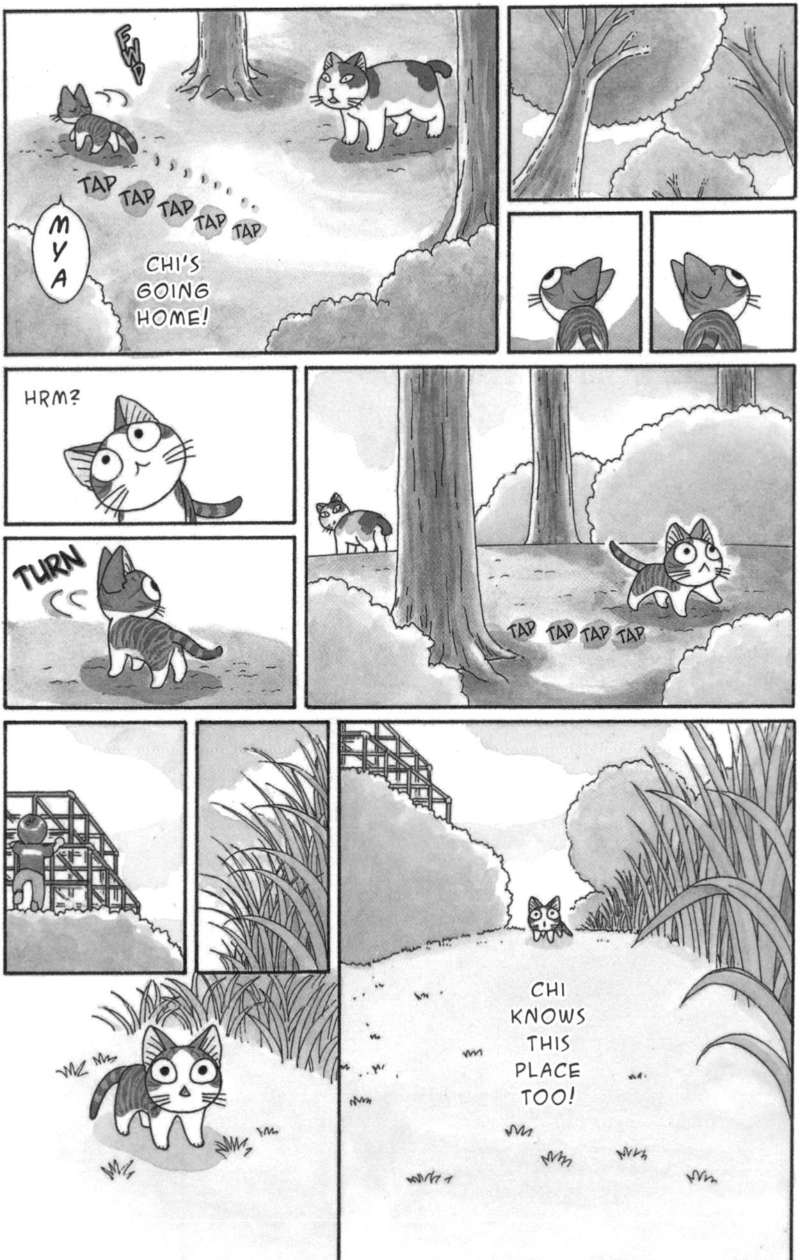
FWP
TAP TAP TAP TAP TAP
MYA
CHI'S GOING HOME!
HRM?
TURN
TAP TAP TAP TAP
CHI KNOWS THIS PLACE TOO!

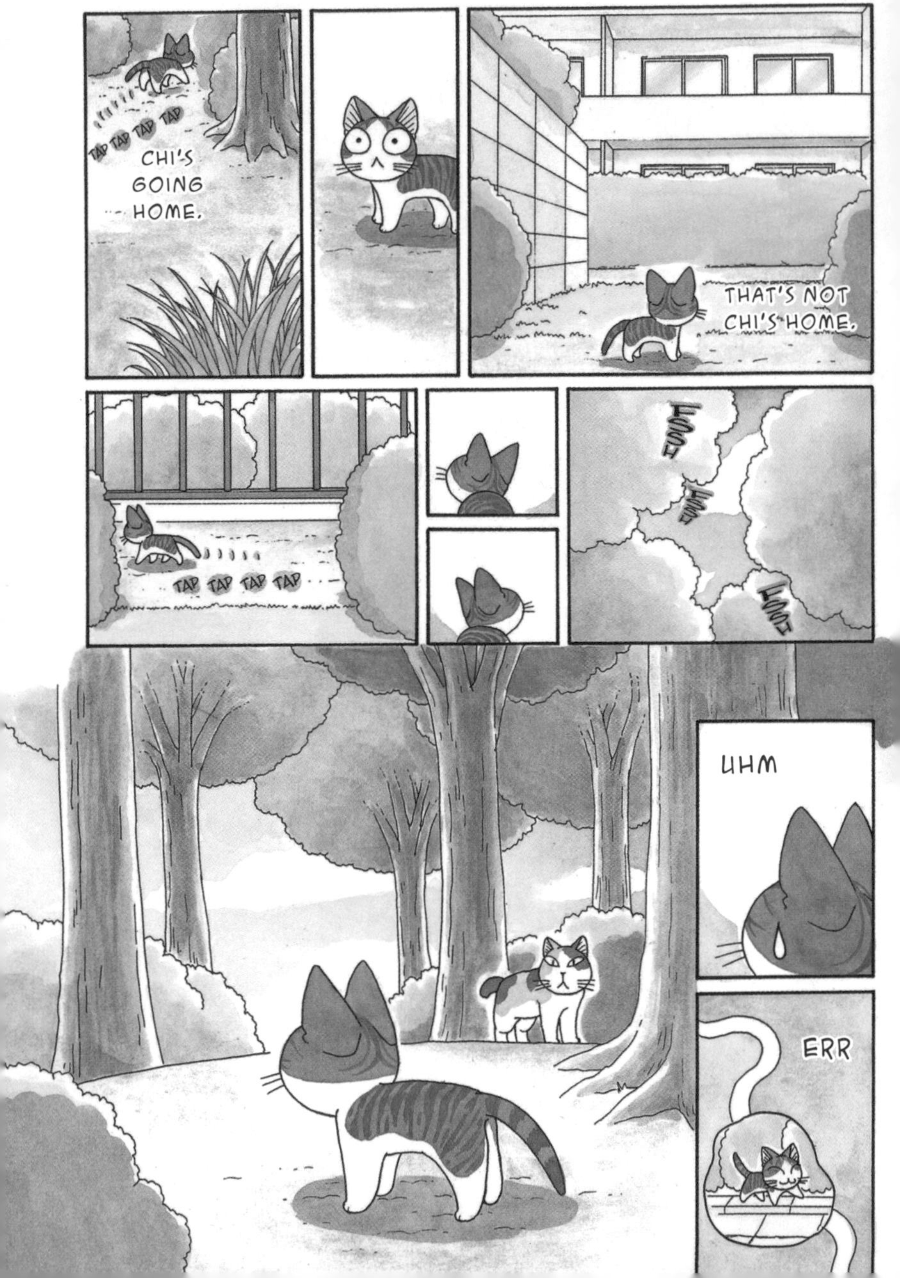
TAP TAP TAP TAP
CHI'S GOING HOME.
THAT'S NOT CHI'S HOME.
TAP TAP TAP TAP
FSSH
FSSH
FSSH
UHM
ERR

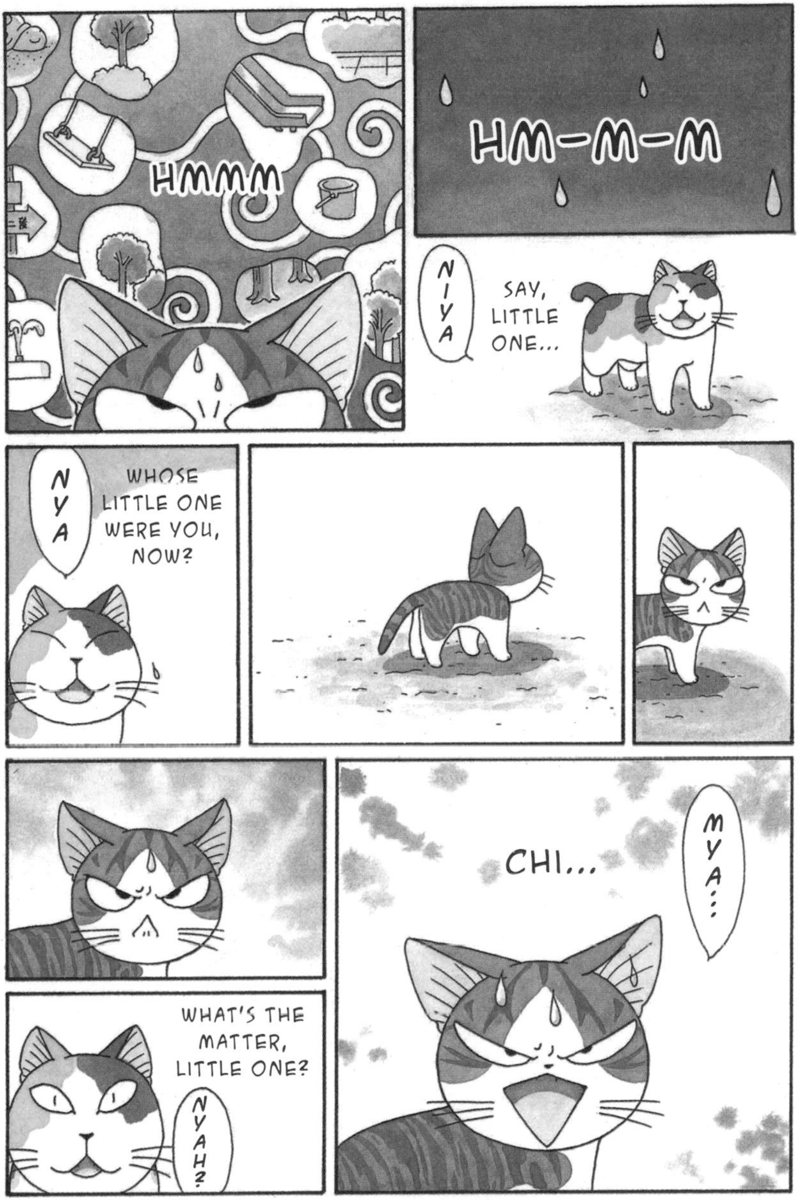
HMMM
HM-M-M
NIYA
SAY, LITTLE ONE...
NYA
WHOSE LITTLE ONE WERE YOU, NOW?
WHAT'S THE MATTER, LITTLE ONE?
NYAH?
CHI...
MYA...

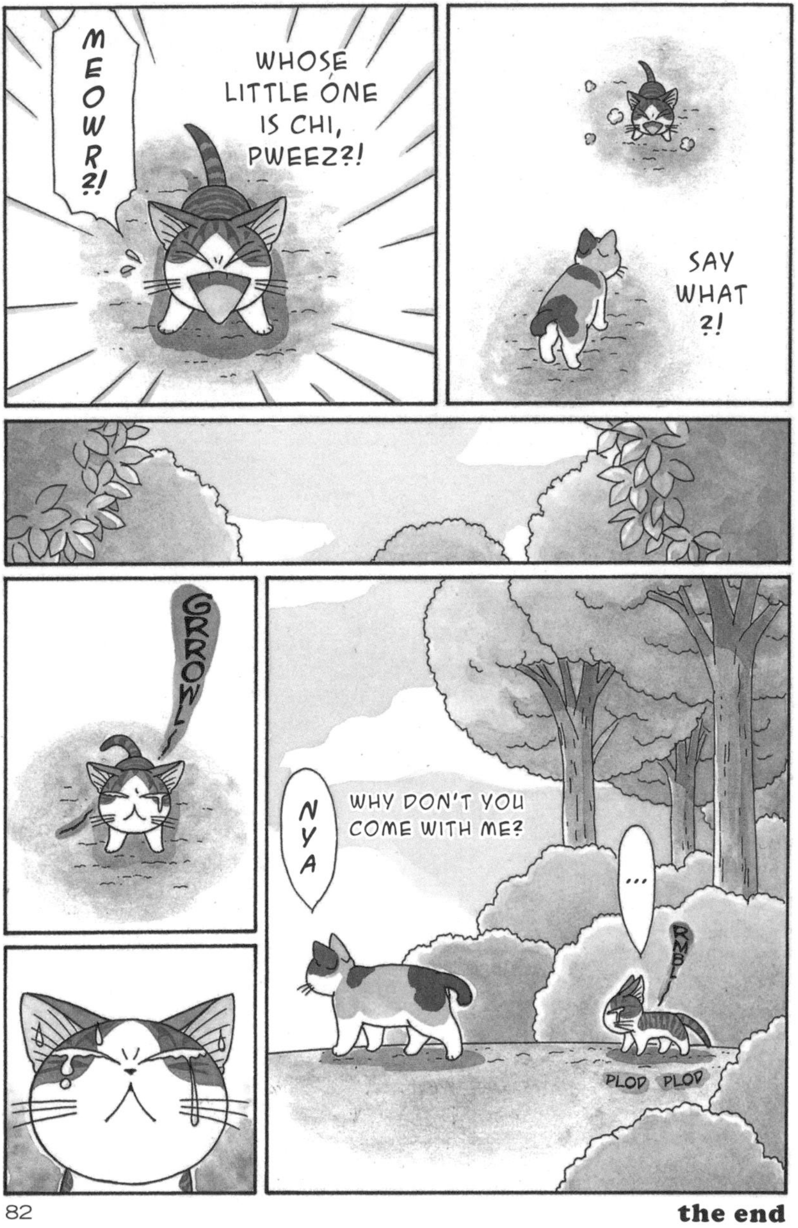
MEOWR?!
WHOSE LITTLE ONE IS CHI, PWEEZ?!
SAY WHAT?!
GRROWL
NYA
WHY DON'T YOU COME WITH ME?
...
RMBL
PLOD PLOD

the end

homemade 85: a cat is invited

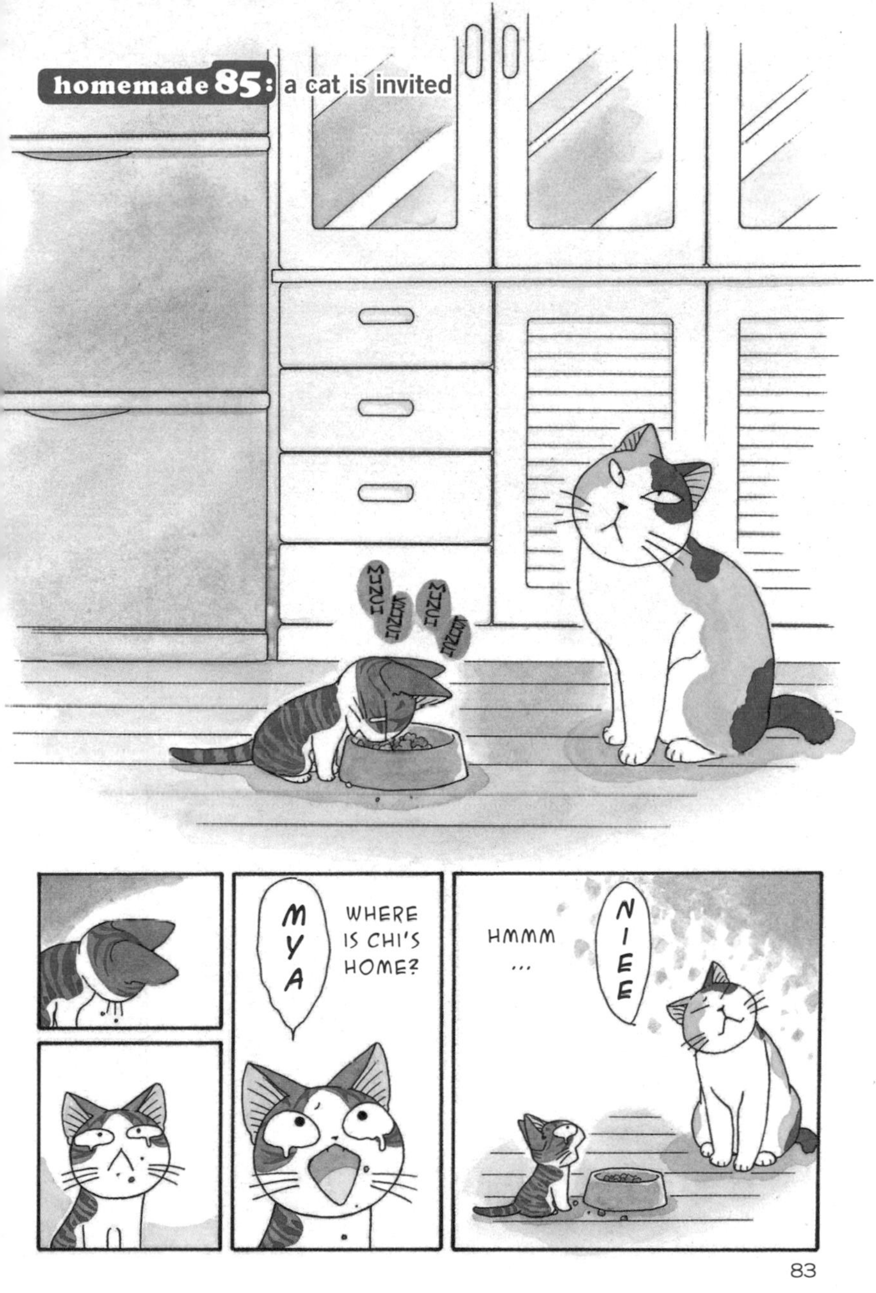
MUNCH
KRUNCH
MUNCH
KRUNCH
MYA
WHERE IS CHI'S HOME?
HMMM ...
NIEE

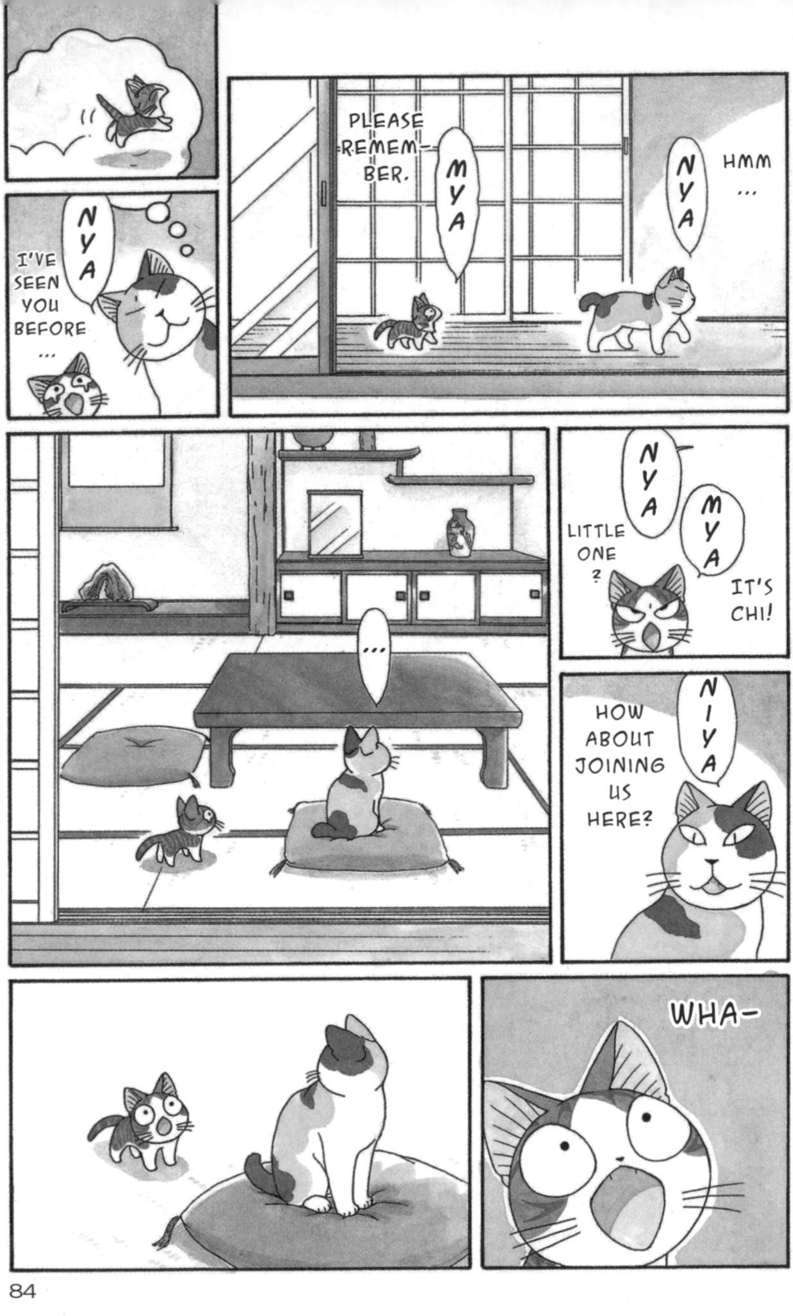

NYA
I'VE SEEN YOU BEFORE ...
PLEASE REMEMBER.
MYA
NYA
HMM ...
...
NYA
LITTLE ONE?
MYA
IT'S CHI!
HOW ABOUT JOINING US HERE?
NIYA
WHA-

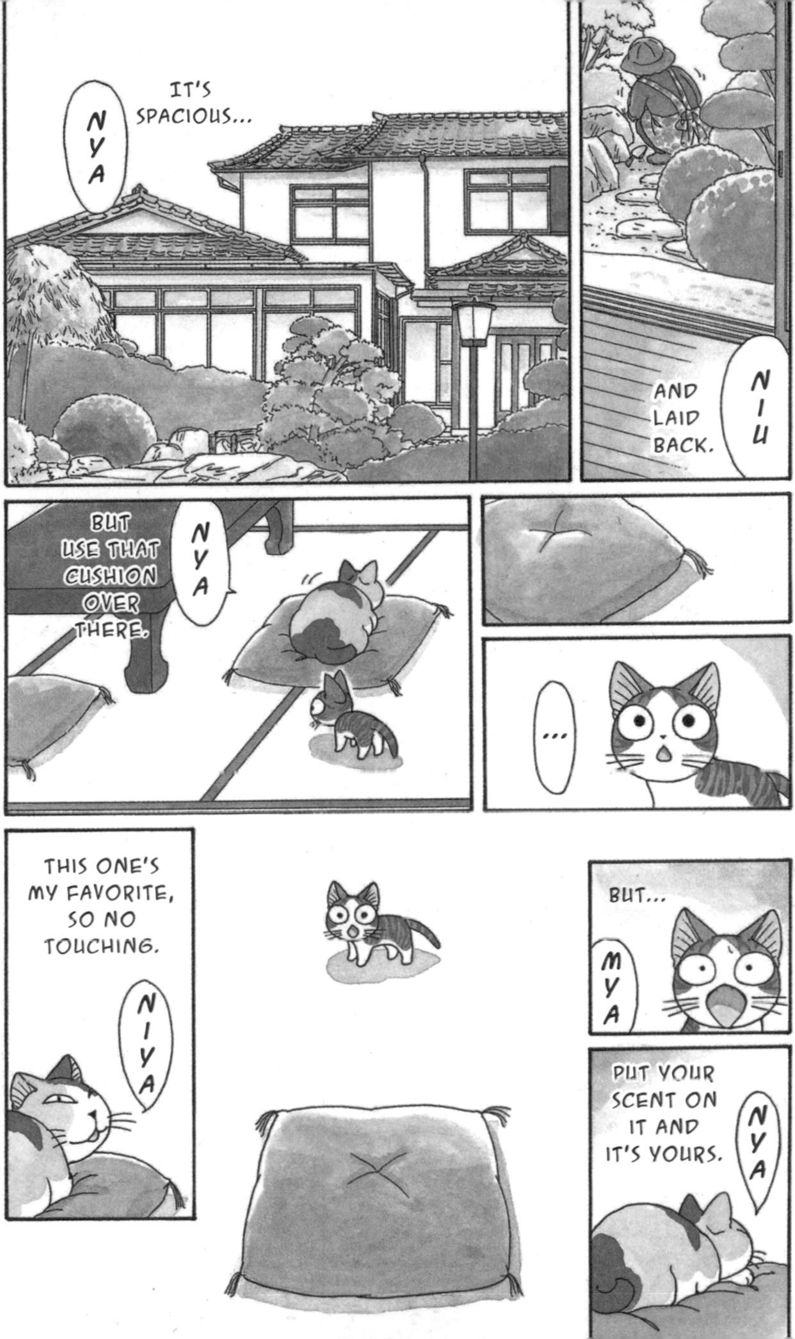
NYA
IT'S SPACIOUS...
AND LAID BACK.
NIU
BUT USE THAT CUSHION OVER THERE.
NYA
...
THIS ONE'S MY FAVORITE, SO NO TOUCHING.
NIYA
BUT...
MYA
PUT YOUR SCENT ON IT AND IT'S YOURS.
NYA

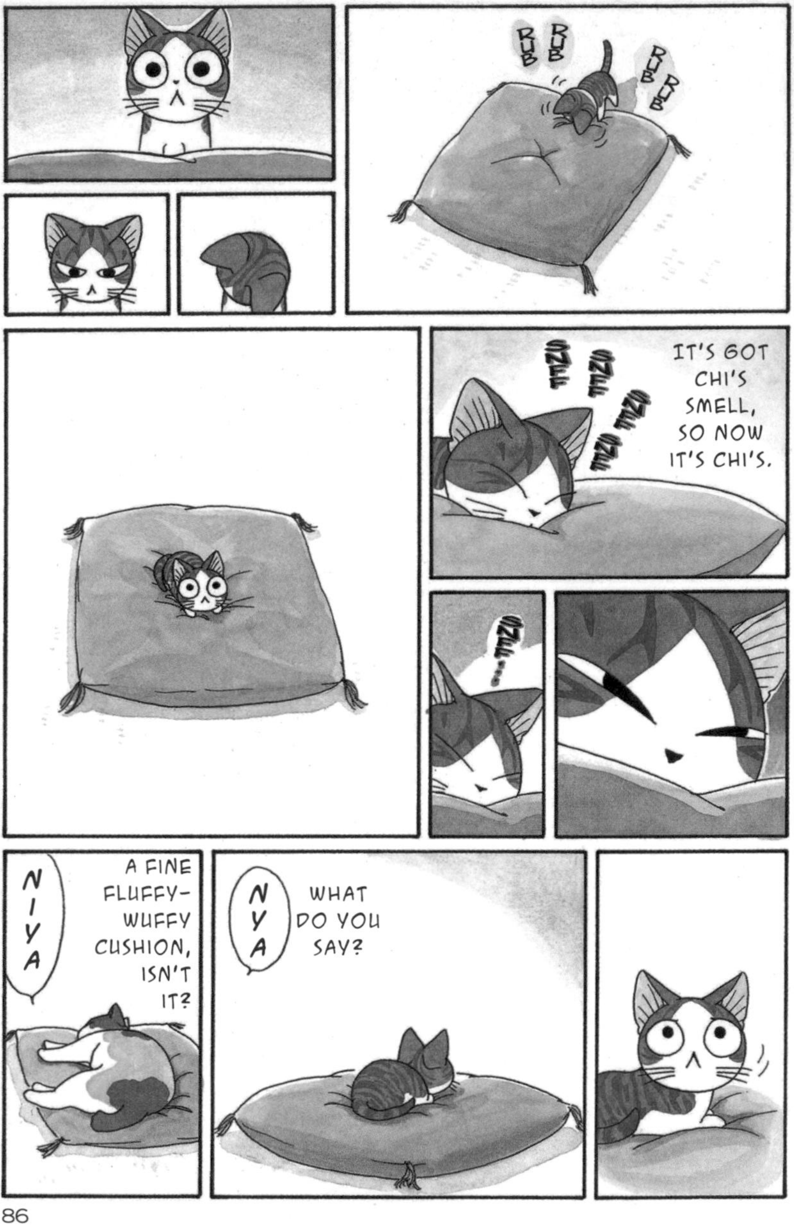
RUB RUB
RUB RUB
SNFF SNFF SNFF SNFF
IT'S GOT CHI'S SMELL, SO NOW IT'S CHI'S.
SNFF...
NIYA
A FINE FLUFFY-WUFFY CUSHION, ISN'T IT?
NYA
WHAT DO YOU SAY?

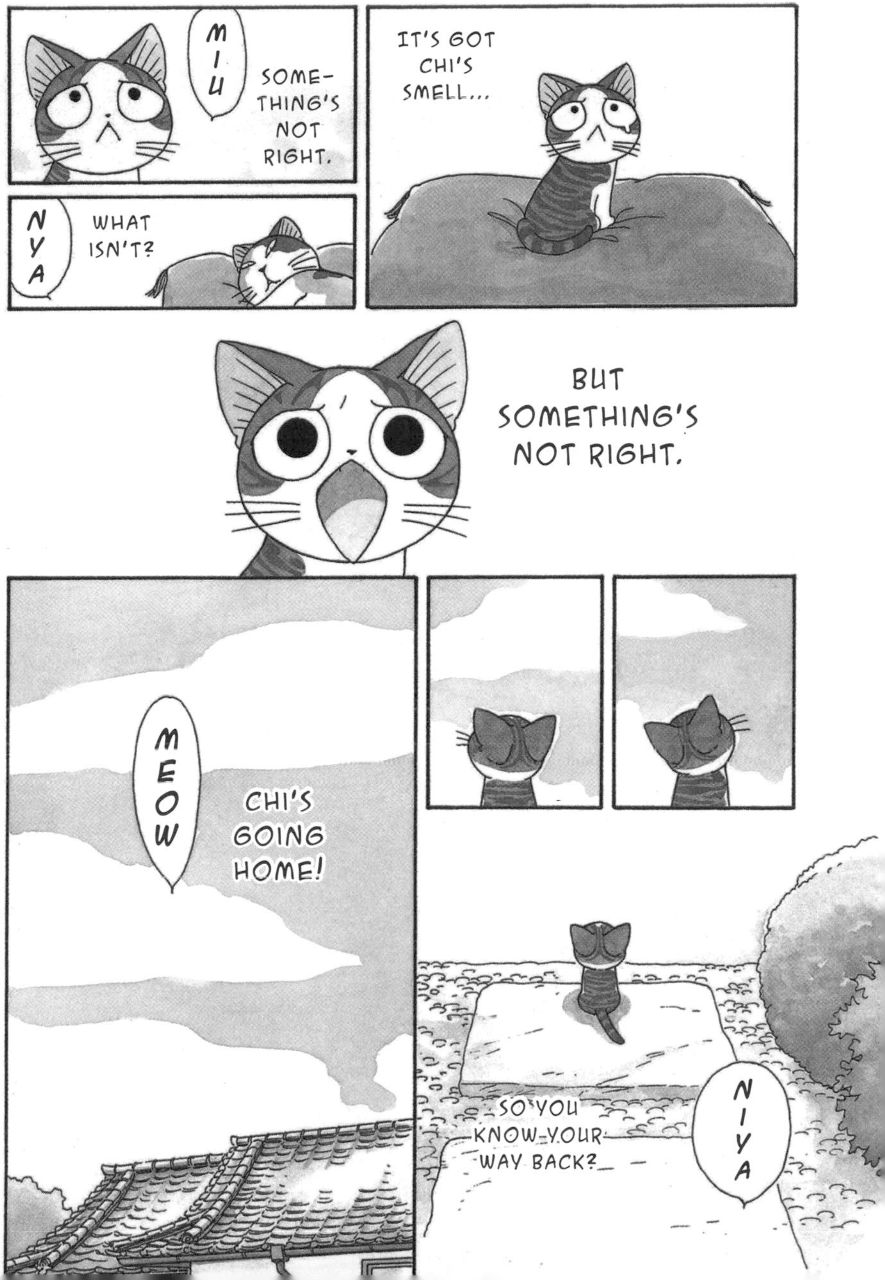
MIU
SOMETHING'S NOT RIGHT.
NYA
WHAT ISN'T?
IT'S GOT CHI'S SMELL...
BUT SOMETHING'S NOT RIGHT.
MEOW
CHI'S GOING HOME!
SO YOU KNOW YOUR WAY BACK?
NIYA

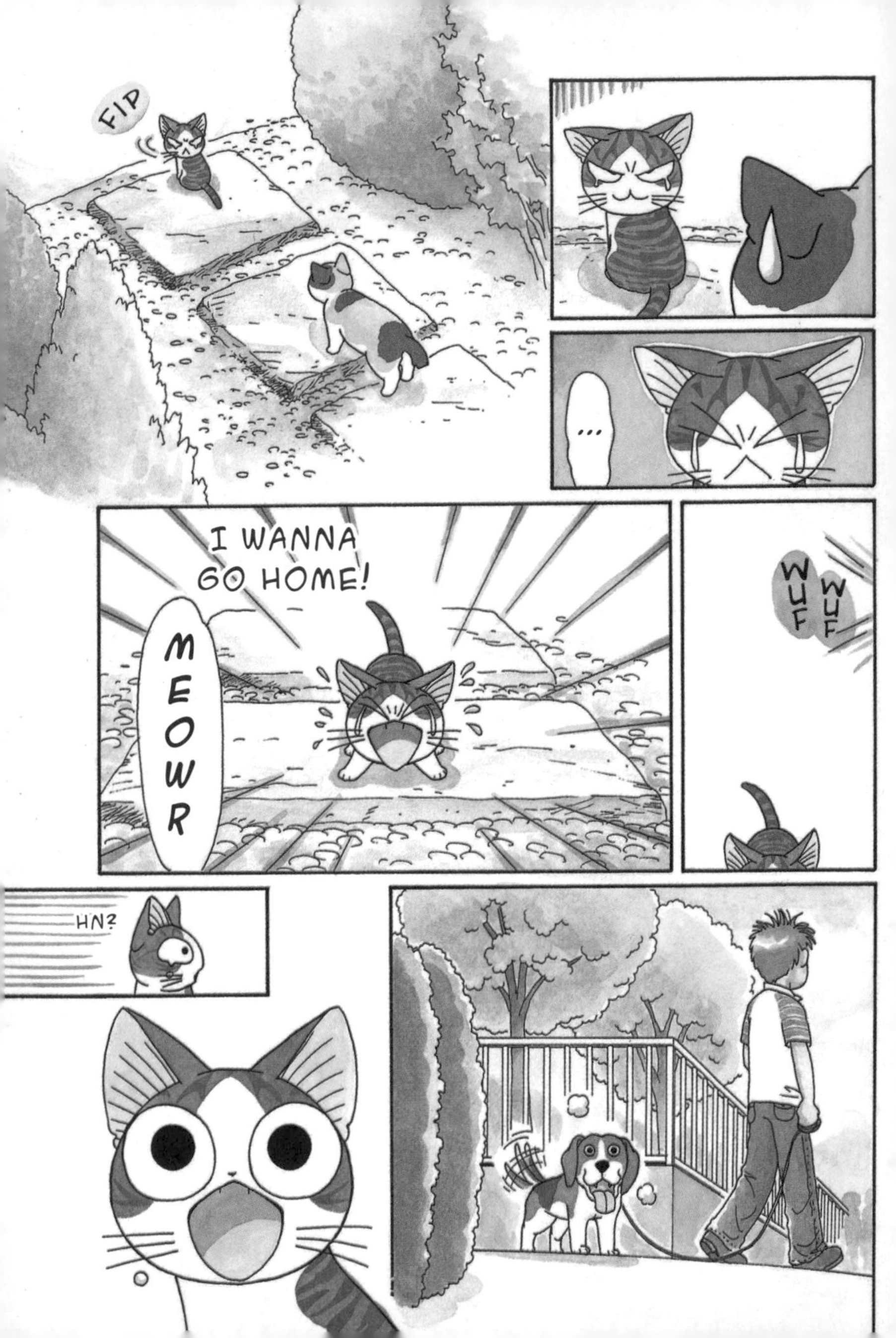
FIP
...
I WANNA GO HOME!
MEOWR
WUF WUF
HN?

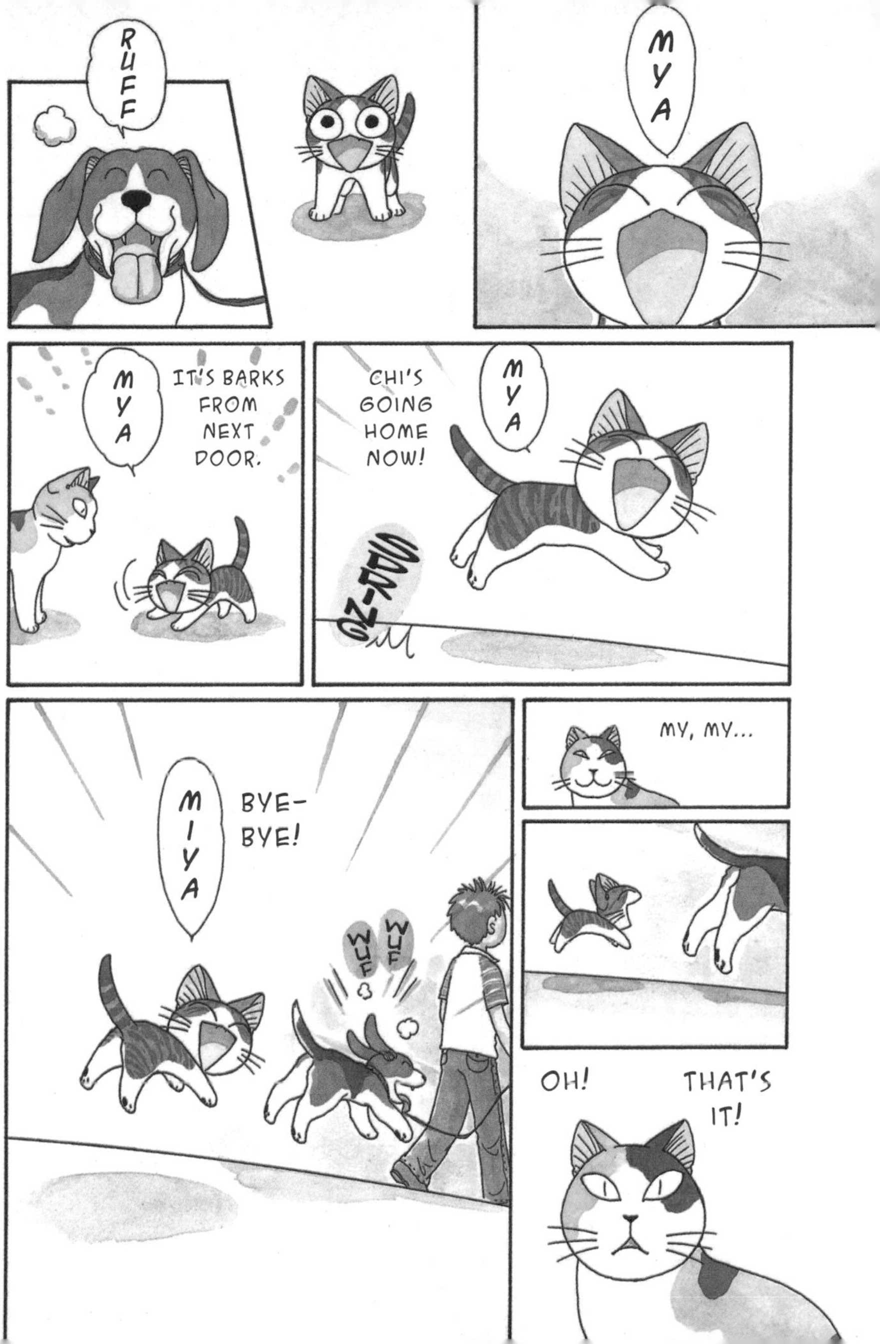
RUFF
MYA
MYA
IT'S BARKS FROM NEXT DOOR.
CHI'S GOING HOME NOW!
MYA
SPRING
MIYA
BYE-BYE!
WUF
WUF
MY, MY...
OH!
THAT'S IT!

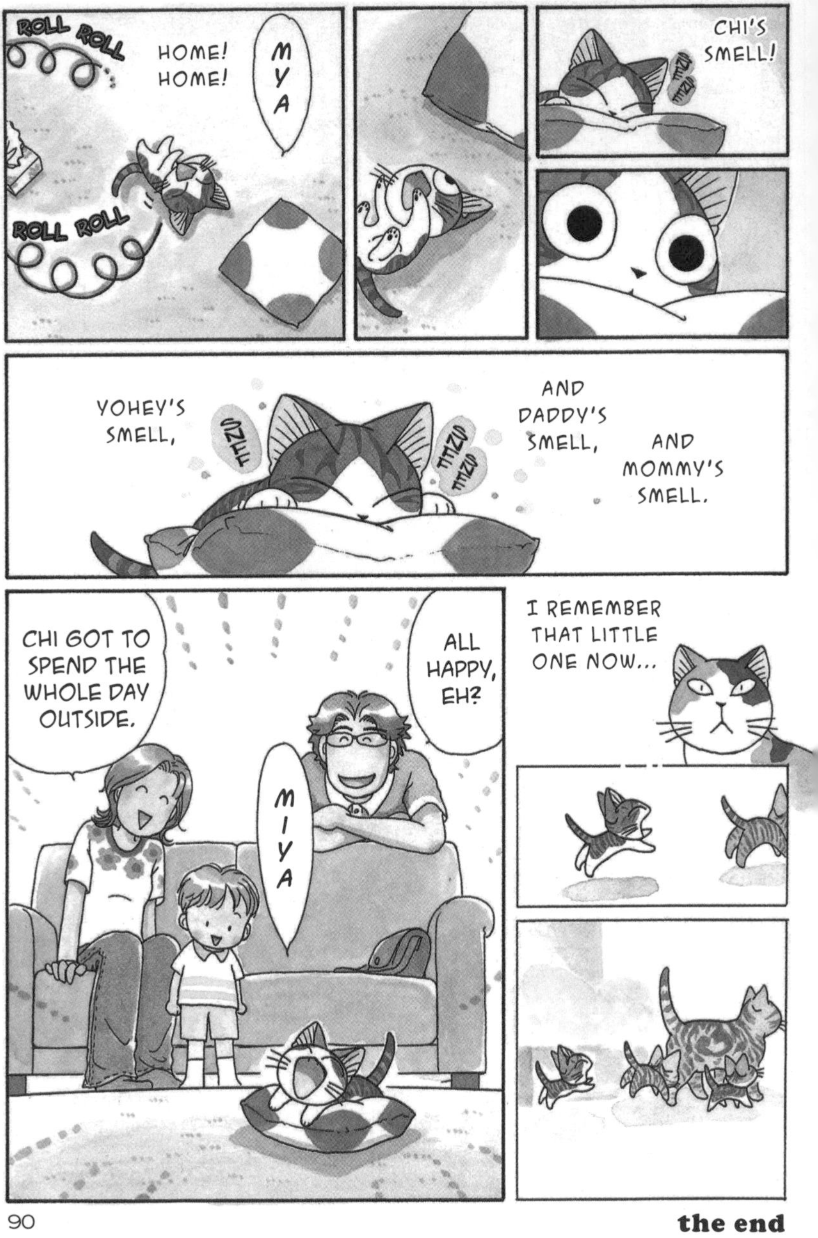
ROLL ROLL
HOME! HOME!
MYA
ROLL ROLL
CHI'S SMELL!
YOHEY'S SMELL,
AND DADDY'S SMELL,
AND MOMMY'S SMELL.
CHI GOT TO SPEND THE WHOLE DAY OUTSIDE.
ALL HAPPY, EH?
MIYA
I REMEMBER THAT LITTLE ONE NOW...

the end

homemade 86: a cat doesn't mesh

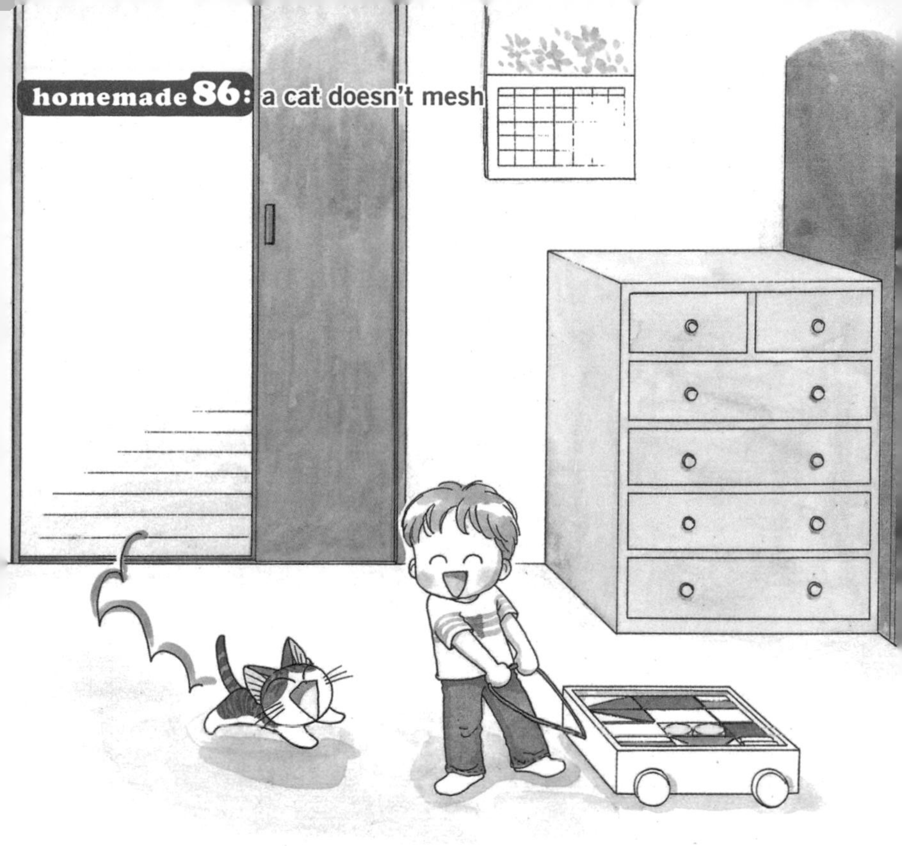

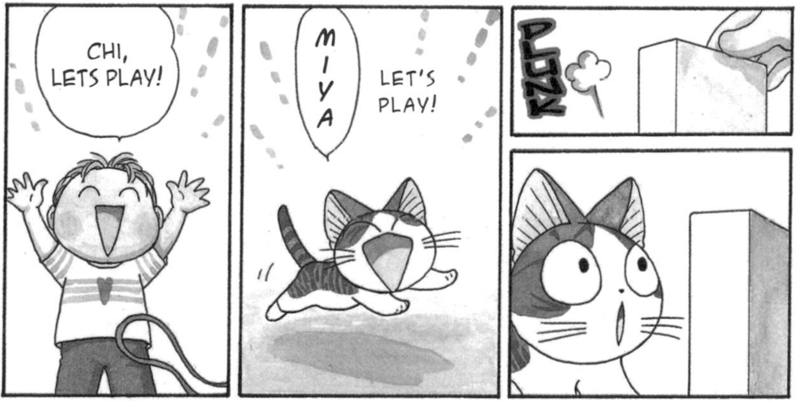
CHI, LETS PLAY!
MIYA
LET'S PLAY!
PLUNK

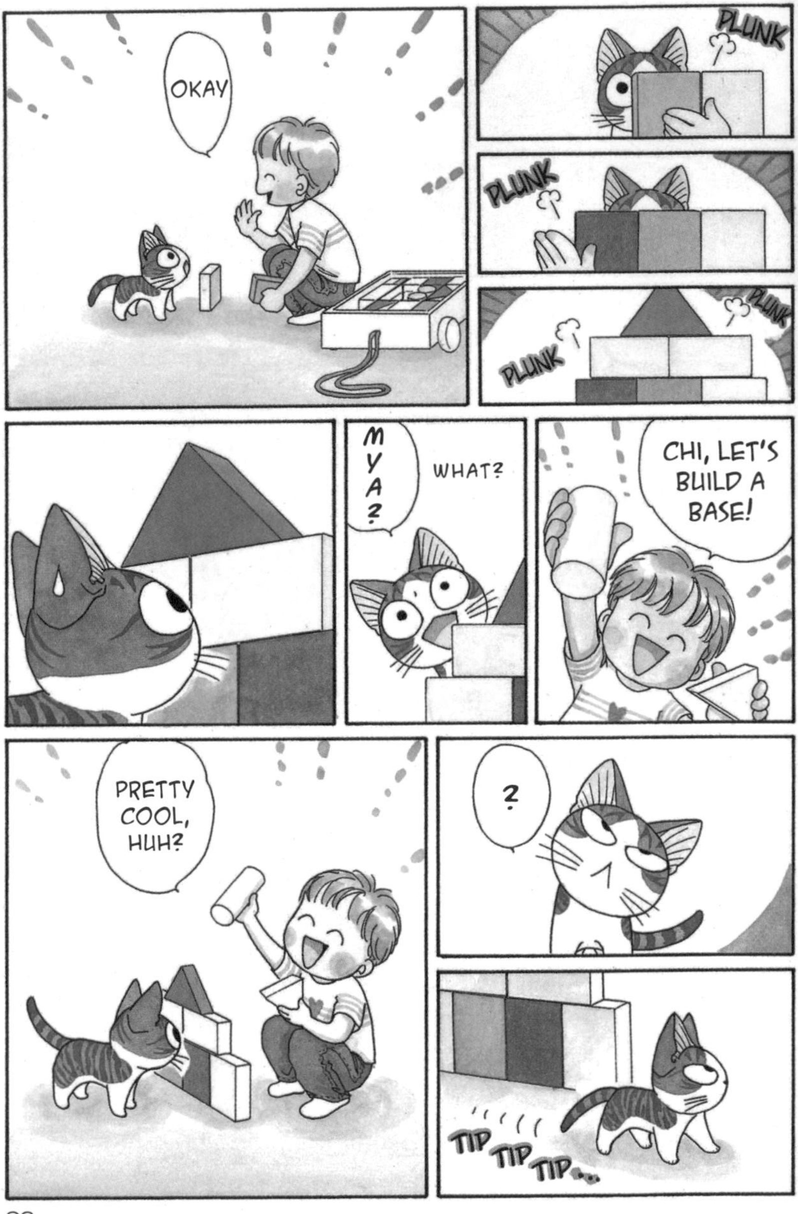
OKAY
PLUNK
PLUNK
PLUNK
PLUNK
MYA?
WHAT?
CHI, LET'S BUILD A BASE!
PRETTY COOL, HUH?
?
TIP TIP TIP...

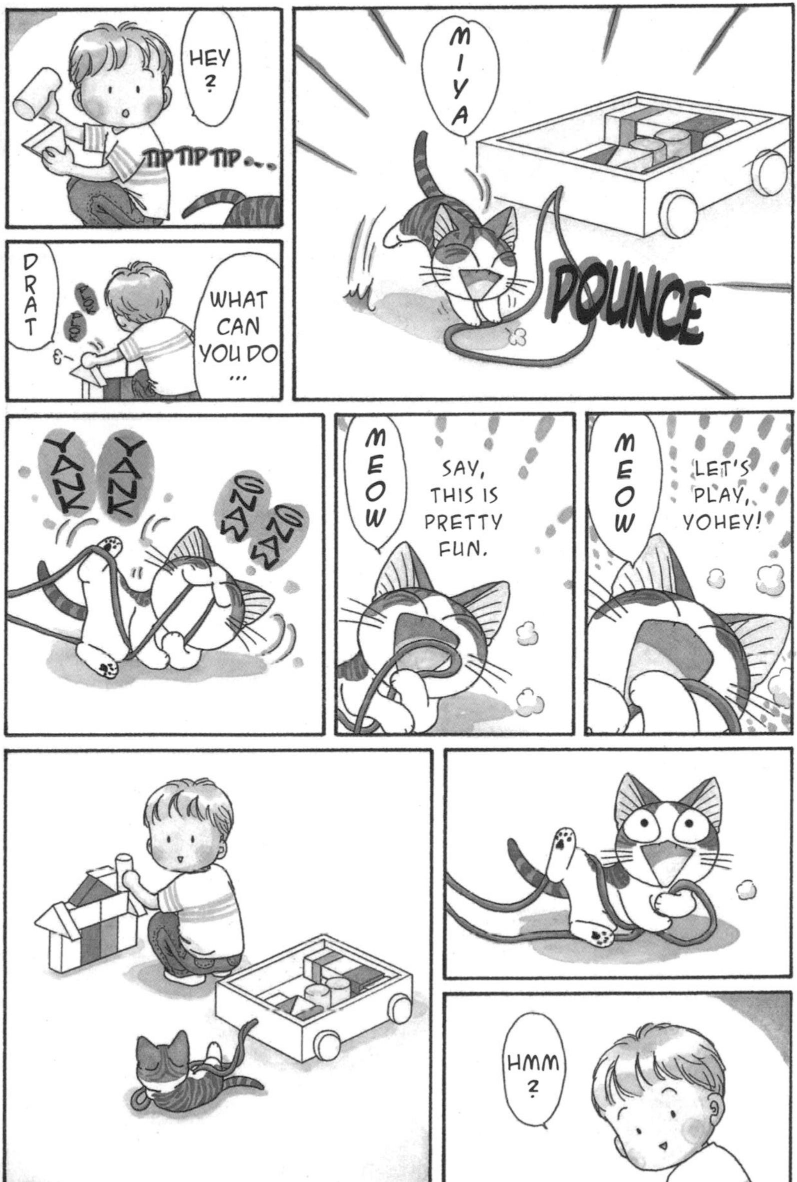
HEY?
TIP TIP TIP...
DRAT
PLOK
PLOK
WHAT CAN YOU DO ...
MIYA
POUNCE
YANK
YANK
GNAW
GNAW
MEOW
SAY, THIS IS PRETTY FUN.
MEOW
LET'S PLAY, YOHEY!
HMM?

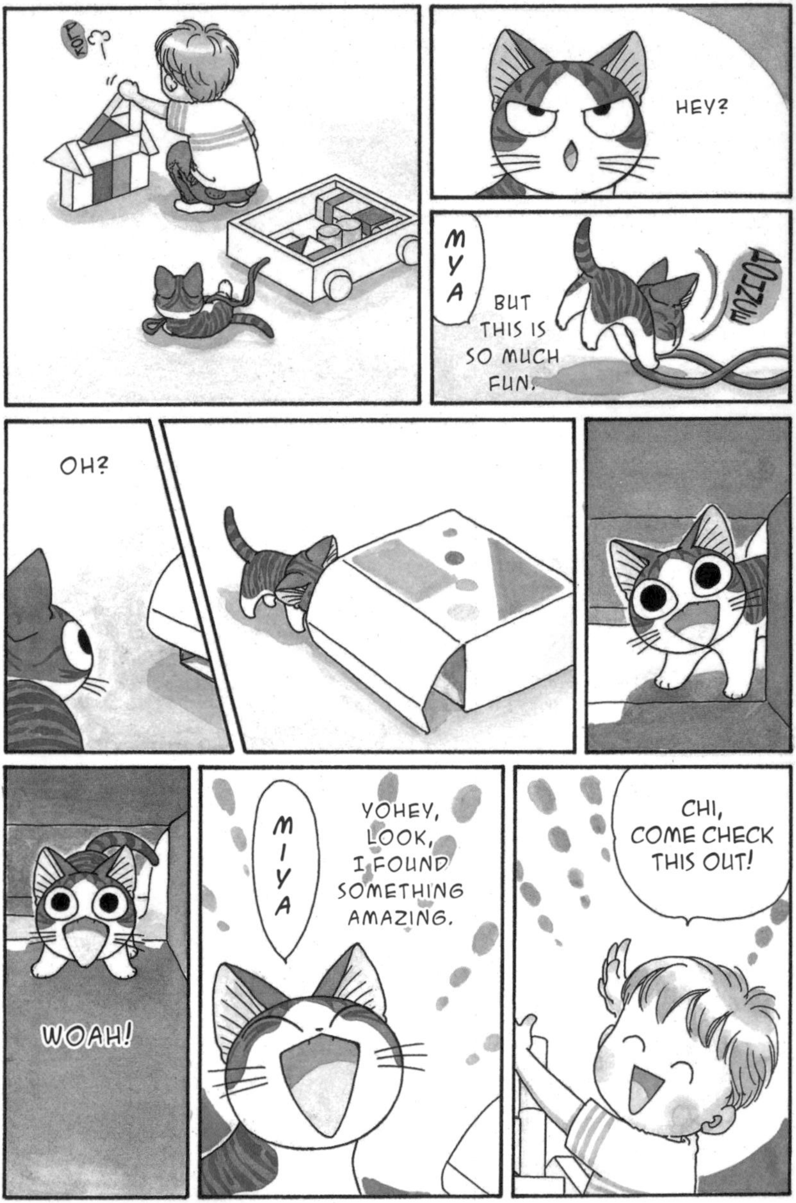
PLOK
HEY?
MYA
BUT THIS IS SO MUCH FUN.
OH?
WOAH!
MIYA
YOHEY, LOOK, I FOUND SOMETHING AMAZING.
CHI, COME CHECK THIS OUT!

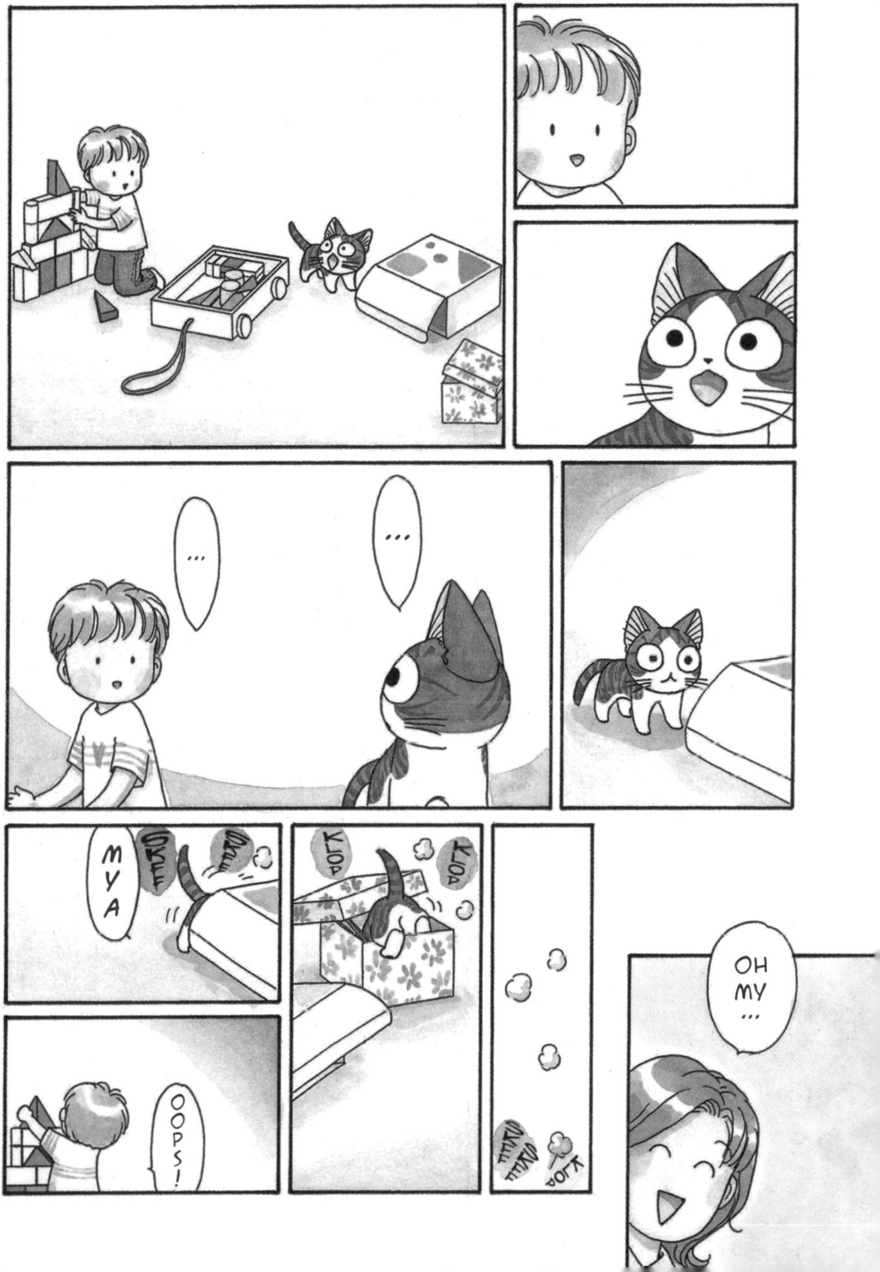
...
...
MYA
SKREE
SKREE
OOPS!
KLOP
KLOP
POLK
OH MY ...

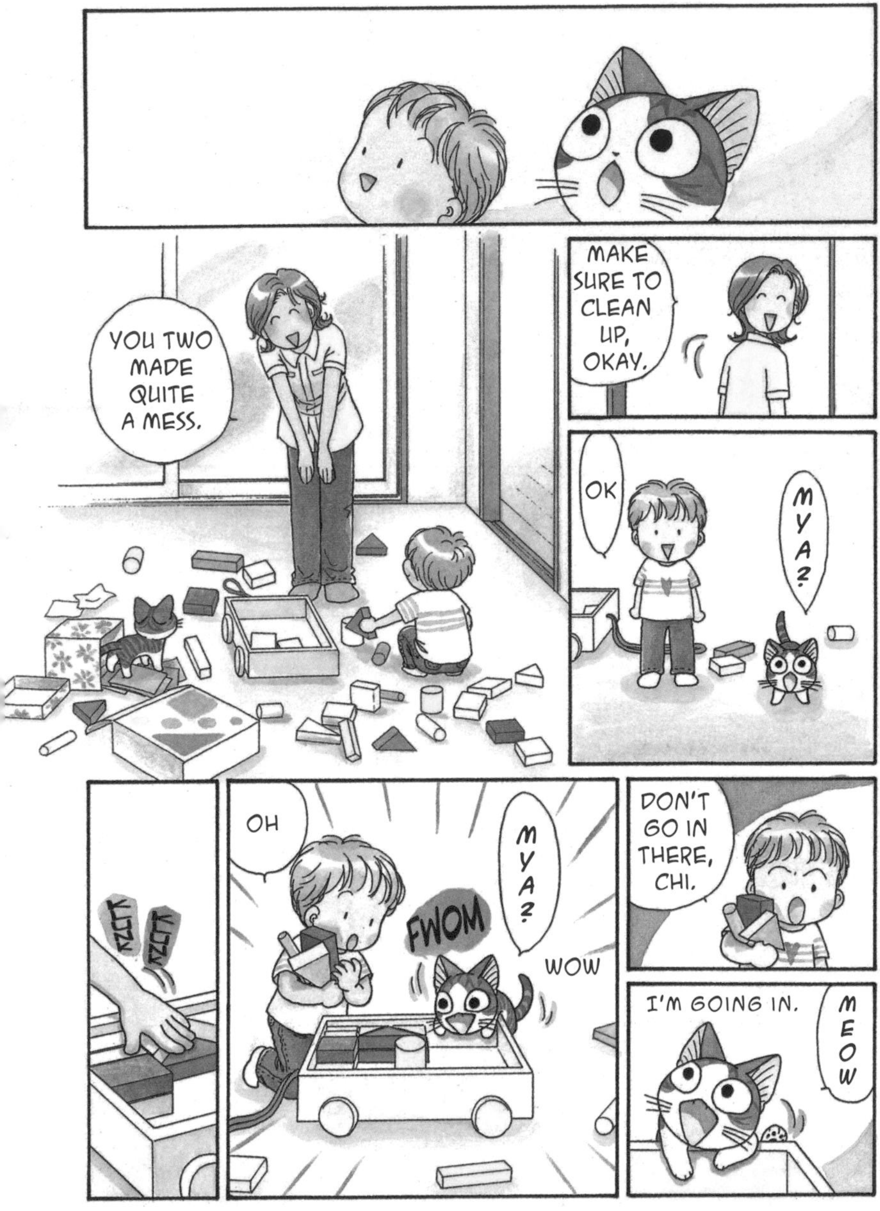
YOU TWO MADE QUITE A MESS.
MAKE SURE TO CLEAN UP, OKAY.
OK
MYA?
OH
FWOM
MYA?
WOW
DON'T GO IN THERE, CHI.
I'M GOING IN.
MEOW

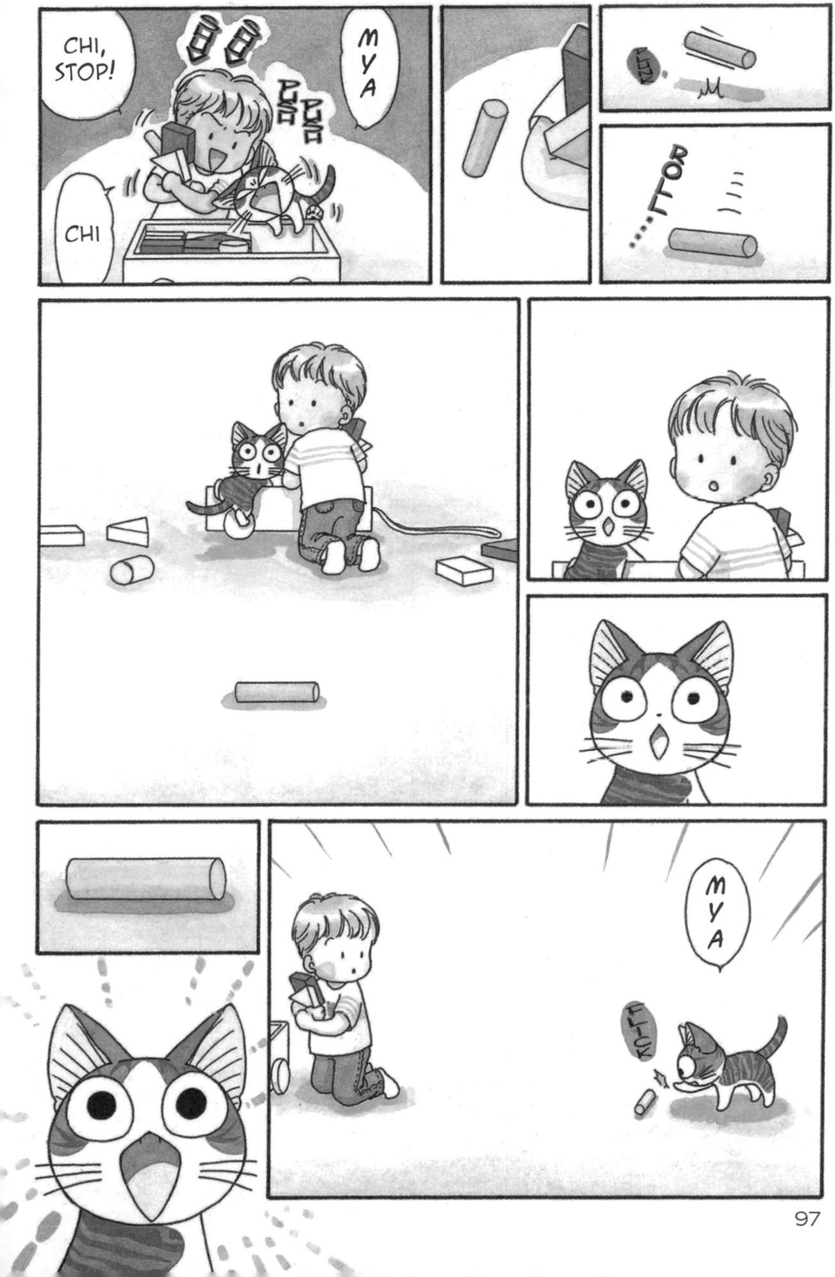
CHI, STOP!
CHI
PUSH PUSH
MYA
ROLL...
MYA
FLICK

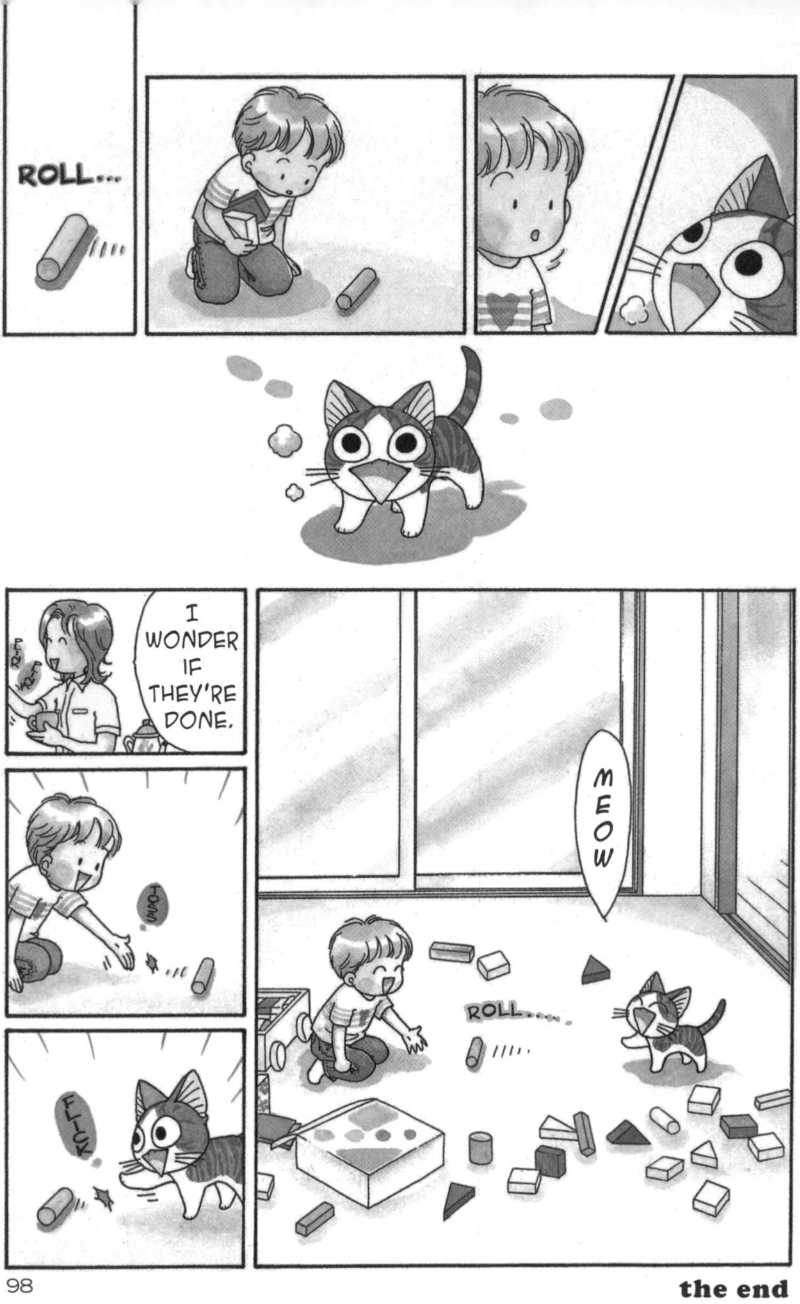
ROLL...
I WONDER IF THEY'RE DONE.
TOSS
FLICK
MEOW
ROLL....

the end

homemade 87: a cat does mesh

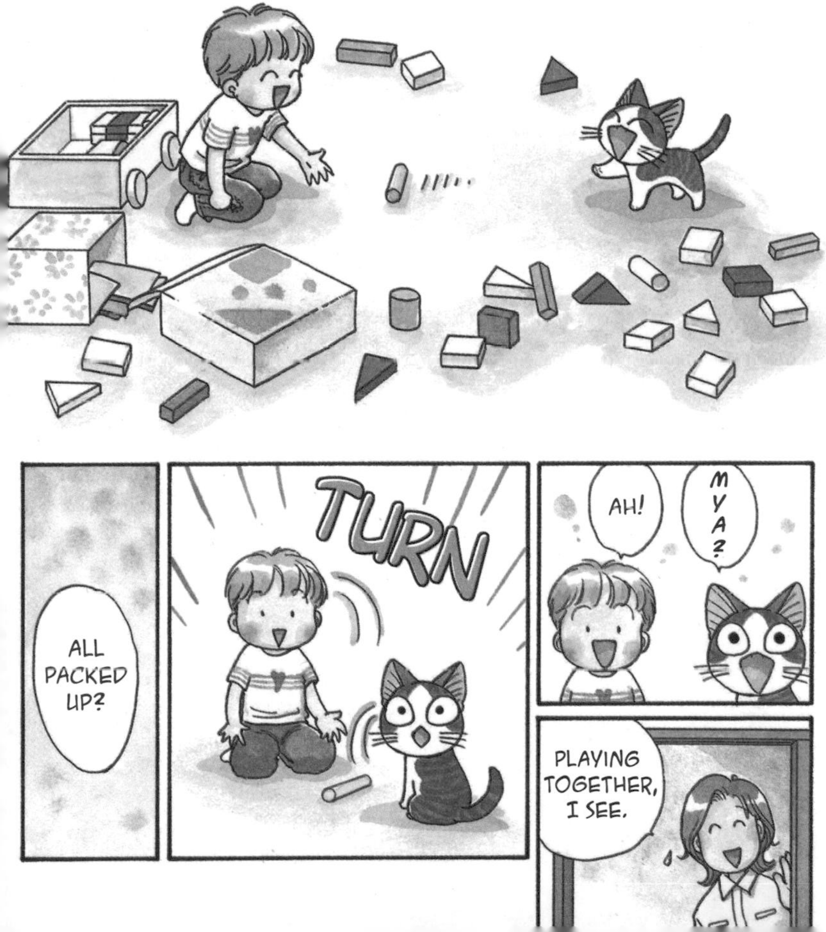
ALL PACKED UP?
TURN
AH!
MYA?
PLAYING TOGETHER, I SEE.

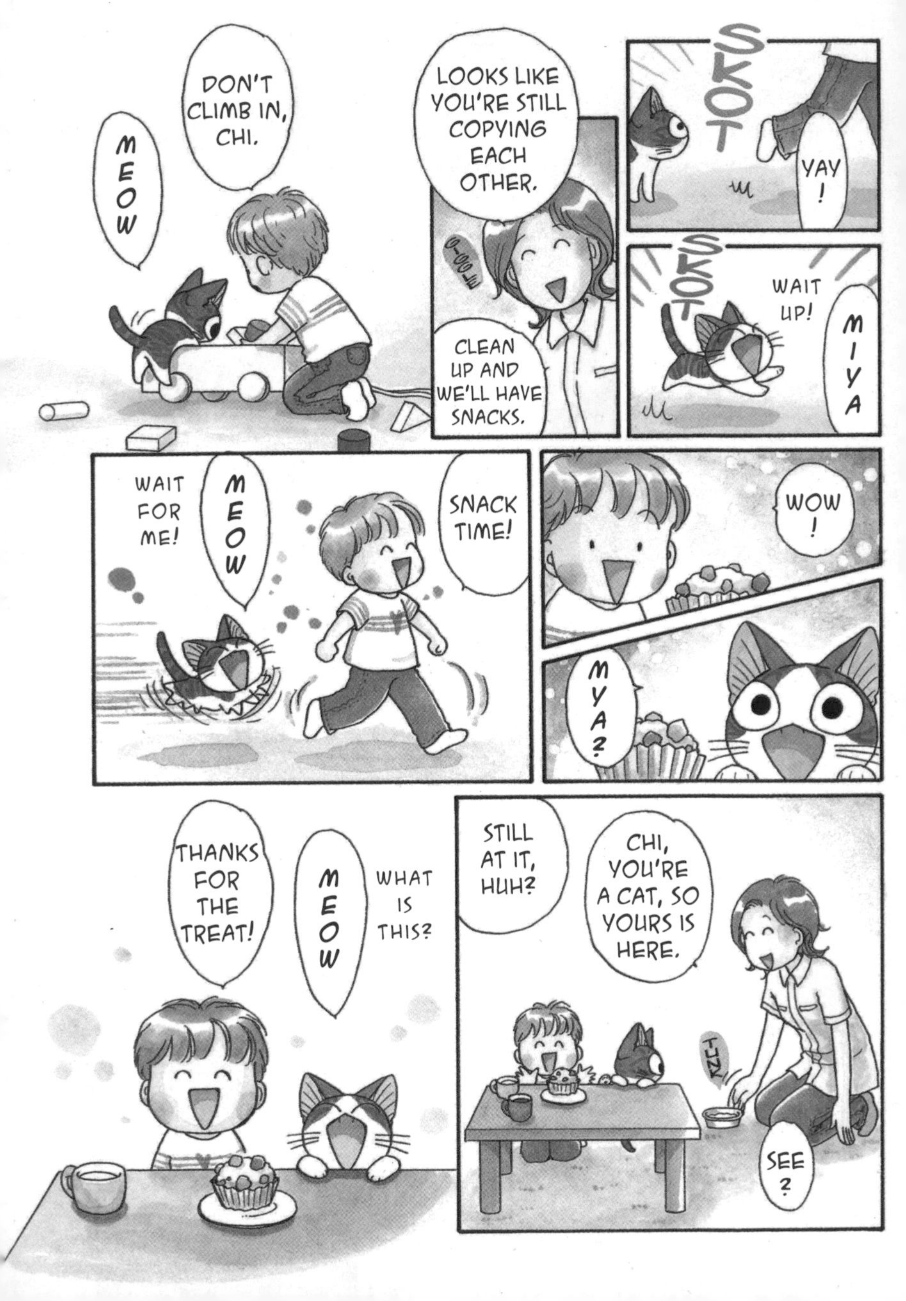
MEOW
DON'T CLIMB IN, CHI.
LOOKS LIKE YOU'RE STILL COPYING EACH OTHER.
GIGGLE
CLEAN UP AND WE'LL HAVE SNACKS.
SKOT
YAY!
SKOT
WAIT UP!
MIYA
WAIT FOR ME!
MEOW
SNACK TIME!
WOW!
MYA?
THANKS FOR THE TREAT!
MEOW
WHAT IS THIS?
STILL AT IT, HUH?
CHI, YOU'RE A CAT, SO YOURS IS HERE.
TUNK
SEE?

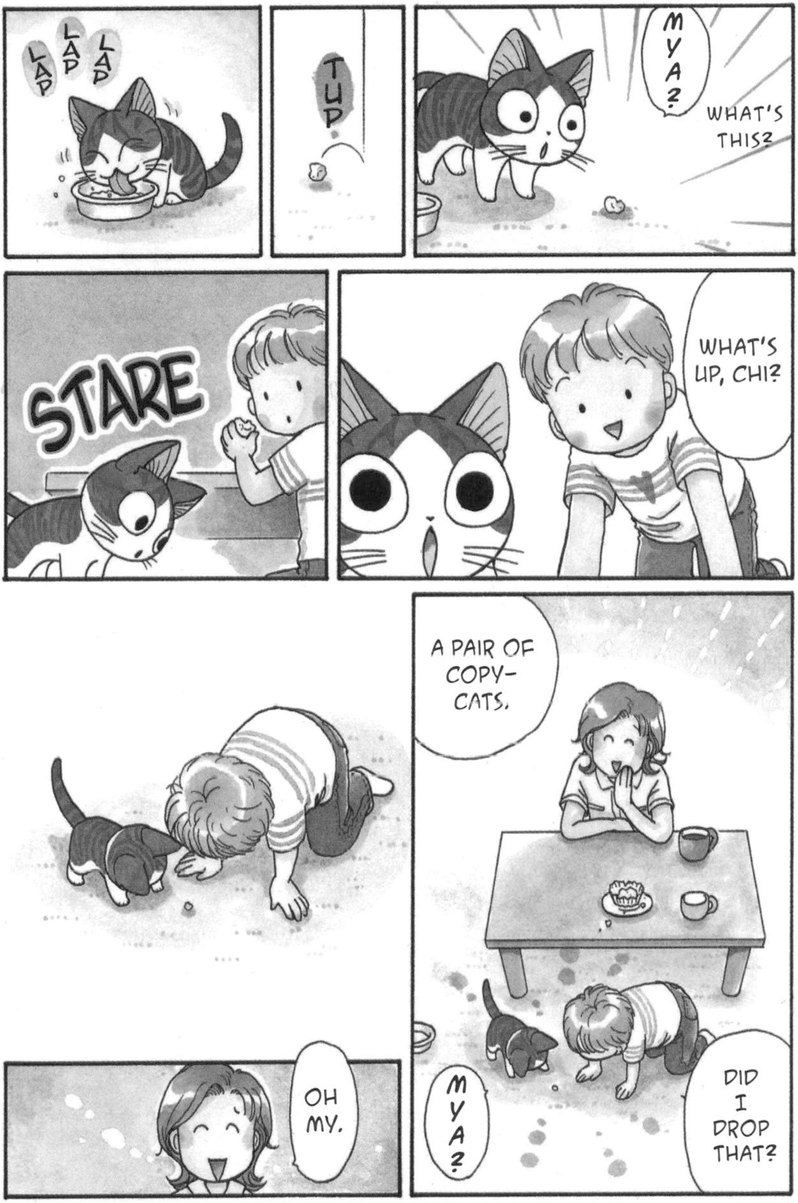
LAP LAP LAP
TUP
MYA?
WHAT'S THIS?
STARE
WHAT'S UP, CHI?
OH MY.
A PAIR OF COPY-CATS.
MYA?
DID I DROP THAT?

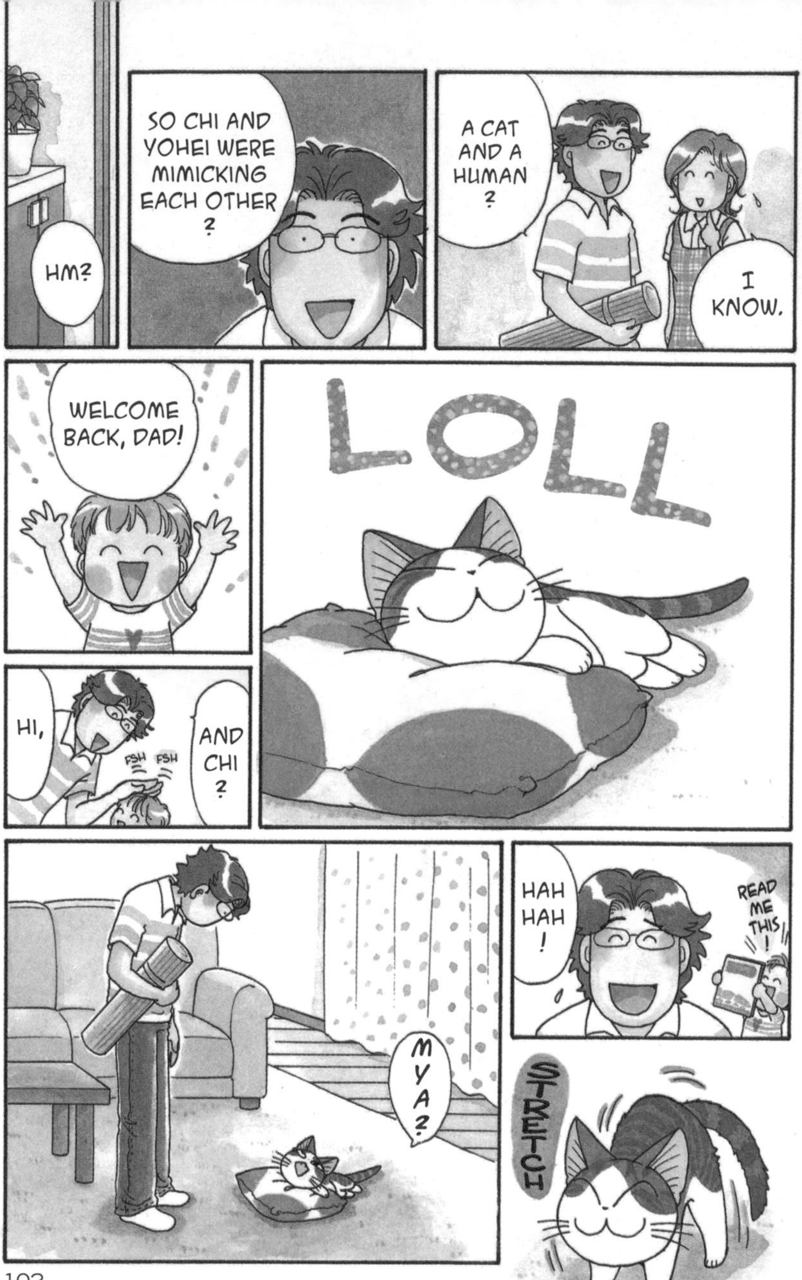
HM?
SO CHI AND YOHEI WERE MIMICKING EACH OTHER?
A CAT AND A HUMAN?
I KNOW.
WELCOME BACK, DAD!
HI,
FSH FSH
AND CHI?
LOLL
MYA?
HAH HAH!
READ ME THIS!
STRETCH

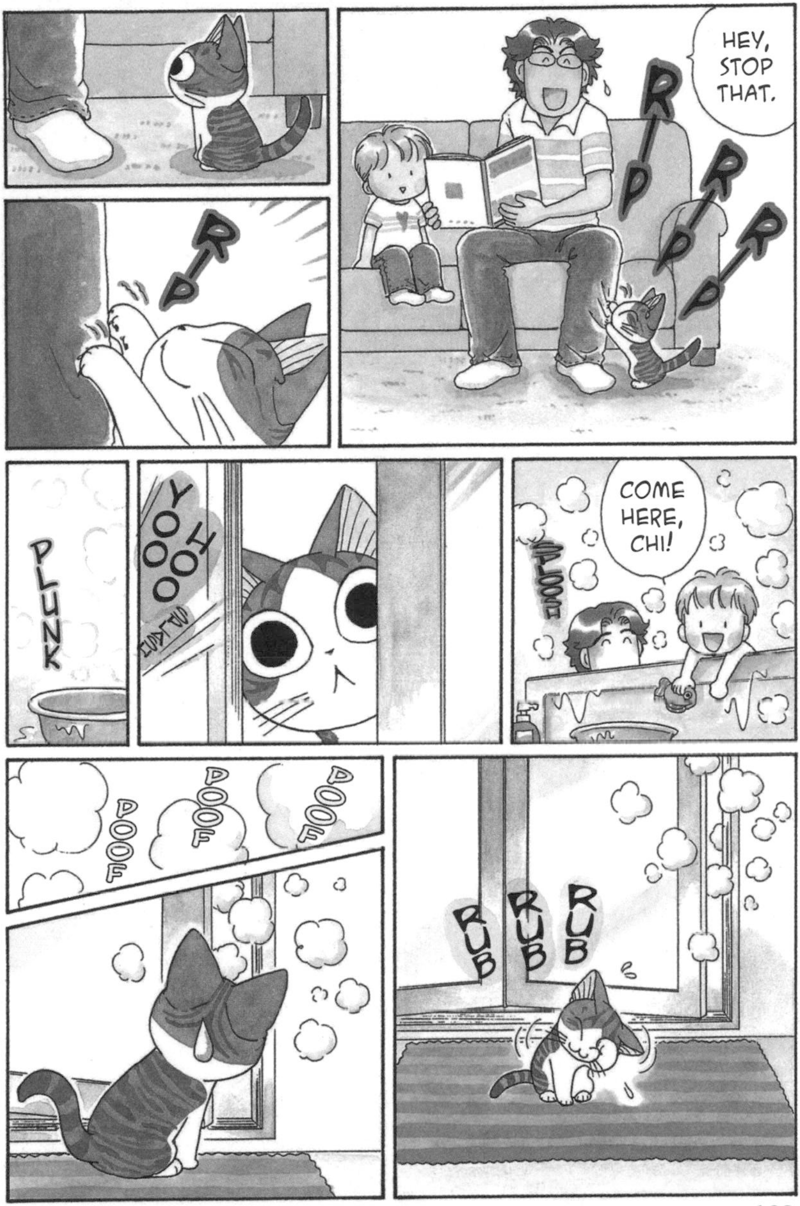
RIP
RIP
HEY, STOP THAT.
RIP
RIP
PLUNK
YOOOOH
COME HERE, CHI!
POOF
POOF
POOF
RUB
RUB
RUB

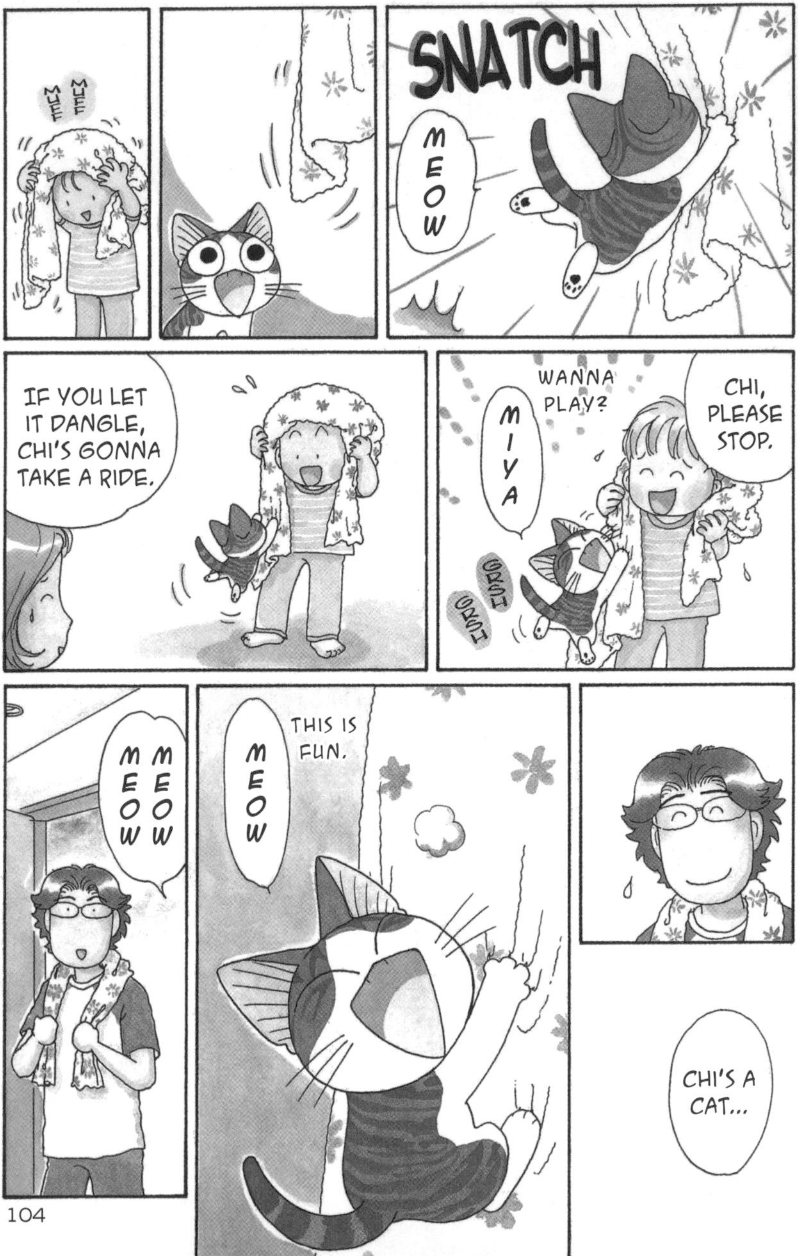

MUFF MUFF
SNATCH
MEOW
IF YOU LET IT DANGLE, CHI'S GONNA TAKE A RIDE.
MIYA
WANNA PLAY?
CHI, PLEASE STOP.
GRSH GRSH
MEOW MEOW
MEOW
THIS IS FUN.
CHI'S A CAT...

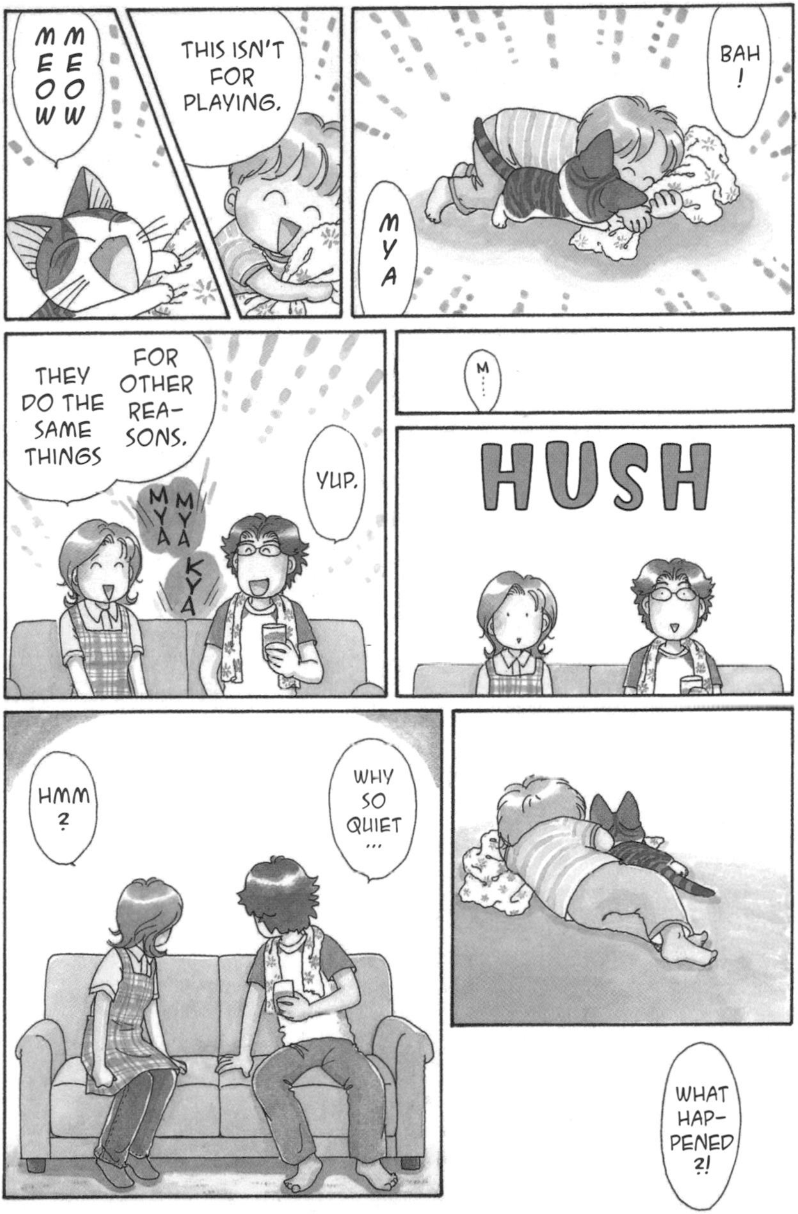
MEOW MEOW
THIS ISN'T FOR PLAYING.
BAH!
MYA
THEY DO THE SAME THINGS FOR OTHER REASONS.
MYA MYA
KYA
YUP.
M...
HUSH
HMM?
WHY SO QUIET...
WHAT HAPPENED?!

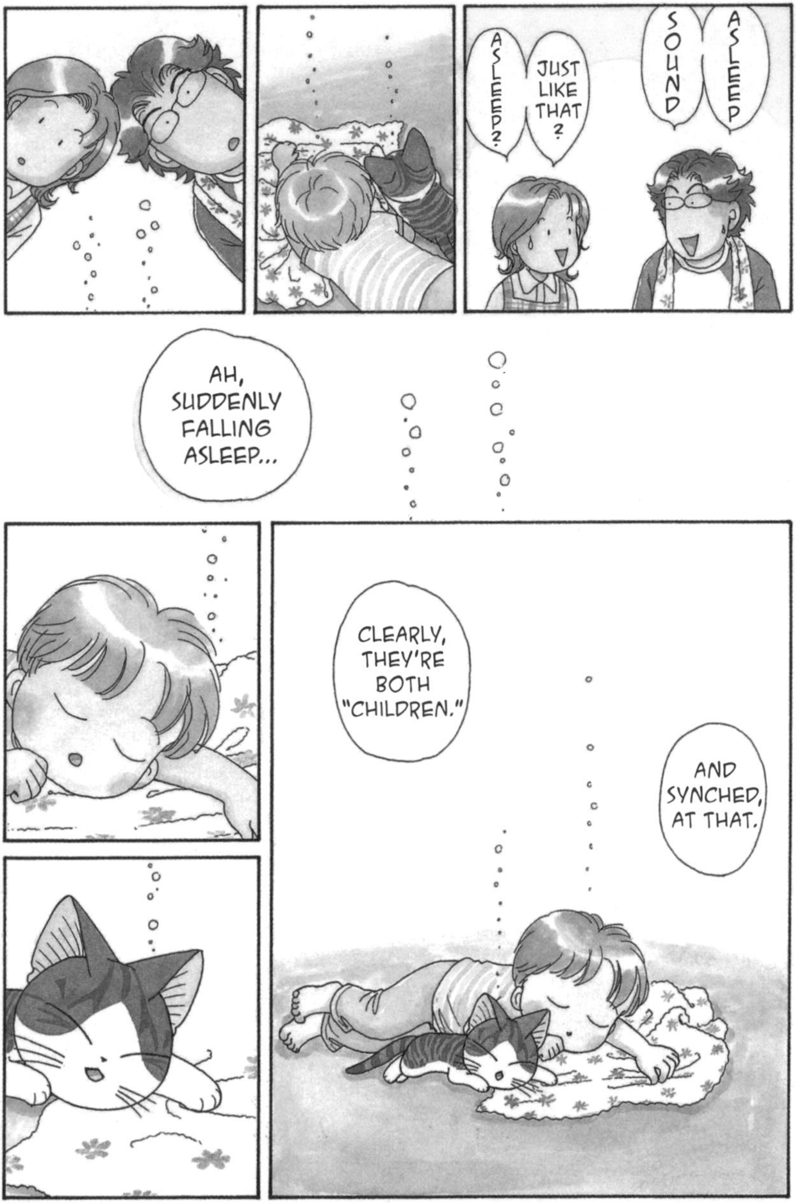
ASLEEP?
JUST LIKE THAT?
SOUND
ASLEEP
AH, SUDDENLY FALLING ASLEEP...
CLEARLY, THEY'RE BOTH "CHILDREN."
AND SYNCHED, AT THAT.

the end

homemade 88: a cat halts

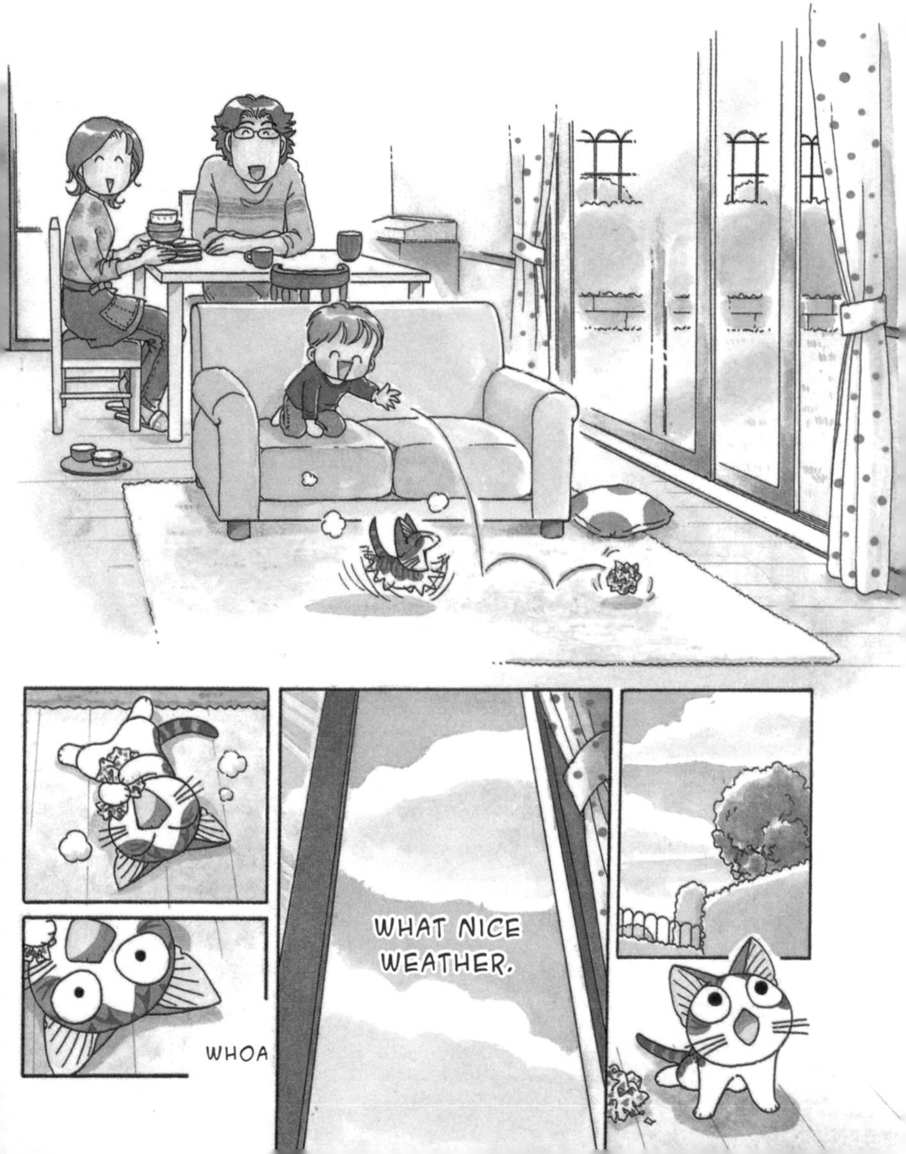
WHOA
WHAT NICE WEATHER.

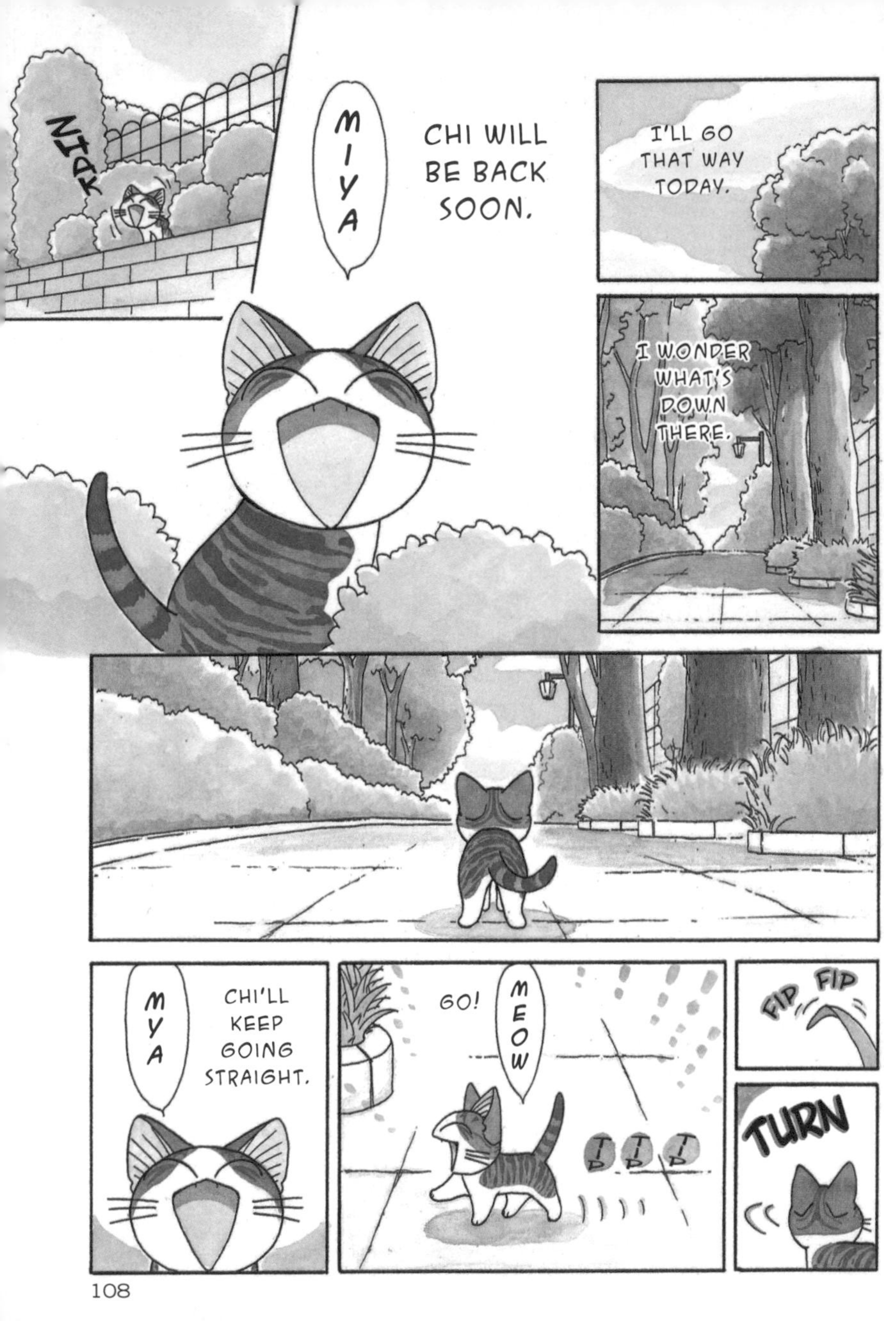
MIYA
CHI WILL BE BACK SOON.
I'LL GO THAT WAY TODAY.
I WONDER WHAT'S DOWN THERE.
MYA
CHI'LL KEEP GOING STRAIGHT.
GO!
MEOW
TIP TIP TIP
FIP FIP
TURN

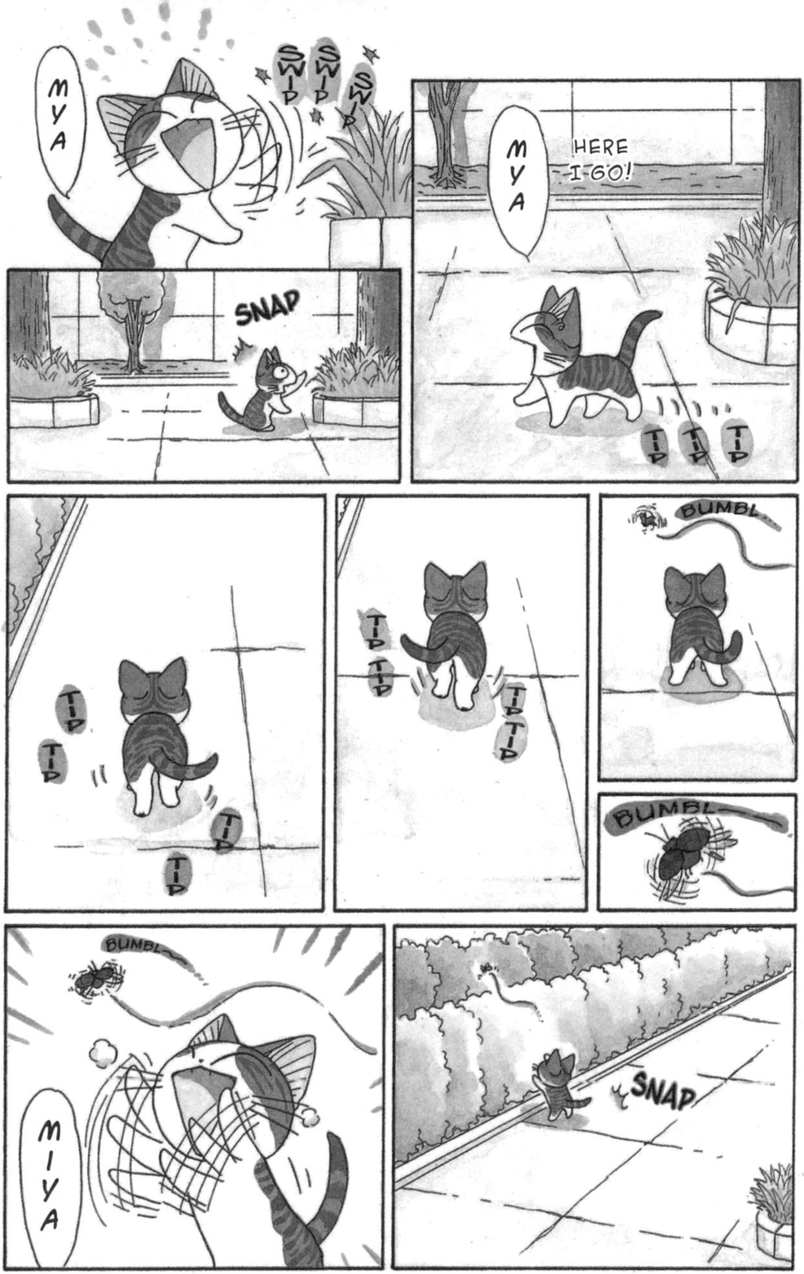
MYA
SWIP SWIP SWIP
SNAP
MYA
HERE I GO!
TIP TIP TIP
TIP
TIP
TIP
TIP
TIP TIP
TIP TIP
BUMBL...
BUMBL
BUMBL
MIYA
SNAP

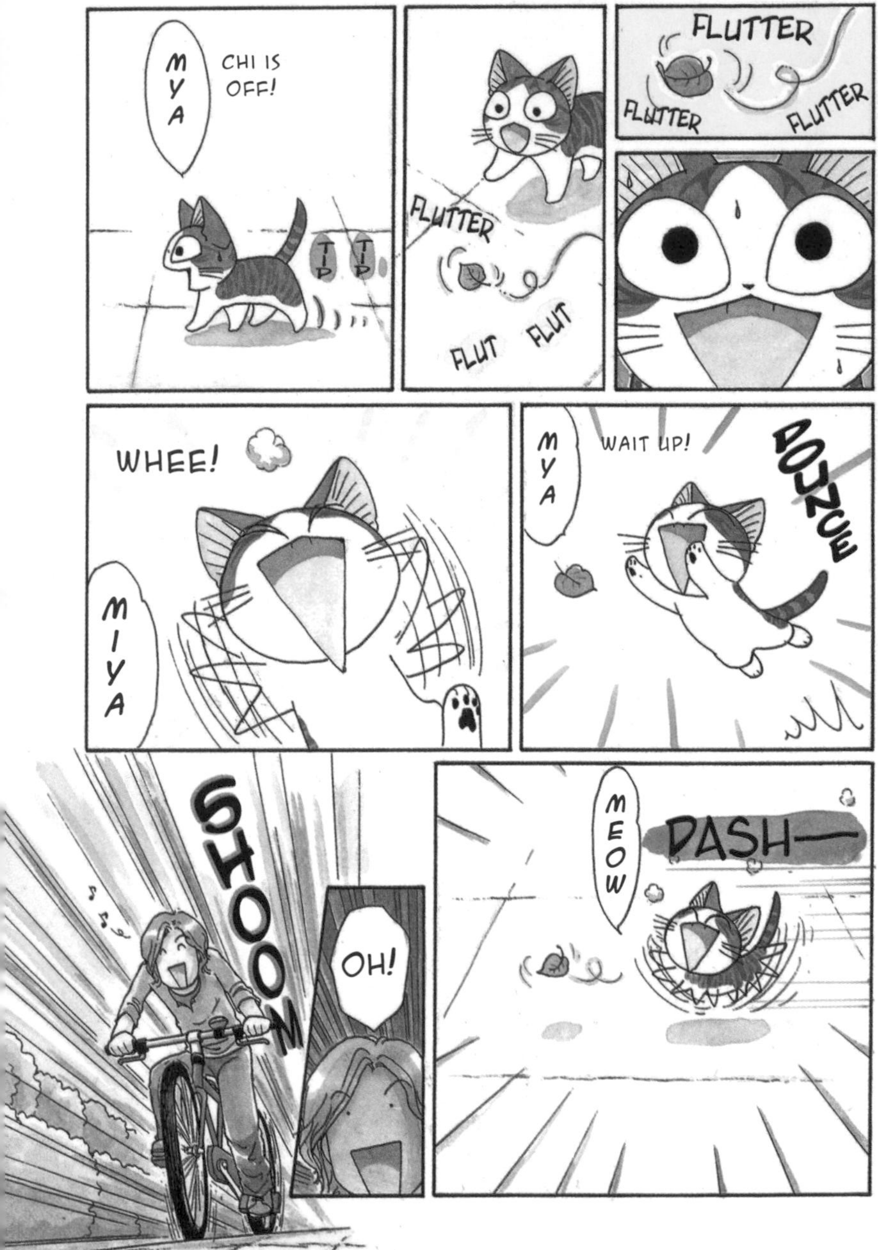
MYA
CHI IS OFF!
TIP TIP
FLUTTER
FLUT FLUT
FLUTTER
FLUTTER FLUTTER
WHEE!
MIYA
MYA
WAIT UP!
BOUNCE
SHOOM
OH!
MEOW
DASH—

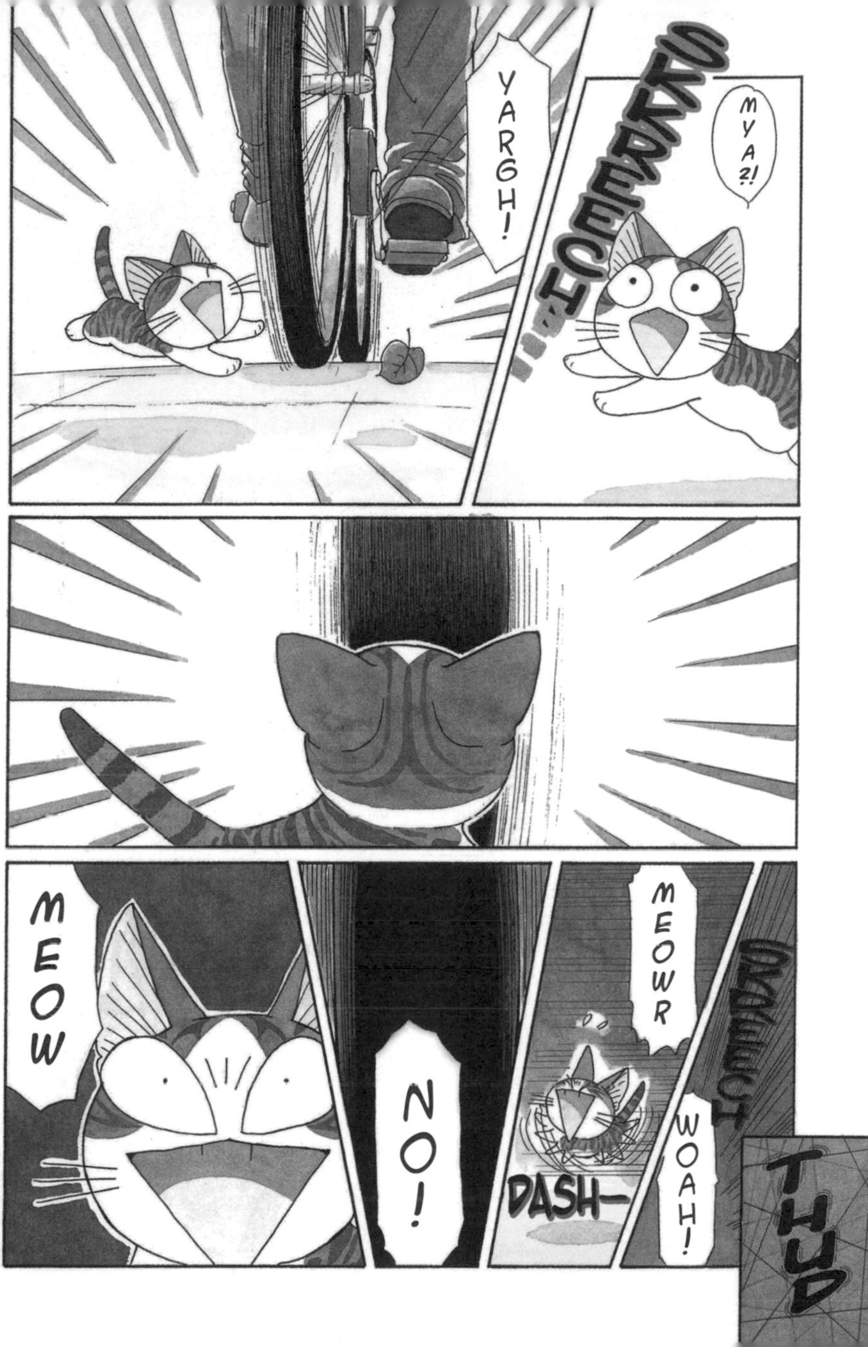

MYA?!
SKREECH
YARGH!
SKREEECH
THUD
MEOWR
WOAH!
DASH—
NO!
MEOW

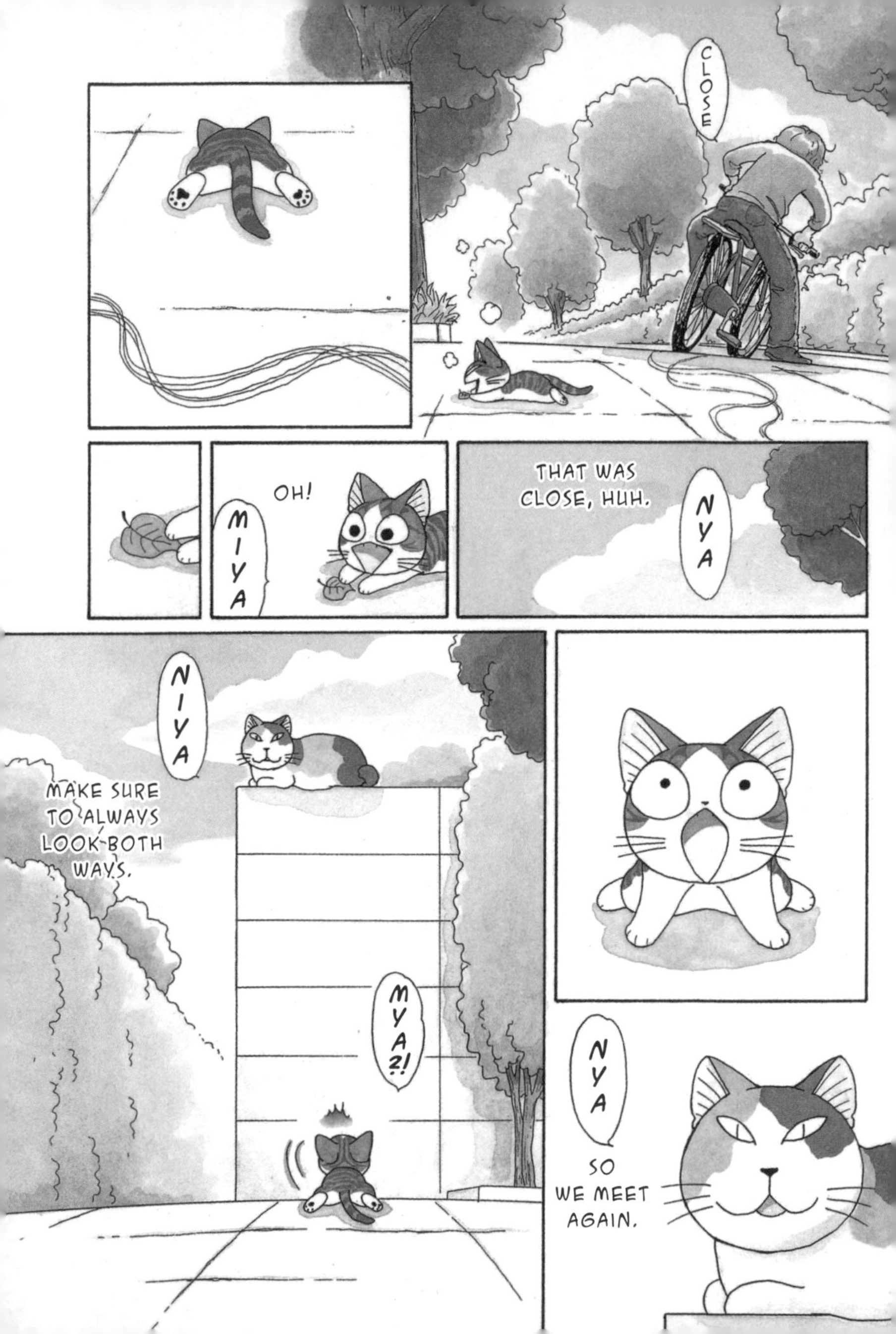
CLOSE
OH!
MIYA
NYA
THAT WAS CLOSE, HUH.
NIYA
MAKE SURE TO ALWAYS LOOK BOTH WAYS.
MYA?!
NYA
SO WE MEET AGAIN.

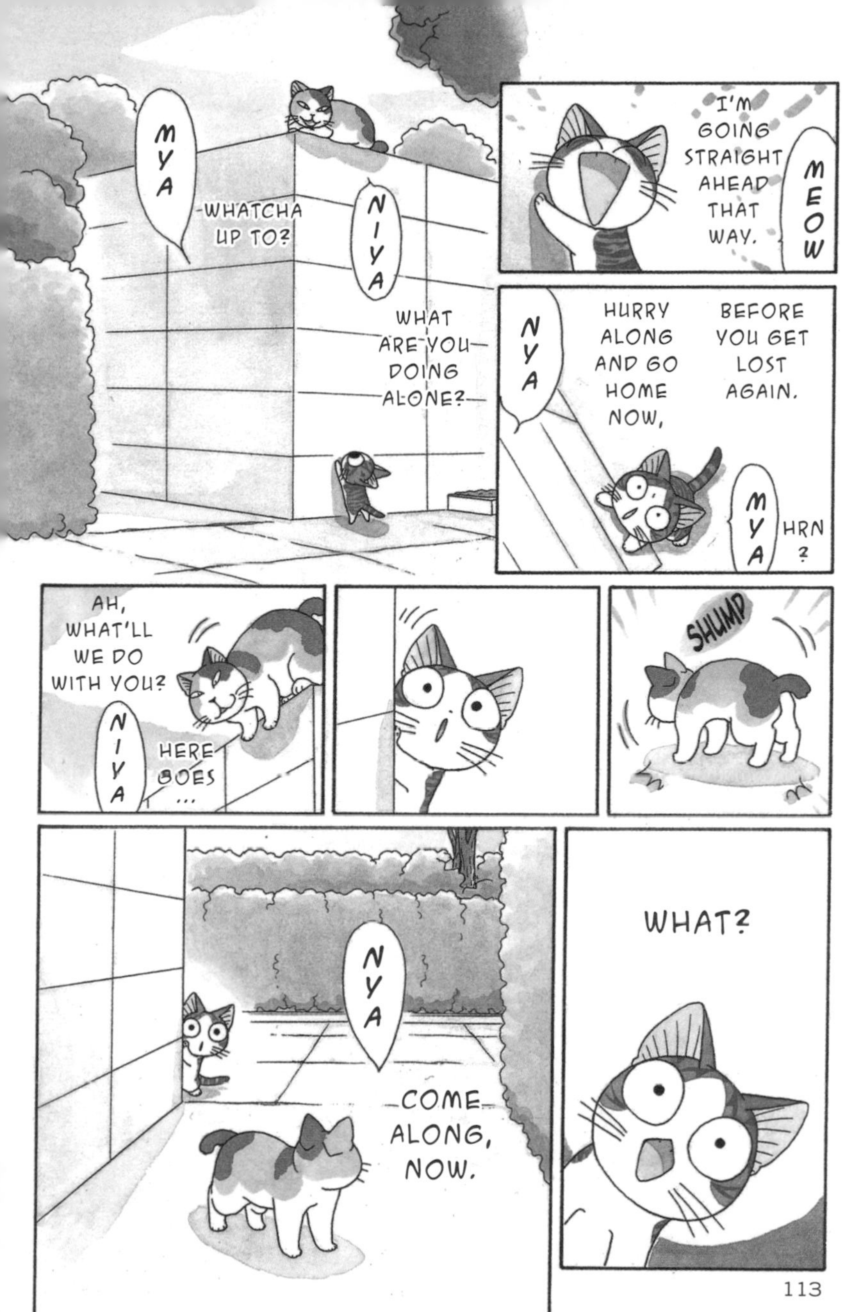
MYA
WHATCHA UP TO?
NIYA
WHAT ARE YOU DOING ALONE?
I'M GOING STRAIGHT AHEAD THAT WAY.
MEOW
NYA
HURRY ALONG AND GO HOME NOW,
BEFORE YOU GET LOST AGAIN.
MYA
HRN?
AH, WHAT'LL WE DO WITH YOU?
NIYA
HERE GOES...
SHUMP
NYA
COME ALONG, NOW.
WHAT?

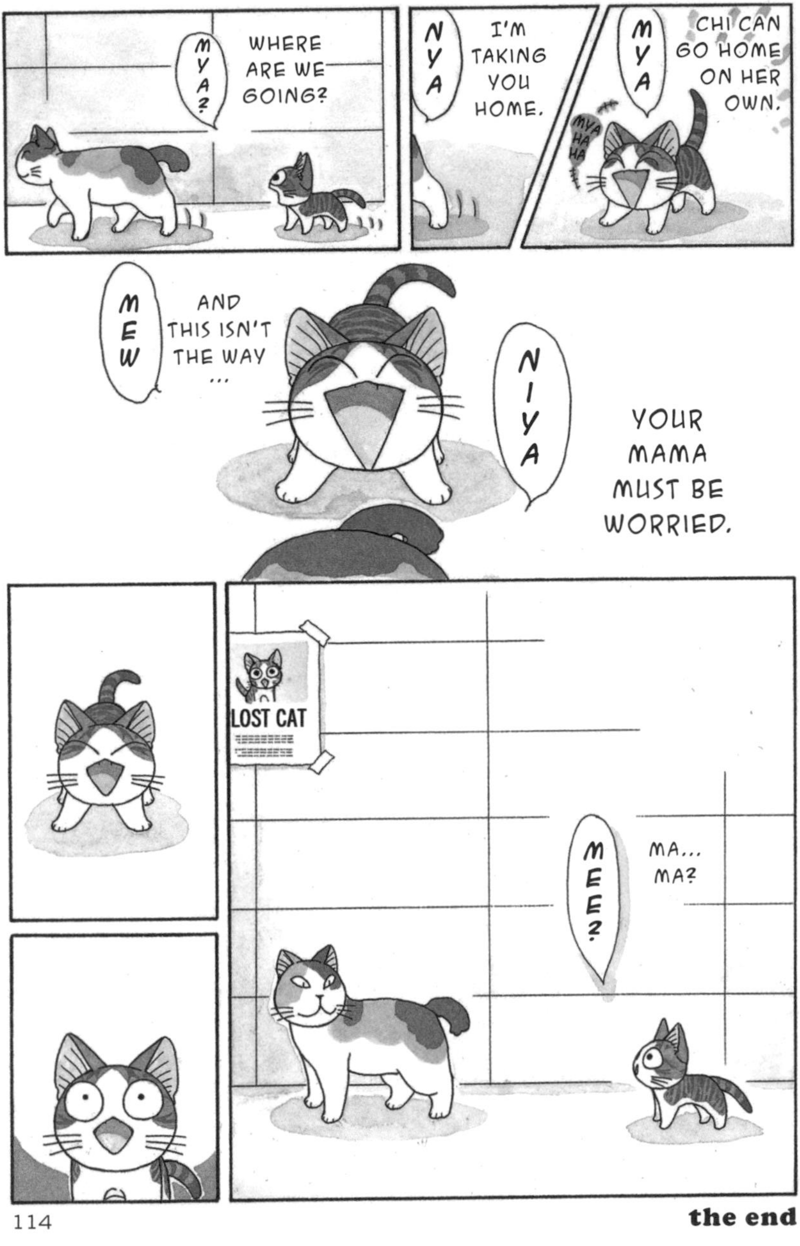
MYA?
WHERE ARE WE GOING?
NYA
I'M TAKING YOU HOME.
MYA
MYA HA HA
CHI CAN GO HOME ON HER OWN.
MEW
AND THIS ISN'T THE WAY ...
NIYA
YOUR MAMA MUST BE WORRIED.
LOST CAT
MEE?
MA... MA?

the end

homemade 89: a cat visits

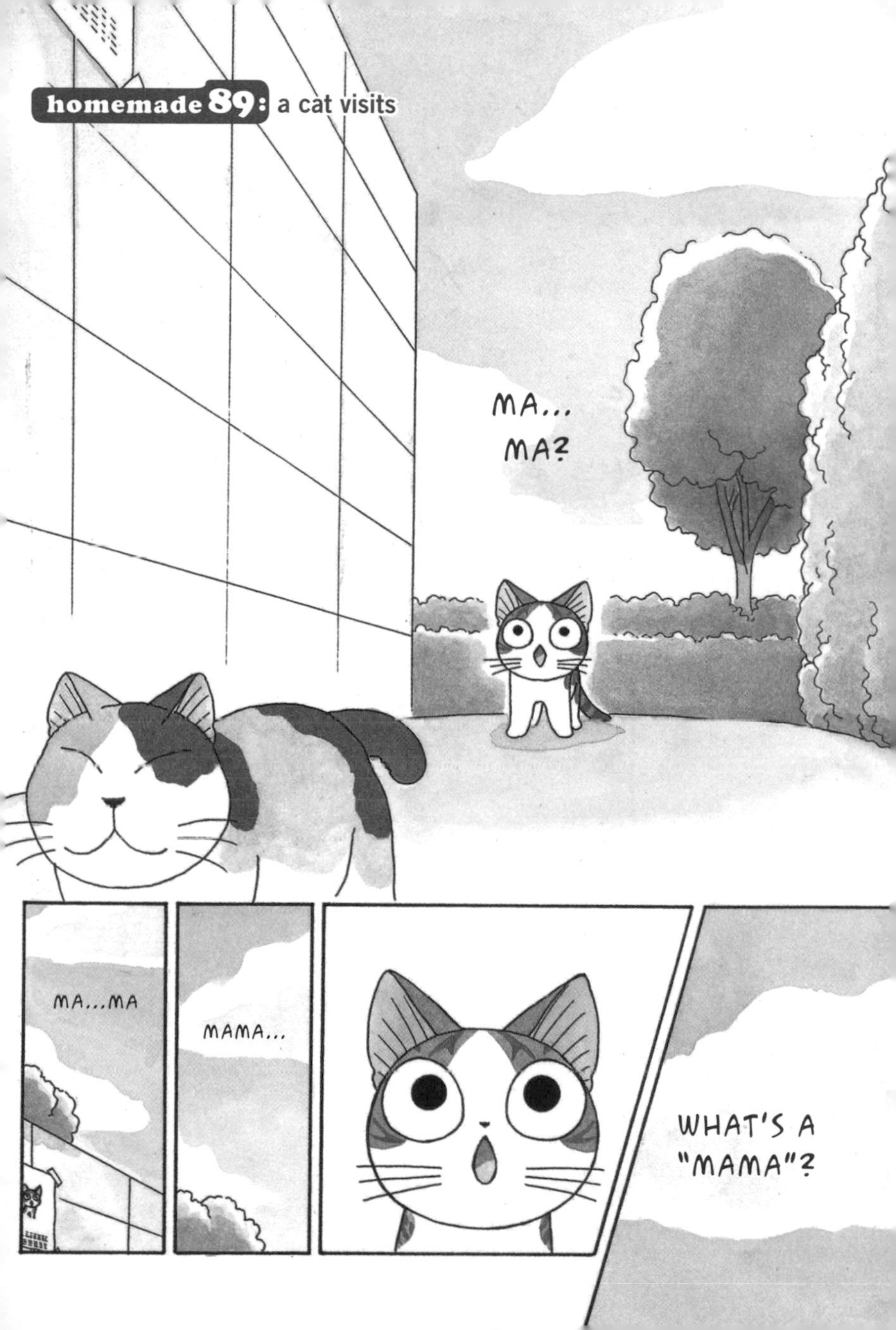
MA...
MA?
MA...MA
MAMA...
WHAT'S A "MAMA"?

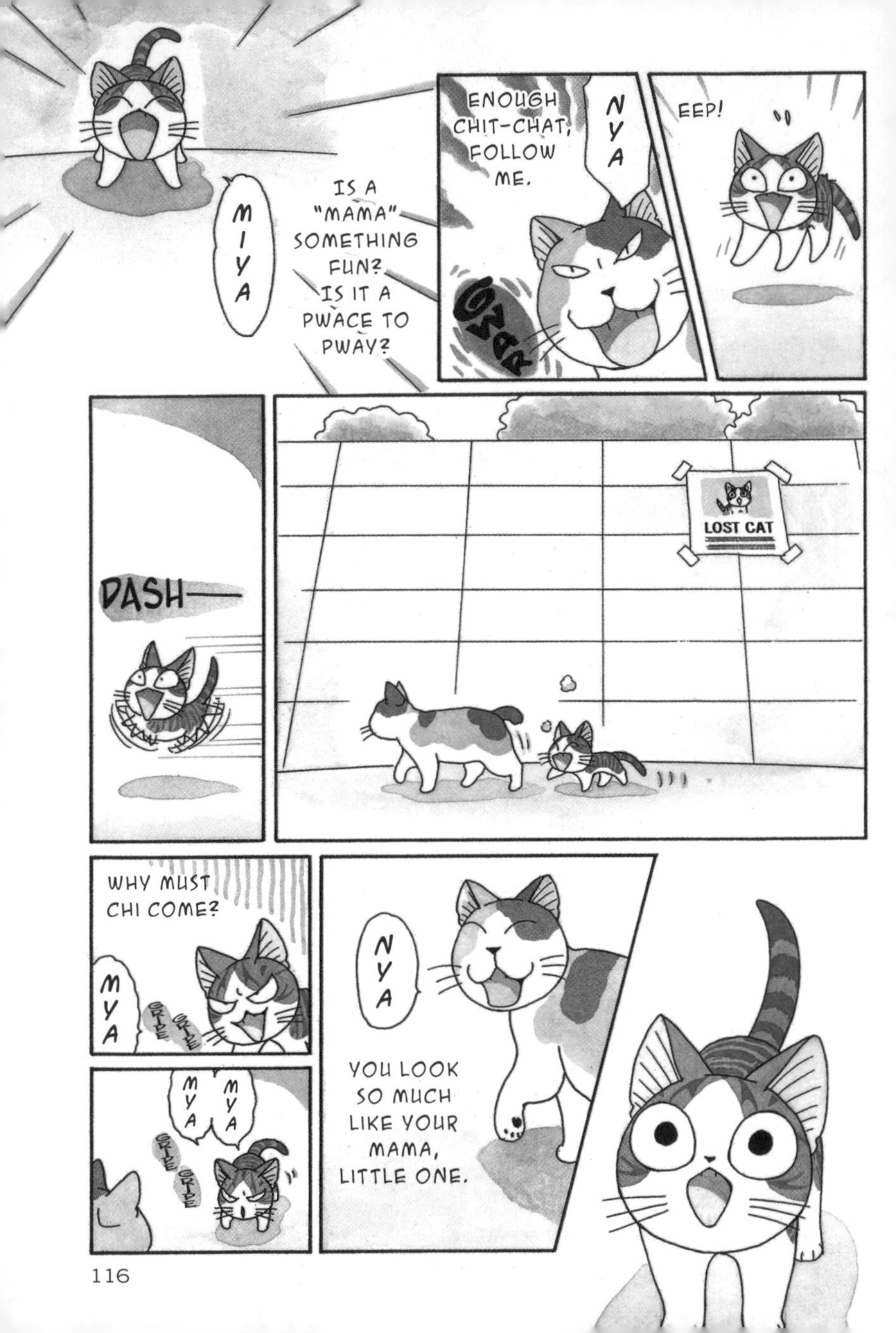
MIYA
IS A "MAMA" SOMETHING FUN? IS IT A PWACE TO PWAY?
ENOUGH CHIT-CHAT, FOLLOW ME.
NYA
GWAR
EEP!
DASH—
LOST CAT
WHY MUST CHI COME?
MYA
GRIPE GRIPE
MYA
MYA
GRIPE GRIPE
NYA
YOU LOOK SO MUCH LIKE YOUR MAMA, LITTLE ONE.

THIS "MAMA" LOOKS LIKE CHI?

MEOW?

NYA

YES

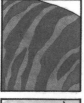

SHOOM SHOOM

POP

HEY HEY

MYA

DASH—

CAT

OF COURSE SHE'S BIG.

NIYA

MIYA

IS IT BIG? IS IT SMAWL?

117

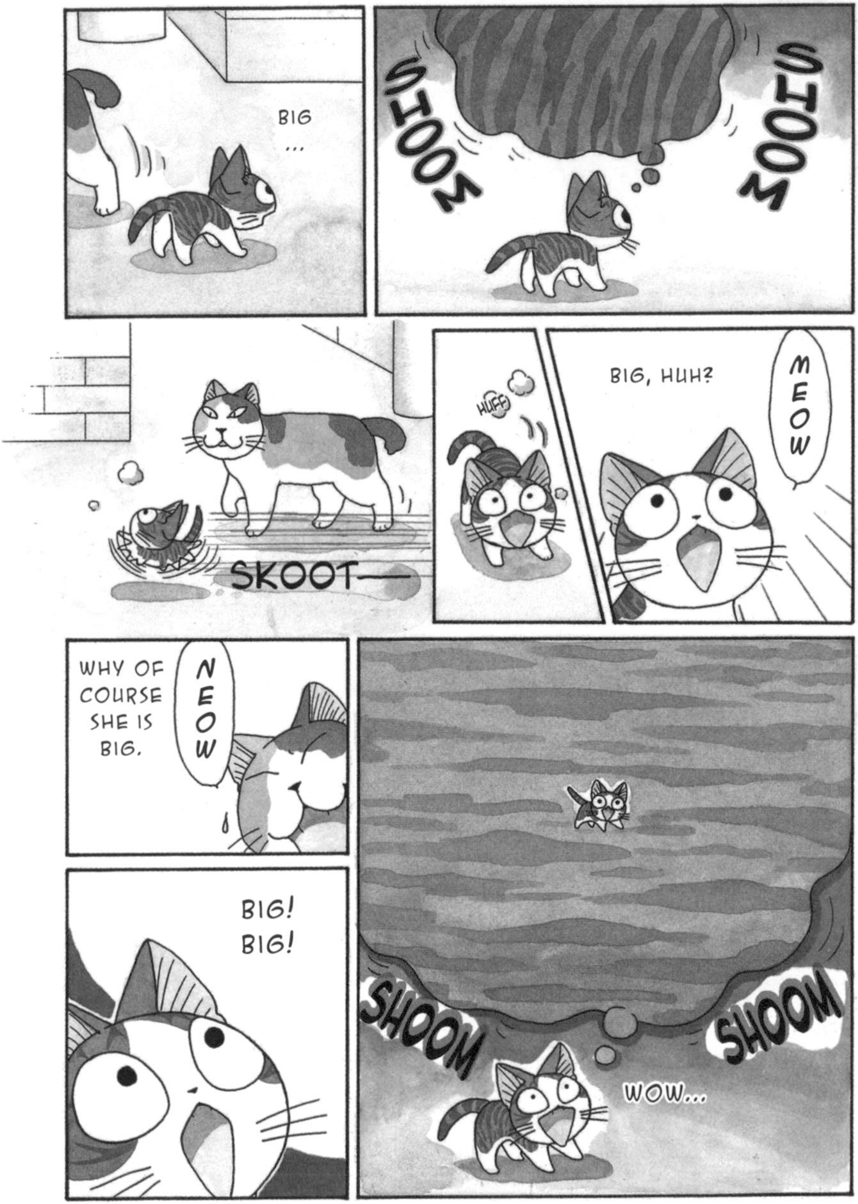
BIG ...
SHOOM
SHOOM
SKOOT—
HUFF
BIG, HUH?
MEOW
WHY OF COURSE SHE IS BIG.
NEOW
BIG! BIG!
SHOOM
SHOOM
WOW...

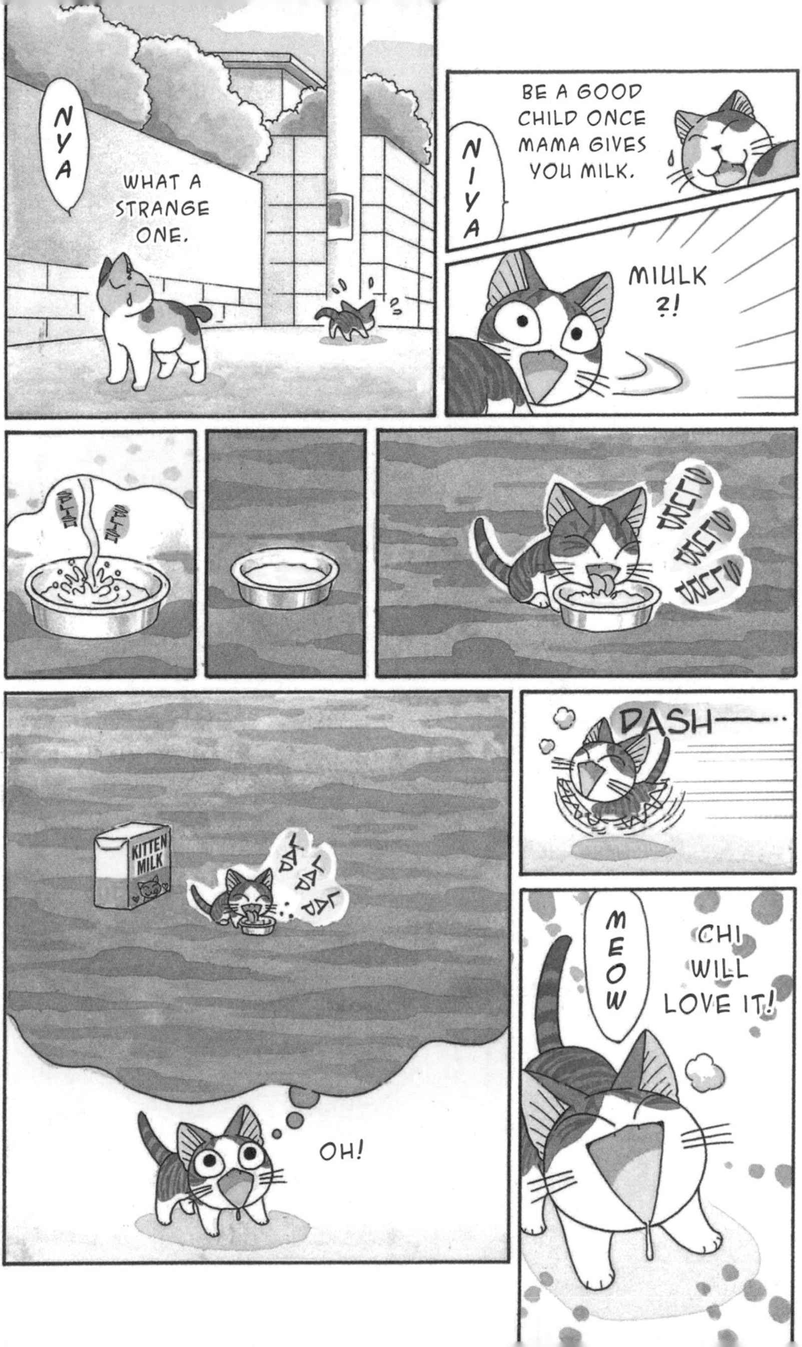
NYA
WHAT A STRANGE ONE.
NIYA
BE A GOOD CHILD ONCE MAMA GIVES YOU MILK.
MIULK ?!
SPLISH
SPLISH
SLURP
SLURP
SLURP
KITTEN MILK
LAP LAP LAP
OH!
DASH——...
MEOW
CHI WILL LOVE IT!

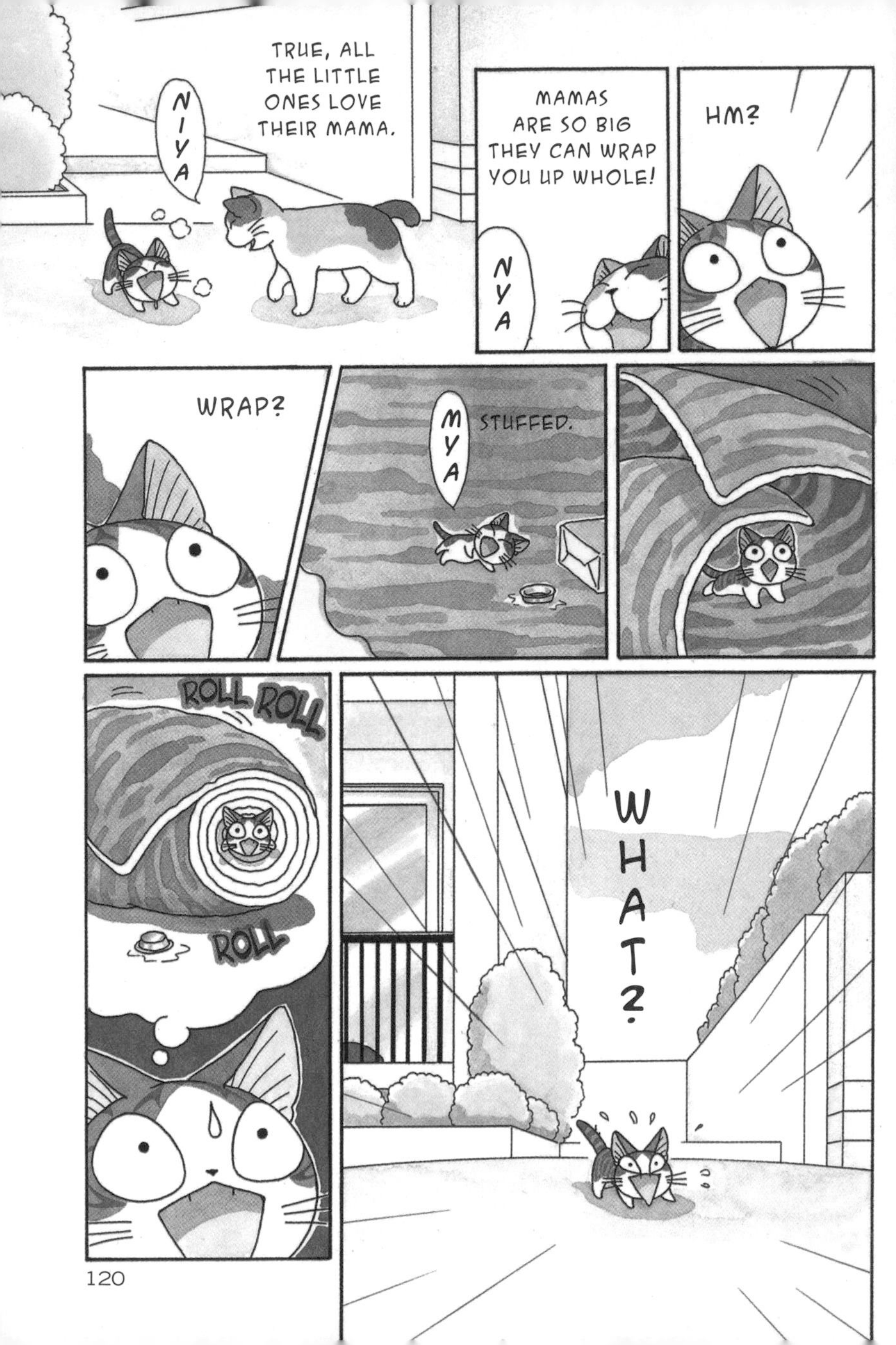
TRUE, ALL THE LITTLE ONES LOVE THEIR MAMA.
NIYA
MAMAS ARE SO BIG THEY CAN WRAP YOU UP WHOLE!
NYA
HM?
WRAP?
MYA
STUFFED.
ROLL ROLL
ROLL
WHAT?

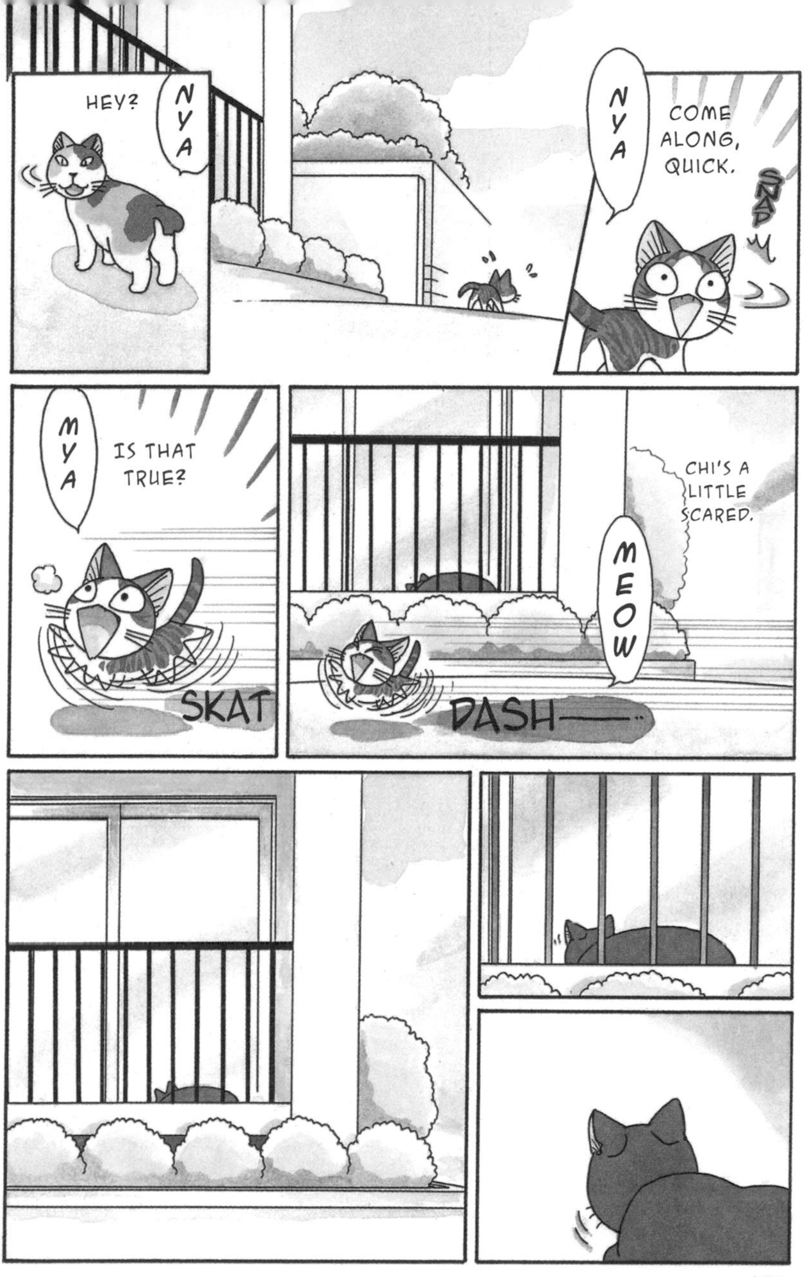
HEY?
NYA
NYA
COME ALONG, QUICK.
SNAP
MYA
IS THAT TRUE?
SKAT
CHI'S A LITTLE SCARED.
MEOW
DASH

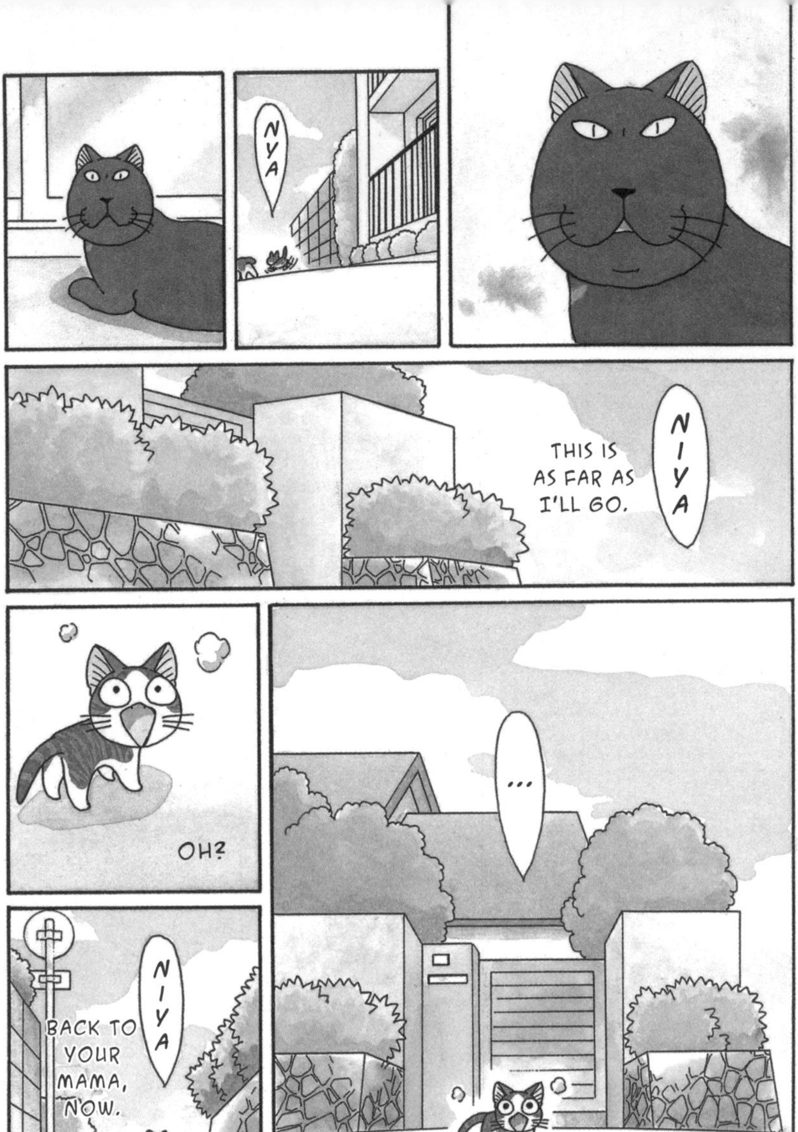
NYA
NIYA
THIS IS AS FAR AS I'LL GO.
OH?
NIYA
BACK TO YOUR MAMA, NOW.
...
the end

homemade 90: a cat is reacquainted

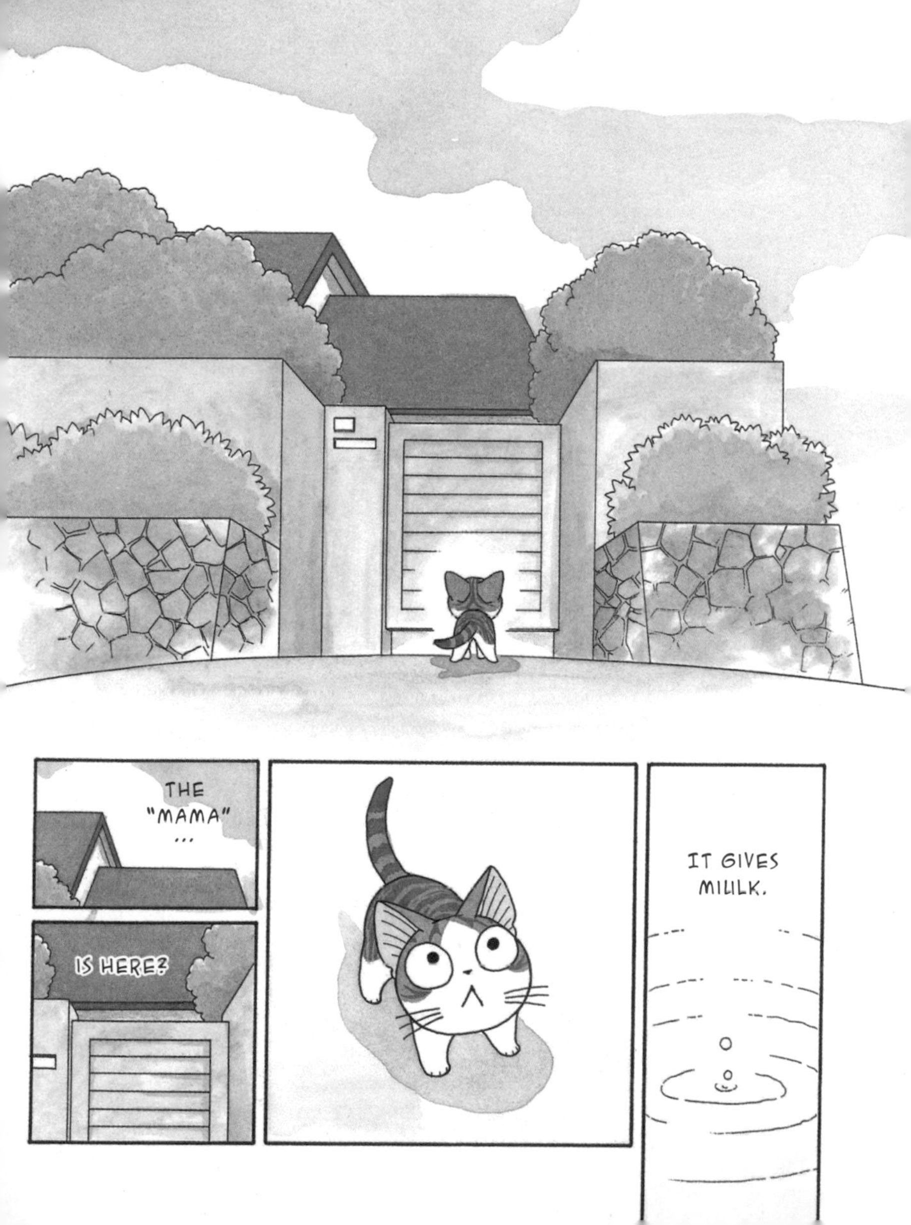
THE "MAMA" ...
IS HERE?
IT GIVES MILILK.

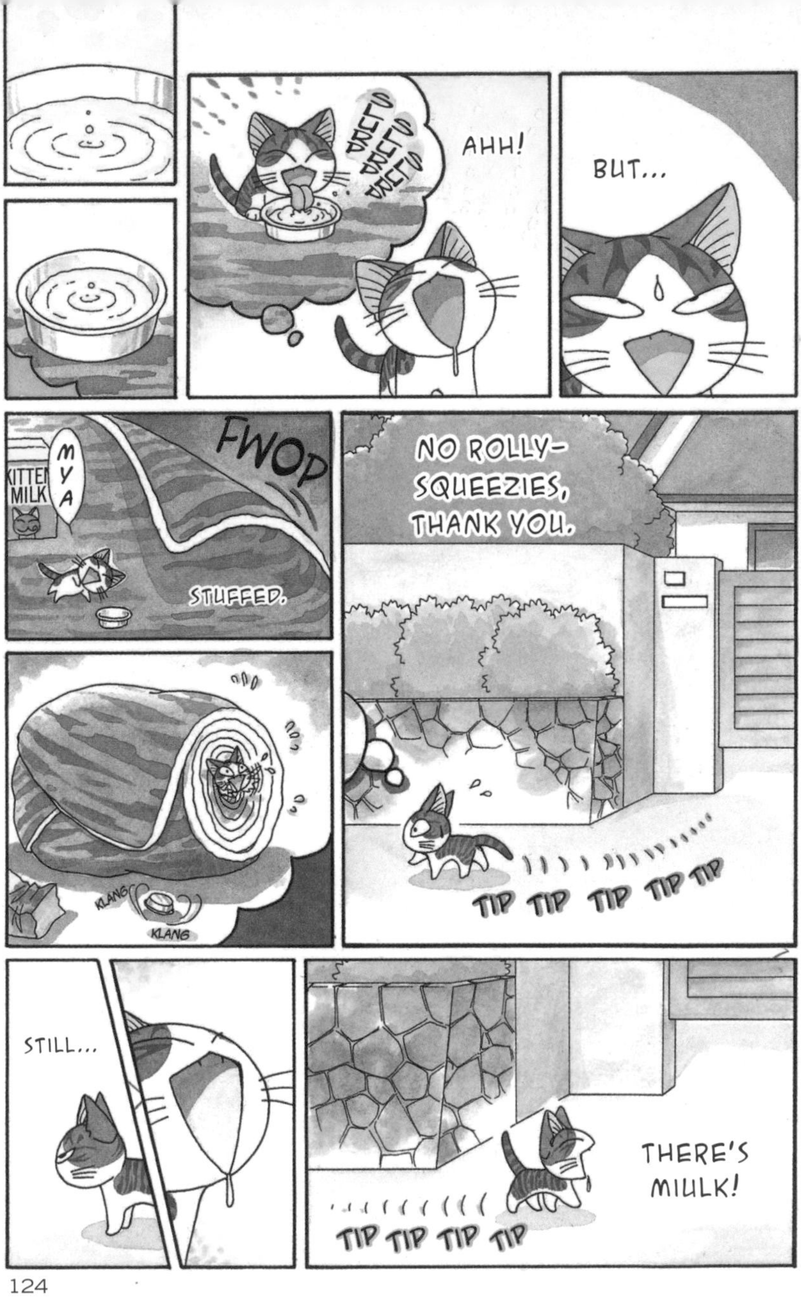
SLURP SLURRP SLURRRP
AHH!
BUT...
MYA
KITTEN MILK
FWOP
STUFFED.
NO ROLLY-SQUEEZIES, THANK YOU.
KLANG
KLANG
TIP TIP TIP TIP TIP
STILL...
THERE'S MIULK!
TIP TIP TIP TIP

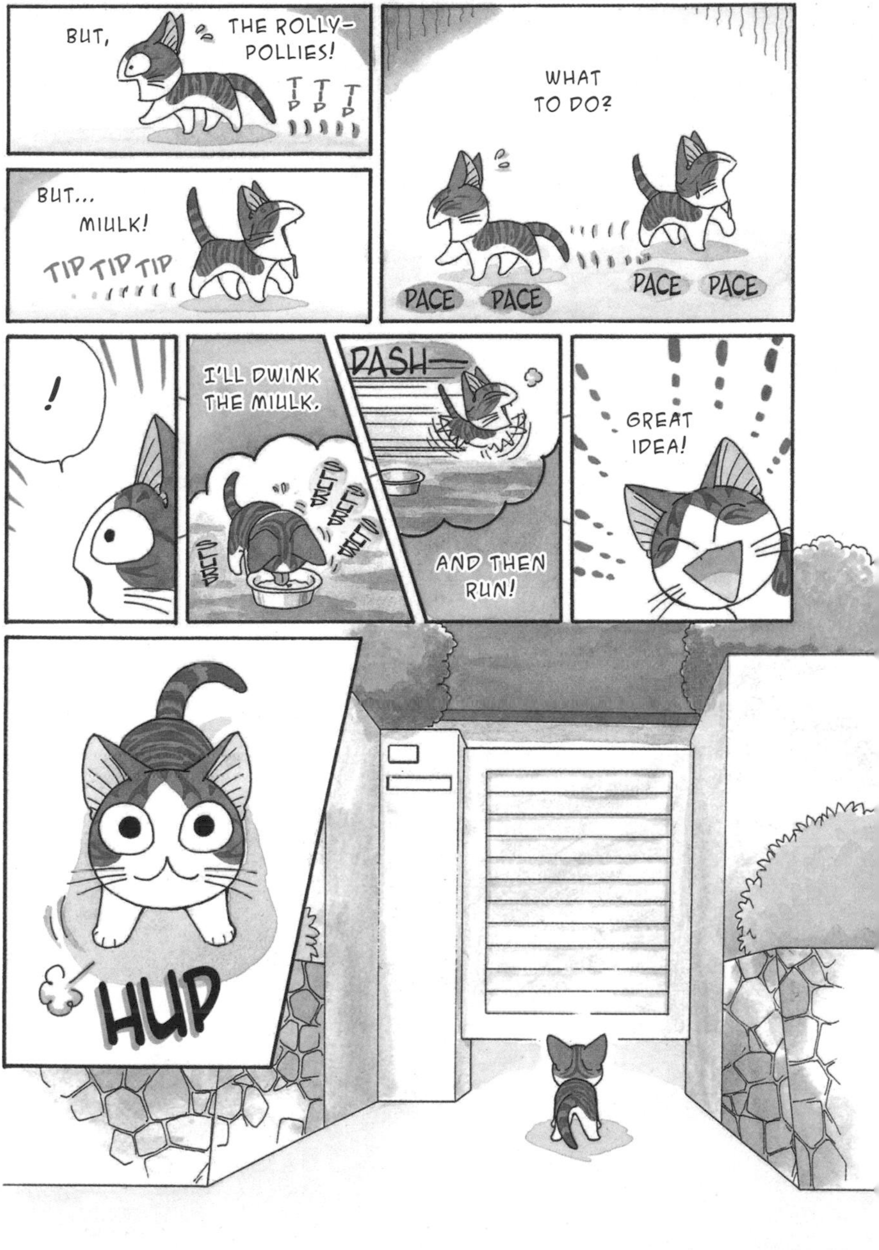
BUT,
THE ROLLY-POLLIES!
TIP TIP TIP
WHAT TO DO?
PACE PACE
PACE PACE
BUT... MIULK!
TIP TIP TIP
!
I'LL DWINK THE MIULK.
SLURP SLURP SLURP SLURP
DASH—
AND THEN RUN!
GREAT IDEA!
HUP

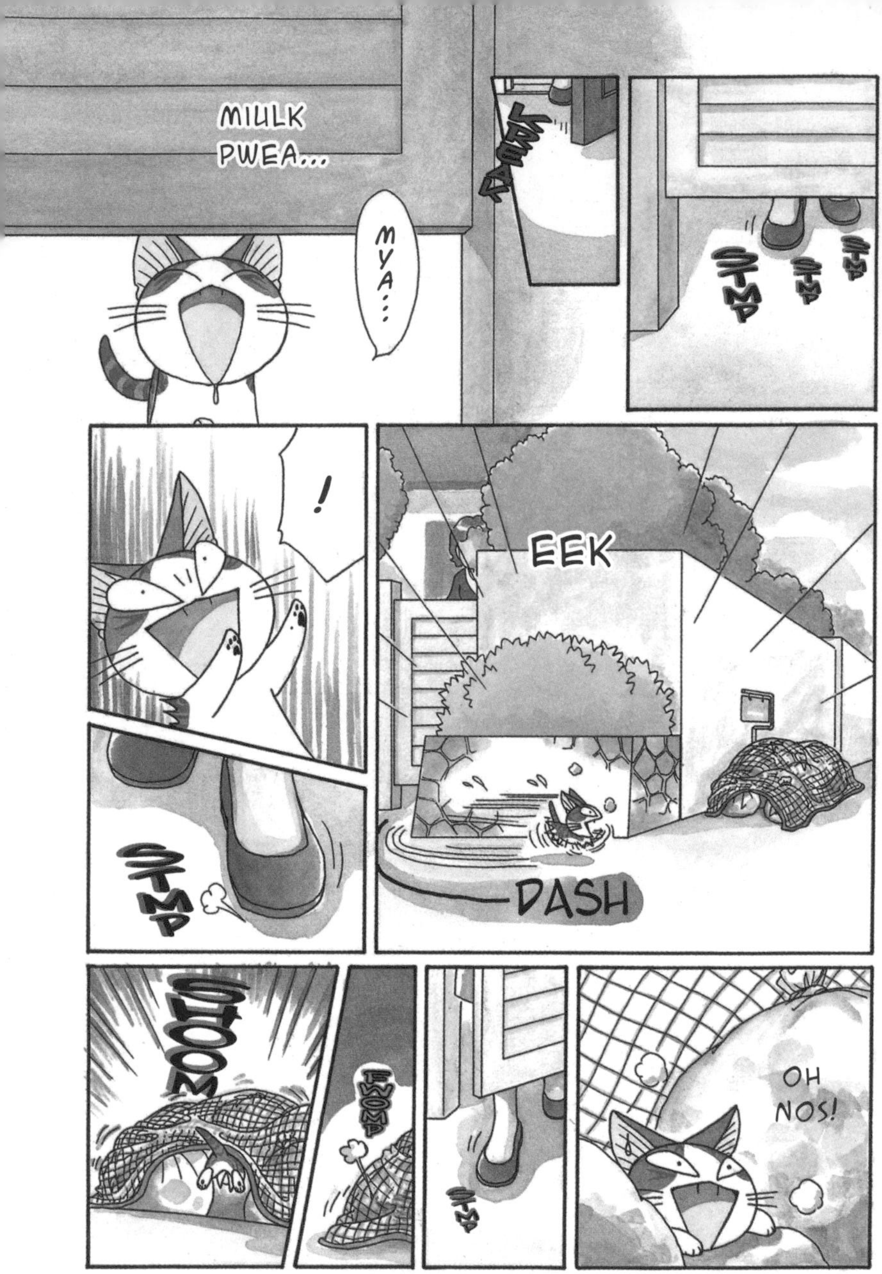
MIULK PWEA...
MYA...
KREAK
STMP
STMP
STMP
!
STMP
EEK
DASH
SHOOOM
FWOMP
STMP
OH NOS!

THE "MAMA" HAS LEGS!!
STMP
STMP
ST
BETTER RUN!
FOOM
FOOM
HEY?!
SWIP
SWIP
SWIP
SWIP
SWIP
SWIP
SWIP
SWIP
SWIP
SWIP
HUFF
HUFF

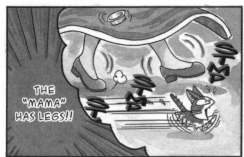

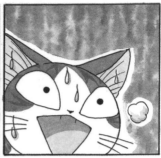

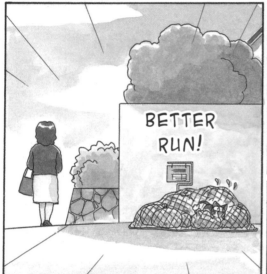

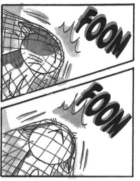

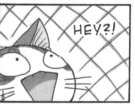

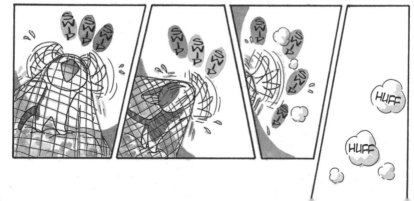

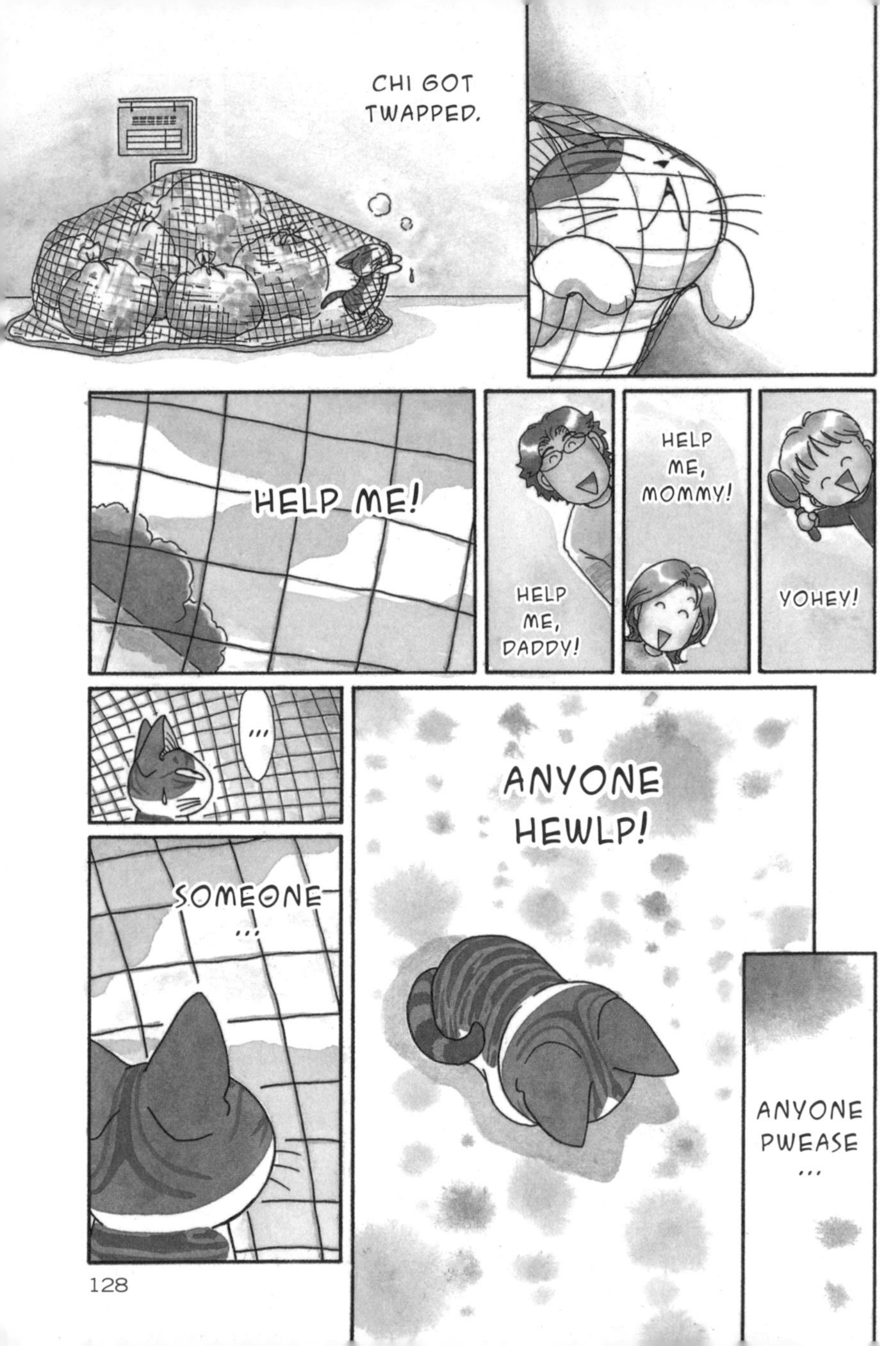
CHI GOT TWAPPED.
HELP ME!
HELP ME, DADDY!
HELP ME, MOMMY!
YOHEY!
...
SOMEONE ...
ANYONE HEWLP!
ANYONE PWEASE ...

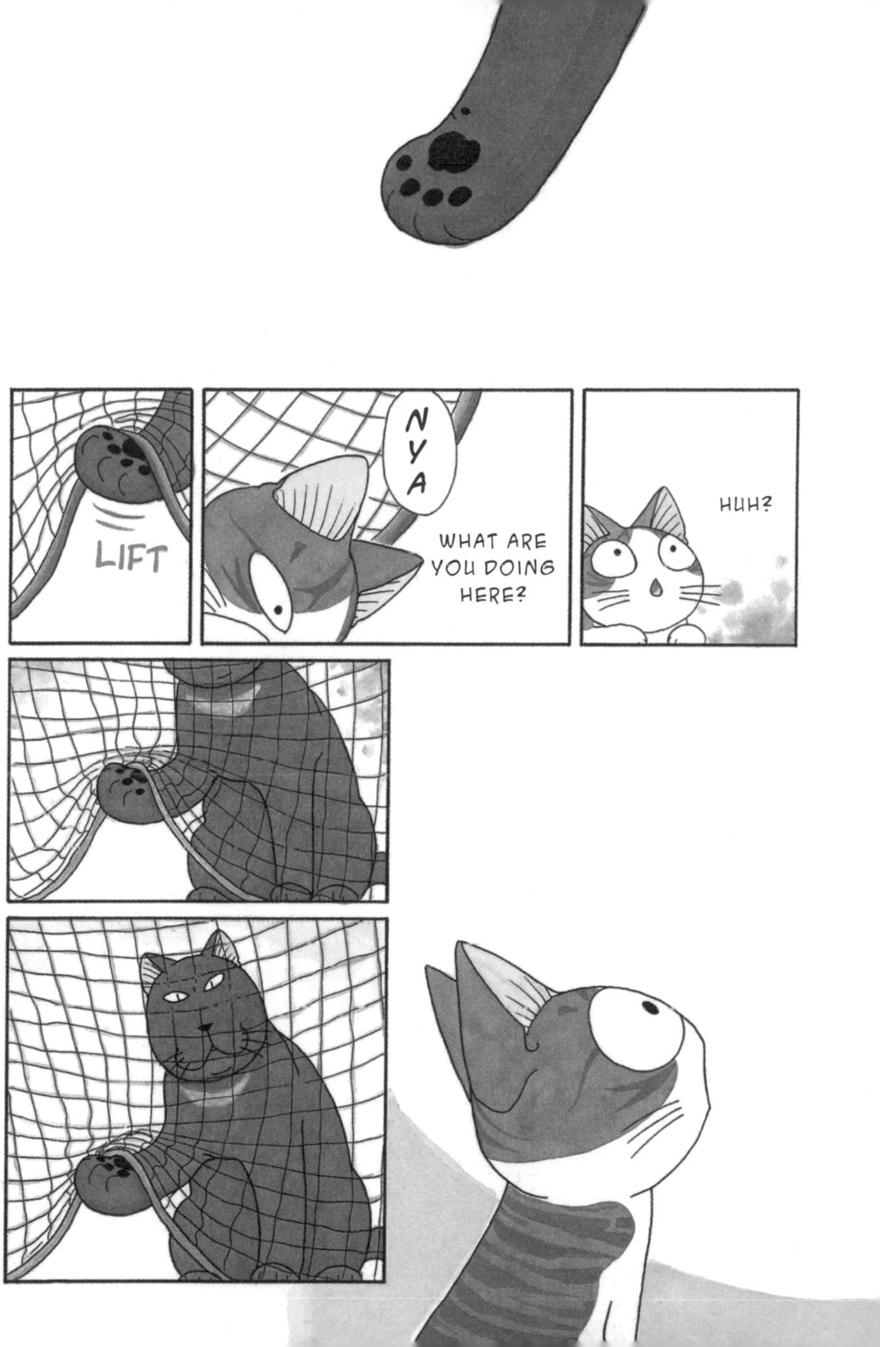

LIFT
NYA
WHAT ARE YOU DOING HERE?
HUH?

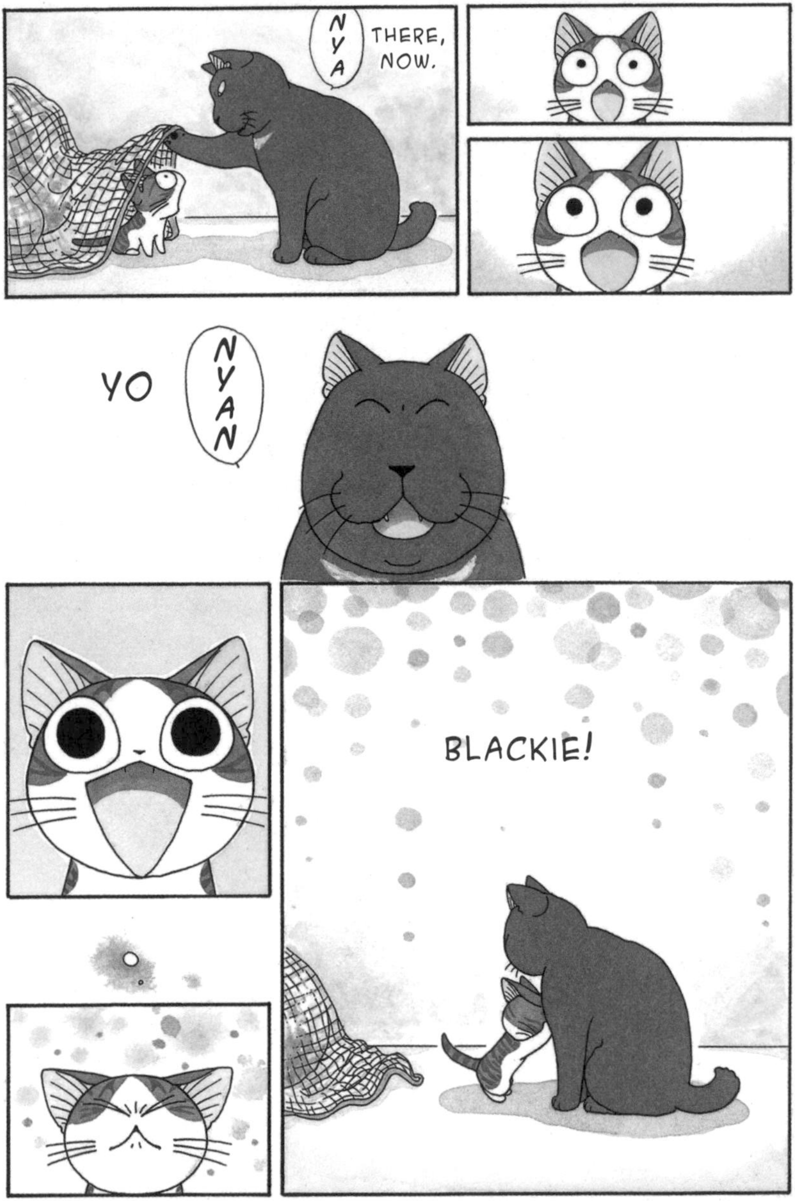
NYA
THERE, NOW.
YO
NYAN
BLACKIE!

the end

homemade 91: a cat receives milk

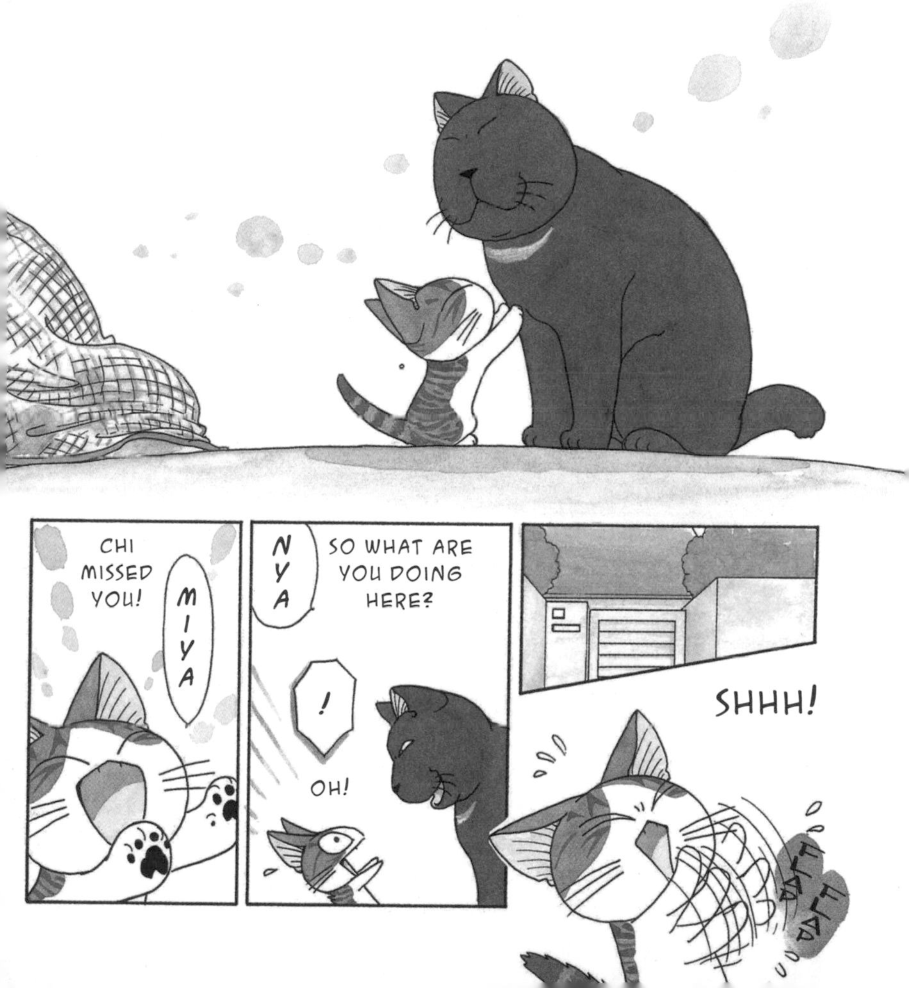
CHI MISSED YOU!
MIYA
NYA
SO WHAT ARE YOU DOING HERE?
!
OH!
SHHH!

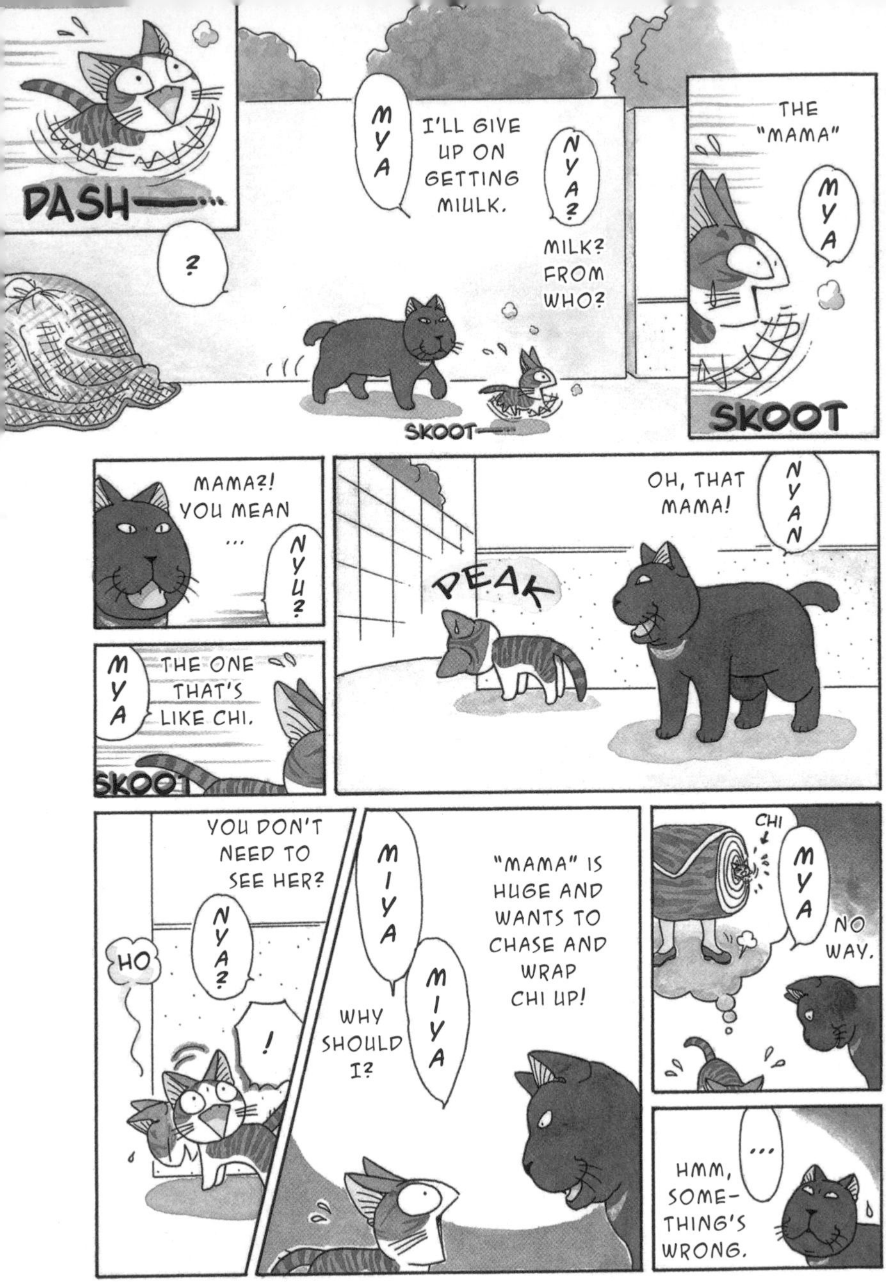
DASH—
MYA
I'LL GIVE UP ON GETTING MIULK.
NYA?
MILK? FROM WHO?
?
SKOOT—
THE "MAMA"
MYA
SKOOT
MAMA?! YOU MEAN ...
NYU?
MYA
THE ONE THAT'S LIKE CHI.
SKOOT
PEAK
OH, THAT MAMA!
NYAN
YOU DON'T NEED TO SEE HER?
NYA?
HO
!
MIYA
"MAMA" IS HUGE AND WANTS TO CHASE AND WRAP CHI UP!
MIYA
WHY SHOULD I?
CHI
MYA
NO WAY.
...
HMM, SOME-THING'S WRONG.

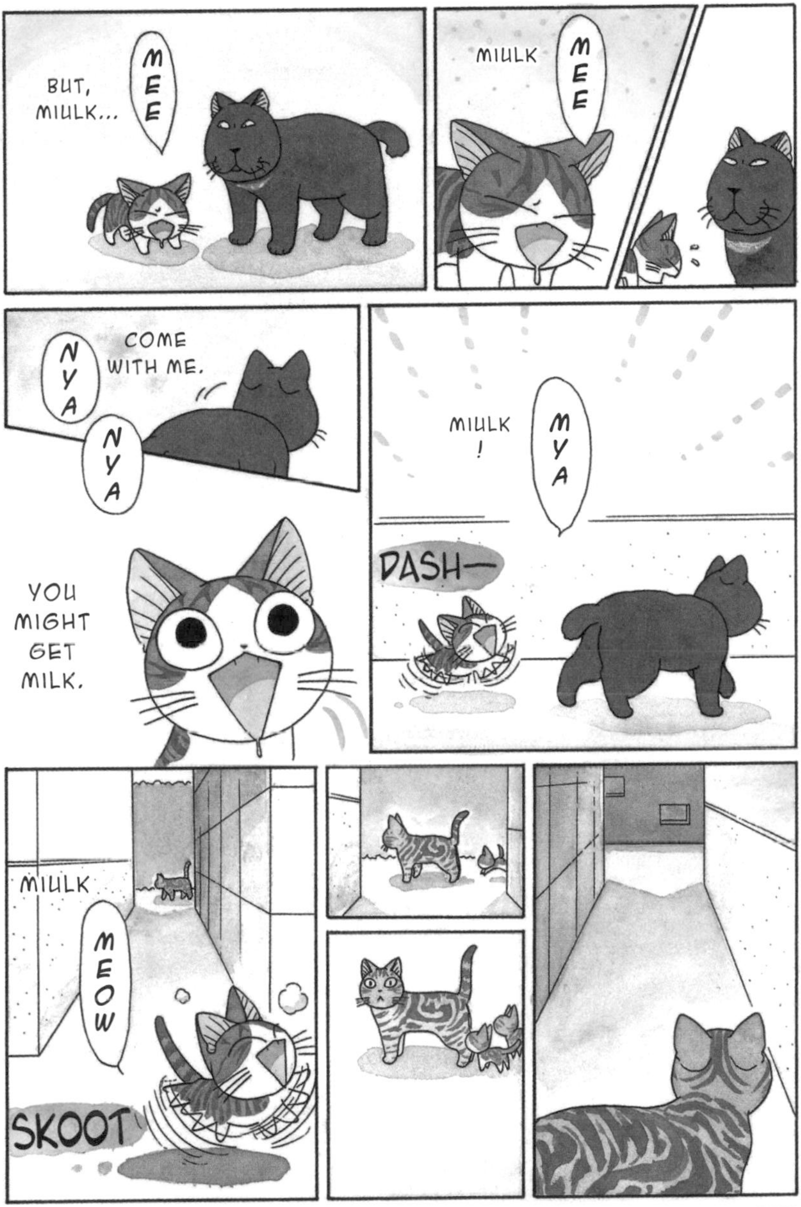
BUT, MIULK...
MEE
MIULK
MEE
NYA
COME WITH ME.
NYA
YOU MIGHT GET MILK.
MIULK !
MYA
DASH—
MIULK
MEOW
SKOOT

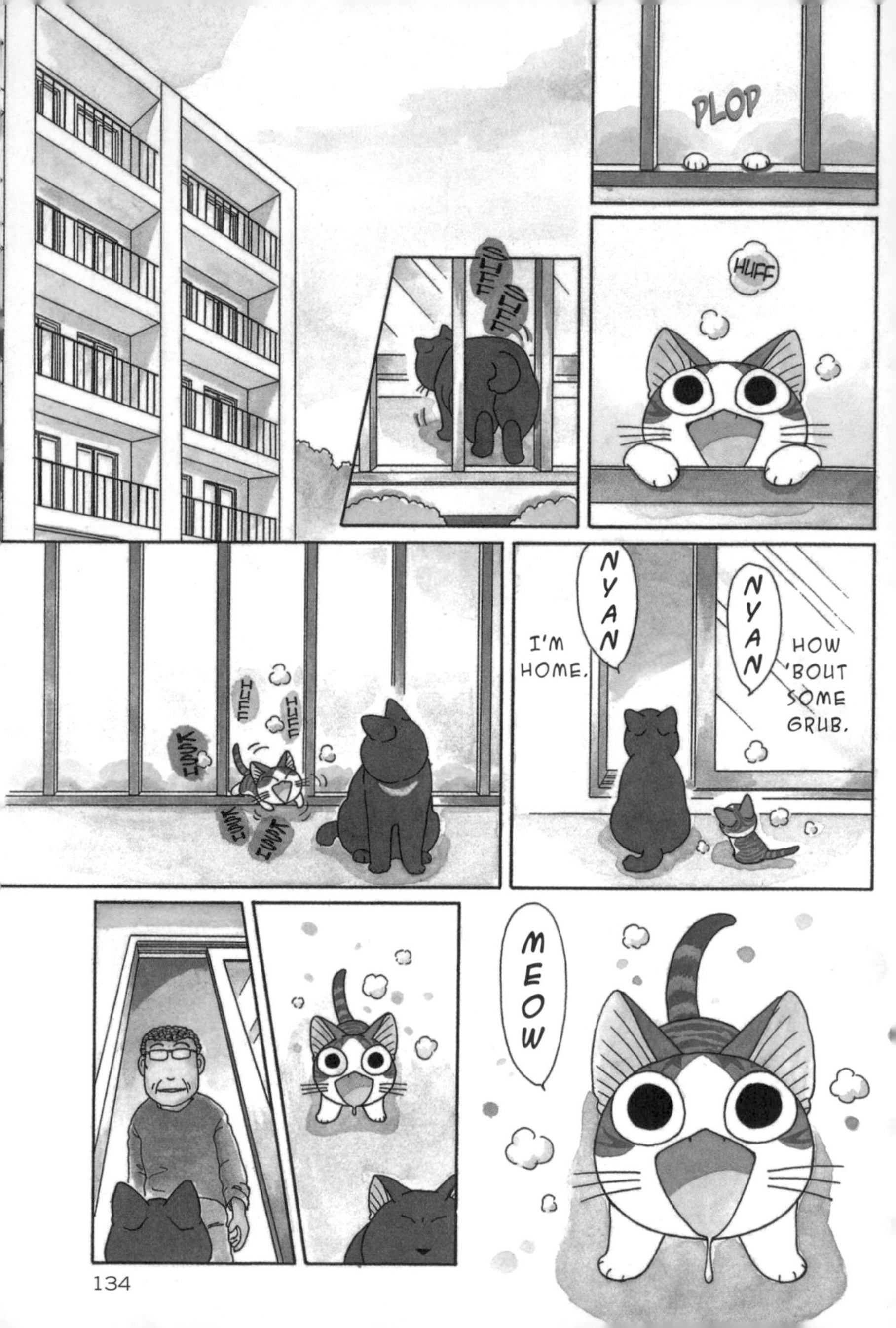
SHUFF
SHUFF
PLOP
HUFF
HUFF
HUFF
THUMP
THUMP
THUMP
NYAN
I'M HOME.
NYAN
HOW 'BOUT SOME GRUB.
MEOW

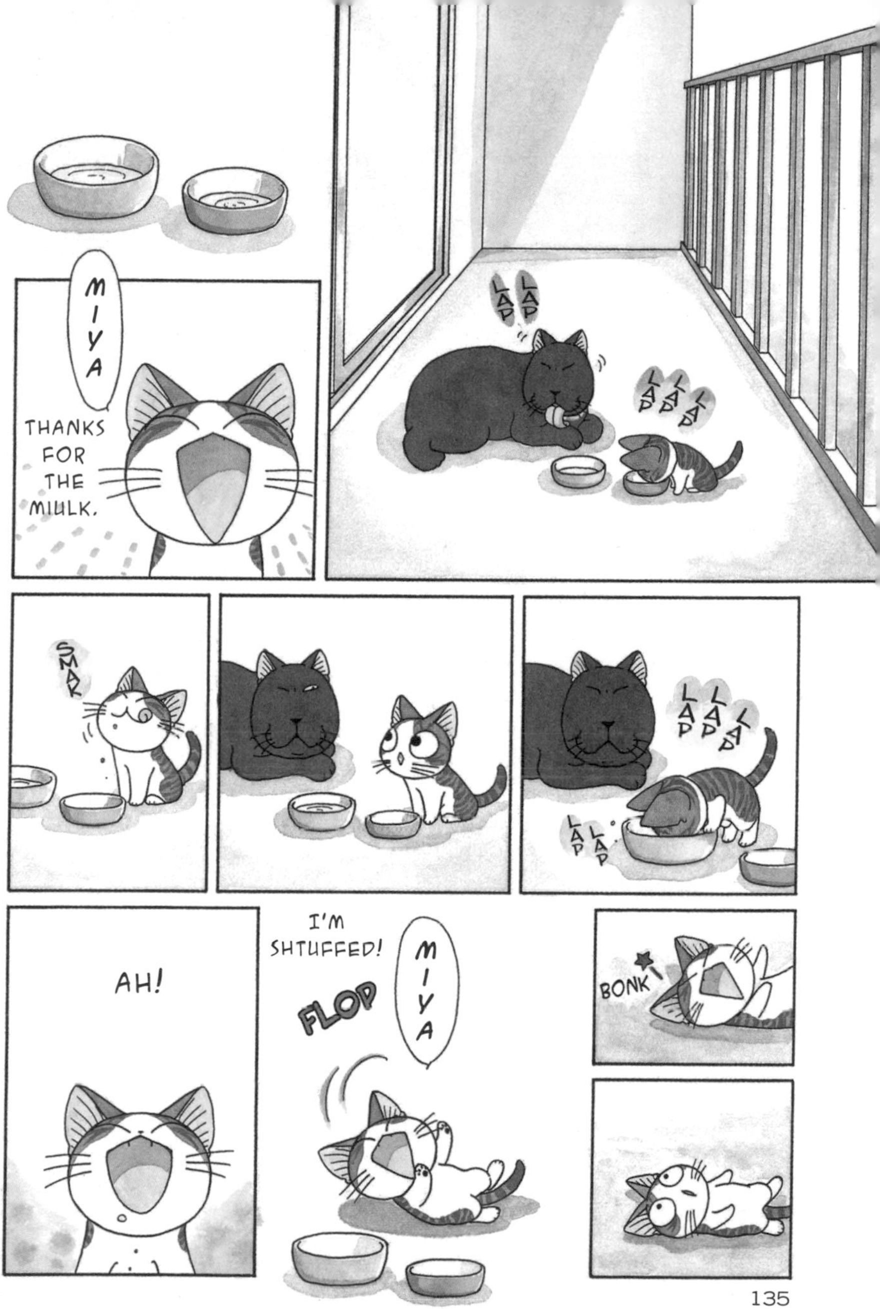
MIYA
THANKS FOR THE MIULK.
LAP LAP
LAP LAP LAP
SMAK
LAP LAP LAP
LAP LAP
AH!
I'M SHTUFFED!
FLOP
MIYA
BONK

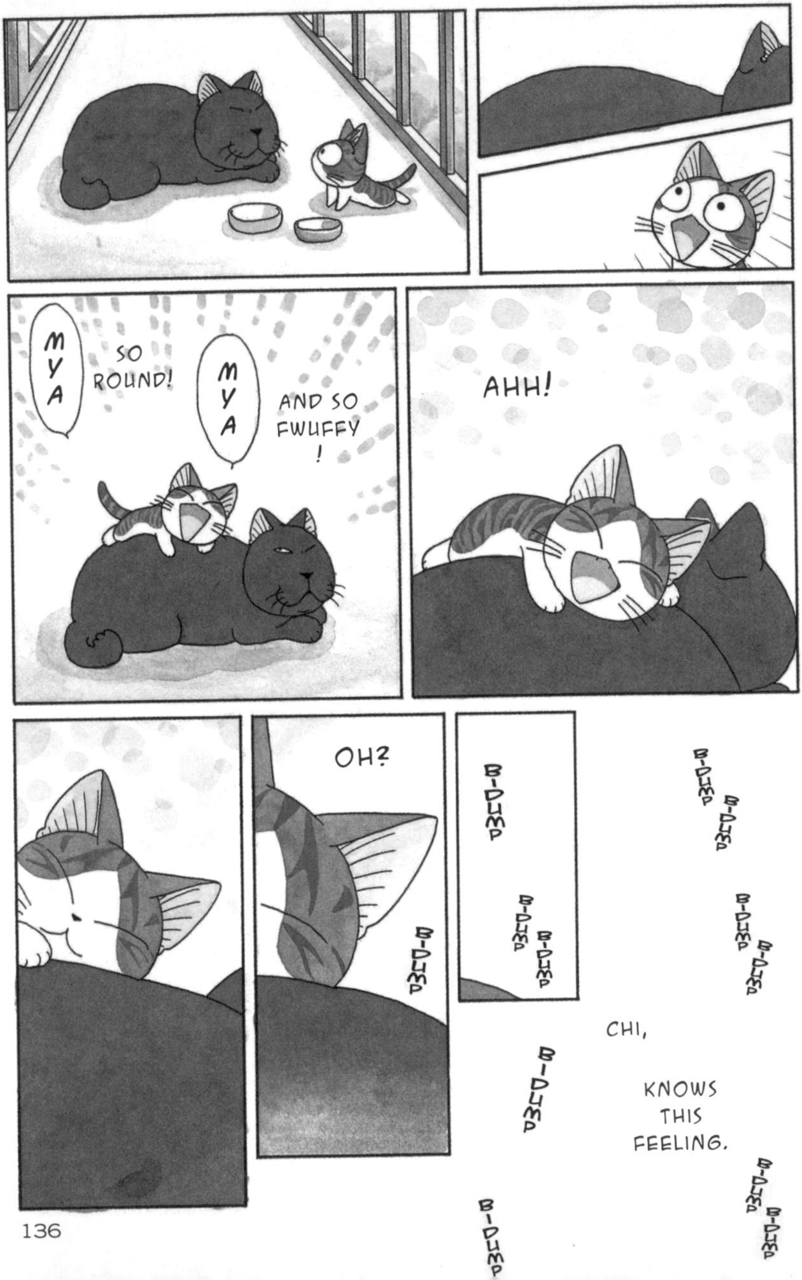
MYA
SO ROUND!
MYA
AND SO FWUFFY!
AHH!
BI-DUMP
OH?
BI-DUMP
BI-DUMP
BI-DUMP
BI-DUMP
BI-DUMP
BI-DUMP
BI-DUMP
CHI,
BI-DUMP
KNOWS THIS FEELING.
BI-DUMP
BI-DUMP
BI-DUMP

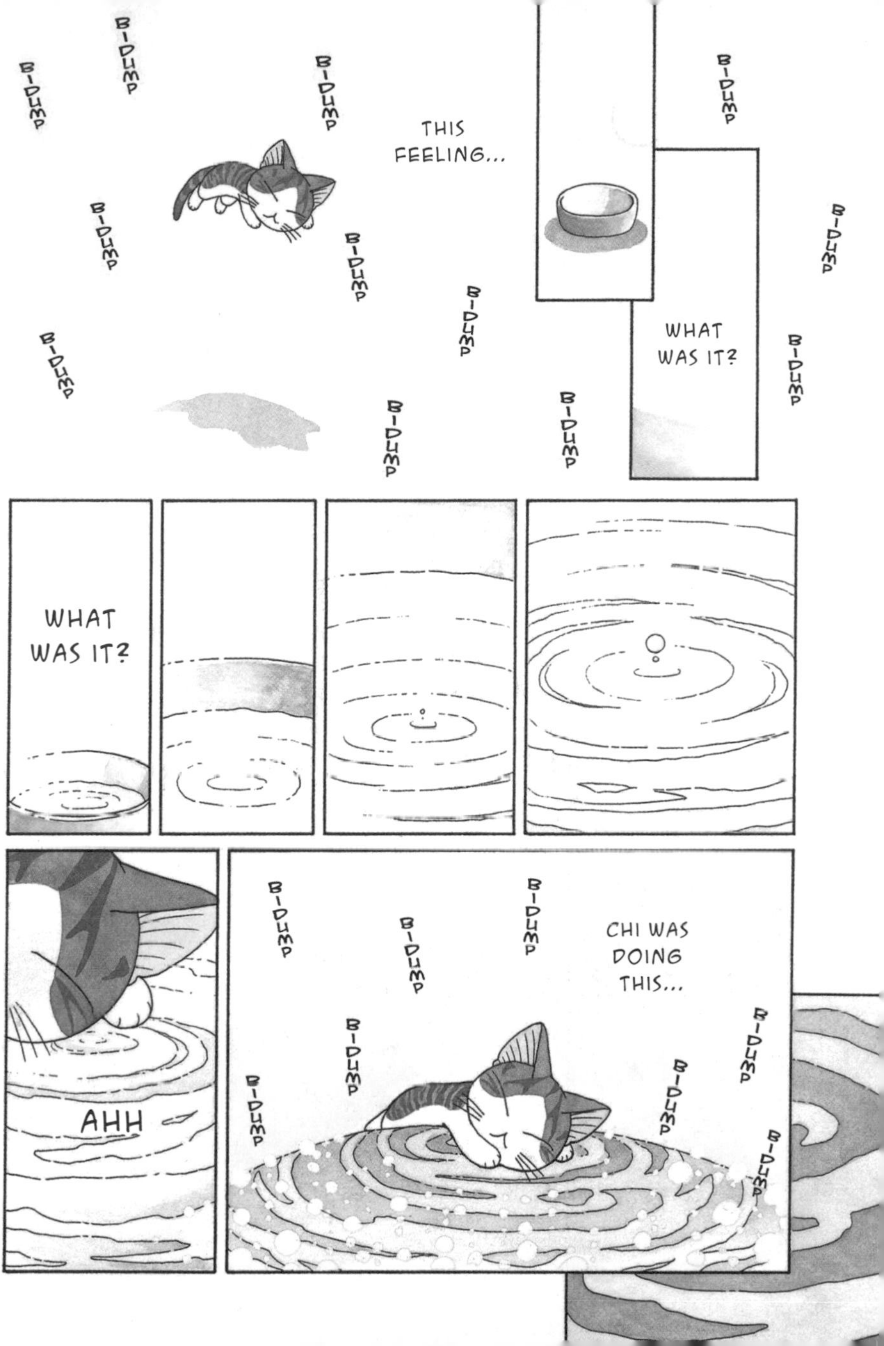
BI-DUMP
BI-DUMP
BI-DUMP
BI-DUMP
BI-DUMP
BI-DUMP
BI-DUMP
BI-DUMP
THIS FEELING...
BI-DUMP
BI-DUMP
WHAT WAS IT?
BI-DUMP
BI-DUMP
WHAT WAS IT?
AHH
BI-DUMP
BI-DUMP
BI-DUMP
BI-DUMP
BI-DUMP
CHI WAS DOING THIS...
BI-DUMP
BI-DUMP
BI-DUMP

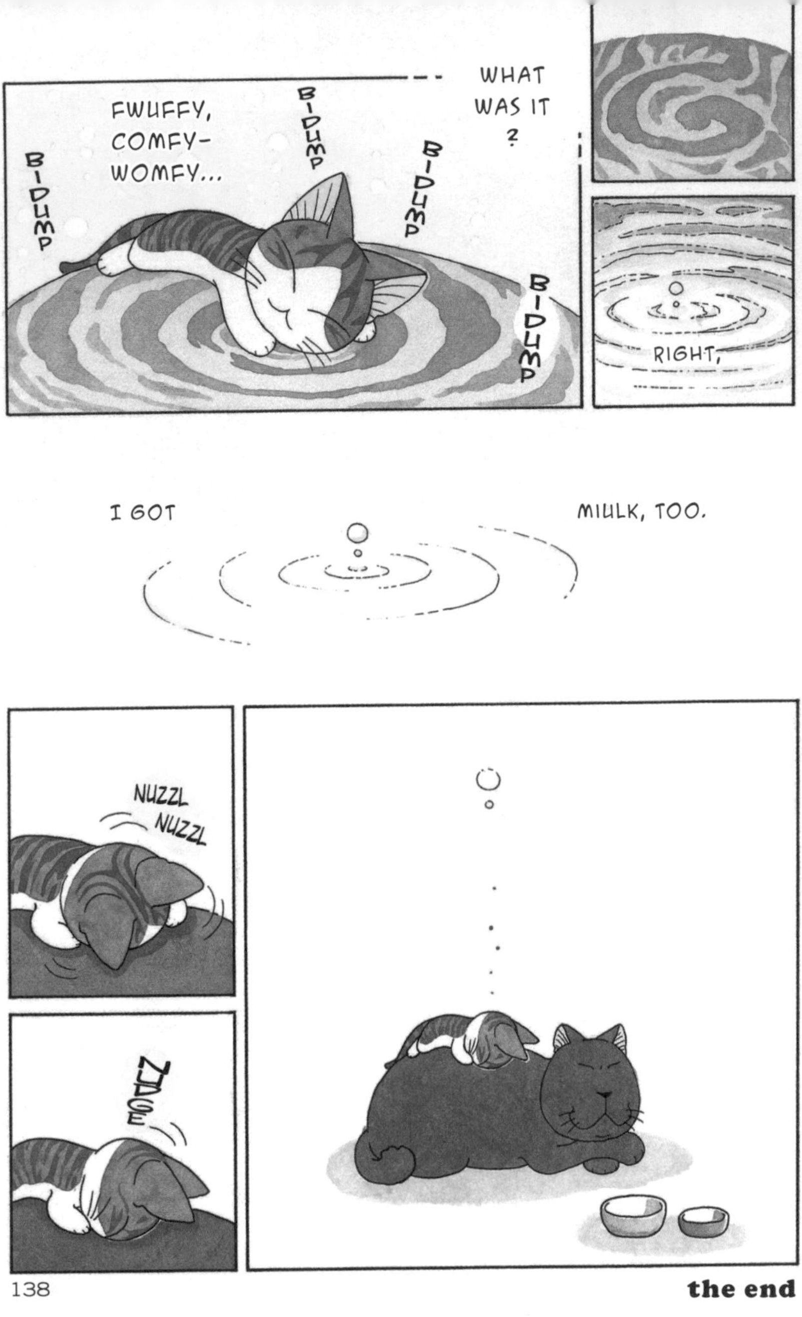
BIDUMP
FWUFFY, COMFY-WOMFY...
BIDUMP
BIDUMP
BIDUMP
WHAT WAS IT ?
RIGHT,
I GOT
MIULK, TOO.
NUZZL NUZZL
NUDGE

the end

homemade 92: a cat is directed home

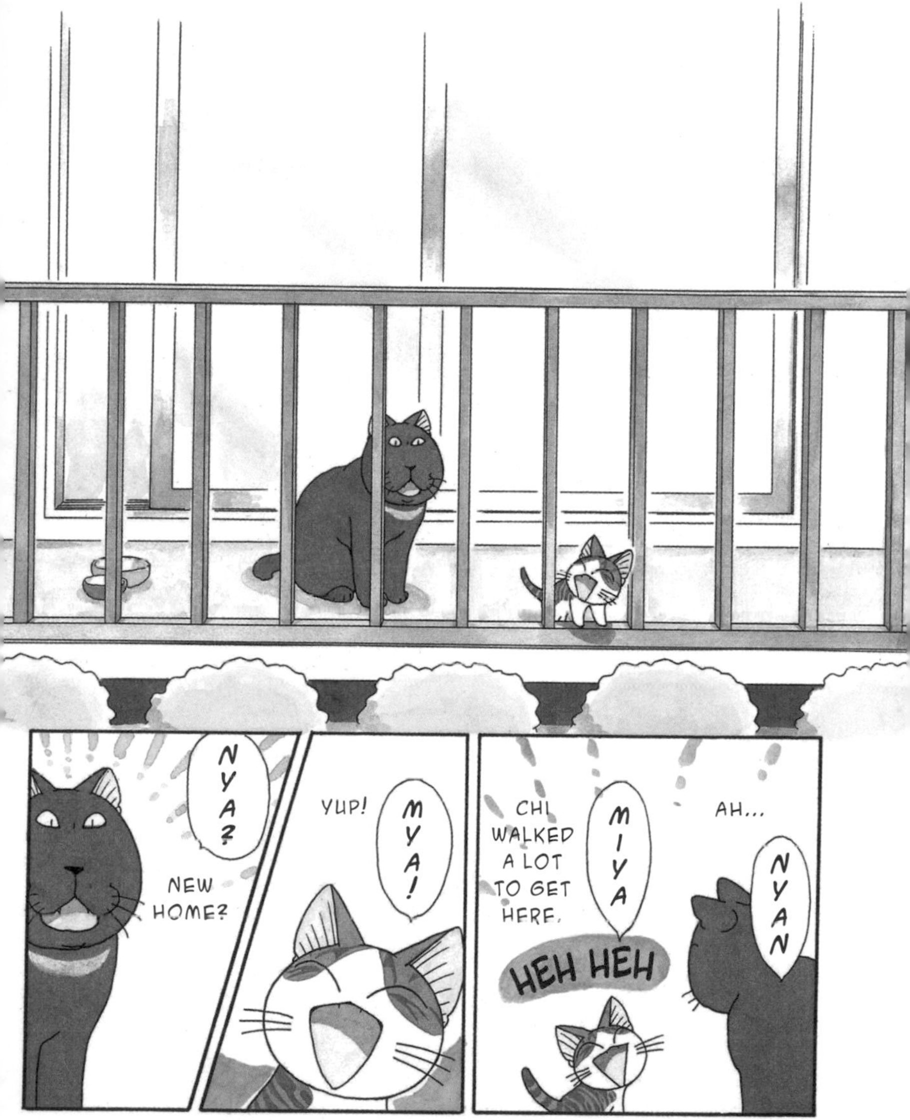
NYA?
NEW HOME?
YUP!
MYA!
CHI WALKED A LOT TO GET HERE.
MIYA
AH...
NYAN
HEH HEH

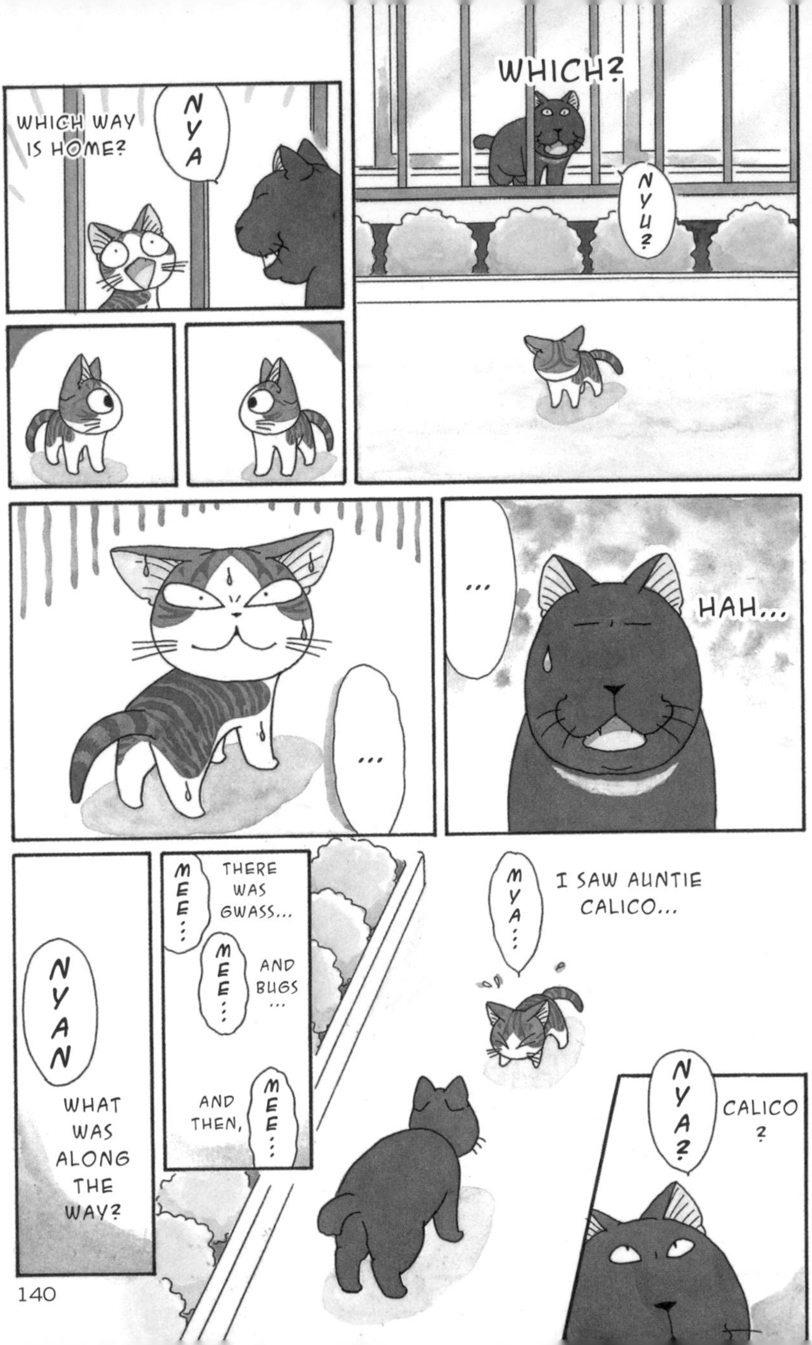
WHICH WAY IS HOME?
NYA
WHICH?
NYU?
...
...
HAH...
NYAN
WHAT WAS ALONG THE WAY?
MEE...
THERE WAS GWASS...
MEE...
AND BUGS...
AND THEN,
MEE...
MYA...
I SAW AUNTIE CALICO...
NYA?
CALICO?

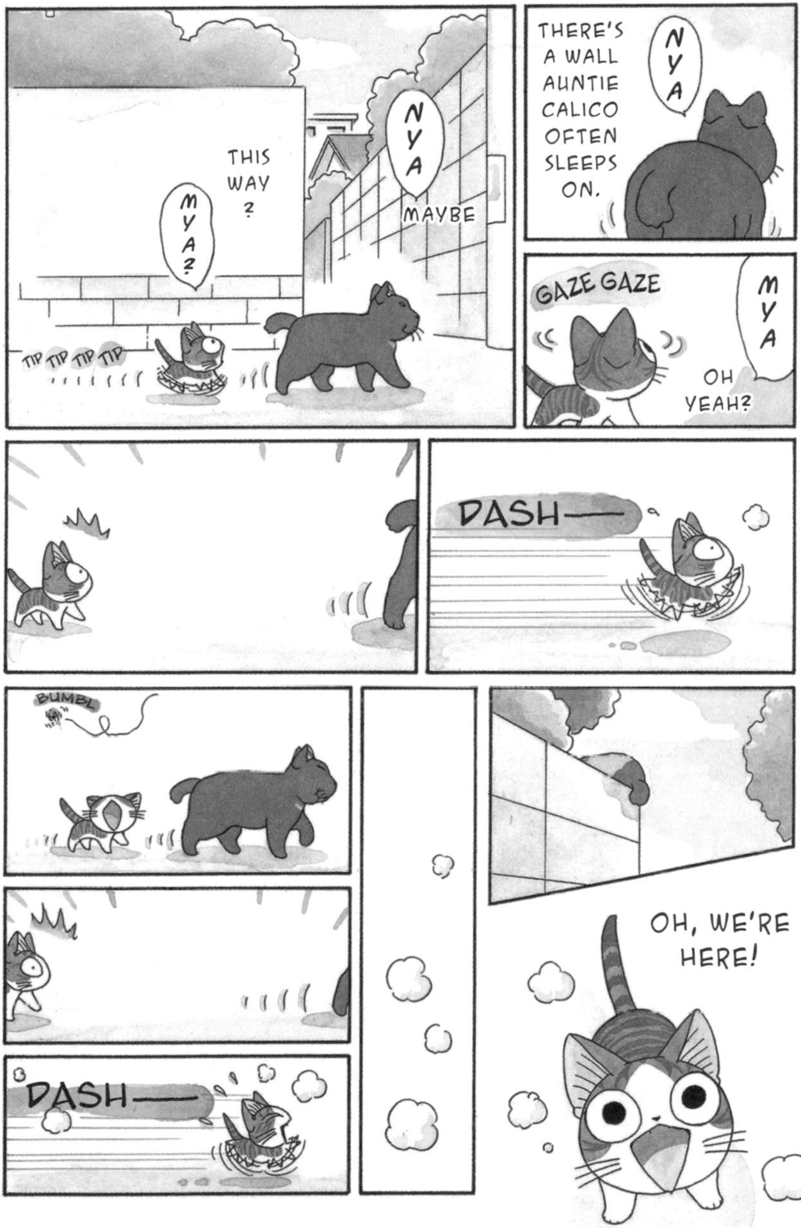
MYA?
THIS WAY?
NYA
MAYBE
TIP TIP TIP TIP
THERE'S A WALL AUNTIE CALICO OFTEN SLEEPS ON.
NYA
GAZE GAZE
MYA
OH YEAH?
DASH—
BUMBL
DASH—
OH, WE'RE HERE!

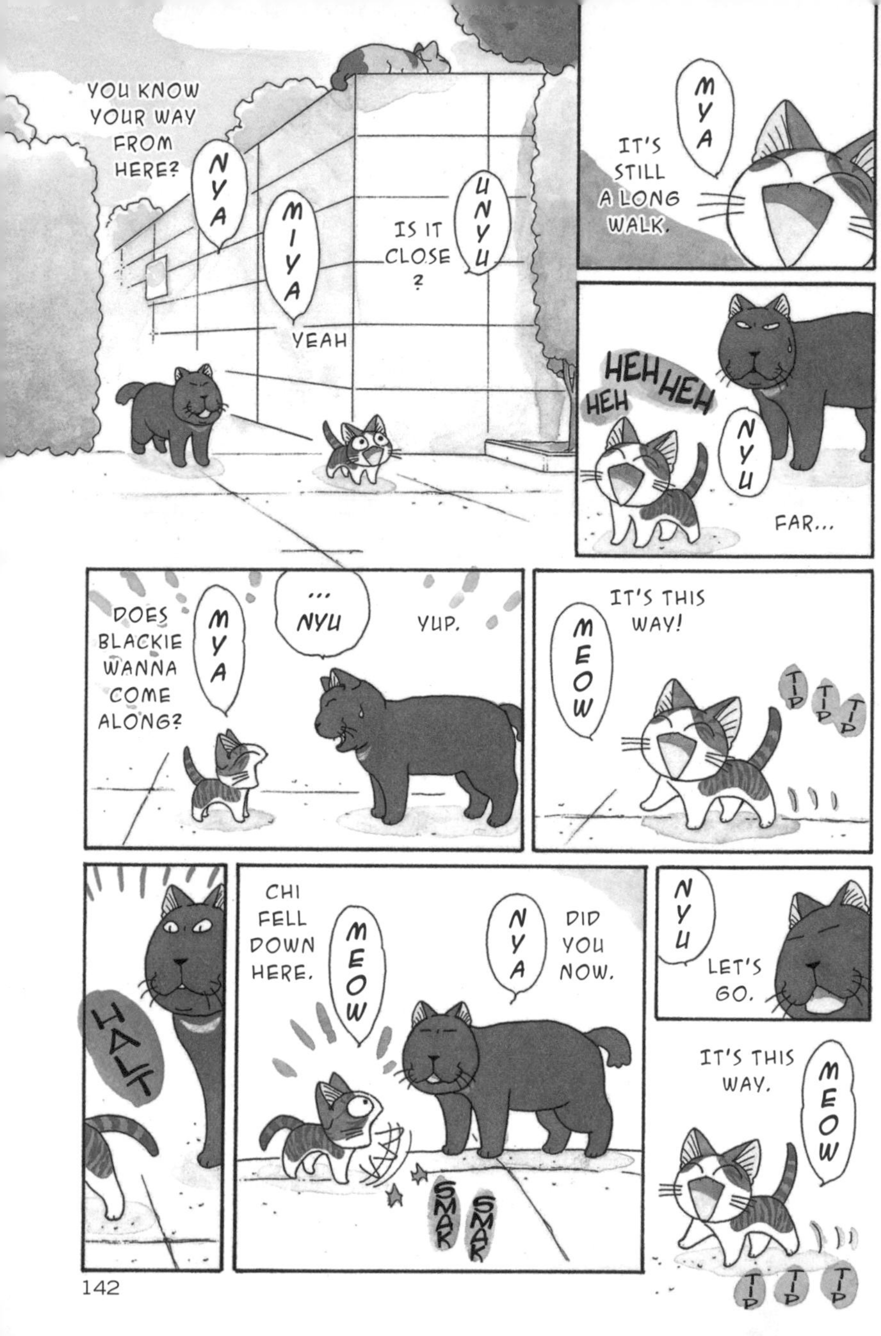
YOU KNOW YOUR WAY FROM HERE?
NYA
MIYA
YEAH
UNYU
IS IT CLOSE?
MYA
IT'S STILL A LONG WALK.
HEH HEH HEH
NYU
FAR...
DOES BLACKIE WANNA COME ALONG?
MYA
... NYU
YUP.
IT'S THIS WAY!
MEOW
TIP TIP TIP
HALT
CHI FELL DOWN HERE.
MEOW
NYA
DID YOU NOW.
SMAK SMAK
NYU
LET'S GO.
IT'S THIS WAY.
MEOW
TIP TIP TIP

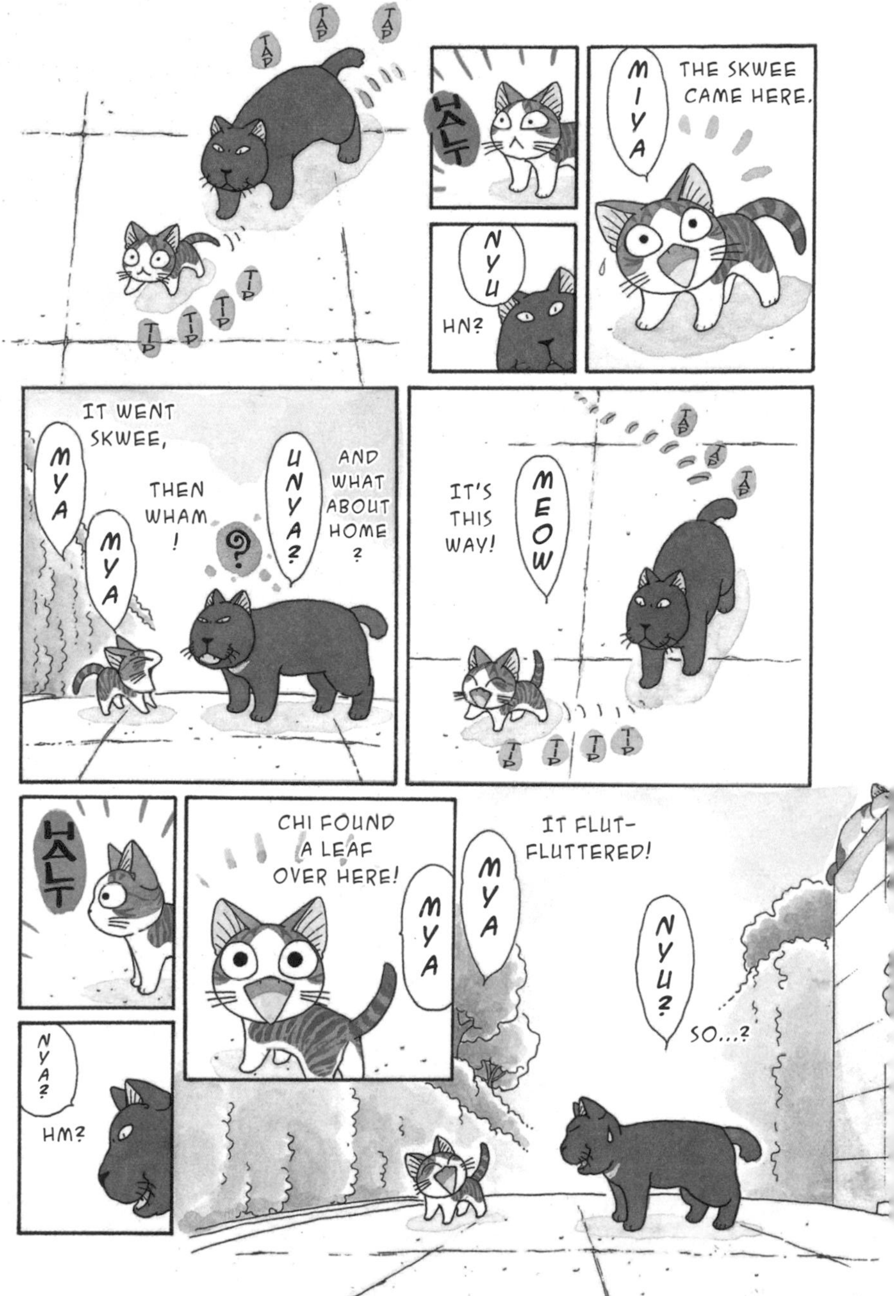
TAP
TAP
TAP
TIP
TIP
TIP
TIP
HALT
NYU
HN?
MIYA
THE SKWEE CAME HERE.
MYA
IT WENT SKWEE,
MYA
THEN WHAM!
UNYA?
AND WHAT ABOUT HOME?
MEOW
IT'S THIS WAY!
TAP
TAP
TAP
TIP
TIP
TIP
TIP
HALT
NYA?
HM?
CHI FOUND A LEAF OVER HERE!
MYA
MYA
IT FLUT-FLUTTERED!
NYU?
SO...?

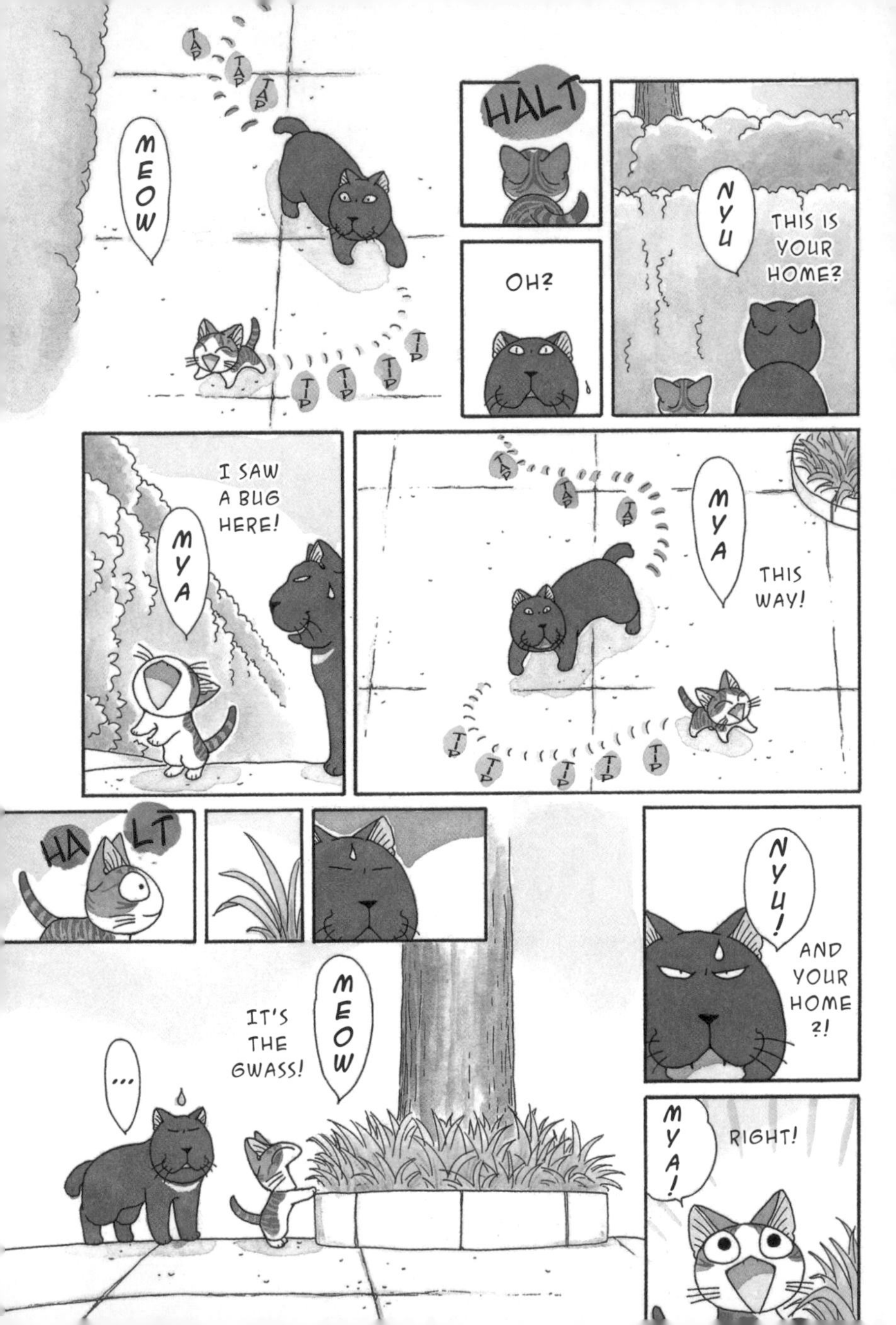
TAP
TAP
TAP
MEOW
TIP
TIP
TIP
TIP
HALT
OH?
NYU
THIS IS YOUR HOME?
I SAW A BUG HERE!
MYA
TAP
TAP
TAP
MYA
THIS WAY!
TIP
TIP
TIP
TIP
TIP
HA LT
...
IT'S THE GWASS!
MEOW
NYU!
AND YOUR HOME ?!
MYA!
RIGHT!

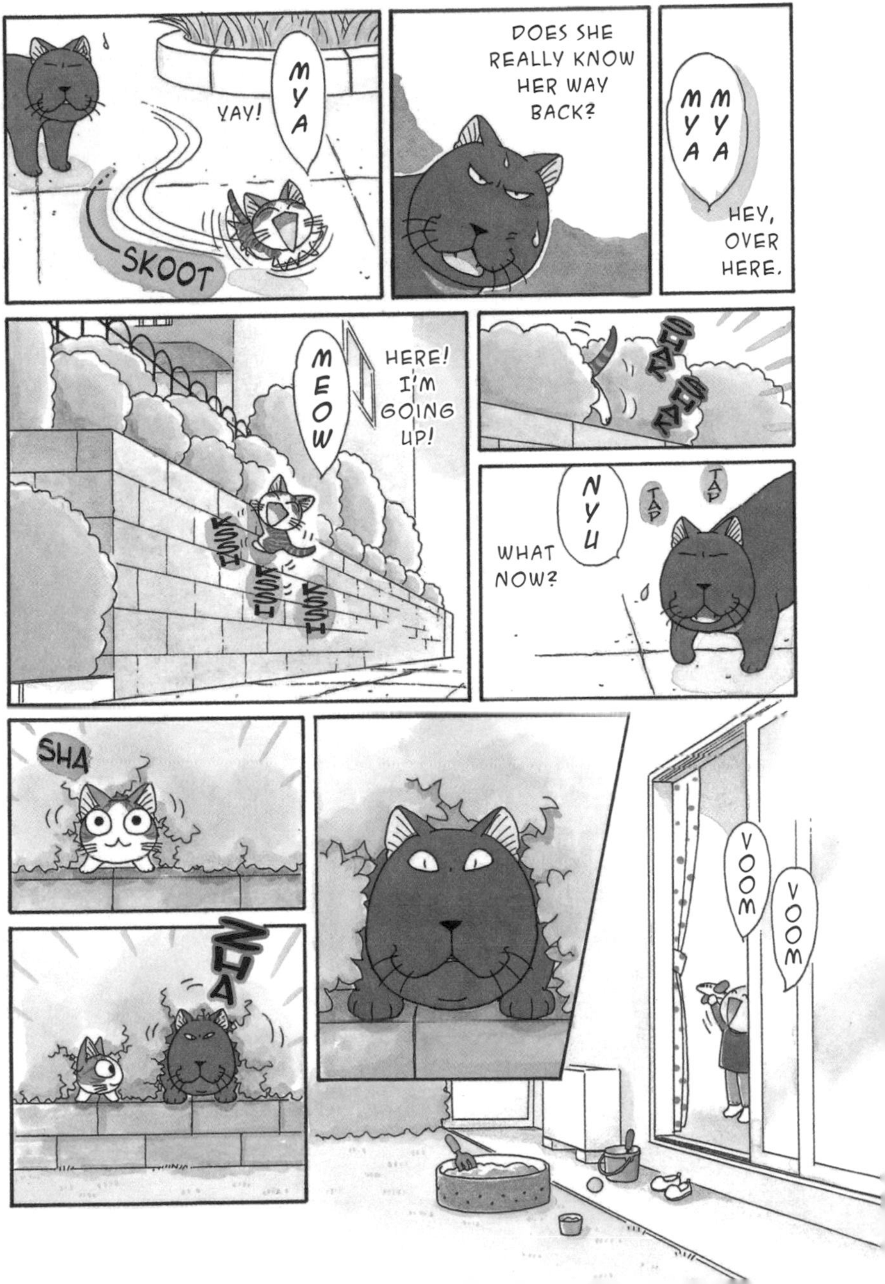
MYA
YAY!
SKOOT
DOES SHE REALLY KNOW HER WAY BACK?
MYA MYA
HEY, OVER HERE.
MEOW
HERE! I'M GOING UP!
KSSH
KSSH
KSSH
SHAK
SHAK
NYU
TAP
TAP
WHAT NOW?
SHA
ZHA
VOOM
VOOM

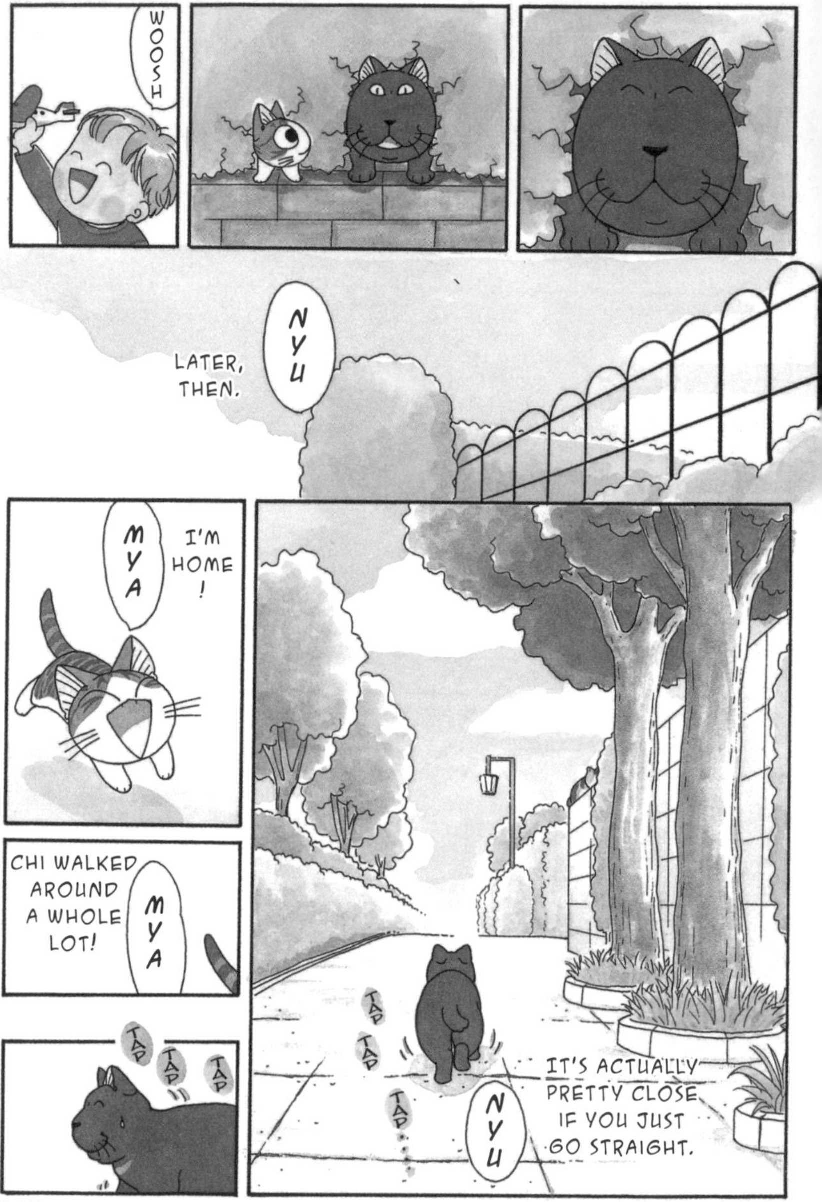
WOOSH
LATER, THEN.
NYU
MYA
I'M HOME!
CHI WALKED AROUND A WHOLE LOT!
MYA
TAP
TAP
TAP
TAP
TAP
TAP
NYU
IT'S ACTUALLY PRETTY CLOSE IF YOU JUST GO STRAIGHT.

the end

Chi is also an anime!!

CSN Chi's Sweet News

news special :

Chi has an anime and a website

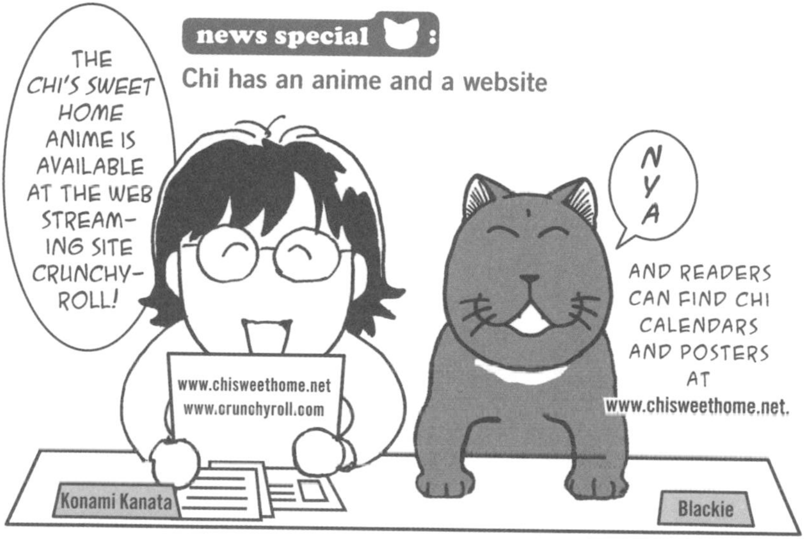
THE CHI'S SWEET HOME ANIME IS AVAILABLE AT THE WEB STREAM-ING SITE CRUNCHY-ROLL!
www.chisweethome.net
www.crunchyroll.com
NYA
AND READERS CAN FIND CHI CALENDARS AND POSTERS AT www.chisweethome.net.
Konami Kanata
Blackie

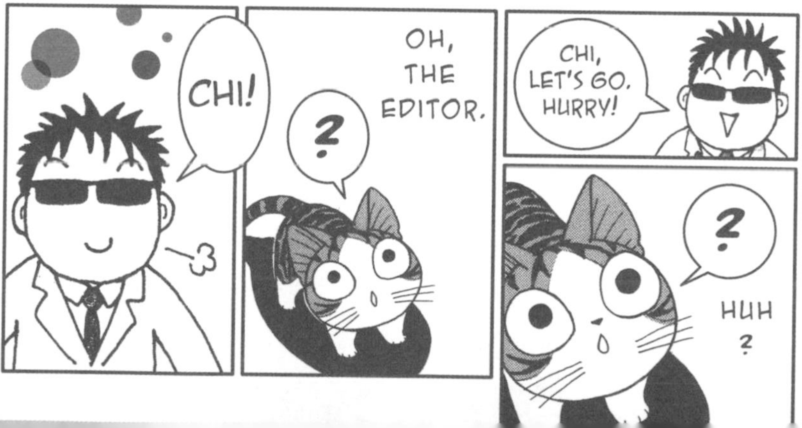
CHI!
?
OH, THE EDITOR.
CHI, LET'S GO. HURRY!
?
HUH ?

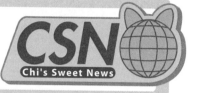

First Look!

The World of *Chi's Sweet Home* finally revealed!

Ever wonder just how Chi's world really looks like? Or where the Mama's home is relative to the Yamadas' apartment? How about the distance from the Yamadas' to the park where Chi and Yohei met? Problem solved! With the following map, now you can properly figure out where the cast of *Chi's Sweet Home* live.

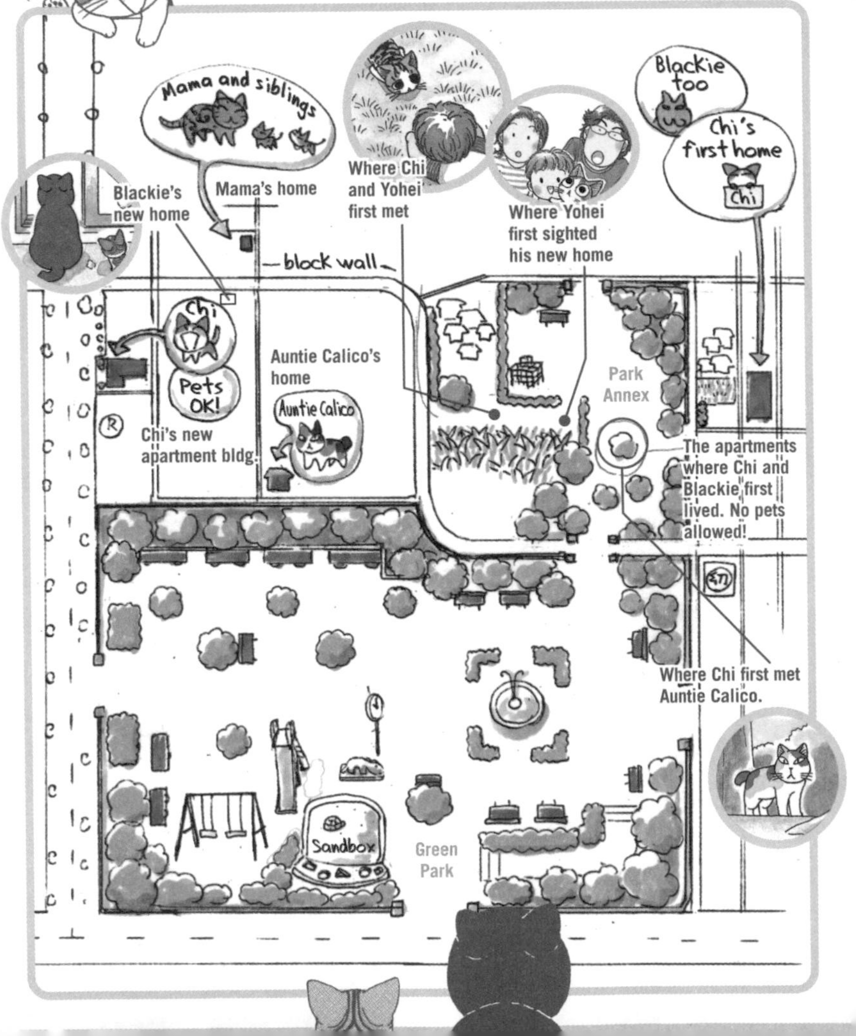
Mama and siblings
Blackie too
Chi's first home
Chi
Blackie's new home
Mama's home
Where Chi and Yohei first met
Where Yohei first sighted his new home
block wall
Chi
Pets OK!
Auntie Calico's home
Auntie Calico
Park Annex
Chi's new apartment bldg.
The apartments where Chi and Blackie first lived. No pets allowed!
Where Chi first met Auntie Calico.
Sandbox
Green Park

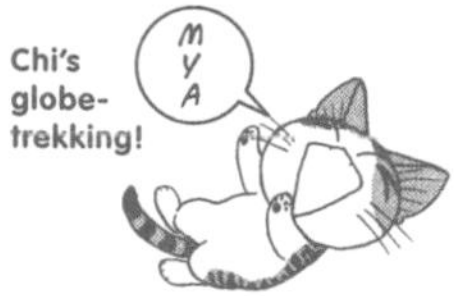
Chi's globe-trekking!
MYA

Chi's on tour!

Emboldened by her travels with her Japanese publisher Kodansha, Chi is now touring the U.S. Follow our cute kitty on her two websites as she travels the globe!

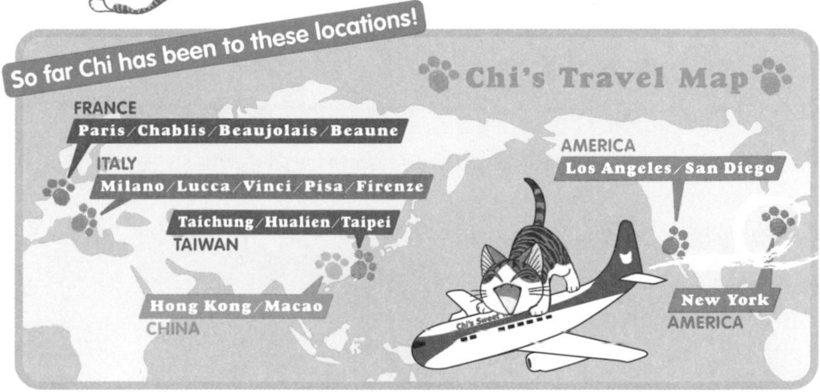
So far Chi has been to these locations!
Chi's Travel Map
FRANCE
Paris/Chablis/Beaujolais/Beaune
ITALY
Milano/Lucca/Vinci/Pisa/Firenze
Taichung/Hualien/Taipei
TAIWAN
Hong Kong/Macao
CHINA
AMERICA
Los Angeles/San Diego
New York
AMERICA

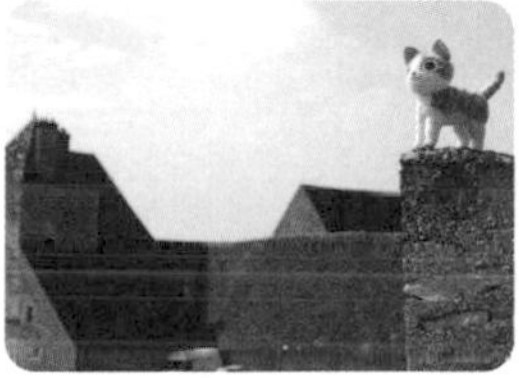

Beaune
strolling through Château Clos de Vougeot

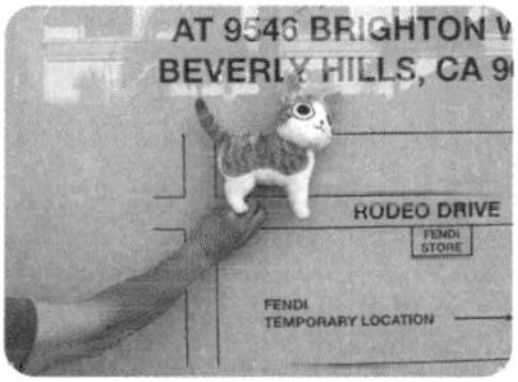
RODEO DRIVE
FENDI STORE
FENDI TEMPORARY LOCATION

Los Angeles
shopping on Rodeo Drive

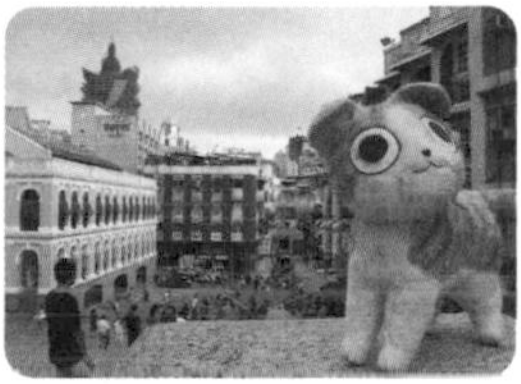

Macao
view from the Ruins of St. Paul's

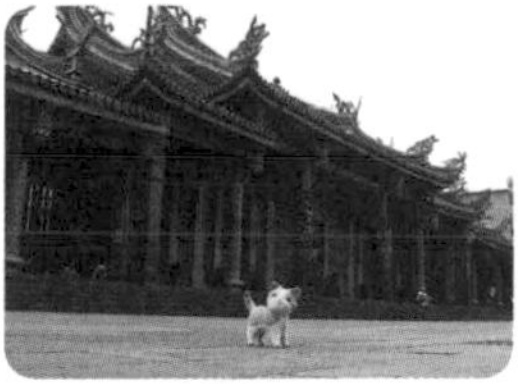

Taipei
at Xingtian Temple

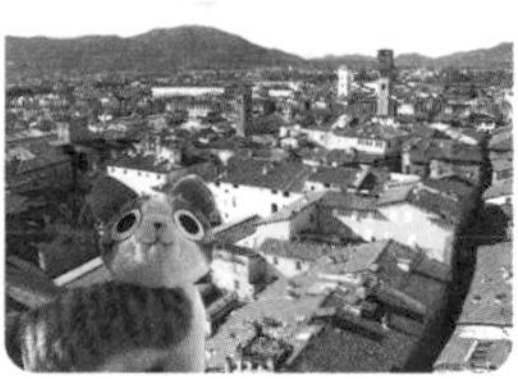

Lucca
view from Guinigi Tower

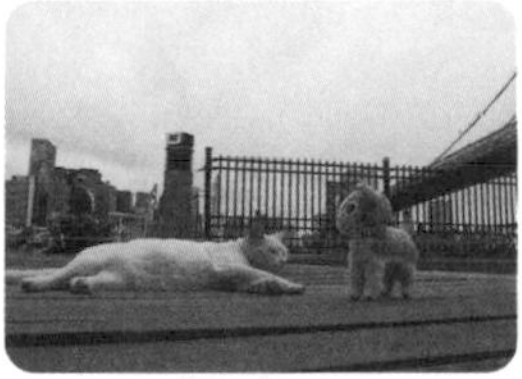

New York
encounter on Brooklyn Bridge

Web URLs:

www.chisweethome.net (English)

http://morningmanga.com/chisweetravel/ (Japanese)

These are just a few of the photos available. Please head on to the sites for more.

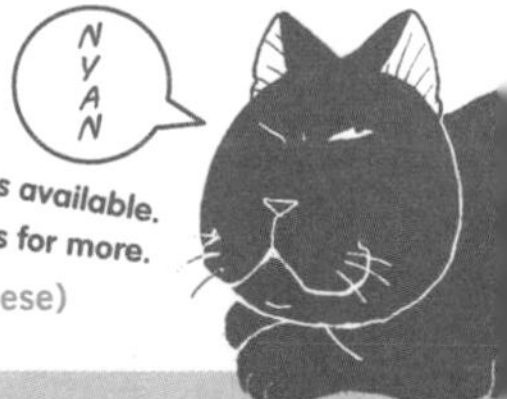
NYAN

TWIN SPI

Space has never seemed so close and yet so far

"It's easy to see why the series was a smash hit in its native land… Each page contains more genuine emotion than an entire space fleet's worth of similarly themed stories."
—*Publishers Weekly*

Now Available Digitally!
16 Volumes, $4.99 each

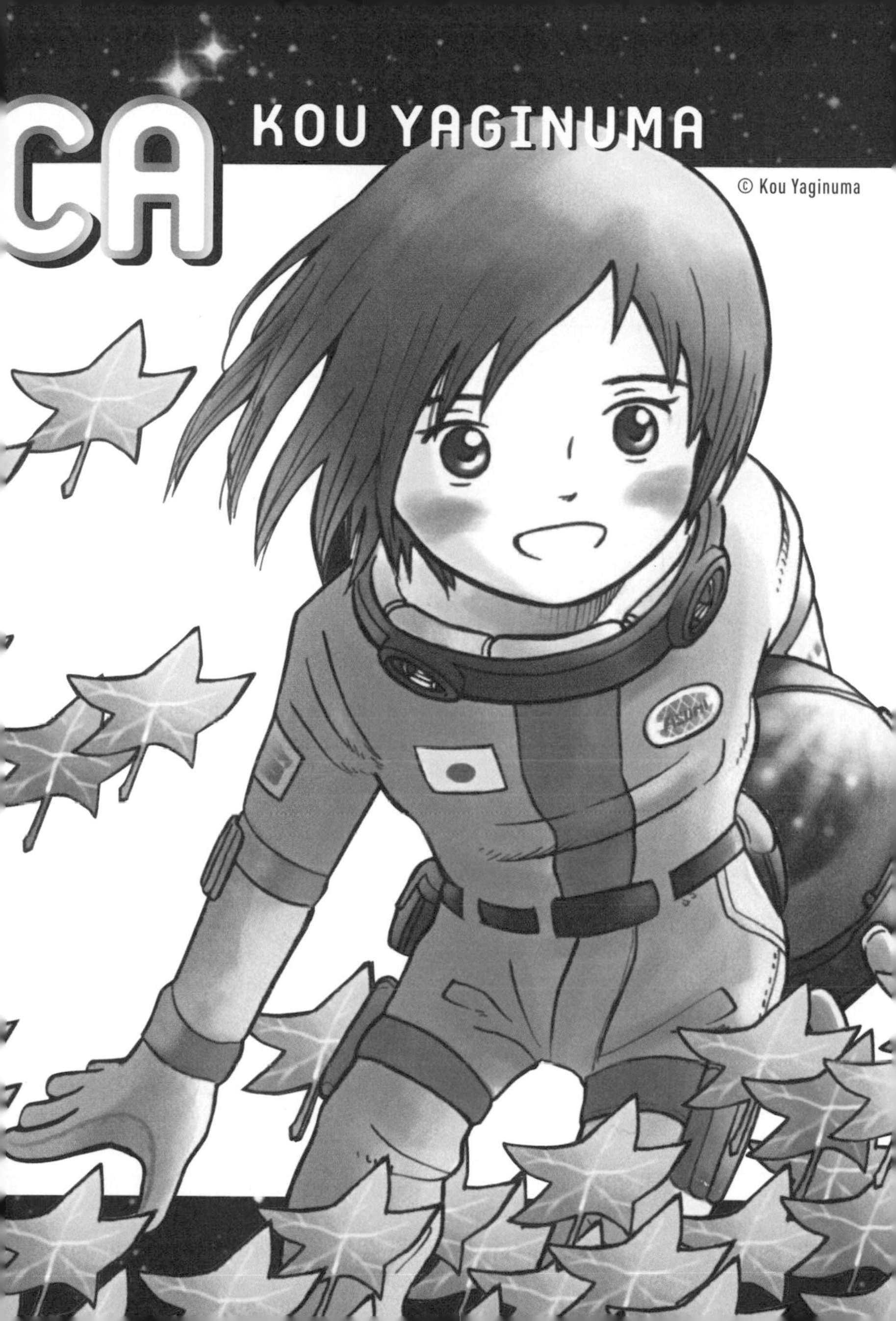
CA
KOU YAGINUMA
© Kou Yaginuma

Chi's Sweet Home, volume 5

Translation - Ed Chavez
Production - Hiroko Mizuno
Glen Isip
Tomoe Tsutsumi

First published in Japan in 2008 by Kodansha, Ltd., Tokyo
Publication for this English edition arranged through Kodansha, Ltd., Tokyo
English language version produced by Vertical, Inc.

Translation provided by Vertical, Inc., 2011
Published by Vertical, Inc., New York

Originally published in Japanese as *Chiizu Suiito Houmu* by Kodansha, Ltd., 2007
Chiizu Suiito Houmu first serialized in *Morning*, Kodansha, Ltd., 2004-

ISBN: 978-1-934287-13-2

Manufactured in the United States of America

First Edition

Third Printing

Vertical, Inc.
451 Park Avenue South, 7th Floor
New York, NY 10016
www.vertical-inc.com

Special thanks to: K. Kitamoto

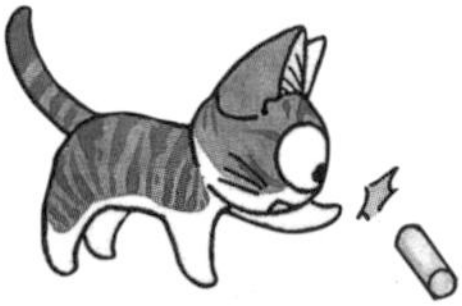